The White Road of the Moon

The White Road of the Moon

RACHEL NEUMEIER

Alfred A. Knopf ✦ New York

THIS IS A BORZOI BOOK PUBLISHED BY ALFRED A. KNOPF

Visit us on the Web! randomhouseteens.com

Educators and librarians, for a variety of teaching tools, visit us at RHTeachersLibrarians.com

Library of Congress Cataloging-in-Publication Data is available upon request.
ISBN 978-0-553-50932-8 (trade) — ISBN 978-0-553-50933-5 (lib. bdg.) — ISBN 978-0-553-50934-2 (ebook)

The text of this book is set in 12.5-point Garamond 3.

Printed in the United States of America
March 2017
10 9 8 7 6 5 4 3 2 1

First Edition

For every teacher who encourages a love of words

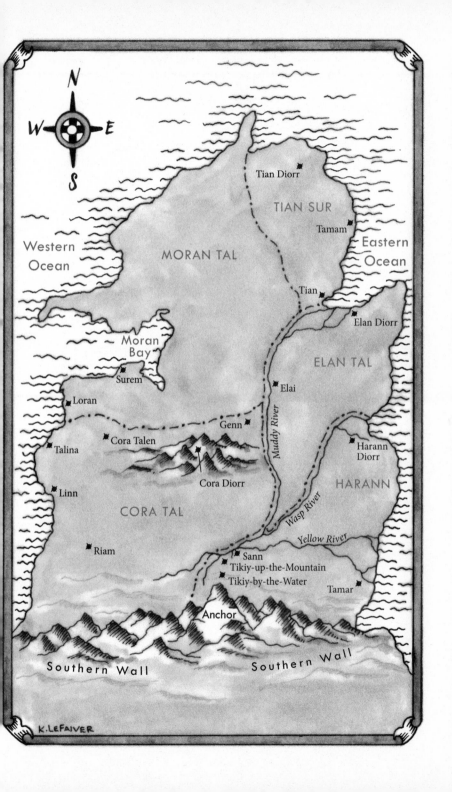

one

There were more than twenty-four hundred people in the town of Tikiy-by-the-Water, but only one of them was alive.

Meridy Turiyn had been alive for just over fifteen years when she came down the path from the village of Tikiy-up-the-Mountain. She came in a rush down the steep trail, with little care for any twisted roots or loose rocks that might wait for an unwary foot. She was too angry to take care, but the hand of the God or familiarity with the path or perhaps simply the sharp reflexes of youth protected her from anything worse than an occasional stumble or missed step. She was forbidden to visit the ghost town of Tikiy-by-the-Water, but she had never much cared about that prohibition.

Aunt Tarana hated any reminder of ghosts or ghost towns, any tale of enchantment or witchery, any echo of history or poetry. Aunt Tarana was a practical woman. That was what she said of herself. At every possible opportunity, it seemed to Meridy, she declared in her loud, firm voice: *Whatever else, anyone can attest that I am a practical woman.* Aunt Tarana had definite ideas about how practical, decent women behaved. She believed that a decent woman kept a neat home and respected her husband; she cultivated appropriate friends and tithed to the local sanctuary; and if she must dabble in an occupation, she made certain it was a respectable one, such as making cheeses or raising bees or making strings of the tiny prayer bells that folk hung from their eaves in hopes of favor from the God.

Most of all, a decent woman kept her mind and the minds of her children fixed firmly on the ordinary, everyday, practical world that everybody could see. *Don't you go teaching my girls any of that fancy poetry, or telling them ridiculous stories about things that likely never were and certainly won't ever be again.* That was what Aunt Tarana had said to her sister, Meridy's mother, Kamay, when Meridy was only five or six. Meridy still remembered that, vividly. Aunt Tarana had been furious because Kamay had led all the girls out into the frigid midwinter night to show them how the moon set directly behind the Anchor of the World, limning the vast mountain with silverglow against sky and shadow. That moment had been beautiful and rare, and Aunt Tarana had ruined it, dragging her daughters away inside, refusing even to *look* at the Anchor.

Aunt Tarana had been angry at Meridy's mother all the time, and after that, Meridy had known it. Tarana had been angry at Kamay for wasting the family's good coin on expensive books, and for insisting on gazing into thin air at things no one else could see, and for bearing an indecently black-eyed daughter to a man she never named. Most of all, Aunt Tarana had been angry at Kamay for having the temerity to die and leave her, Tarana, to bring up the child. All this Meridy knew.

Kamay had died when Meridy was only eleven, of a fever that rose and rose and would not break.

A witch might have lifted that fever, but Aunt Tarana said a witch would let Kamay die so as to bind her ghost. Witches had no power to bring the *ethereal* into the *real* without a ghost to help, and so every witch alive wanted to bind ghosts, and that meant they wanted people to die. Witches were all just a step away from being murderers, Aunt Tarana said. She said that was why the decent folk of Tikiy had driven out any witches who dared openly practice their witchery. Meridy couldn't help but understand that Aunt Tarana more than half believed Kamay should have been driven out, too, even though she'd never done anything wrong in her whole life except hear the quick dead, which anyone might, and occasionally admit to a glimpse of the *ethereal*. And, of course, bear a black-eyed daughter, a daughter uncommonly dark, even for a village in the shadow of the Wall where for hundreds and hundreds of years a trace of Southern blood had been no rare thing. Meridy couldn't help understand that this was her mother's greatest offense of all.

It wouldn't necessarily have taken a witch to heal Kamay. A priest, witch-eyed or not, might have lifted the fever, for any priest might serve as a conduit for the God to reach into the mortal world, just as a ghost made a way for a witch to reach into the realms of dream and memory. The nearest sanctuary was in Sann, not so very far away, but Aunt Tarana wouldn't send for help. She said priests were almost as much a danger to the dying as witches, even the ones who weren't witches themselves. She said decent people kept to the practical world and didn't clamor at the God for every little thing.

Aunt Tarana didn't trust anyone who might touch the magic and dreams and memory that lay in the *ethereal*. She never trusted anyone who could bring dreams or hopes or prayers across the boundary into the *real*, the living world of solid weight and present time. Not even if they did it to heal the sick.

3

So Aunt Tarana insisted the fever would lift on its own. But it did not.

In tales, the prick of a rose thorn might cause a person to fall into an enchanted sleep so that her soul drifted free and untethered; the fragrance of a rose might recall the soul and wake the sleeper. But even if such tales were true, it was not the season for roses. Meridy tried rose pomanders and rose jam, but nothing she did helped at all. The roses failing, she hoped to hold her mother's soul beyond death as a witch could, by binding her soul to the *real* and preventing it from taking the White Road of the Moon into death. But despite her black eyes, Meridy couldn't do that either. Her mother died, and though Meridy watched by her bedside and refused to leave her, she never even glimpsed her departing ghost. There was nothing she could do.

Afterward, Aunt Tarana sold all her mother's scrolls and books to the first peddler who came through Tikiy. *I have to have you here with my girls, I suppose, but I'll have none of those notions of my sister's,* Aunt Tarana had told Meridy. With her whole world broken into bewildering pieces around her, Meridy had been too shocked to protest, and so she had nothing left of her mother save the stories her mother had told her, the wonder and magic she carried in imagination and memory.

You should be grateful, Aunt Tarana had told her. *High time someone took you in hand and taught you to behave like a respectable girl. No decent man likes a woman who puts on airs and talks a lot of nonsense about poetry.* But Meridy found it impossible to be grateful.

Aunt Tarana's husband had passed into the realm of the God a year or so before Meridy's mother, and so it was a household of women and girls. Aunt Tarana's daughters, all older than Meridy, first resented her because they had to share between just two rooms, and one more girl meant that much less space for the rest of them; and then they detested her because she could quote all the classic epics in the original Viènè; and more than that they hated her because her dark coloring made it obvious her nameless father had been a man carrying a lot of Southern blood. Most of all, they feared her because of her black eyes.

Initially Meridy was too numbed by grief to notice that her cousins hated her, and then later she despised them and didn't care what they thought, any more than she cared what Aunt Tarana thought.

She hadn't realized she needed to care, until today. She *ought* to have realized. She knew, she *knew* that Aunt Tarana was always sweet as clover honey when she was getting ready to do something awful. Four years of living in her aunt's home had been more than long enough to teach her that. And yet she hadn't guessed, even though Aunt Tarana had spent the morning making molasses toffee, which Meridy especially liked, and had allowed Meridy to help. But even the molasses candy hadn't warned her. She had been taken completely by surprise.

Though she shouldn't have been surprised at all. Of course, nothing could be more likely than that Aunt Tarana would take the chance to hand her black-eyed niece over to any craftswoman who needed an apprentice at the moment Meridy turned fifteen, by law old enough to sign marriage lines or inherit property or bind herself to an apprenticeship contract. Aunt Tarana didn't care what happened to Meridy, just so long as she could be rid of her inconvenient niece once and for all and forget she had ever had a sister.

So Meridy was supposed to be packing her few belongings and making ready to present herself to Tikiy's soap maker at noon tomorrow.

The soap maker was a grim old woman, twice Aunt Tarana's age, with no living children of her own. Her house was up at the highest edge of the village, where the trees and meadows gave way to bare rock, because although the finished soaps were fragrant with lavender or roses or verbena, the actual process of making soap was unpleasant, stinking work, and no one wanted to live too near a soap maker's house. Though Meridy did not know the soap maker well enough to like or dislike her, she couldn't imagine living in the old woman's cottage or helping her with her work. She could guess too well what her apprenticeship would be, especially since the soap maker was also a laundress. Meridy would spend all the days of her apprenticeship carrying endless buckets of water and even more endless bundles of firewood. She would burn wood down to ash to make the lye, and boil the fat of sheep or pigs or the occasional bear for hours and hours to render and clean it. She'd stir huge cauldrons until her arms ached, she'd burn herself with lye, her hands would turn red and rough from washing other people's worst-soiled clothing, and at the end of every day, what would she have to show for her labor? *Soap.*

In the old days of great deeds and sorcery, before the witch-king Tai-Enchar had betrayed High King Miranuanol in the hour of his greatest need and shattered the whole Kingdom with his greed and pride and ambition, Meridy would have . . . she would have found an injured horse and healed it and ridden north out of the mountains . . . no, not actually a horse but a fire horse, one of the savage tusked beasts that legend claimed only kings and heroes and Southerners could ride. If Meridy had to so obviously bear the stamp of Southern blood, why shouldn't she have some benefit from it? She'd have found a beautiful red-gold mare with an injured foot, tamed her until she would take meat gently from Meridy's hand, and never try to bite. Then Meridy would have ridden her away from Tikiy, straight across the breadth of the land. She would have presented herself to the High King, won a place in his court, learned all the ways of memory and dream and magic, and become not merely a witch but a sorceress. Everyone would have known her name, and they'd have known her mother's name, too. Kamay Turiyn would have been remembered forever. Everyone would say, *Oh, yes, just a modest village woman from the far South, but she taught her daughter everything she needed to know to rise in the world.*

Two hundred years ago, all that might have been possible. Well, probably not the fire horse, but the rest of it. Meridy could picture it perfectly in her mind: the High King and his court bright and vivid in Moran Diorr, the gracious City of Bells. She had told the old stories over to herself a hundred times since her mother's death. *By the grace of the God, the high kings ruled for a thousand years.* That was how the old stories began. *It was an age of greatness; it was an age of heroes.*

But then Tai-Enchar had ruined everything.

If Meridy had been at the High King's court, maybe . . . well, no doubt she'd have drowned with everyone else when Tai-Enchar's treachery broke open the great storm of sorcery and Moran Diorr sank beneath the waves. The sea had rolled in and silenced all the bells, and everyone had died. Even so, she wished she had lived in those days, the great days, the days of high kings and great sorcery and crashing battles, when men—yes, and women, too—did great deeds, and the things they did *mattered.*

But there was no High King anymore. Moran Diorr had

drowned, and the unified lands of the High Kingdom had shattered into all the little warring principalities. The stories of the old Kingdom were all the more bitter because now, in this lesser time, there was no place for great deeds and shining magic. Meridy had been born too late, and now there was nothing in her future but a hard, boring, tedious apprenticeship to the soap maker.

She came down through the ruined outskirts of Tikiy-by-the-Water, half tumbled out into the sunstruck glade where once the town green had spread, and caught her balance against the broken gatepost that marked the entrance to the center of the ruined town. She was breathing quickly, more from anger than with the exertion of her fast descent down the mountain trail, and so she leaned there for a moment, catching her breath and looking for the storyteller who had his place here by the gates. She let her gaze soften and unfocus, blinking the bustling town of the past into place over and through the dead remains of the present.

The old storyteller, Ambica, looked up from his bench just inside the gates, in the shade cast by a graceful beech. Neither bench nor tree was actually there, of course. But both had been there once. What Meridy saw was the memory they had left behind.

Before his death, Ambica had sold stories to passersby as other men might sell their cheeses or their skills at pot mending. But he had not lived his life here in the shadow of the mountains. If one believed his tales, Ambica had been everywhere and done everything. He'd been a living man at just the time Meridy most longed for, the time of High King Miranuanol, before Tikiy-by-the-Water had been destroyed by the retreating Southerners, as so many small towns and villages had during those last furious days of the war. Now those towns and all their people existed merely as memories and dreams of what they had once been. Though High King Miranuanol had saved the rest of his kingdom. He had spent all the strength of the Kingdom to drive the Southerners back into the southern desert for *just long enough,* and then he and his sorcerers had raised the great Wall to stand forever between the Kingdom and the South. If Meridy had lived in those days, she could have learned to be a sorcerer and helped raise up the Wall and the great Anchor, and even if Tai-Enchar's treachery had killed her, too, at least it would have been a glorious death.

And maybe she'd have become quick, like Ambica, and lingered to see the new age dawn.

Though this last wasn't necessarily a comfortable idea. Being anchored by a ghost town meant you'd never be able to leave it; the alternative, being anchored to the living world by one's husband or sister or whomever, might not be quite so confining, but it meant you'd have to stay by your anchor. In Tikiy, that meant you'd probably never travel more than a few days' walk from your home. Besides, everyone knew the lingering dead couldn't touch or affect the *real* world unless they were bound by a witch. And a witch could compel a ghost against her will, so if the witch was evil, that would be terrible.

Even so, sometimes Meridy couldn't help but think it might not be so bad to become quick instead of taking the White Road of the Moon, the God's Road—to linger for a short time or for ages—if only she could have *lived* first. Lived through great and exciting days, played a part in stories that would be remembered for hundreds of years.

At least, with her mother's blood and her black eyes, she could not only see Ambica and listen to his stories but also glimpse the world that had once been.

The storyteller knew he was a ghost, but he claimed to be in no hurry to take the Moon's Road. There were so many ghosts here that they had no trouble maintaining their bustling town, so they forgot they were dead and lingered in their common memory of Tikiy. Ambica knew he was dead, but he lingered, too, half in the memory of the town and half in his stories of a world long vanished.

The stories he told were set in the world before the Southern Wall had been raised up. The world was a smaller place now, filled with smaller people, like Aunt Tarana, who had never in her whole life been farther from Tikiy than the trading post on the Yellow River Road and who thought the most important thing in the world was seeing her daughters well married to craftsmen instead of muddy-handed farmers. And disposing of her black-eyed niece in the most expedient manner possible.

Meridy was still too angry to think about that.

She moved to sit on the blanket spread before Ambica's bench—bright in memory, half visible to Meridy's black eyes, barely there to any touch—and smiled back. It was easy to smile at Ambica, even when she was angry. He was so good-humored himself and always pleased to see her, and that made it hard for Meridy to hold on to her bad temper. Even today. That was why she'd come down the mountain. Well, and she had always found the presence of the dead far more welcome than that of the living. Especially *Aunt Tarana*. Especially *today*. She tried to scowl at Ambica, but she could feel it was no use.

"Ah, Mery, bramble-child!" he said to her. He called her

by little-names sometimes, as though he were no older than she, especially when she was in a temper. No one else ever did. Meridy would not have answered anybody else who tried. He patted her hand. "I had a story for you, one I've never told you before, a good one, all bright courage and noble sacrifice and tragic death, but there's no time, no time. You've someone seeking you."

"Seeking me?" Meridy thought she must have misunderstood. The lingering dead of Tikiy did not think enough about the living to seek out anyone.

"Ah, well, seeking any witch, I think," Ambica amended. "A ghost, he is, seeking you or one like you: someone with eyes that see behind the world. Fretful, he was. I told him you'd do. I told him there's not much your black eyes look past. I said I'd send you along, bramble-girl." He patted her knee with one bony hand, smiling at her as though he'd done her a favor.

Meridy stared at him. "You're telling me a *ghost* came here from *somewhere else,* deliberately *looking* for a witch, someone who can bind ghosts?" This seemed so unlikely that she could hardly frame the questions that pressed suddenly behind her teeth.

The quick dead, the ghosts who turned away from the White Road of the Moon and lingered instead in the *real,* were usually bound to the place of their death. If they left it, then unless a living person anchored them, ghosts would forget themselves, and eventually shred away on the wind, lost to the world and the God alike. A wife, a brother, a child— any of the living might anchor someone after he died, even though they couldn't see him and could hardly hear the thin, breathless whisper of his voice. But if anchored by a wife or brother or child, a ghost could turn away from the world and

11

take the God's Road. That choice was always there for such a ghost. No ordinary person could hold one of the quick dead back from that choice once a ghost had decided to depart the *real* and go to the God.

It was different for a witch, because a witch could anchor one of the quick dead, bind him, and use him as a conduit between the *real* and the *ethereal*. That was the source of all of a witch's magic, so witches sought out the lingering dead and bound them whether they wished to be anchored or not. Meridy could not quite imagine why a ghost would deliberately risk such servitude by seeking out an unknown witch.

Getting to her feet, Meridy stared away, into the ruined town and the half-glimpsed memory of it the ghosts of Tikiy recalled, layered one above the other, looking for someone she did not know. Someone she did not recognize.

"Go on, bramble-child," Ambica urged her. "But be careful! He's got depth to him, that one. He's carrying a story on his shoulders, and not a light burden, or I miss my guess."

"Yes," Meridy said again, not really listening. She *was* curious, about this ghost and about the anchor who must have brought him here. So she headed straight into the ghost town. Or as straight as she could while picking her way through crumbled streets and around ruined homes.

She found Ambica's stranger in one of her favorite spots in the whole town: the crumbling base of the central fountain. He appeared quite at his ease for all Ambica had said he was fretful. He seemed a boy about her own age. That surprised her. The ghosts of children rarely lingered. But he was obviously a ghost and obviously someone she had never before seen, so who else could he be but Ambica's impatient stranger?

Meridy paused between part of a broken wall and a tree

that had grown up through the remnants of a foundation, just to study him. The ghost boy was leaning back on his elbow, staring down into the depths of the dry fountain, one hand resting on the head of a big brindled wolfhound. The dog was also a ghost, but no more familiar to Meridy than the boy himself. As dogs were sacred to the God, after death they went as they pleased between the world of men and the God's realm. But this one clearly belonged with the boy.

Where shadows fell across boy and dog, the two ghosts were hard to see, even for her, but the noon sunlight caught out the boy's head and shoulder in more detail. The light glistened off dust motes in the air, delicately limning the place where he almost was. Even at this distance and only half visible, his expression was abstracted.

Then the boy looked up and saw her. He straightened, gazing right at her, meeting her eyes. The dog, too, sat up alertly, pricking his ears.

Meridy started forward. She couldn't see anyone living. She didn't understand how the boy could have come here by himself, but if a living person had brought him, then where was that person? Tension clenched her stomach. Meeting someone like herself, maybe a witch . . . someone older, someone who knew things and wanted things and had perhaps even come here *looking* for her, or for someone like her. It was bound to be complicated.

Still, she could see no one except the ghost boy and his dog.

Meridy cast a quick glance around the town square, but she saw only a few townsfolk, familiar ghosts all, going about their simple days. They paid no attention to her, absorbed in their own memories; she was too familiar to them to draw more than an occasional indifferent nod. She saw no one else,

13

no one living who might anchor a ghost, no one who might pose a challenge or a threat.

The ghost boy had risen to his feet. He was clearly waiting for her to join him at the fountain. At last Meridy allowed curiosity to lead her forward.

It became more possible to distinguish details of the ghost's appearance as she approached the fountain. The boy was tall, by his height and the cast of his features of pure northern blood. His clothing was not village clothing: the dyes must have been clear and strong to produce those echoes of blues and violets, and the style was not familiar, his shirt close fitted at the wrist and neck and loose everywhere else.

His expression was both tense and contained. He had a measuring look about him, as though he had set himself to judge her, and Tikiy, and all its other ghosts; as though he had a *right* to judge them all. He looked somehow less solid and at the same time more vivid than the ghosts Meridy knew, and she thought Ambica was right: there was a depth to him. Although he had died young, this one was an *old* ghost. The dog was clearly his dog. She wondered if they had died at the same time, and how it had happened.

The dog dropped his head and laid back his ears in a friendly way. His tail stirred, though of course the dust and dead leaves did not shift in answer.

Close by the boy's hand, on the cracked tiles of the fountain's rim, lay a rose. The pink and white tiles were an echo of the wealth Tikiy had once possessed, though the colors were faded now, with ferns growing in the cracks. In contrast to the tiles, the rose looked perfect. Too beautiful, too perfect to be *real,* the rose was blood dark against the tiles.

If enough of the ghosts of Tikiy had been near the fountain, their gathered memories could have restored it to the beauty it had enjoyed in their day and Meridy might have seen it as they saw it. But there were few ghosts nearby, save for this one she did not know. A ghost boy, a crumbled fountain, and a single perfect rose lying on the broken tiles.

The ghost boy gave Meridy a careful, gauging look. Then he picked up the rose and offered it to her with a courtly gesture. Resisting the urge to touch it, Meridy put her hands behind her back. It was an *ethereal* rose, of course, and would melt away if she touched it. But it was beautiful. It looked, in fact, exactly like the sort of rose that might restore the soul to someone who was dying. If she had been able to make one like it out of dreams and memory . . .

The shadow of grief brushed her, but she was old enough now to know that the stories about roses were just stories, and fever was fever. After a minute, she sat down on the rim of the fountain and let the ghost thread the rose into her hair. His touch was cold and light, almost imperceptible, like being brushed by a dream of cobwebs. If Meridy kept her hands away from the rose and pretended that it wasn't there, it would probably last a little while before fading.

The ghost boy, glimmering in the sunlight, told her, in the feathery, breathless voice of the quick, "There's an injured man in the woods. Down by the ruined mill."

Meridy looked at him carefully. "Your anchor?"

The ghost shrugged. His tone was cool, assured, unimpassioned, by no means the tone of any boy his apparent age. "Does it matter? He's hurt. Perhaps he's dying. Will you leave him there to die?"

This boy had come here looking for her. He had gone to a good deal of trouble, in fact, to find help for this man who must be his anchor. He'd made her an *ethereal* rose, even. That spoke well for the man. Whatever he was to this boy, whether he was a witch or a priest or a sorcerer, Meridy couldn't believe he was wicked. She was fairly certain she didn't want to meet a priest, who might well, considering her black eyes, try to pen her up in some sanctuary and make her take vows to the God. On the other hand . . . curiosity tugged at her. And the boy was right. She had no reason to care about this stranger, but if the man was hurt, she couldn't refuse to help him, either. She winced away from imagining what it would be like to lie helpless in the cold woods and know that you were dying.

She stood up.

The ghost boy immediately faded out, becoming nearly imperceptible even to her. Impatient, that was clear. Intolerant of questions. "Hurry," his airless voice murmured.

Meridy shrugged, to show that she didn't care one way or the other, and headed for the mill. Fine. She would bring this man to the town inn and make a fire; old and ruined as it was, the inn in Tikiy-by-the-Water still possessed a sound roof and walls. He might die anyway, if he'd been lying alone too long and was too sick or too fevered, but at least he could die where it was warm. So she walked down through the woods toward the old mill, pretending not to hurry but walking fast for all that, following the flickery corner-of-the-eye motion of the ghost boy.

two

The man certainly was hurt. Meridy, in her first summing glance, thought he might already be dead. A closer look showed that he was merely unconscious. As the boy had said, he was wounded: bleeding sluggishly from a long slash on his thigh and more freely from another cut on his side. The wounds did not look like they had been made by any animal or accident. They looked like they had been dealt by a knife, or perhaps even a sword. There was a knife, in fact, close by one outflung hand. It gleamed dully in the mud: no cook's knife but a fighting dagger. No one in Tikiy carried such a weapon. Meridy knew of no one who even owned a fighting knife. Skinning blades and everyday belt tools had quite a different look about them, which was not something she had been aware of before, but it was obvious enough now.

Meridy cast an uneasy look around, but there were no signs that this man's enemies, whoever they might be, were anywhere near. Nor, even more curious, were there any signs to show how the man had come to be here. No broken shrubs or crushed undergrowth spoke of any recent battle. There was blood on the man's clothing, but very little on the ground. He might have come out of the air, stepped off the White Road itself, to fall and die alone in a ghost town at the edge of the world.

Meridy knew less of sorcerers than she knew of witches, and she knew little enough of witches, but she could recognize the working of magic when it was this obvious. She regarded the man uneasily. He didn't look powerful. He looked only exhausted and ill and likely to die, if he was not cared for properly.

Crouching down beside him, she touched his throat. The skin was cool and damp, not a good sign, but not the worst possible, either. The man did not respond to the touch. She thought of the *ethereal* rose, probably still tucked in her hair. But the man's heartbeat seemed steady and strong enough, though a little fast.

Muttering an exasperated curse under her breath, Meridy shook the man lightly. He moved a little, and his mouth twitched. Meridy looked at the ghost boy, standing nearby, nearly invisible in the woven shadows of the trees. "Can't you heal him?"

"No," the boy said, clipped and impatient. "Healing takes the aware assistance of a witch—and he's not a witch, anyway. You need to get him somewhere warm. Then I'll help you heal him, if it comes to that."

"Huh," Meridy muttered. He meant he'd let her bind him, a secondary binding if this man was already his anchor. It was still an unexpected offer. She didn't say that she didn't know how to heal anyone, that it would never have occurred to anyone in Tikiy-up-the-Mountain to ask for her help. That in Tikiy-up-the-Mountain, some people not only believed that a witch could bind the quick dead—which was true—but thought a witch could steal your soul and make you into a ghost while your body still walked and spoke and went about its days like a normal person, which as far as she knew was completely false. Though Aunt Tarana probably thought a girl with black eyes, even her own niece, was just waiting for a chance to do exactly that.

She looked back at the man, considering. He couldn't stay here in the damp, or he would surely die. Witches used ghosts to reach into the *ethereal* somehow, and their power to heal came from that; but even if the boy had been bound to her, which he wasn't, Meridy didn't know how any of that actually worked. And she certainly couldn't *carry* a grown man.

Meridy gingerly picked up the knife and tossed it some distance away. Then she leaned forward and pressed her hand firmly against the cut in the man's side.

He curled forward with a cry and caught her wrist with one hand, his grip much stronger than Meridy had expected. But after her first involuntary jerk away, she stopped herself and moved instead to offer support. The man's hand, so strong at first, rapidly weakened; she set her knee behind his shoulder to keep him up. "I can't carry you," she told him. "If you want to live, you must walk. I'll help, and it's not far."

The man stared at her wordlessly. His eyes were not black but a surprising, vivid blue. But his gaze was quite blank, as though he were still unconscious or the next thing to it.

"Or you can lie here in the mud and finish dying," Meridy said, refusing to be intimidated by either the man or the circumstances. "At the rate you're going, it won't take long."

Awareness slowly filtered back into the man's face. He made a small sound and struggled to get his feet under him. Meridy threw her strength into the struggle, and then he was up, swaying. The ghost boy watched critically but offered no advice.

The walk back up the hill was a nightmare of mud and

loose rocks and desperate sharp breaths as the injured man slipped, and caught himself, and slipped again. Blood dripped on the path. Meridy kept her head down and her eyes on the path, and she pretended to herself that it was just one more step, and then just one more, until the ghost boy flickered quickly in front of her, lifting his hands, and they *were* there, with the door to the inn a few paces away and a crowd of curious ghosts fluttering dimly within.

Between them, Meridy and the man managed to get up the few steps and inside and at last to the hearth of the nearest fireplace, where the man sank down as gratefully as though the stone hearth were a feather mattress. Meridy left him for a moment while she kindled a fire, thankful that on her last visit she had for once bothered to put wood by for future use. She fetched water and put a kettle over the fire to make tea, found the threadbare blankets in the corner where she stored them, and came back to the bench.

The man was fumbling with the clasp of his wet cloak, trying to get it off. His hands were shaking so badly that he could not manage the task but only made the cut on his side bleed faster. Meridy impatiently unfastened the clasp herself, getting his shirt off also while she was about it. The man was soon wrapped in the blankets, his violent shaking slowly winding down to a kind of gentle quivering. Meridy made tea and brought it to him in her best cracked mug, and he took it with hands that were only a little unsteady. She watched long enough to be sure he wouldn't drop the mug, then drew her boot knife and began to cut her cleanest blanket into bandages.

An hour later, the man, bandaged and no longer shivering, was working on a second mug of tea and the last of the slightly stale rolls Meridy had brought for her lunch. Meridy sat on the floor, her arms wrapped around her drawn-up legs, and watched him. The innkeeper's wife bustled around them both, building up the fire till it roared with *ethereal* flame and laying out transparent dishes loaded with *ethereal* food. It gave Meridy an odd sort of double vision, the innkeeper's wife's memories of this inn as it had been imposed over the faded reality. The ghost boy sat on a nearby table, watching, his expression closed and hard to read. His dog lay beside him, stretched out almost the whole length of the table, his enormous straight-jawed head resting on equally enormous paws, watching everything with evident approval. The dog's tail thumped soundlessly whenever Meridy looked at him. He certainly seemed friendlier than the boy.

The flagstone Meridy sat on was cold despite the fire. She was trying to ignore this discomfort by concentrating firmly on the man. Like the boy, he seemed to be of pure northern blood. His hair, drying, was quite curly and fair as sunlight, rare this far south.

He couldn't be a witch, not with blue eyes, but he wore no priest's medal at his throat. Not a witch, not a priest, yet he still anchored a ghost. . . . Any ordinary person might anchor someone they'd loved, a ghost who'd chosen to forsake the God's Road and linger, quick, in the *real* world after death. But Meridy didn't believe that could be the explanation in this case. The ghost boy was too old, had been quick too long. No ordinary person could hold a ghost for so long, keep him so much himself for so long, stop him for so long from either taking the White Road of the Moon or losing himself in the *real*.

No, she thought this man must actually be a sorcerer. If that was so, his magic would be rooted in the *real*. He would be able to affect the world directly, rather than depending on this ghost of his to help him touch the *ethereal* so he could bring dreams and imagination into the *real*. Yet he'd bound this ghost and held him, even though he probably didn't need him as a conduit for his magic. Meridy knew what that meant, or thought she did: according to Ambica's stories, the magic of a sorcerer like this might not be limited to the *real* world. He would probably also be able to reach from the *real* into the *ethereal*, the other way around from what a witch did. He would be different from anyone she'd ever met. Certainly he'd have no reason to be afraid of an untrained girl like Meridy, even if she was a black-eyed witch.

People mistrusted witches because they could bind a ghost, keep it from taking the God's Road; because they were rumored to be able to steal the souls of the living; because they mostly carried too much of the Southerner's foreign blood; and because too many witches had once followed Tai-Enchar when he'd betrayed the High King and the Kingdom. But in all the old tales, sorcerers were actually more powerful and unpredictable.

According to the tales, some sorcerers started as witches and then also learned to touch the *real* world without needing to work through ghosts. That was what Meridy had dreamed of learning to do, if she'd born during a higher, brighter age. But other sorcerers weren't witches at all, and those were the ones who were supposed to be more powerful. Some were said to be able not only to root their magic in the *real* world but also to step from the *real* into the *ethereal* realms and back again. Some were said to be able to take other people with them, somehow make them into servants or slaves. Or something. Tales offered wildly different ideas about exactly what happened to ordinary people who fell afoul of a wicked sorcerer. But sensible people were wise to be cautious around sorcerers; on that, all the tales agreed.

Yet it was hard to picture an actual sorcerer dying in the woods alone, or tucked up by the hearth of a ruined inn. The man's shirt, hung now near the fire to dry, was plain homespun, not so much better than the shirts they made in Tikiy. Surely a sorcerer would be wealthy. It was all very puzzling.

The man finished the roll and the tea and looked around the inn, right past and through the ghost boy—now lounging more at ease on the table, his elbows on his knees and his chin resting on his laced fingers—and also past the innkeeper's wife, and the innkeeper, and the clutter of other ghosts who had gathered near. Well, blue eyes. She shouldn't have expected he would see any of them, even if he was a sorcerer. And maybe he wasn't. She still wasn't sure.

There was a drawn look to his face. Lines of exhaustion and pain touched the corners of his mouth and his eyes, but there was something else there as well, less readable; Meridy thought it might be irony. His expression was oddly distant, as if most of his attention were on something else. Yet at the same time, for all this abstraction, he looked about the worn rafters and worn stones of the inn with a kind of wondering astonishment, as though of all places he might have found help, this ruined inn was surely the least expected. Above all, he no longer seemed like a man wandering close to the White Road.

The cornflower gaze finally fell upon Meridy. Fine eyebrows arched slightly in wondering appraisal. Meridy felt herself flushing. She could imagine what he must think of her, highborn as he plainly was, and faced now with a black-eyed village girl carrying the obvious stamp of Southern blood: the dusky skin and flyaway black hair, the broad-boned face and stocky frame. He wouldn't be surprised by her eyes. Southern blood for witchery, as the saying went, and northern blood for sorcery. She, at least, must seem a fitting occupant of this crumbling Tikiy inn, where otherwise only ghosts dwelt. Anger at the thought stiffened her back and let her meet his eyes as directly as she imagined her mother might have.

"An *ethereal* rose?" the man said at last. "I suppose we must be relieved you had no need of it, though I appreciate the thought. Did you make it yourself?"

Meridy, without thinking, lifted a hand to touch it and felt it dissolve beneath her fingertips. Her face warmed with embarrassment at her carelessness.

The ghost boy said coolly, "I made it for her. It seemed you might need it, as you were so incautious as to be wounded so far from any reasonable hope of help."

The man lifted one fine eyebrow but declined to answer this. "Forgive the manner of my acquaintance," he said to Meridy. "And believe me grateful for your attention. It was most good of you to offer assistance." His voice, in contrast to his worn appearance, was beautiful: rich and warm and expressive. His accent, quick and smooth and light on the ends of words, was nothing that he had learned in the shadow of the Anchor of the World.

Meridy inclined her head slightly, not at all sure she welcomed such flowery gratitude. She said, deliberately echoing his formality, "Perhaps you would be good enough to tell me who you are, and where you are from, and what you are doing here."

The innkeeper's wife said softly, "He's from up the north road, dear. Maybe Linn or Talina, or even Surem up in Moran Tal. See that fine skin and that pretty hair? You only see hair like that on northern men." The innkeeper's wife faded in and out of visibility in gentle waves, but her voice was perfectly audible for a ghost's. She added wistfully, "I knew a man from Surem, once, I did. Hair like that, gold on corn silk, just like that, but it was a long time ago. . . ." She faded gently away into memory.

The man looked around, startled. "This is a ghost town, then? It doesn't have quite the usual feel. *'Dorahd y hana caniy'*—"

"—*'umano y rahid caniy siërrid,'*" Meridy finished blandly. "A trifle overdramatic, I think, although in the moonlight one does pick up a certain odd feeling at times. Still, I think Barihd captured the idea better in *U Munohd, U Cahy*. Where did you say you're from?"

The man smiled a little. "Persistent child."

"And well-read, to cap *your* quotes," commented the ghost boy, his tone neutral but his gaze lingering on Meridy's worn skirts and work-roughened hands. "I must commend your teachers, girl. And your dedication to poetry, to learn those lines in the original Viënè."

The boy did not say, *Astonishing, for a mere village girl.* But Meridy heard that implication and resented it. She ignored him, keeping her own gaze on the living man instead.

"Kamam," the man said, with just the merest trace of amusement carried in that beautiful voice. "I'm from Kamam, originally."

'The city walls that, in the setting sun, Recall the running flames that cast the ramparts down; And let within the conquering sword. . . .'

Meridy interrupted him, giving the ghost boy her haughtiest look as she completed the lines:

'Red stone fever-hot, streets full of blood, Fear trapped in the shadows of the walls, Wind-caught the voices of the dead.'

"I've heard that it's beautiful, but not as grim as Laor Sinn made it sound. Who are you? If you're from Kamam, then you're from Tian Sur." From the other end of the world, in fact: as far north as one could possibly get without falling into the sea. "What are you doing *here*?"

But the man only asked, "Heard from whom?"

Meridy shrugged. "The ghosts tell me stories. One of them, Ambica, used to be a poet himself, I think."

"Did he?" the man said thoughtfully. "And bold enough to criticize Laor Tai-Sinn, king of poets. The rebuilt part of Kamam is lovely, but your Ambica is right that it doesn't hold memories. It was in the ruins of the old city that Laor Sinn heard the voices of the dead. Since we have wandered onto the subject, perhaps you would be good enough to tell me whether you are able actually to *see* the quick dead as well as hear their tales?"

He was asking whether she was actually a witch or merely dark eyed. That much was obvious. "Why should you care?" Meridy asked warily. "It's nothing to do with you."

"She can certainly see us," said the ghost boy, brief and decisive. "But it's more than that. She's *heavy*. Light breaks around her. She could learn to step into the realms of dreams, I've no doubt of it, and if she did, I believe the moonlight there would also run around her like water around a stone."

"Indeed," said the man. He glanced in the boy's general direction, though he plainly couldn't see him. "Witches for bringing dreams into the *real*, sorcerers for carrying the *real*

26

away into the realm of dreams, as they say. Interesting. And she was born so far out of the way that . . . no one . . . ever discovered her."

"Wonderful," said Meridy, giving both living man and quick boy her best annoyed look for talking about her like she wasn't even present, though she was too interested in who could possibly be meant by that fraught *no one* to be angry. She said, hoping to draw one or the other of them, "I'm glad to be *interesting,* I'm sure, and I suppose *you're* claiming to be a sorcerer, is that right? Or are you a priest?"

The boy gave her a tiny shrug.

"Forgive me if I have worried you, child," the man said, clearly amused. "I'm not precisely a sorcerer, or a priest. Not in the ordinary sense. Not tinker, not soldier, not candlemaker—no one you need worry about, I assure you. But it's interesting, finding a girl like you here, so far out of the way. A girl, moreover, who seeks out the ghosts of poets and storytellers. Indeed, perhaps that's why . . ." His hand went to his side in an unthinking gesture.

Meridy stiffened. "I didn't have anything to do with your being hurt."

"Certainly not," the man said at once. "I did not mean to imply any such suspicion, child. I was only thinking that the God clearly saw fit to put me in your way. I don't for a moment imagine it's chance that cast me from the realms of dream into the *real* at nearly the very doorstep of an untrained witch-girl such as yourself."

" 'So once more swift on the goalless road the traveler proceed—' " began the ghost boy.

"Well, well, that's neither here nor there, just at the moment, perhaps," the man cut in smoothly.

Meridy thought for a moment and then said triumphantly, "That's from Ilonn Tivona's epic about the death of the sorceress Aseraiëth! I know that one. Her road led neither to the realm of the God nor back into the *real;* it didn't lead anywhere but looped in a circle, so she was trapped between realms, half living and half dead. I could never decide whether the poet meant us to be sorry for her or not. He didn't make her sound very nice."

The man's mouth twitched. "Well," he said to the boy, "you're the one who declared her well-read. You might have taken that a bit more to heart."

"But what does that *mean?*" demanded Meridy. "All that about you finding yourself here, I mean. You don't think the God actually guided your steps?"

"Who can say? The God does have these little whims. I wonder whether you would be so kind as to tell me where exactly it is that I find myself. Somewhere in the deep South, of course, to have Linn referred to as a northern city, but precisely what locale?"

She hesitated, but she could think of no reason not to tell him. "Tikiy. The nearest big city is Riam, and that's days and days away. Ten days, maybe twelve, maybe more. Sann is the closest town, but it's still three days' walk and not very big."

"As far south as that." The man sounded as though he were coming to terms with something he had half expected but not truly believed. "In the shadow of the Anchor, on the very edge of the world!" He regarded her with still more interest.

Meridy eyed him. "You know, you haven't explained how you came to be bleeding to death in the woods outside Tikiy."

The cornflower eyes narrowed with warm amusement. "Well, child, I think perhaps I was indeed finding you."

"Because the God put you in my path."

"Is that so difficult to believe? Doesn't the God turn events toward the right path? You are, I believe, quite a powerful young witch." His glance was uncomfortably acute, and he added, his tone still light and yet with an underlying seriousness to it, "How fortunate that you were born in the shadow of the Wall. Indeed, in a village so small that you could grow up untroubled, in these days when so many young witches meet an unfortunate fate just as they come into their gift."

Meridy scowled at him, annoyed that he could make her feel ignorant and bewildered. "Oh, do they? How does that come about? And what business is it of yours? You're not a witch. *Are* you a priest? You're not wearing a medal." Not that it mattered. She didn't *care* whether he was a priest, *or* a sorcerer either, just so long as he didn't interfere with her.

The man only smiled at her. "You may call me Carad Mereth, if you like. And I have been a priest, from time to time."

"Oh, *from time to time*? And I don't believe Carad Mereth can possibly be your name." In Viënè it meant "storm crow," and Meridy flatly refused to believe it was anybody's name.

"It's one of my names, in fact. And if you live long enough, you may find, my prickly child, that one may indeed be a priest from time to time."

She had an impression, stronger than ever, that the man was laughing at her, but though she looked at him carefully, his manner remained perfectly sober.

"And *your* name, child? If you will do me the favor to offer it to me?"

"You can call me Imariy," Meridy said coldly. "If you like." The term was not a name at all, but a word that specifically referred to nameless things.

The ghost boy smiled, a swift, surprising expression, and gave her a little salute, just a flick of one finger, as if she had scored a point in some tricky and unfamiliar game. Carad Mereth's eyes crinkled with humor, though she knew he couldn't have seen that gesture. He said, "More poetic than mine, at least. Very well, my impressively well-read nameless child. I'm pleased to make your acquaintance."

He bowed slightly, from his seated position. The gesture did not look the least bit affected. He might as well have been in the constant practice of bowing to threadbare girls in ruined village inns. There was no way this man had gotten his manners in any farmer's house.

She asked, "Are you a sorcerer, those times when you're not a priest? Can you step from the *real* into the *ethereal*? Is that how you got here, by crossing into dreams and then crossing back?" That would explain a lot, actually.

"I am not precisely a sorcerer—"

"He certainly is," said the ghost boy, almost loud enough to be heard by the living, from his perch on a nearby table.

The man peered around irritably. "I beg your pardon?"

The ghost boy shrugged, not seeming impressed.

While at least one of them seemed forthcoming, Meridy said, "You're his anchor, even if you're not a witch. All right, I know anyone can anchor a ghost. But he's too old to be kin to you, so how can you hold him? Sorcerers can't usually bind ghosts; they work with the *real,* mostly. Unless they're also witches, I mean, except you aren't. But somehow you've bound him anyway, haven't you?"

Carad Mereth, leaning wearily against the broken stones of the hearth, answered, "It's more or less true that no one but a witch can use one of the quick dead as a conduit between the *ethereal* and the *real.* However, it's not quite so true that

only a witch can bind a ghost. Such categories are the arbi-
trary creations of men, as they say, and the God does not often
trouble to consult our philosophies."

Meridy nodded. "So you're a sorcerer who's bound a ghost.
An old ghost, held long past his time." She didn't say, *So you're
the kind of sorcerer everyone admired and feared most in the old
stories, aren't you?* He probably knew what she meant, though,
judging from the tilt of his eyebrow.

The ghost boy laughed without sound. "Even raised here
at the edge of the world, she knows better than to be distracted by facile evasion."

The man shrugged, looking faintly irritated. "I have a few
skills I've collected in my life, that's all. I do what is put before
me to do, in whatever way I am able to do it. As do we all."

Meridy studied him. The man raised his eyebrows back
at her, copying her expression as though he could not imagine
how she could possibly have any further questions. Meridy
started to speak—and paused. She had a thousand questions
yet that she wanted to ask, so many that they all jumbled
together and she could not think how to frame any of them.

"Of your generosity," Carad Mereth said in the pause,
"might you be kind enough to build up the fire a trifle? This
does hurt a good deal." He gestured vaguely toward his side.
"I would like to think warmth might be of some use."

Meridy had built the fire up high right at the beginning,
so now she was almost out of wood. She would have to leave
the half-roofed inn to gather more. She was almost certain
that was the point: get her out of the way so he could talk to
his ghost without her overhearing.

Then she was ashamed of her suspicions. Maybe he did
want her out of the way for a little while, this man who said
his name was Storm Crow and insisted he wasn't a sorcerer,

him with his blue eyes and his old ghost. But he did look cold, despite the fire. His face was still drawn and tired, and Meridy knew that injury and blood loss could lead to fever even in summer. So she pushed herself to her feet and, because she didn't want him to think he had successfully distracted her from the question, told him, "I'll be back in just a minute. And then you can tell me what purpose brought you to the edge of the world."

"Yes," he murmured, lounging back on the warm hearth as though it were a couch and looking already half asleep.

three

The sunlight was startlingly bright after the dimness of the inn. Meridy glanced around indecisively, not sure which way to go to find wood. Off toward the center of town was closer, but usually dead wood was more abundant at the edge of town, where the forest had long been encroaching. She was aware of an unaccustomed excitement, which she was too self-conscious about to give free rein. Sorcerers and magic! She was certain Carad Mereth was a sorcerer. All that nonsense about being a priest just some of the time! He didn't seem wicked. If he was a sorcerer, maybe he would explain how a witch learned to be a sorcerer. Maybe he knew, even if he wasn't a witch himself. If she could learn that, she wouldn't need the help of a ghost to reach into the *ethereal*. That would show Aunt Tarana—it would show everybody. If she could be a sorcerer, she wouldn't have to worry about being apprenticed to a soap maker.

And the poetry! She'd never met anybody but Ambica who would refer to Laor Tai-Sinn, who would even know that *tai* was a way of saying *king*. He'd quoted the poet so casually, he must know the classics well, better than she did; he could teach her poetry and history, too.

She longed to know what he might be saying to his ghost, but she was not a child to listen at the door to see if she could overhear anything interesting. She couldn't hear anything anyway, other than a low, indistinct murmur of voices. So she might as well gather wood after all, and if she was quick, maybe they would still be talking when she came back.

She ran down the inn steps, careful of the uneven places, and hurried toward the center of town, hunting for dead branches that would be easy to break and carry. It took longer than she had hoped to collect a good armful. To her surprise, before she was finished, she caught a shadowy flicker out of the corner of her eye and found that the ghost dog had come after her. He stood like a king's dog from some story, calm and alert, his tail waving slowly, but his ears were canted back as though he was not quite certain of his welcome. So of course she had to put down half the wood she'd gathered and rub his insubstantial ears.

Then when she would have gone back to gathering wood, the dog leaned his bodiless bulk against her hip, demanding more attention. She didn't have to bend down at all to pet him. Yet for all his size, he was an elegant creature. His eyes were set deep beneath wiry brows; his jaw and the planes of his skull were level and strong; his shoulders sloped well back from his long neck. Again she thought of the tall hounds that were shown, in illuminated histories, as the companions of kings.

"Were you ever a king's dog?" she asked him, smiling at this fancy. "You're a long, long way from any king's court now, aren't you?"

The dog wagged his tail and leaned on her harder, almost enough for her to imagine that she felt his weight. If he'd been a living dog, she was sure he would have pushed her right over. So she had to pet him again and assure him he was a fine dog even if he was a ghost, and so gathering the wood took a little longer still.

Given all that, she supposed she shouldn't have been astonished to find, when at length she made her way back to the shelter of the inn, that Carad Mereth was gone. But she was astonished.

Meridy frowned around the empty room, her vision shifting between the dilapidated, half-rotted wood and dusty stone of the present building and the polished, clean, cluttered image of the cherished past. Naturally the ghost boy was gone; that didn't surprise Meridy a bit. But the dog had followed her and was still here. That surprised her a good deal. She had been sure he was the boy's dog. But he stood in the doorway, blocking none of the afternoon light, and showed no signs that he knew he had been abandoned and no inclination to try to follow his master.

Other than the dog, there were bloodstains on the hearth where Carad Mereth had lain, and bits of torn blankets scattered on the floor, and that was all.

"Ambica!" Meridy said out loud, turned on her heel, and stalked out of the inn.

The ghost dog leaped down from the porch and trotted along with her. Meridy could not believe the boy had left him behind, and resented it fiercely on the wolfhound's behalf, but the dog, to her puzzlement, seemed cheerful. His head was up and his ears attentive to everything that moved, ghost or bird or swift flickering lizard, but he moved confidently, not with the cringing nervousness of a dog that knows it has been abandoned. He came to nose at her hand from time to time, to make her pet him, but with an air of reassuring her rather than seeking reassurance. In the way of any ghost dog, he seemed to want the company of a living person, and she suspected she'd bound him without realizing what she'd done. She certainly hadn't chanted his name or declared her intention to anchor him to the world, the way witches did in Ambica's stories. On the other hand, she didn't know how much of that was necessary and how much poets just made up because it sounded impressive.

If she'd accidentally made herself an anchor for the dog, it was a little disturbing, but at least he didn't seem to mind, and she was glad of it. Glad he was with her, glad he seemed willing to stay by her. She ran her hand over his half-perceptible ears and hoped he *was* anchored and would stay close.

Ambica smiled when she approached, and he held up a rose. The afternoon sun caught dust motes in the air, outlining his thin hand with a fine pale light but turning the flower blood-red. Meridy set her hands on her hips and glowered at him. "You hear everything, old man. Tell me, why a rose? Did you *know* the ghost boy who gave me the other?"

Ambica crinkled his eyes at her, amused. "Why not a rose, thorny child? Every house needs its sign, and it's the scent of roses that summons the soul and wakes the sleeping dead, isn't that what the poets say? I'll wager you've been woken from *your* sleep, eh, child?"

Meridy snorted.

"Maybe I knew him and maybe I didn't; how can I tell?" Ambica went on, more abstracted now. "I remember stories better than my own life. But I saw that old ghost make his rose for you. He's no one who died here, that one. He died long ago. Long ago." He blinked, recalling himself to the present. "Well, well, and you met his anchor, then, and helped the man? Good. Yes, that's good."

"Now he's gone!" Meridy snapped. "They're both gone, and what do you know about it?"

"Well, well, not much, but there's nothing so very astounding in their going. Sharp set, that boy, and his anchor no less so, or I miss my guess." He peered at her with shrewd interest. "Did he give you his name, that ghost boy? Did his anchor give you his right name?"

"He said his name was Carad Mereth. He was a sorcerer, I think. Or a priest. Although he said he wasn't—or only some of the time. How can you be a priest only some of the time?"

A translucent hand fluttered. "Perhaps the God calls to his soul only now and again; who can tell? Carad Mereth, did he say? From the tales, that will be. The bird that flies before the storm; the bird that brings the storm trailing from the tips of its wings. What color were his eyes?"

"Not black."

"So he would not be a witch, although—yes, perhaps a sorcerer."

"I know. *Are* sorcerers always wicked?"

Ambica laughed at her. "No, no, of course not, no more than witches. Sorcerers are like anyone else, good and bad and mostly in between. I knew half a handful of sorcerers, once. Deira Cias, who was a priest before he came into the skill, and never stopped listening for the voice of the God—so you see? He certainly wasn't evil. He never trusted Tai-Enchar, argued against his influence with the High King. . . . Perhaps that was the voice of the God there as well. This was in the old days, of course, when Tai-Enchar was merely one more lesser king and answered to the High King's rule, or so men thought. These were the days before he betrayed Miranua-nol, betrayed us all, tried to raise up his witches to rule men and himself to rule over all." Ambica had fallen easily into a storyteller's cadence, and he went on with measured phrases: "In those days, the Southerners still came by ones and twos, trading gemstones and iron and spices for the dyes and alum and pearls of the Kingdom. In those days, no one mistrusted Southern blood or feared witches' treachery."

"I know," said Meridy. "You've told me."

But the story carried Ambica forward anyway, as sometimes happened. "But then the days of peace gave way to days of war, and the Southerners rode across the desert lands in their armies, perhaps for lust to conquer or perhaps pressed by some disaster in their unknown homeland; who can say? Then the Southerners came in their thousands and their tens of thousands, with sword and flame, mounted on vicious sharp-clawed fire horses as terrible as their riders, and they conquered all the southern part of the Kingdom, driving the folk of those lands into the north. . . ."

Meridy had heard all this many times before. She said impatiently, "Yes, but sorcerers? You said you knew Deira Cias. Whom else did you know?"

Ambica blinked, recalled to the actual moment. He said thoughtfully, "No one called Carad Mereth. I knew Usamie, who could speak to any creature living or quick but hardly ever said a word to any man, though there were plenty as tried her silence. She was a beauty, was Usamie. I told her a story, once, and she laughed out loud at the ending. Aseraiëth, now, she was one of Tai-Enchar's allies at the end, to her shame. She had been Laìdomìdan's lover—did I ever tell you that story?"

"I don't think so. . . ."

"Well, she fell under the witch-king's sway, she did, or maybe led him into treachery herself. I don't think anyone ever knew the truth of it. Ambitious, that was Aseraiëth, for all her fair beauty. I thought Laìdomìdan would win her heart, but Tai-Enchar promised her power, and she wanted that more than love." Ambica was silent for a moment, remembering. He went on at last in a quieter tone, "Not that Laìdomìdan wasn't ambitious on his own account. I remember him laying down the law with that arrogance of his to High King Miranuanol himself. He could do *arrogance* up fancy when he chose, could that one; no wonder he and Aseraiëth were lovers for that time."

Meridy snorted. "My Carad Mereth was arrogant enough to fit right in, I think. I suppose those sorcerers are all long dead."

"Oh, aye, those were the great ones when I was young myself—near as young as you are now, Mery, my girl. Young enough to go out on the roads of the land with a light heart and an empty pocket, just as you're going now."

Meridy stared at him. But then she realized it was true. She *was* going. Now, this hour. She was going to walk away, leave Aunt Tarana's house just as her aunt had wanted, but on her own terms, with nothing to remind her of her aunt's bitter charity and no apprenticeship contract to constrain where she would go. She had not even known it until now, and yet she was not even surprised.

Ambica tilted his head, a smile pulling at the corner of his mouth. "Ah, that village up the mountain was never any place for you! I remember Kamay, who gave you her black eyes and her cleverness with poetry and her crooked smile." His face went a little vague on that recollection, with the difficulty the lingering dead had with time and memories, but he added, "She used to come talk to me, too, though she saw the *ethereal* only in glimpses. Your eyes she had, but only a trace of Southern blood. You, now, you can call the *ethereal* to your hand. You can almost reach out of the *real* to touch the *ethereal*. Perhaps you will, someday. I'd have liked to see you come into your strength, young Mery."

"You'll miss me. I'm sorry for that."

"Ah?" The old man blinked back at her. "I've my memories, bramble-girl. And the road out there runs both ways, so it does. Remember that." The spidery hand lifted again, to wave her on. "So go on, go on, young Mery, my rose-child-all-thorns. Take the first turning and see where it leads—but be careful! Don't be too proud to take help where it's offered; give it back where it's needed; and pay attention to any dreams you have in which the moon is full."

"Yes, Ambica," Meridy said obediently. She found she was smiling after all. She felt light, somehow, and no longer angry with Carad Mereth. She was hardly even angry with Aunt Tarana, now that she knew she was going to leave Tikiy and not go back to her aunt's house.

"And never patronize your elders!" Ambica told her severely.

"Of course not, Ambica."

The sun at his back turned the storyteller translucent as glass, but his voice was still clear. "Well, then, be sure to visit Moran Diorr while you're about it, my girl. The City of Bells is a wonder of the world, so it is."

Fishes swam now among the towers of Moran Diorr. Eels lived in the High King's hall; anemones swayed among the jewels and the bones. Ambica had told Meridy that tale himself, but she forbore to remind him now. The memories of the long dead were always chancy. She said instead, "I will if I can! And you, old man, think up a new tale to tell me, for when I get back." It was, she realized, the truest goodbye she had to say to anyone in either the old Tikiy or the newer village. That made her stop smiling.

She ducked away quickly and went, before the gathering brightness of the day could make her eyes water. Behind her she heard the murmur of Ambica's voice, spinning out a story: *Once there was a briar-girl, born from the kiss of sunlight upon the rarest sort of rose. . . .*

She half wanted to listen, but she hesitated only a second and then went on after all.

Meridy did not climb the path back toward Aunt Tarana's house and Tikiy-up-the-Mountain. She went the other way, the way she had never gone in all her life, across the stones laid into the stream and down the path on the other side of Tikiy-by-the-Water, following the rippling little creek north toward the Yellow River, which she had never seen save as a line on a map.

She picked her way over and around the fragmented stones that had once paved a wider road, a great highway from the time before the mountains of the Wall had been raised up, with the Anchor to hold the Wall fast forever against Southern magic. Even now some of those ancient paving stones remained visible, though broken by frost and pushed up here and there by great knobby tree roots, half hidden in places by the accumulated soil and leaves of the passing years.

The ghost dog came with her, through the ragged lanes to the edge of town, around the tumbled stones of the town wall, and down the path. He had taken her as his anchor to the living world, plainly so, though Meridy hadn't done anything to bind him, not that she knew of. Sometimes he trotted before her and sometimes he ranged off to one side or the other, slipping in and out of visibility as he padded through patches of sunlight and shadows, but he never left her. She was glad. Because she might have left Tikiy on her own and for her own reasons, but as long as the dog was with her, she didn't feel too much alone. And she felt, somehow, that he might know even where he was going, though she didn't. After all, the dog wasn't from Tikiy. He was from the broader world, and now he was going back to that broader world. And she could tell from his cheerful gait and his waving tail that *he* wasn't afraid.

four

Just under three hours after leaving Tikiy-by-the-Water, Meridy climbed over a fallen tree, clambered around an inconvenient pile of boulders that must have tumbled down last winter and that no one had bothered to move out of the way, and stepped at last onto the hard-packed earth of the Yellow River Road. She stamped her foot on it, proving its solidity: she was really standing here, on an actual road that led away from the mountain villages and out into the world. The river itself, beyond the road, was broader and slower than she had expected: here where the foothills of the Southern Wall abruptly gave way to gentler land, the river had room to stretch out. The water was indeed an earthy yellow, the froth where the stream came down a paler ivory.

First she looked out across the river. Then she stood with one hand resting on the ghost dog's half-present back and gazed down the road to the east, then turned and looked along it to the west. The road ran as far as she could see in both directions. It ran broad and nearly straight through the woodlands, only turned a little this way and that to accommodate the rougher foothills. It was the first true road she had ever seen; neither uneven wagon track nor ancient highway overgrown by centuries of forest. The lowering sun ran down the road, gilding the dust and turning the Yellow River ruddy.

Meridy had spent long solitary afternoons following in her mind the windings of the Yellow River Road. She knew that from here the Yellow River ran east to where the Wasp River joined it, and then went on farther east, past all the small towns and villages of the foothills, until eventually it came to Tamar, on the eastern coast, and so to the sea. She would like to see the sea—she couldn't even imagine it—but she knew she didn't want to go east.

If she turned west, the Yellow River Road would soon leave the Yellow River behind, cross from Harann into the principality of Cora Tal, and enter the lands of stories and histories. If she went that way, this road would lead her all the way to Riam. Riam! She wanted to see it: a city that had lain cradled in the western hills since the time of the high kings. Hardly anyone from Tikiy had ever been so far. Meridy longed to go there.

And from Riam . . . she hardly dared imagine it, but Riam was the gateway to the whole north. From Riam, the Riamne Highway curved north and west, and then farther north and farther west, touching the Western Ocean at Loran and then passing from the principality of Cora Tal into Moran Tal. It was called the Suremne Highway then, but it was all the same road. It did not end until it culminated finally in Surem on the shore of Moran Bay.

Ambica's stories crowded into Meridy's memory: stories of the High King's city, Moran Diorr, which had drowned when Tai-Enchar betrayed the Kingdom and the High King. The witch-king had wanted the Southerners to conquer the

Kingdom; he'd wanted to establish a different sort of king-dom, one where witches ruled over ordinary men and he ruled over all. And so when High King Miranuanol had cast the great sorcery to drive back the Southerners and raise up the Southern Wall so they could never return, Tai-Enchar had turned against him and broken his hold on all the power of that sorcerous working. And the sorcery had shattered and Moran Diorr had sunk down, and the ocean had rolled in over them all.

Meridy could almost see the great sprawling city of Moran Diorr in her mind's eye. She longed to look over the bay that hid the drowned city. She had always wanted that: to see Surem, and Moran Bay where Moran Diorr lay under the waves—to get out of the shadow of the Anchor and see all the famous and wonderful places in the world.

But now she also thought, scuffing her boot uneasily through the dust of the Yellow River Road, that seeing roads on maps was not the same as standing on them. It was a good deal safer to look at a road on paper than it was actually to walk on one, at least for a girl traveling on her own. Or almost on her own. She stroked the ghost dog's barely perceptible head and smiled down at him. He was a great comfort, but he was a ghost, after all, not a living dog. There must be brig-ands along these roads; not many, surely, but some. The men of Tikiy-up-the-Mountain had caught a dozen and hanged them, not so many years ago. . . . Meridy remembered people talking about that for many weeks afterward. The thought of running into brigands frightened her.

But trying to go across country would be even worse. Much slower, for one thing, and then there were wolves—not so dangerous, especially in summer, but griffins might have come down from the heights. And there were fire horses in these mountains, bigger and worse-tempered and more savage than either wolves or griffins, or so people said. Fire horses killed sheep, usually in late winter when game was poor, but unlike wolves, sometimes they killed the shepherds as well. Meridy might have dreamed of taming a beautiful fire horse, but now she had to admit that, to a girl alone, fire horses were almost as frightening as brigands.

"West, then, on the road," Meridy said to the ghost dog. He looked at her, tilting his head to the side as though he were considering what she said, and she laughed and ran her hand along his jaw and down his elegant neck. "As long as you agree!" she told him. Then, turning into the setting sun, Meridy started walking along the side of the road, dust puffing up with every step. The dog walked with her, but his paws did not disturb the dust, except every now and then, when he left an enormous paw print alongside her boots' scuff marks. She smiled, noticing that, certain now she had indeed anchored the wolfhound, even without knowing how or performing any sort of ritual. She knew there *was* some kind of ritual, but the old tales were scant of detail—maybe to stop any random village girl from learning how to bind the lingering dead.

But she had bound the dog, and she was very glad of it, because he meant she wasn't alone on this road.

She thought she would walk a little while and then stop by the river and eat the hard bread that was all she had with her and maybe fish for a while. Fish liked to bite at dusk. She was lucky she'd kept spare line in Tikiy-by-the-Water, or else she'd have no hope tonight of anything but a bite of bread, and little hope of anything at all tomorrow. She was glad of the blanket she carried, too, threadbare as it was. It would not be cold at night, but a blanket was a comfort, if not so great a comfort as a dog.

Two days later, Meridy was still walking along the road, but she was beginning to think that her worries about brigands and ferocious animals had been needless. She had crossed the Yellow River and left it behind her, continuing west into more open country. She thought she was probably now in Cora Tal, though to her eye it looked much the same as Harann. Streams still came down from her left, dashing out of the foothills, so water was not a difficulty. But she was not going to find fish in quick, shallow streams like those. Frogs, maybe. Or snakes. She tried not to worry about the possibility of snakes.

She had so far met no other people at all, respectable or otherwise. The only signs of animal life had been little birds, and once a rabbit, and from time to time faint glimpses of translucent ghost shimmer, where some creature had died suddenly and not yet gone to the God.

Judging by tracks in the dust, it seemed that recently there had been quite a bit of traffic on the road, and she thought one large group was no more than an hour or two ahead of her. It might be possible to catch up with it. She wondered if she should try. But at the moment, nothing moved; the air was sticky with a foretaste of high summer. Meridy was sleepy. She had stopped once to pick a few narrow leaves from a redneedle bush and chewed them while she walked. The sharp flavor was pleasant, but real food would have been even more welcome. She had nothing left of the fish she'd caught yesterday.

Coming around a long bend, Meridy was pleased to see

a small creek across the road. It dashed down from the hills in a fast, narrow waterfall, spread out within shallow banks as it crossed the road, and quickened again on the other side, tumbling out toward the drier country to the east. Stepping-stones had been placed through the stream for convenience in crossing. Meridy picked the biggest, knelt on it, and started turning over smaller rocks. She was rewarded almost at once with a big crayfish, which she picked neatly out of the water. She dropped it into her skirt and looked for more. The ghost dog grew bored and wandered out of sight, but Meridy kept turning over rocks. The creek was productive; a quarter hour of searching yielded a dozen more large crayfish and one small one that she tossed back. She picked a handful of wild sorrel to go with them. Steamed in their shells, the crayfish would make a perfectly good meal. Pity she had no butter.

She found a comfortable place off the road, sheltered under a large pine, to make a fire, with dry needles for tinder. Even with the needles, it took a little while to get the fire kindled and to cook the crayfish, but it was nice to sit still for a while.

She had finished eating, and was just starting to kick dirt over her fire, when a drawling voice behind her made her whirl.

"Well, well, not competition after all, is it?" There were four men in the little clearing, all with drawn knives or swords. Their clothing was worn and ragged, but it had been of good quality once—doubtless stolen from wealthier men. The one who had spoken was in the lead. "Go tell the others what we got here," he added to one of his companions. The man grinned nastily and jogged off through the woods.

The leader wore mail over his shirt, and ill kept as his clothing was, Meridy could see that the mail was in good shape, which meant he was a fighter, and not too stupid. He and his men spread out now, cutting her off from the road. Not that it mattered, since she had no one to run to for help.

"All on your own, girl? Didn't know better than to pick wood that smokes?" asked the leader. The contempt in his voice made Meridy want to hit him—or run. She did neither. She stood still and tried to think. How could she have thought it such a fine idea to leave Tikiy? Would being a soap maker's apprentice have been so bad, really? She took a quick breath, and another, struggling to steady herself.

"Village brat, by that skirt and them shoes," one of the others, with a scar across his face just below his eye, commented disdainfully. "And too much Southern blood in her. Look at her: brown as a nut, and she won't clean up anyways special."

The scarred man was almost as dark-complexioned and probably as common-born as Meridy, but he obviously felt no kindness for a girl, even one who shared his Southern blood. She looked around hopelessly for a way out, knowing she wouldn't find one.

The leader shrugged. "She'd clean up good enough for a man as isn't too particular. Specially if she's a virgin. You a virgin, girl?"

"Yes." Meridy didn't have any trouble at all putting a quiver in her voice. If they decided not to touch her, it might be best to give up quietly and try to get away later.

"Do we care?" That was Scar again. "There's not so much price difference. And look at the eyes on her—black as pitch on a moonless night."

"Oh, well, I can think of places they ain't so picky," the third man said. He had his dirty hair in a loose braid, a style

Meridy hadn't seen before on a man. "Places where they don't care if a girl's brown or milk pale, nor if her eyes are black, decent brown, or red as coals."

"Maro's, you mean," said the leader. "Them don't care if a girl's a virgin, neither. I say we do her ourselves, keep her till we've got enough goods to make the trip worthwhile, and take her along to Riam. We can sell her to Maro as already trained."

Meridy hooked her small knife out of her boot, threw it hard at Braid—he was closest—and leaped to grab the lowest branches of the pine at her back. The leader's fingers brushed her foot, and she convulsed upward and clawed her way to a secure perch on sheer terror.

"Little bitch!" To her utter surprise, Braid was clutching the hilt of her knife, which was buried in his stomach. She wondered faintly if it had been a big enough knife to kill him and, if so, how long it would take him to die.

The leader glared at her, ignoring the wounded man. "Get down here, girl-bitch!"

It wasn't funny, but Meridy laughed in pure astonishment that he thought she might obey. The leader reddened and jumped for the lowest limb of the tree. Meridy grabbed a thin branch and whipped him across the face with the needled end as hard as she could, and he lost his grip, cursing. She climbed a little higher. Did they have bows? She didn't see any. And then she did as Scar turned: a small crossbow, but more than adequate.

The leader looked at it, looked at her, and smiled. It was the meanest smile Meridy had ever seen.

"Shoot her in the legs or the hands," he said. "Be careful not to kill her. I want her alive."

"It'll ruin her value," Scar pointed out.

The leader was still smiling. "Screw her value."

Scar shrugged and set a quarrel in the crossbow. Meridy took a deep breath and edged around to put the trunk of the tree between her and the bow. It was amazing how much thinner the tree suddenly looked. Braid, still gripping the knife in his stomach, made a coughing sound and fell to his knees. The leader glanced that way in evident annoyance, stepped over, and cut Braid's throat with the skill of long practice, stepping back to avoid the blood. Meridy didn't throw up, but it was an effort.

Scar lifted the crossbow. Meridy stared at him . . . and out of the corner of her eye saw a flicker, both like and unlike a glimmer of sunlight through the leaves. She blinked. The first quarrel pinned her skirt to a branch. Meridy jumped and made a small noise embarrassingly like a whimper, but she didn't look away from the movement she thought she had seen.

Then a large paw print appeared in the scuffed soil below the tree. Meridy caught her breath. Concentrating, she made out the shimmer of light along one powerful shoulder and flank. A second quarrel, deflected by the breeze, hit a branch directly in front of her knee. She flinched, losing the almost-image. Then smoke from her cooking fire blew across the ghost dog, and Meridy blinked and stared at it with fierce concentration, remembering stories in which witches used smoke or mist or dust to help demarcate the *ethereal,* help bring what they alone could see into the *real* so that anyone could see it. She had never tried to do anything like that herself, but she'd never been so scared, either. So she stared at the pale wisps from her smoldering fire and encouraged the diffuse smoke to outline the dog so anybody could see him—most of all so the brigands could see him. She made him a little more *real* than he had been, and a little more, and bent the *ethereal* into the *real*. And there he was: visible and suddenly almost *real*, a tall smoke-and-silver brindled wolfhound, looking much bigger now, tall and aggressive, with his hackles raised like a war dog from an old and violent tale.

Now that they were able to see him, both the brigands stared. Scar half lowered his bow.

Meridy drew one hard breath and shouted, "*Good* dog! *Get* them!"

Scar took a step backward.

The dog hit him at chest height. The outlaw went sprawling, too surprised to make a sound. Transparent fangs tore his throat out, and for a second spraying blood outlined the head and shoulders of the ghost dog, letting Meridy pull him farther into the *real*. The outlaw leader grabbed his sword up and slashed at the wolfhound. But the blade passed right through a half-visible back and thudded into the ground, pulling the man off balance, and the dog closed powerful jaws on his side, just above the hip, and shook him violently. The crack of his snapping spine was clear even over his scream.

Then there was a pause, during which nothing seemed to make a sound except the last harsh breaths of the dying outlaw leader. When even that stopped, the world seemed infinitely still.

Meridy clung to the branch and shook. The ghost dog crept to the base of the tree, making himself small, afraid, she could tell, that she would be mad at him. Probably he was not actually trained as a war dog and wasn't supposed to bite people. Meridy ripped her skirt free from the quarrel and managed to climb down from the tree without killing herself. She collapsed at its base, unable to stand. The dog came and put his weightless head in her lap. She put her arms around where he almost was and told him what a good dog he was, what a fine dog. Then she cried. The dog wiggled and licked her face and became more and more solid, there in the shadows of the trees, every translucent hair glimmering with its own *ethereal* light.

When Meridy had more or less recovered, she gathered up her things and repacked them, even the knife that she had thrown at Braid. It scraped sickeningly over the bone of his pelvis as she pulled it out, and she had to stop to throw up in the bushes. But she still went through the outlaws' pouches and took their coins. She didn't know how much all the coins were worth—there seemed a lot of different kinds—but she took them anyway. She also took the small crossbow and all the quarrels she could find. Then she went back to the road. Her legs were still shaky, but she knew she had to get far away. The fourth outlaw had been sent back to their group. Eventually they would start to wonder what the delay was.

That was the day she named the ghost dog. She named him Iëhiy, which was the name of a king's hound in one of the old tales. In Viënè it meant "lifted by fire" and might refer to smoke, or sparks, or souls.

Three days later, Meridy sat high on a hillside and watched a company of wagons set up camp by the road. She had retreated off the road after meeting the brigands, to watch for a westbound party that might be willing to let her travel with them, and that looked like the kind of people with whom Meridy would feel safe. She had thoroughly lost her appetite for traveling alone, but she was equally nervous about choosing the wrong kind of travelers to join. She was also a little bit worried because she had only the coins she'd taken from the outlaws to offer for her passage and she didn't know how much those were worth, or whether she might be able to ask for work in exchange for leave to travel with a caravan. It had never occurred to her to ask Ambica for everyday details about practical things. Now she was sorry for that.

This company looked good. There had been two other parties, and she liked the look of this one best. It was a merchant's train, judging by the wagons heavily laden with barrels, bales, and crates. There were fourteen wagons, plus about forty mounted men. Most of these were clearly guards, who looked tough, well armed, and disciplined. Four women were with the company, three driving wagons and the other watching over a gaggle of children. It was the children and the women that made Meridy decide to go down and try to get a place with the party.

She looked around for Iëhiy. The ghost dog was lounging in the shade of bayberry shrubs, nearly invisible even to her. The leaves of the bayberry sent a lacework of afternoon sunlight flickering across his back and legs, as though not quite sure that anything was there to reflect them. At her glance, the dog lifted his head attentively. Dust motes in the sunlight caught the outline of his head as it came into the direct light. Entirely transparent, he was nevertheless plain to her sight, like a dog carved of ice or fine glass. Leaves behind him were perfectly visible, though a little distorted and wavery.

"Well," Meridy told him, "I hope no one down there has eyes to see you, or they'll think I know how to bind ghosts, and you know how people feel about that. Well . . . we'll risk it. You want to come with me?" She stood up. The dog scrambled to his feet, tail waving enthusiastically. "Silly question, hmmm?" said Meridy. "Come on, little one. Don't bark, now."

Iëhiy, who had hardly barked once since he had been with

her and would not be heard if he did, raced in pleased circles around Meridy as she started down the hill. He came in closer as they got nearer the wagons and, as though conscious of his dignity, was right at her side by the time a rider noticed her and approached them.

The man reined up a short length away and stared at Meridy, frowning. He was broad-shouldered and powerfully built, and even with him on horseback it was obvious he was tall as well as big. He looked to be in his forties. Meridy thought he was probably not yet fifty, though his hair, coarse and nearly black and with plenty of curl to it, had lots of gray hairs mixed with the dark. He had a thin scar running from the corner of his mouth across his jaw, but despite his frown it didn't make him look mean, the way the outlaws had looked. Judging by his coloring, darker than any possible tan, he had some Southern blood behind him, though he'd clearly gotten all the height of his Kingdom ancestors. His eyes were brown.

"Surely you're not out here on the road alone, my girl?" the man demanded. He looked her over carefully, then lifted his gaze to examine the hills behind Meridy. Apparently reassured that no one was there, he studied her once more, looking rather askance at her black eyes and her slightly tattered condition. He gave no sign of noticing Iëhiy.

The dog, for his part, regarded the guard alertly, but his tail waved gently, which was reassuring.

"Have you parents hereabouts? Or a husband?" The man sounded doubtful on that last; girls as young as Meridy did sometimes marry, but most girls waited till they were a little older.

"No, sir," said Meridy, and lied smoothly. "My father was taken into the God's hand when I was little, and my mother just last week. I mean to join an aunt of mine in Riam, if I can get there. I hoped your people might let me travel with this party?"

The man still frowned. "Where are you from, then, girl?"

"Tikiy, sir. A village back in the hills, that way." She pointed vaguely. "But I don't have any kin near here. If I can't get to my aunt, I'll have to go to some closer town, Sann maybe, and ask for a place at the inn. . . ." She let this trail off.

The guard knew what kind of work a young girl without family or friends was likely to get. His frown eased. "I'm sorry to hear of your loss," he told her. "You'd better come talk to the owner. Be polite, hear?"

"Yes, sir," murmured Meridy as politely as she knew how.

But the guard hesitated another moment, looking at her. "You a witch?" he asked at last.

"No, sir," Meridy assured him. She'd thought out beforehand what to say to that question. "I see things sometimes, when the moon is full, but that's all."

The guard raised his eyebrows but didn't outright accuse her of lying the way a villager might have. He tipped his head toward the camp and repeated, "You'd better come talk to the owner."

Meridy walked beside the guard's horse to the campsite. Preparations for the night's camp hadn't stopped with her appearance, but they had slowed as wary guards scanned for any danger Meridy might have brought with her. As the man brought her in, the activity picked up again. Her escort waved a couple of the other guards out to scout, just in case.

The owner bustled over, a small, plump man with midfair coloring and a rather vague round face. He frowned anxiously as he looked from the guard to Meridy and back again, but

Meridy thought his face looked more accustomed to smiling. "What's this, hey?" he said. "What's this, then, Niniol?"

"She's from some local village," said the guard. "She'd like permission to travel with your train, excellent sir. She's heading for Riam, by your leave."

"That right?" The owner peered at her. "Is that right, my dear?" He spoke slowly and loudly, as if afraid she might be deaf or stupid. If he noticed her eyes, he didn't seem to think they were worthy of comment.

"That's ri— I mean, yes, indeed, excellent sir." Meridy offered him a small bow. "I'm trying to get to my aunt in Riam, excellent sir, and it's not safe to travel alone."

"Not safe to travel alone?" repeated the merchant. "No, no, certainly not at all safe, not safe at all. Of course you must travel with us, my dear. Why, I can hardly believe you ever thought of traveling to Riam on your own! You are alone, you said? She is alone, Niniol?"

He blinked at the guard, who sent a discreet sidelong smile at Meridy and said soberly, "Quite alone, excellent sir."

"Quite alone," mumbled the merchant. He bellowed, "Maraift!" so suddenly that Meridy jumped slightly.

The plump, fair woman who had been supervising the children arrived in a flurry of skirts. She surveyed Meridy with wide blue eyes. "Why, my dear, are you all alone?"

"Quite alone, excellent lady," Meridy assured her blandly.

The guard, Niniol, smothered a grin behind his hand.

"But, my dear, how dangerous!"

"She'd like to travel with us," interjected her husband.

Meridy started to say she could pay and would try to be no trouble, but the woman swamped her attempt to speak. "But of course she would, Derren, my dear, and of course she must! Why, the poor child! Imagine traveling *alone.*" Maraift shuddered visibly. "Why don't you just come sit by the fire, child, and have a mug of mulled cider? Just the thing when it's a bit nippy, I always say, don't you think so? And these evenings can be cool, can't they, even this time of year."

Meridy found herself enveloped in a warm cloud of concern and wafted toward the roaring bonfire at the center of the camp. She had hardly blinked before she found herself settled among cushions spread on a large rug at the fireside, a mug of hot spiced cider held in both hands, and four children of varying ages staring at her with wide-eyed interest. Iëhiy lay at her side, his weightless head pillowed on her thigh. His obvious comfort helped ease Meridy's own tension.

"Now, my dear," said the woman warmly, "supper will just be a moment. I'm sure you're starving. I'm Maraift, as I'm sure you heard my husband say, that is, Maraift Gehliy. My husband over there is Derren Gehliy, and these are my children, but I don't expect you'll care to hear all their names just at the moment, my dear, at least if you're like me and can't remember such things. Mind like a sieve, that's me. And your name, my dear?"

"Meridy Turiyn," Meridy said into this flood of words. "I'm traveling to my aunt in Riam, by your kind permission, excellent lady."

"Of course you are, dear. At least, that's where we're going, Riam, I mean, not your aunt's, so I expect that's where you're going, if you're traveling with us. But you mustn't call me excellent lady the whole way, it would get so tiresome, don't you think? I'm Maraift to everyone, my dear." The woman patted Meridy's hand maternally, without the faintest sign of disapproval of her Southern blood or black eyes. "I'm so pleased you're with us, Meridy, dear, because Jaift does so enjoy other girls her age to talk with." She nodded toward a tall honey-blond girl with a baby on one hip and a long wooden spoon in her hand, stirring a large pot of something that smelled delicious.

"That's Jaift there, with my youngest. Jaift is my second-oldest, dear, and we're hoping to find her a nice husband in Riam. My oldest daughter's husband didn't care to come into Derren's business—well, who can blame him with a good place as a district manager for the Eine Bank? But it does leave us in a spot, without enough young people learning the business, you know." She paused expectantly.

"Um, yes," said Meridy.

"So naturally we're hoping to find a nice young man who can take a proper interest in the business." Maraift effortlessly took back the conversation. "The Derem family in Riam has a nice boy the right age, but of course young people today just *insist* upon meeting before deciding anything. Well, I suppose that *is* sensible—look at what happened to dear Erenniy's boy when he married that unfortunate girl from Genn. But it *is* inconvenient to gather up the whole peck-and-pack and make the journey. Still, it's a treat for the little ones; they've never been to Riam before, you know. I don't suppose you've ever been there either, my dear."

"Um, no," Meridy admitted.

"Oh, well, dear, I'm sure you'll enjoy it. It's a great city, you know. Quite splendid, at least if you like large cities. It can be a little overwhelming, I always think. Not at all like our own city, Tamar, which I always say is more *comfortable* than impressive, you know, but then there's a lot to be said for comfort, don't you think so, dear? Especially for everyday life."

"I guess so," agreed Meridy, beginning to be slightly mes-merized by Maraift's kind deluges.

"Besides, if we want something splendid to look at in Tamar, there's always the sea. Stormy or sunlit, there's nothing like the sea for beauty, I always say. Though it is a pity Tamar always smells of fish. I sometimes think we could make a fortune in perfumes and incense, but then such things are so expensive to buy in the first place that perhaps no one could afford to take them off our hands once we got them to Tamar, so I suppose it's a good thing we haven't bought them up in great amounts. Besides, everyone does get used to the fish eventually. That's what we do, of course. Dried fish, salted fish, fish oil, my dear, you have no idea. And cider, to be sure, apples are the other thing we do well in Tamar. Why, I don't doubt but what some of the cider we have here in these very wagons will end on the prince's own table in Cora Diorr. Oh, look, here's supper." Maraift interrupted herself to take the bowls offered her by Jaift and pass one to Meridy.

Jaift smiled at Meridy, a show of friendliness Meridy didn't trust for a second. Derren Gehliy and Maraift, maybe; they were adults, and belonged to a merchant family, and probably were used to being nice to all kinds of people. But Meridy had never met a girl close to her own age who wasn't eager to show everyone how much better she was than a fatherless black-eyed girl.

Jaift's eyes were a perfectly ordinary blue, her skin fair, her expression a touch vague. If she disapproved of her mother's kindness to a village girl or was taken aback by the color of Meridy's eyes, she didn't let it show. Of course, she didn't know about Meridy's learning poetry yet, or about her unnamed father. But she didn't linger to ask questions, either, turning back to the cooking pots after only a slight hesitation.

Meridy gazed after Jaift for a moment, not quite able to

figure out what puzzled her but feeling obscurely that *something* about Jaift's manner had been odd. Then she tasted the thick stew. The main ingredient seemed to be fish, with potatoes and onions. "This is delicious," she said sincerely. Iëhiy sighed wistfully. He knew he couldn't eat *real* food, but he would have liked to try anyway. Meridy rubbed his flank with her foot comfortingly. She might have made a spoonful *ethereal* for him, but not in front of other people, especially strangers, no matter how friendly they might seem.

Looking up again, Meridy found Jaift studying her from over by the fire, no longer seeming in the least vague. But when their eyes met, the other girl only smiled politely, nodded, and turned to stir a pot as though she weren't at all interested in the girl her parents had befriended.

"I'm glad you like it, dear," Maraift was saying. "Jaift does have a nice bit of skill with spices. Why, I can't tell you how the sauces improved the second she was old enough to stand on tiptoe and stir the pots. Of course, it rather annoyed the cook until she started begging for lessons in pastry making. That did the trick. Not entirely a master with sauces, is our cook, but a sorcerer with cakes and confections and such. Jaift used to skimp on her other lessons in favor of spending time in the kitchens, but as I told Derren, any girl can pick up embroidery and deportment and accounting along the way, and music isn't really that important, but a talent in cookery, now that will hold a husband's interest. Not that Derren ever taxes me with my lack in that direction, the dear man, but of course we've always had cooks."

Meridy allowed Maraift's comfortable babble to wash over her in soft, warm waves. She ate the stew and hard bread, occasionally murmuring agreement when a pause presented itself. As full dark came down, she let herself be wrapped in a blanket and gently deposited near the other children under one of the wagons. Fingers of moonlight lay under the wagon, lending a gentle illumination that let her see Iëhiy, gleaming palely, stretched out beside her. Feeling safe for the first time in days, Meridy fell instantly to sleep.

five

Meridy woke with a jerk. She wasn't sure what had woken her—something sudden and loud, she thought, like someone shouting in her ear. At first she thought someone actually had shouted, a half-familiar voice, but now she seemed to be completely alone. In fact, it was quiet. Stunningly quiet. The silence before the world began might have been like this: a great roaring silence that was the very antithesis of sound. And yet there *was* a kind of sound here, when she listened: a murmur not quite heard, at the edge of her awareness. The sound sand might make, rushing through a timing glass.

Meridy opened her eyes.

She was not beneath the wagon with the Gehliy children. She was on her feet, standing on the edge of a broad, pale road that ran straight as an arrow's flight as far as she could see to her right and to her left. She knew without turning that a dark immensity rested at her back, an infinite wall of night. At her feet, Iëhiy sat perfectly still, brindled in smoke and charcoal, looking almost like a living dog. He had an air of expectation, as though waiting for something to happen. Meridy, glancing down at him, discovered that she too had a sense of anticipation, although she had no idea what it was that either of them expected.

Light rose from the surface of the road and met the moonlight pouring down from above. The moon rode full and pale in the dark sky, veiled now and again by streamers of blowing cloud—though when Meridy had left Tikiy, the moon had been barely past new and could not now be full. But it was, in this place.

A girl came into view, walking along the road, from Meridy's right hand toward her left. Blurred and formless at first, the girl did not actually seem to *approach* so much as simply to grow more distinct, as though the light of the road were shaping her out of itself and lending her reality. Meridy knew as soon as she saw her that this was what she had waited for.

The girl didn't seem to see Meridy. Her gaze was blank, as though she saw nothing at all. As she came near, Meridy saw that she was a ghost, though in this place she had none of the transparency that ordinarily characterized the quick dead, so Meridy knew she herself must have stepped out of the *real* world and into some realm of dreams.

The girl—or young woman (she looked older than Meridy, maybe nineteen or twenty)—had a straight dark brown plait falling down her back, bound every eight inches or so with a fine golden chain. Her eyes were an odd green-bronze color, set in a delicately pretty face. Judging by her fine light skin, she undoubtedly had pure Kingdom ancestors back a thousand years, but Meridy would have known the girl was highborn even if she'd been as colorless as a lingering ghost, for her dress was more elegant than anything Meridy had ever seen and she wore several thin gold bangles on her right wrist. But she walked hesitantly, seeming unsure from step to step whether the road would be there to meet her feet. Meridy could tell the girl still did not see her, although she had now come quite close.

It seemed suddenly insupportable that the ghost should go blindly past. Without thought, as though the movement were as inevitable as the falling of a cast stone back to the earth, Meridy reached out and took the hand of the ghost before she could pass by. Iëhiy stood up, his tail waving slightly, looking attentive and pleased.

The ghost made no effort to pull away from Meridy but turned her head slowly. "Can you help me?" she asked. "I think I've lost my way. I see the Road, I see the way to the God, but there's something . . . someone. . . . I need to go back to the world." Her voice was clear and plain, not like the voiceless whisper of an ordinary ghost, but her words fell into the great silence and were muted instantly to nothing. It made it hard to remember what she had said—it made it almost hard to believe she had said anything at all.

"You won't come back to life either way, you know," Meridy warned her. "The White Road runs only one direction— unless the God opens a hand, and I think that only happens in poems."

"I know," said the girl. "I know, but it doesn't matter. I need to go back. It's my . . . it's my brother, I think." Her voice gained clarity and decision. "It's my brother. He needs me. He doesn't have anyone else. Not anymore."

Meridy nodded, accepting this. "What's your name?" she asked.

The girl looked blankly into nothing. "I don't remember," she said at last.

Meridy turned, still without conscious volition, to look along the road to her left. It seemed she could see along this road forever, as though there were no horizon and no limit to her gaze. She almost thought she could see someone there, almost hear a voice. . . . "Listen," she said to the girl. "I think your brother is calling to you from the living world."

As from very far away, a voice cried, "Diöllin!" Meridy thought it was a young boy's voice, though it might have been a girl's. It wasn't loud, but there was a solidity to it that Diöllin's voice entirely lacked. He must be this girl's anchor.

When Meridy had tried to call her own mother back from this road, she had probably sounded like that boy. But her mother had not heard her calling. No one had been standing by the White Road to seize her mother's hand and bid her listen. Meridy's throat tightened with a grief she had thought she had forgotten, and she turned her face away, swallowing hard.

"Diöllin!" called the boy again, from beyond the moonlight.

"Oh," said the girl. "Yes. I hear him now." She took a step, then hesitated.

Meridy swallowed again. "You can go," she managed to say, her voice not quite level. And then, more fiercely, she said, "Go on! Go on! While you remember the one who calls you."

"Yes," said the ghost. She began to take a step forward but paused, glancing once more the other way, where the White Road of the Moon rushed away, toward the realm of the God.

"Diöllin!" called the voice a third time, shrill and afraid, as from the depths of the earth.

"Yes," the girl said again, turning back toward her brother, this time sounding certain and almost fierce. "Oh, yes! I have to go." She pulled her hand free from Meridy's grip and hurried away, half running, down the pale road, following the voice that had laid an almost-visible light though the dark, like a candle held up to signal to a traveler. Color bled away from her body as she walked, until Meridy lost sight of her entirely, a translucent ghost as pale as the Road.

She woke, blinking, in the unfamiliar darkness beneath the wagon, wrapped in an extra blanket besides her own, with the only light in all the world that of the waxing moon and the stars and, not too far away, the banked embers of the cooking fires. There was no trace of vision or dream in the perfectly ordinary night, except the echo it had left in her memory. *Diöllin.* Meridy thought she had heard that name somewhere, but she could not remember the tale now. Frowning, she lifted herself on one elbow and peered out from under the wagon. She could hear the Gehliy children breathing deeply in sleep nearby—one of them was snoring gently. Beyond the wagon were quiet voices, and the gentle swish of boots through grass as the guards kept their watch. From farther away came the muted stamp of a restless horse. There was no trace of any magic in the night; no hint of anything other than the firmly *real* . . . always excepting Iëhiy, of course. The wolfhound thumped his tail gently against Meridy's thigh, a pressure she could almost feel, if she paid attention to it.

She rubbed his ears and crept out from under the wagon, sat down on the ground, and looked for a while up at the stars, and the half moon.

Sighing, Meridy brought her gaze down to the mortal world. After another moment, she crawled back under the wagon and lay down again, pulling up the blanket. She was very sleepy. She didn't know whether or not to hope for more dreams. But she did not dream again that night.

The day dawned clear and bright. Meridy, waking once more beneath the Gehliy family's wagon, had a second of confused disorientation before she remembered where she was. The wagon, yes. Maraift and Derren and their family, and a lot of wagons and people, enough to be safe from any brigands or wolves or fire horses. Yes. She was safe, and on the road to Riam, and from there who knew where? Excitement stirred, the same that had buoyed her since she'd first seen the Yellow River and the long road that led into the world. She clambered out from under the wagon to see what the morning promised.

The muted shout of the last watch of guards waking their fellows was still hanging in the quiet air, and the picketed horses were snorting impatiently at the men working their way along the line with the morning grain. A couple of guards were making breakfast porridge. Meridy noticed Jaift wandering past the cooking pots and pausing to stir them.

Sure enough, when she collected a bowl of the porridge, it was definitely a cut above the usual—creamier or thicker or something, Meridy wasn't quite sure. Iëhiy leaned his weightless head against her hip and rolled his eyes up to her, begging. Meridy glanced around surreptitiously. No one appeared to be watching. She bent a bit of the porridge out of the *real* and dropped it off her spoon. She'd been practicing such changes a lot in the past few days. The hound caught the dollop before it hit the ground and, tail waving, begged for more.

"Not now," Meridy whispered. "Behave!"

Ignoring this command, Iëhiy sat up on his hind legs, a ridiculously cute sight when the dog had surely outweighed her when he'd been alive. He was irresistible. She tipped another spoonful of porridge out of the *real* into the *ethereal*. Iëhiy snapped it up and lolled his tongue out in canine good humor. It was a terrible encouragement of bad manners, but after all Meridy truly did need to practice working with the *real* and the *ethereal*. She dropped another dollop.

But then she realized Jaift had come back again and was now looking in her direction. Plainly the other girl hadn't noticed anything strange—she was absentmindedly watching a couple of the men bringing horses from the picket lines to the wagons—but still, it was impossible to give Iëhiy any more porridge. Especially since he didn't actually need food at all. Meridy ate the rest of the bowlful herself.

Derren Gehliy made his appearance before Meridy was quite finished with her breakfast. Meridy watched the merchant shake his head over one hitch, where one of the lead horses had apparently come up lame. He finally ordered the horse unharnessed and put on a lead and some of the weight redistributed to other wagons to spare the short hitch. Meridy was surprised that it wasn't the caravan guards who had seen the problem but the merchant himself. He hadn't seemed so perceptive to her. Meridy made a mental note to be careful about Iëhiy when Derren was watching.

Then Maraift bustled over. "You did look exhausted last night," she said comfortably. "But you look much better this morning. Just put that bowl with the others to be washed, dear, and let me introduce you to the children. Now that you're properly awake you may be able to remember all the names, though of course you can simply ask again if you forget." She led Meridy firmly toward her children. They stood in a clump, six of them, ranging in age from Jaift right down to an infant a younger girl was holding. They all stared at Meridy with an intensity of interest she couldn't help but find daunting. She jerked her chin up and glowered back at them, trying to take courage from Iëhiy's cheerfully waving tail. But *he* didn't know how cruel girls could be to each other.

"Now, you've met Jaift," continued Maraift, also seeming oblivious to the possibility that her children might resent or despise the stranger she was foisting on them. "And these two young terrors are Cory and Cehy, they're twins as you can see, and this is Jihiy with the baby, and this one is Little Derren, after my husband, of course. My dears, this is Meridy Turiyn. I'm sure you'll all get along famously." She gave a pleasant nod and swished away in a cloud of skirts and hospitality, taking the baby with her. It took a shameful effort for Meridy not to run after her.

After the barest moment, Jaift stepped forward and offered her hand to Meridy. She was perhaps a few years older than Meridy, a tall girl, as tall as most men, but she carried her height with confidence, as though she knew every other girl longed to be just that tall. She was pretty, in a straightforward sort of way. She wore a dark green blouse, a split traveling skirt in dark brown, and practical brown knee boots that laced up the front. Her wheaten hair, a shade lighter than her mother's, was braided back with the ends tucked invisibly under, a style Meridy hadn't seen before.

Meridy was fairly certain she could guess what Jaift thought of *her*: a plain, dark village girl with near-black hair that always tangled no matter what she tried to do with it. Boys the twins' age didn't usually go out of their way to be mean to a girl—they would hardly have noticed girls at all, yet—and the other children were probably too young to care. But Meridy knew Jaift must be scornful of a hard-worn dress that had obviously, even in its best days, never been anything but a village girl's homespun. A girl like Jaift, practically the next thing to highborn, would hate her for being dark and common even if her smoky-black eyes didn't suggest the strong possibility that she might be a witch.

She brushed the offered palm lightly with her own and said, trying not to sound too grim about it, "I'm pleased to know you, Jaift Gehliy."

"And I you, Meridy Turiyn." The merchant's daughter *sounded* perfectly friendly. "It will be pleasant to have a girl my age along for the rest of the journey. Perhaps you will ride with me? You could take one of the remounts."

Meridy felt her face heat. "I'm sorry," she said, trying not to sound resentful. "I don't know how to ride."

She was sure Jaift had asked her just to show up her lack of skill, but the Gehliys' daughter blinked in what seemed honest surprise and said after a second, with no sign of scorn, "Perhaps we could both walk, then. Or would you like me to teach you to ride?"

Meridy looked at the horses to give herself time to think. She didn't want to try to be friendly with Jaift. She knew the merchant's daughter probably intended to embarrass her. And horses looked much bigger when you thought about getting up on one than when you saw them in a pasture or in front of a wagon. But Meridy had always wished she knew how to ride. She remembered her daydreams of taming a beautiful fire horse and riding proudly across the land, and stupid as it was, she still wanted to learn. Even though she would never have chosen a girl nearly her own age as a teacher, she said at last, "That would be very kind of you."

Cory, or maybe Cehy, pushed in. "I ride better than Jaift does," the boy declared. "Are you a witch like Uncle Daven?"

"I'm a better teacher, and you've no manners," said Jaift tartly. "Go have one of the remounts saddled for Meridy. Mind, not that idiot colt you've been teaching bad habits! Jihiy, better catch Little Derren before he wanders too far!" As the younger children all darted away, she added to Meridy,

"I'm sorry, but Cory didn't mean anything by it, you know! Uncle Daven's a priest, and our favorite uncle. The children *are* likely to ask you for stories, I'm afraid. They think that's what witches do—tell stories and do tricks."

Meridy cautiously answered Jaift's easy smile. She still didn't trust that appearance of friendliness, but it made her feel better, somehow, to know there was a *reason* the Gehliy family seemed so untroubled by her black eyes. She wasn't sure whether she was sorry the uncle wasn't traveling with the family or not.

Jaift's smile was starting to fade. Meridy glanced at Iëhiy, who was sitting with his ears slanted back in a friendly expression that made it clear he, at least, was perfectly ready to be friends. At last, half persuaded by the wolfhound's attitude, Meridy said cautiously, "I could probably tell a story, if the children want." She had heard plenty of Ambica's stories often enough to remember them.

Jaift was immediately friendly again. "They'd like that! We've all heard each other's stories far too many times."

Niniol rode up before Meridy had to answer this, leading a stocky cider-colored gelding. He gave Meridy a nod and Jaift a respectful salute. "Your brother said you wanted a horse for your guest, miss. This is my own remount. I think he'll answer."

"Thank you, Niniol," Jaift said, taking the reins. "We'll take good care of him."

The guard tipped Meridy a friendly wink and rode off.

Meridy stared after him, wondering. If Iëhiy seemed to accept the goodwill of the Gehliy family, even Jaift; and if Niniol was willing to lend his own horse . . . maybe this wasn't going to be quite as bad as she'd feared.

Then Meridy looked again at the horse. "He seems a little, um, large," she ventured, and instantly winced inwardly, though she tried not to show it.

She had expected mockery, but Jaift's smile seemed open and friendly. "He's smaller than you are where it counts—in his head. That's the first thing you should keep in mind about horses." She handed Meridy a bit of bread from her pocket. "Want to get acquainted? Give him this, flat on your palm."

It might have been a trick, except Meridy knew that truly was how you offered treats to a horse. She gingerly extended her hand, and the horse lipped the bread delicately off her fingers, blowing gently in her face. She patted his neck and thought that, after all, he wasn't *that* much taller than Iëhiy. Perhaps she could treat this animal like a large dog. The wolfhound, as if summoned by the thought, insinuated himself jealously under her hand. Meridy patted him, too, then looked quickly to see if Jaift had noticed.

The other girl was checking something about the gelding's bridle and didn't appear to have seen anything odd. Now she turned back and asked, "Shall I give you a leg up?"

For the first time, there seemed a slight reserve to her tone, and Meridy hesitated. But she didn't think she could get up by herself. "If you don't mind . . ."

Jaift smiled at her, the stiffness vanishing until Meridy wasn't sure any constraint had been there at all. "Of course I don't mind! Go ahead and grab his mane—it won't hurt him." Cupping Meridy's knee, she heaved her up and said, "Good—you see? That wasn't hard, and there you are. How does it feel?"

Meridy looked around. She felt *much* higher up than she had expected. But after a moment, when the horse didn't do anything sudden or startling, she started to relax a little, feeling that this might work after all.

"Now," said Jaift, "sit up straight. Lean back if you want him to slow down or stop. Your leg should be here." She took Meridy's ankle and firmly moved her leg back. "Keep your head up. You nudge with your feet to go. Don't kick, just nudge. You tighten the right rein to turn him right, the left to turn him left, and both together to get him to stop. Don't jerk. It only takes gentle pressure."

"All right," Meridy answered tensely. At least she doubted that Niniol would have purposefully given her a difficult or dangerous horse. So far the animal was standing quietly, though his ears rotated back toward Meridy, perhaps wondering what she was waiting for. She pressed her legs firmly against his sides. He stepped forward gently and she pulled back on the reins in startled reflex. The gelding stopped, ears cocked back at her attentively.

"There, you see?" said Jaift. "Hold on while I get my mare. You can ride him in circles, if you like." And she walked off toward the horse lines, leaving Meridy by herself.

Meridy did not panic, but she didn't try to get the gelding to move, either. She sat perfectly still and thanked the God for the great good fortune of being given a particularly amicable animal. And, apparently, a particularly amicable family of merchants. She was almost starting to think even Jaift might not be so bad. Maybe the daughters of wealthy merchants weren't the same as village girls. Or maybe the God had in fact guided Meridy's steps.

It wasn't just that the Gehliy family seemed genuinely nice. What mattered was that not one of them knew Meridy from little green acorns. They didn't know her mother had never named her father—maybe that was why they were nice to her. And they had an uncle who was a witch, so they didn't mind the color of her eyes. She was sure that was important.

Here among these people, Meridy could actually tell any story about herself and her past that she pleased. Free from her past! There should have been unadulterated delight in the thought, and there *was* pleasure in it; but Meridy discovered that it gave her an odd unrooted sort of feeling, too. Surely she wasn't missing Tikiy?

She told herself firmly not to be ridiculous and, as Jaift returned, carefully nudged her borrowed horse into a walk to join her.

six

The whole camp moved out almost as soon as Jaift was mounted, the wagons rumbling forward in close formation and the riders spreading out around them. Derren Gehliy rode a stocky bay horse up and down along the train of wagons. Maraift, with the baby on her ample lap, waved cheerfully as her wagon passed Jaift and Meridy. Jaift led the way to fall in to one side of her mother's wagon. Iëhiy paced beside Meridy's horse, keeping up effortlessly. The twins tore by on a matched pair of spotted brown-and-white horses, riding fast beside the road, yelling and whooping. A pair of guards rode after them with a long-suffering attitude.

Jaift laughed and shook her head. "Riding herd on those two is wearing out the guards, poor things. But I think they like it, however much they complain. It breaks the monotony, you know. It does get boring on a trip like this. It's nearly a four-week trip at caravan speed."

Meridy made a noncommittal sound.

"That's one reason I was glad when Mother said you would be traveling with us. Were you honestly planning to walk all the way to Riam by yourself?"

"I'd have had to, wouldn't I, if I hadn't met your party?"

Jaift gazed at her with open admiration, not seeming to mind Meridy's edged tone. "Wouldn't you have been scared to death? You should maintain more tension in the reins than that. You ought to be barely able to feel his mouth. That's right, good, that's much better. What if you'd run into outlaws?"

Meridy flashed on Braid with her knife in his belly, and Scar falling after Iëhiy had torn out his throat. She swallowed hard and focused on her horse's neck. "I'm very glad your father let me ride with you."

"Oh, he had to, once Mother made up her mind. Mother would never have let him hear the end of it if he'd turned you away."

"Your mother seems kind."

"She is. Heels down. So is Father, really." Jaift hesitated. "Your parents are both in the hand of the God, Mother said. I'm sorry. That must be hard for you."

Trying not to snap at the other girl, Meridy said tightly, "It happens. I'll get by."

"Of course," Jaift answered quickly. "I'm sorry." She visibly searched for another subject. "Have you ever been to Riam before?"

"No." It was Meridy's turn to hesitate. Jaift hadn't said or done one nasty thing, and her own suspicions were starting to feel mean-spirited. Yet she didn't even know how to talk to girls who were trying to be friendly. "Your mother said you were hoping to find a husband there," she offered at last.

"A Derem son, Timias." Jaift sounded relieved at this change of topic. "Yes. At least he's only a little older than I am."

"You don't mind getting married?" Meridy realized as she asked the question that Jaift might justifiably be offended.

But Jaift only shrugged. "Sometimes I used to think I might follow my uncle's path."

"Your uncle the priest? You thought of being a priestess?" Meridy asked in surprise. Not many girls followed that path—she'd never known one who had, but then, priests seldom came through little villages like Tikiy, only once or twice a year to send any lingering ghost to the God, and to bless new cottages and new wells, new marriages and new babies.

Jaift shrugged again. "Well, yes, I thought I might. But marrying this Derem boy would be good for the business, I suppose. The boys will be our uncle's heirs—that's already been settled. Which is fine, but there's not another girl after me except Jihiy, and she's so little still, it'll be years before she could marry. I like doing the accounts, anyway. He'll be coming to Tamar if we do marry, so I wouldn't have to leave my family. That would be nice."

Meridy didn't answer. How different it must be, to be surrounded by your own family, which wanted you to be a part of it. . . .

"Heels down," Jaift reminded her. "Or sometimes it helps to think of it as lifting your toes."

Meridy gave her a wary look, but Jaift's tone had been matter-of-fact rather than scornful. She tried to push her heels down.

"Good," said Jaift. "How about you? Were there any young men in your village you were sorry to leave?"

"No," Meridy said, more emphatically than she'd intended.

Jaift laughed. "Oh! A boy broke your heart, did he? Some tall, brooding boy with a smile just for you. Or else your kin wanted you to marry where you didn't want to, so you ran away from home—"

"No!" snapped Meridy.

"I'm sorry!" Jaift seemed taken aback by Meridy's sharp answer. "I was just, just—" She waved an apologetic hand. "I like imagining stories about people, that's all. I didn't mean any of that. I'm sorry."

Now it was Meridy's turn to be embarrassed. She said in a much more conciliatory tone, "No, I was stupid." She tried to think of something else to say. "I wanted to see Riam," she muttered.

Jaift brightened immediately. "Oh, yes, so do I! It's a much bigger city than Tamar, you know. Does your aunt in Riam have a business of her own that you're going to help her with?"

Meridy was starting to really dislike her pretend aunt. The woman was getting more complicated all the time. No doubt Meridy was going to have to make up an uncle, too, and a couple of cousins, and a flourishing business of some sort. She had no idea what people even did in a city like Riam. "I'd like to travel," she said. At least that was true. "I want to see some of the famous places from the classics. I don't think I could have stayed in the village *one more day*." It was more honesty than she had intended to offer.

"Well, maybe *you* could be a priestess," suggested Jaift. "You could travel all over the principalities, the way they do, seeking out folk who need the blessing of the God—"

"A priestess! I don't think so."

"Oh, well," Jaift said peaceably, but this time didn't seem as startled by Meridy's tone. She said, "I suppose it only seems natural because of your eyes." But then she gave Meridy a quick glance and changed the subject immediately: "You've read the classics? Which ones? I don't know any girls who read anything but household accounts."

But when Meridy looked at her suspiciously, Jaift still

didn't seem scornful, merely curious. Of course, she'd said her uncle told stories. Maybe Jaift thought it was normal for a person with black eyes to know the classics. Or maybe an educated merchant's daughter who had learned to do accounts actually thought a girl might simply like history and classics.

Deliberately testing to see how the other girl would react, Meridy said, " *'Thaliaë-se na hiyän laiysënaè, usamèa temeshanan eis rehluè someriaè Diaël-aè eriëth na-en homithiän. Deira'ea meriy na'a rehesen. Teganei uänai-se chariësen, hiliën goho'il se iyrier homithiän. . . .'* " She trailed off, flushing at Jaift's astonished stare and bracing herself for a scathing comment about unfeminine girls and village brats who got above themselves and pretended to be clever.

"But that's amazing!" Jaift exclaimed. "It's Viënè, isn't it? It sounds so pretty! I never managed to remember more than a few words of Viënè, though Father wanted us to learn it. What does that mean?"

After a moment, Meridy answered, "It's old. It's from a cycle of poems by a woman named Loès Nehen. There are several different translations. I'm afraid none of them are as good as the original." She fixed her eyes on her horse's ears and recited, this time finishing the poem: " 'In the dim light of the coming dawn, I know we watch the night withdraw from opposite sides of the world. I pursue the shadows of my dreams. Memories tangle in moonbeams, soon forgotten in the waking world. I know you are watching these same skies, where sunlight, like a vision, comes slantwise across the face of the world and sets the city aglow.' " She added awkwardly, "She lived in Moran Diorr, the poet who wrote those words to the one she loved. Before the sea came in and drowned the city and separated them forever."

"It's quite beautiful!" Jaift exclaimed. "And sad. Whose translation is that?"

Meridy flushed again, more deeply this time.

"Yours?" cried Jaift. "But that's amazing! I couldn't do that in a hundred years!"

"The hard thing," said Meridy hesitantly, "is to keep the rhythm and still approach the meaning. A lot of the words in Viënè don't have equivalents today, not all the way down to nuance. And the grammar is quite different, of course."

"Well, it sounded good to me."

Oh, Jaift found a too-educated village girl *impressive.* But that was better than open scorn. Meridy shrugged, trying to look as though she were willing to be friends, but that it meant nothing much to her either way.

A surprisingly comfortable silence fell. Iëhiy came back to pace at her side, sunlight glimmering over and through him. Occasionally a paw print appeared in the dust, but no one except Meridy noticed. Niniol rode by once, gave her an assessing look, and said, "You're a quick study, miss. Your hands aren't half bad. I wish all my students were so apt." He noticed another guard signaling him from farther back in the train, gave a casual salute, and reined off again.

"He's nice, isn't he?" commented Jaift. "He's been with our house a long time. He taught me to ride when I got my first pony."

"I thought he was only a guard?"

Jaift shrugged. "It's true he heads the guards when my father's on the road, but between trains, Niniol supervises the house guards at home. Heels down. He used to be a captain in some lord's personal guard, but he got married to a woman from Tamar and she wanted to live near her family."

She laughed a little. "I had the most terrible passion for him when I was a little girl."

"Really?" Meridy was slightly shocked the Gehliys' daughter would admit something like that. Surely a wealthy merchant's daughter was expected to look much higher than a mere guard captain, especially one so dark complexioned, obviously with a strong trace of Southern blood. Of course the guard captain *was* good-looking and plainly competent, but Niniol was not only part Southern but obviously older, and undoubtedly common born as well.

"Oh, yes. He never laughed, either, just let it wear off naturally. If you ask me, Jihiy is the one with the passion these days. She follows him around disgracefully when we're at home, but of course she can't while we're on the road. I mean, I expect she'd like to, but she couldn't possibly keep up."

Having seen the constant movements of the guard leader about his duties, Meridy could believe it. She asked curiously, "Have you ever been attacked on the road?"

Jaift shrugged. "Not me personally, but yes, we've had our trains attacked occasionally."

Meridy shivered involuntarily.

"Not often," Jaift said quickly. "And not caravans as big as this one. We're too well armed, and there are too many of us for outlaws to be much of a threat. And when we *have* been attacked, the guards have always turned the brigands back without any trouble. But it's true we have to be careful—everyone has to be careful, especially here, between the Yellow River and Riam. You know the prince of Harann doesn't seriously claim any lands west of Sann, and the prince of Cora Tal isn't much interested in anything southeast of Riam, so there's sometimes trouble in between, especially these days when all the princes are arguing about where exactly the borders ought to be and no one's troops will deal with someone else's brigands. But Niniol's completely trustworthy, and he always hires good men."

Meridy nodded. She knew, probably better than Jaift, how Tai-Enchar's long-ago betrayal of the High King had shattered the High Kingdom and led to the emergence of a whole flurry of petty kingdoms, some hardly encompassing more than a single city. She knew how those little kingdoms had warred and feuded and quarreled until finally the five modern principalities had emerged. The largest three were Cora Tal, Moran Tal, and Elan Tal, which had allied and broken apart and redrawn their boundaries fifty times and even today owned among them the best land of the old High Kingdom. And then there were the two lesser principalities: Tian Sur, at the far end of the world, and of course Harann, to which Tikiy belonged, more or less, though as far as she could tell no one in the mountain villages actually knew or cared where the boundaries might lie. But she didn't know much about the current political situation. She remembered that the prince of Harann was one of the Luviodes, Sethan Luviode, she thought; and that the prince of Cora Tal was named Diöllonuor, a wonderful old-fashioned name that rolled off the tongue like poetry. But she hadn't known anything about the current tension between the two princes, or what that rivalry might mean to ordinary people. By this time, she was almost not surprised by Jaift's tact in explaining.

"You're lucky you met us. I can't imagine traveling alone. Heels down, Mery."

Meridy twitched slightly at Jaift's casual use of that little-name, unsure whether she meant to be friendly or condescending. But Jaift's manner was so open that after a moment she just tried to sink her weight more into her heels and admitted, "I wasn't really happy about the idea either."

"Was your village such a terrible place to live?"

Meridy glanced at her and away. "I don't suppose it would be so bad for someone with family there. I don't expect any place is especially nice if you don't have family or friends there." She added, "I guess lack of family isn't a problem for you."

"You couldn't be more right," agreed Jaift emphatically. "Not with all this lot, and all of them younger than me." She sighed gloomily, then brightened. "At least getting married will get me some privacy. My own bedroom! Think of that!" Then Jaift, glancing over, asked in surprise, "What is it, Mery? Are you . . ." Her voice changed, taking on a tension very different from her earlier manner. "Are you all right?"

Meridy, fixedly watching a bright sparkle in the air next to Iëhiy, said, "I'm fine."

Just as she spoke, the ghost boy from Tikiy flickered into being. This time he didn't offer Meridy any *ethereal* roses, but he patted Iëhiy, who, tail waving wildly, seemed delighted to see him. Meridy glared at him, fiercely jealous.

"Do you—" Jaift began, then stopped, looking rather blankly from Meridy to the ghost boy.

"Everything is *perfectly fine*," Meridy snapped, and then stared at Jaift, wondering if the other girl could possibly have actually looked at the ghost boy. Jaift, with her blue eyes! It was impossible, and Meridy knew it was impossible—a girl Jaift's age could not conceivably be a sorceress—she must be looking at something else. Yes, now she was staring away at her twin brothers, who were trying to get their horses to rear, something that surely wasn't allowed, which must be why Jaift looked tense and upset.

The ghost boy, kneeling with his arm around Iëhiy, looked up and contradicted Meridy with the arrogance Meridy remembered from their last meeting. "You're nothing like fine. You'd better look sharp, girl. There's an ambush that's going to be sprung on you in only a few minutes."

Meridy, her grip tightening on the reins involuntarily, stopped her horse without thinking.

Jaift had also drawn up her mare. "Meridy?" she asked tensely.

The ghost boy said rapidly, "There's more than forty men. They're hiding there"—he pointed—"and there, and some over there, and you're already past some of them. A lot of them have bows. But their master is a greater peril to you than any brigand! You must not fall under his sway."

Well, *that* was certainly helpful. Meridy resisted the urge to shout at the ghost, and instead said forcefully to Jaift, "Can you get Niniol over here *right now. Quietly.*"

Jaift didn't hesitate for even a second. Turning her mare, she called in a clear, cheerful tone, "Niniol!"

Hardly a minute later, the guard captain cantered up. "Is there a problem, young miss?" The look he cast toward Meridy was faintly suspicious.

The ghost boy had come up to stand beside Meridy's horse. He looked at her steadily. Meridy took a deep breath and said to Niniol, "There's soon going to be an ambush. More than forty men, a lot with bows." She nodded discreetly toward the places the boy had pointed out.

To Meridy's surprise, Jaift added at once, "I'm sure she's right! I'm sure she's telling the truth!"

Niniol stared back and forth between them. Then he laughed as though the girls had said something funny, but he said grimly through his broad smile, "Get to cover under the wagons." He rode casually back among his men. Meridy saw him clap one of them on the shoulder and speak briefly. They separated, and the men started to sort themselves unobtrusively into fighting order.

Meridy and Jaift rode toward the wagons.

The ghost boy flicked into visibility directly in front of Meridy. "Duck!"

Meridy bent low over her gelding's neck—and beside her, so did Jaift, tucking down to her horse's neck. A short little crossbow quarrel hissed wickedly over their heads and skittered through the dust.

Jaift swung down from her mare, caught Meridy's hand, and dragged her down, pulling her toward the nearest wagon. Another quarrel hissed past them and *thunk*ed into the side of the wagon just as Jaift scrambled under it. Meridy ducked after her, immediately squirming around to see what was happening.

There were suddenly quarrels everywhere. Guards galloped past, crouched in their saddles; others ran behind the wagons for cover, reaching for their own crossbows. Meridy saw a guard hauling one of the twins, she didn't know which one, toward a wagon. The man took a quarrel in the back as he reached it, and he pitched forward, falling hard. The boy turned and tried to drag the man under the wagon with him, but the guard shook his head, pushing the twin toward the relative safety of the wagon, and another quarrel struck him in the neck. He collapsed, limp and boneless, and a second later Meridy saw his ghost pull free and vanish in a blaze of invisible light, gone down the White Road into the hand of the God.

Meridy scanned the wagons, looking for Maraift and the other children. She saw Derren Gehliy, a knife in his hand, standing over Jihiy, who had a quarrel in her leg. One of the attackers rode at them, but a guard intercepted him and knocked him out of the saddle before he could reach them. Derren picked his daughter up and made a dash for the wagons. He made it, throwing the little girl under a wagon before turning to face another of the brigands. Niniol came out of nowhere and gutted the attacker with a quick, vicious stroke of his sword, immediately disappearing again into the melee. The merchant scrambled for the wagon where Maraift sheltered with the baby.

"Oh, may the God preserve us!" Jaift cried suddenly. She pointed to where Little Derren, not far away, was crawling out from under a dead man. The boy stood up and turned in a circle, screaming. Meridy caught her breath.

A mounted attacker rode at the little boy, aiming a sword cut at him, and since this time there was no smoke, Meridy desperately grabbed up a handful of the fine dust from the road and threw it over Iëhiy, letting the dust help define him. It worked even better than she'd hoped. Every mote caught the sunlight, and she used the hinted visibility to reinforce her own sight so she could pull him into the *real*. Then she pointed urgently at Little Derren, and the dog went that way with a snarl that was almost audible. Iëhiy knocked the rider out of the saddle and crushed his throat with one fast chomp of his jaws. He flickered in and out of the *real* as Meridy's concentration wavered, invisible and visible as he leaped through swirls of dust. A guard snatched up Little Derren from horseback, parried a stroke from an outlaw, and retreated. Iëhiy snapped at another attacker's horse, driving it back, and the guard reached Meridy's wagon. Beside her, Jaift reached out to take Little Derren as the guard handed him down. The guard reined away again. Iëhiy had vanished into the fighting—Meridy couldn't see him anywhere and thought that he might have gone *ethereal* again.

Dead men were everywhere, both guards and brigands. Ghost after ghost pulled free of their bodies. Some trembled into nothingness immediately. Others tried to keep fighting with *ethereal* weapons, not realizing they were dead. Some horse ghosts were also climbing dazedly to their feet and galloping away, before flickering out of sight, gone onto the White Road and to the God's realm.

The ghost boy wavered into existence at Meridy's side, unexpected enough that she jumped and hit her head on the floorboards of the wagon. He said, breathless and quick, "He's sent one of his servitors. These brigands are being driven back, but the servitor will hold them and rally them and use them, living men and dead alike—"

"What do you mean?" Meridy demanded.

But the ghost boy only said imperatively, "You must kill the witch-king's servitor! The brigands aren't the true threat— they're merely a tool; you must disembody Tai-Enchar! Then you may be rid of his influence for at least a day or two." He shredded back into the air before Meridy could yell at him that she didn't understand any of that.

"*Whose* servitor?" began Jaift, but then she pointed to where an outlaw had come into view, one of the twins across his saddle in front of him.

Meridy caught her breath as the other boy ran out from his hiding place, snatched up a fallen sword, and ran at the outlaw. Niniol, shouting, rode after him. The outlaw knocked the sword out of the boy's hand and struck him on the temple with the hilt of his own blade. Niniol, lifting his sword to attack the man, took a quarrel in the face and dropped limply off his horse, dead before he hit the ground. The outlaw laughed and started to drag the twin up onto his horse on top of his brother.

Niniol's ghost pulled away from his body and got shakily to his feet. He took a step toward the outlaw, slashing at him with an *ethereal* sword. It passed through the oblivious attacker without resistance. Niniol staggered and fell to his knees, crying out in despair and rage. His cry was the thin, voiceless cry of a ghost.

Then, beyond Niniol, something peculiar began to happen to the air. There was a soundless concussion, and another, and a patch of air simultaneously seemed to gain substance and lose *reality*. The air in that area wavered and rippled, like water or some strange kind of sheer, transparent cloth, and the light and air and dust folded away and folded back again, and a man stepped through that area of distorted space into the middle of the road, glancing around with cool appraisal. This man wasn't a brigand, not *just* a brigand. He wasn't any ordinary man. He looked as though all this death and violence meant nothing to him, but it wasn't only that indifference that made him frightening. Even from this distance, Meridy could see that the man had black eyes and, stranger still, that he had one shadow that lay out like a shadow should, against the position of the sun, but also another shadow that wavered away toward the north, as though in response to a quite different and paler sun way down in the sky in the wrong direction.

The man spared a cold glance for Niniol. Then he beckoned, and Niniol flinched and got to his feet and took a step toward him, though his face set hard with resistance.

Meridy might not know about servitors, but she knew every cruel tale ever told about the witch-king, and she could see, now, how a handful of other ghosts crowded behind the black-eyed man. She knew he must be binding the ghosts of the men who had fallen here, that he must be binding them for his own purposes, preventing them from taking the White Road. He was going to bind Niniol, too. Maybe he already had.

"May the God preserve us!" said Jaift, low, like it was really a prayer. "Meridy! Can't you do anything?"

Meridy squirmed out from beneath the wagon, ran out to Niniol, scooped up a double handful of dust, and threw it over him. Sunlight caught and tangled in the dust and around him, limning him in light that was at once both *real* and *ethereal*. "Niniol!" Meridy cried. "Niniol! By your name I call you and bind you to the world!" *That* was something the other witch couldn't do: she was the one who knew his name. Meridy threw more dust to help catch the light and show the *real* world exactly where Niniol was, so that when he moved, the sunlight curved around him almost as it would around a living man. Figuring out what the dust was for helped; she saw how only a little dust would do, as long as she balanced the *real* against the *ethereal* just right.

The double-shadowed man, obviously the witch-king's servitor, had turned in surprise. He smiled, unimpressed by anything she'd done. Then he stepped toward Meridy, lifting his hand. She scrambled backward, knowing she could not get out of his way fast enough. But Niniol, shimmering in the sunlight that glinted off clouds of suspended dust, jerked his head up, twitched his sword experimentally, grimaced in determination, squared his stance, pivoted, lunged, and took their enemy's head off with one lunge.

The blood was as red as any man's blood, and the head *bounced*. Meridy screamed, a thin sound that embarrassed her. She pressed a hand over her mouth, staring at Niniol. *He* didn't look upset. He looked grim, and determined.

With the servitor dead, the bound ghosts of the dead men were already dispersing. But even if the ghost boy didn't consider them a threat, the brigands were still there, and threat enough, surely. Standing in the open was obviously a terrible idea. A quarrel went through Niniol's shoulder, but harmlessly, thumping solidly into the ground. Meridy hastily caught a ghost horse, ducking away from another quarrel that whipped past. She brought the ghost horse to Niniol, using dust and sunlight to show the world where the animal was and bring it into the *real*. This wasn't even difficult anymore. She hadn't thought she'd ever be grateful for the brigands by the stream, for their forcing her to find out how to use smoke and dust and such liminal things to bring ghosts into the *real*. At least she was grateful she'd learned she might do such things before this horrible day. "Stay close to me," she warned Niniol, "or I may not be able to keep you in the *real*."

Niniol vaulted into the saddle without a word and rode for the nearest attackers. Dust swirled thickly around him, which helped Meridy maintain him in the *real*. Now that the double-shadowed man was gone, Niniol cut a terrible swath through the outlaws and no one could stop him. Although his sword could touch living men, the brigands' weapons were harmless to him. Iëhiy came into view and Meridy bent him back into the *real,* too, and sent him to help Niniol. A moment later the outlaws were in full retreat. The remaining guards swept into a ragged mop-up action.

Meridy pressed her fists against her head and strained to hold her ghosts in the *real*.

Jaift tentatively touched her shoulder. "Meridy?"

Meridy lost her hold on the ghosts. To the living without eyes to see, Niniol and the wolfhound must have seemed to blink out like candles in a strong wind; even to her, they seemed suddenly insubstantial. She felt strangely insubstantial herself, as though she had fallen partway into the *ethereal,* and she had a crashing headache. But it didn't matter. The outlaws were in full rout now, and the danger was over.

seven

Meridy straightened with a groan, suddenly aware of bruises she hadn't noticed acquiring. She hadn't fought at all—she'd only run and ducked under the wagon—but she felt like she'd been beaten all over.

Slowly, the survivors reappeared from under wagons or behind bales. Derren lifted his wife tenderly down from her wagon and went to help Jihiy from her hiding place. Jaift ran to embrace her mother.

Meridy didn't follow. She could imagine what they must all think of her. *Everyone* would know she was a true witch, now. Jaift would tell her parents about the ghost boy, what he'd said. She would tell them about that horrifying double-shadowed witch who had tried to bind Niniol; she might even remember the ghost boy had said the man was Tai-Enchar's servant. Servitor. Meridy didn't know what a *servitor* even was and doubted Jaift did, either, but Jaift might well have recognized the name of the witch-king. Two hundred years had passed since Tai-Enchar had betrayed High King Miranuanol and shattered the High Kingdom and himself gone down into ruin for his malicious ambition, but his was still a name anyone might recognize.

Worse, Jaift would surely warn her parents that Meridy might have drawn the attack on them in the first place. That wasn't fair. Or it was, in a way, but how could Meridy have guessed anything like this might happen?

Everything had been good, and it had all gone wrong. So fast. Everything was ruined, and Meridy didn't even understand how it could have happened. The brigands had been horrible, but if it had been only an attack by brigands, at least it wouldn't be *her fault*.

And she didn't understand how blue-eyed Jaift had seen the ghost boy in the first place. Meridy increasingly felt she didn't understand *anything*.

Guards moved among the fallen, sorting the dead from the wounded, wary of the body of the double-shadowed servitor, though in death he seemed just . . . ordinary. The men moved their own wounded gently aside and bound the injured brigands to await questioning. One of the men pulled the quarrel that had killed Niniol out of his face and threw a cloak over the body. Niniol's ghost watched with a profoundly unsettled expression. Meridy didn't blame him. She felt sick and shaky herself, and she wasn't even hurt.

Very few of the other ghosts were still present. Meridy saw no trace of the servitor's ghost, for which she was grateful. Most of the ghosts would have already taken the White Road to the God's realm; some would have fled back to their homes, to hover around their wives or children or brothers for a few days before disappearing into the God's hand. One or two might linger, quick, for a longer time, caught by fury or fear or simple surprise between the *real* world and the *ethereal* realms, until a priest sent them on or a witch bound them or luck led them to a ghost town, where they might make a place for themselves amid the combined memories of the ghosts who dwelt there.

Niniol came slowly over to Meridy. Iëhiy, trailing at his heels, pressed past him and flopped wearily down on her feet, panting as though he had been tired out by his exertions, though of course a ghost dog couldn't actually get tired.

"I can't see anyone clearly but you," Niniol told her, his voice thin. "And the dog. Everything else is sort of vague and . . . flickery." His voice was the familiar bodiless whisper of the quick dead, but still recognizably his own voice even so. He ran a translucent hand through colorless hair, obviously still partly in shock from his sudden death.

Meridy glanced around, but no one seemed to be paying her particular attention. They were all too busy about their own tasks in the aftermath of the battle. Besides, what did it matter now? There had been plenty of witnesses to her bringing the ghosts into the *real*. Starting with Jaift, whose blue eyes were completely misleading, and that was just not fair— witches were supposed to have *black* eyes.

But Meridy shrugged all that aside because she was sorry for Niniol. "That's normal," she said, as kindly as she could. "I've anchored you—I've bound you to the living world. I'm sorry. I couldn't think of anything else to do. I'm pretty sure that means you'll see the *real* more clearly when you're near me. If you get too far away from me, you'll probably find everything becomes vaguer as you . . ." She hesitated, but of course she had to warn him. "As you start to fade. If the White Road doesn't open for you, if you can't find me, if you can't find something else that holds you, you could . . . lose yourself. The tales say. It's important for the quick dead to stay close to their anchors, unless they *want* to fade. Into a whisper on the wind and then nothing." She hesitated. "I *am* sorry. Jaift said you were married? Your wife might serve as another anchor for you, even if she's not a witch."

"I *was* married. She passed down the White Road. . . ." Niniol looked around, squinting as though he half expected to see the God's Road open up before him.

Meridy wouldn't have been surprised, but she saw nothing, and apparently he didn't either. She said tentatively, trying to reassure him, "I'm sure you'll find your way to the White Road. It'll open for you eventually and you can join her in the God's realm. I would let you go, you know. Of course I would."

Niniol looked around but appeared to see no shining road of light opening up before him. He said after a moment, "Well, I'm glad enough you could hold me. Believe me. I thought the . . . other witch had me. After I . . . died." Niniol touched his face with the tips of his fingers. "I can almost feel the quarrel still." He shuddered helplessly.

"You killed him. You saved the twins. And everyone else, I think."

Dropping his hand, Niniol shook his head. "It was your warning that made it possible to salvage anything from that mess." He tried to smile. "Late as it was in coming."

"I'm sorry. I did warn you as soon as I found out. I wish it had been sooner."

"So do I."

Jaift came up, hesitant but nodding to Niniol as well as Meridy. "I'm sorry," she said to Niniol. "Are you . . . That is, I'm sorry."

Niniol ducked his head, not seeming at all surprised that Jaift was addressing him. "Happens," he said gruffly. "Just not to me, before." His face tightened, probably with the memory of his death, but he squared his shoulders and added, "Could have been a lot worse. For a minute there, I thought it *was* going to be a lot worse."

"Yes, it was terrifying," Jaift said earnestly. "And so peculiar." She turned to Meridy. "I've never seen anything like that man before. But the . . . the *witch-king's* servitor? What does that even *mean*? The witch-king's been dead for two hundred years!"

Meridy had no idea, but she'd obviously been right about Jaift recognizing Tai-Enchar's name. But that wasn't what she most wanted to know. She said, trying not to sound too accusing, "You saw him too—you saw how strange his shadow was! You can see Niniol. And you *were* looking at Iëhiy before! Even though your eyes are blue!"

"Oh, well," Jaift said unhappily. "I only see things, you know." She nervously rubbed her eyelids, then dropped her hand and met Meridy's eyes. "I'm not really a witch. Not *really*. I'm . . . I see and hear ghosts, yes, but I don't know how to actually *do* anything. Not like you. You made Niniol *real*. That was so . . . I couldn't have done that."

Meridy stared at the other girl, wondering if Jaift was telling the truth or thought she was.

Jaift ducked her head and went on quickly, "My uncle—he did it when I was a baby. Turned my eyes blue to match my mother's eyes. He told me. Obviously I don't remember."

Meridy couldn't imagine how a witch could do anything like that. Maybe Jaift's uncle was actually a sorcerer as well as a witch. "Do your parents know?" But she realized they must. Why else would they have been so nice to a black-eyed village girl who turned up asking for shelter?

"Yes, I suppose." Jaift did not sound quite sure. She glanced over her shoulder at her family, gathered together now in a little knot, then back at Meridy. "I mean, of course they know, but they don't—no one ever—we don't *talk* about it. My uncle, no one minds him—after all, he's a priest—but it's different for me. Even if I can't *do* anything. Which I can't. And Jihiy was hit, you know. In the leg. With a quarrel."

"Oh," said Meridy, suddenly understanding. She was more than willing to help if she could, especially if it made Derren and Maraift less likely to blame her for Jihiy's getting injured in the first place. She looked past Jaift, toward the other Gehliy children, gathered into a tight knot with their parents hovering over them. They were all staring at her, but now Meridy she could see how anxious they looked. Not angry. At least, not yet. Maybe they were too shocked to be angry, yet. Meridy turned questioningly to Niniol.

"I don't know," he said quietly, his voice the breathless murmur of a ghost. "But I would be willing to try."

Meridy nodded and followed Jaift slowly toward the family group. "Maraift," she said, nodding to the woman, and then to Derren, "Excellent sir." She didn't know what she expected. She tried to look mature and responsible and not the least bit like a horrible witch who might steal a little girl's soul while she healed her. She was vividly aware of the sidelong looks she was getting from all directions. The children were more honest: they stared openly. Except Jihiy, who rocked back and forth, a nasty little quarrel standing in her leg.

Jaift moved to kneel and put her arm around her sister. She looked at Meridy with a helpless expression. "*I* can't do *anything,*" she said again. "I don't know how."

Derren Gehliy was pressing a cloth against his cheek, where he had evidently been cut. But the plump merchant spoke with more dignity than Meridy would have believed possible.

"I gather we're all much in your debt. If you hadn't warned

Niniol"—he glanced toward the body, an automatic flinching glance that the rest of them, including Niniol's ghost, copied involuntarily—"we'd all be dead, I think. You are a . . ." He hesitated over *witch* and said instead, "You are able to . . . to bind and command ghosts? To, ah, heal?"

"I don't know, excellent sir," Meridy said warily. "I've always been able to see ghosts. But I've never actually *tried* to . . . to do anything else."

"No, no, I shouldn't think so," answered the merchant, blinking. "Of course not." He glanced down at his injured daughter. "But I know that is something, ah, that can sometimes be done."

Meridy could hardly refuse. She said uncomfortably, "I'll try, of course."

"I'll be glad to try, too," agreed Niniol. "It's my men who need you most."

"Niniol says he'll try, too, excellent sir."

"Niniol?" said Maraift, and again everyone helplessly glanced over at the body.

"I feel sick," Niniol muttered.

"Take deep breaths," Meridy advised him, hoping it might help him feel more normal even if he didn't actually need to breathe any longer.

Jihiy was biting her lip. "My leg hurts," she said in a small, embarrassed voice. "It hurts a *lot*."

Maraift sat down on the ground with a total disregard of her skirts and put an arm around her young daughter. "Oh, sweet, I know it does. Hang on a bit and we'll make it better."

Meridy said uncomfortably, "I may not . . ." But she couldn't finish.

"I know, dear," said Maraift. "But I'm sure you'll try your best."

Derren Gehliy touched Jihiy's hair gently and threw a beseeching look at Meridy.

Meridy sat down next to Jihiy. Jaift wordlessly shooed the other children out of the way, though she herself retreated only a step or two and then hovered uncertainly.

Meridy nodded to her to indicate she should stay. She said to Maraift, "I've never—" and stopped. Uncertainty was not what any of them needed right now. "This shouldn't take long," she said instead, with confidence she was a long way from feeling.

Niniol hunkered down in the dirt next to them. His broad hands flexed as he kept himself from reaching, hopelessly, to touch Jihiy in comfort. "Could you let me get a look at the wound, miss?" he asked Meridy.

Meridy folded back the little girl's skirt. Four inches of the quarrel stood obscenely out from her leg, broken off a handspan from the head. Jihiy shut her eyes and leaned against her mother.

"I don't know much about this kind of healing," said Niniol, "but for regular physicking, I know that quarrel has got to come out."

"How?" asked Meridy.

Niniol shook his head. "If I were doing it, I'd cut to get the point out. Just pulling would do more damage. Then the wound would have to be packed with that healer's powder to keep fever out. But I don't know about ghost healing."

"I think we should probably get it out," Meridy said reluctantly. "I don't think I can do it, though."

"Get Inden Temen to do it," said Niniol. "He's done some work like this before, helping physickers. So have I, but—" He cut that off. "Inden's helping with the other wounded right now."

"Can you get Inden Temen over here?" Meridy asked Maraift.

Maraift didn't get up. She simply lifted her head and shouted, "Inden!"

The guard came up a minute later, scrubbing blood from his hands with a cloth. He looked at Jihiy, slanted a quick look at Meridy, and said to Maraift, "I'm sorry, excellent lady. I should have come to see your daughter before tending the men."

"Not at all," said Maraift. "Of course you had to make sure none of the men were dying before looking at, at"—she swallowed, got control of herself, and went on—"lesser injuries. Meridy wants you to get the arrow out before she tries to heal Jihiy." It was, for Maraift, a miracle of brevity and precision.

"Oh," said the man. He darted another quick look at Meridy. "Are—are there ghosts around here, then, excellent miss?"

"Only Niniol," said Meridy a touch maliciously, "and he's right beside you."

Inden jumped and looked around nervously.

"Tell the fool to steady up and remember he's a professional," growled Niniol.

Meridy repeated this.

"I'll be blessed," said Inden, staring at her. "That's the captain, all right, the bastard. Begging your pardon, sir," he added hastily to the air. He knelt to inspect the wound. "Now, you just rest quiet, my girl," he said to Jihiy. "This'll hurt some, but it's got to be done. Excellent lady, better give the kid something to bite on. Miss, if you'll hold her leg still?"

Maraift took a fold of her skirt and told Jihiy to bite it. Meridy gingerly gripped the little girl's knee and calf.

Jihiy bit on the cloth and the soldier made one fast cut. Jihiy gave a muffled scream against the cloth, and then Inden tossed the quarrel aside and pressed a bandage against the sudden flow of blood.

Meridy put her hands over the wound. "Try to help me," she said to Niniol, and sent up a wordless prayer to the God. Inden backed away.

Nothing happened. Niniol swore under his breath.

"You're doing it wrong," said a cool, critical voice behind them.

Jaift straightened and lifted her chin, and Niniol spun around, an *ethereal* sword glittering suddenly in his hand, like light and air.

"That's a, well, sort of a friend of mine," Meridy said quickly. "I met him just before I left home."

The ghost boy gave Jaift a thoughtful look, slipped by Niniol without paying him the least attention, and knelt by the little girl. Sunlit dust motes traced his hands and the curve of his face, caught sparkling in his hair. He looked both more present than Niniol and less *real.* He must be, Meridy thought again, a very old ghost. She wondered once more who he was.

The boy put his translucent hands over the wound. "Put your hands over mine," he told Meridy. "Don't think about the leg the way it is now; think about how it should be. Only sorcerers can take the *real* into the *ethereal;* that's what you need me for. I'll heal the little girl in the *ethereal* and then you'll bring her back into the *real.* Is that clear?"

It was clear enough, but Meridy protested, "I thought a ghost could only help his anchor heal someone—only help his anchor work magic at all."

"You *are* my anchor now," the ghost boy said impatiently.

"One of them, at least. Making you my anchor enables our friend to act more freely elsewhere; that's why he did it. That, and it enables me to keep an eye on you. Do you want to help this child or not?"

Meridy felt herself flushing. She asked, more meekly than was usual for her, "How do I get the healed part to stay *real* after it's done?"

"Once it's part of her, the little girl will hold it in the *real* by herself, exactly as though it'd healed naturally. Now, watch carefully, because I'm only going to have time to do this once," the ghost boy added to Niniol. He leaned forward over Jihiy. So did Meridy. So, a trifle uncertainly, did Jaift, edging forward for a better view.

Jihiy glimmered, faintly transparent. The torn flesh of her leg smoothed out until only a scar was left. Jihiy cried. Meridy couldn't tell whether the magic actually hurt her, or whether she was only frightened. The second the leg looked normal, Meridy blew a pinch of dust over it to help outline the *ethereal,* and she pulled girl back into the *real.* For a second she thought the healing was going to dissolve when she let it go, but the ghost boy had been right: It wavered for only an instant before settling thoroughly into the *real,* leaving not even a scar. With a surprised look, Jihiy hiccuped and stopped crying. Maraift hugged her and scrubbed a hand across her own eyes, blinking back tears of relief.

The ghost boy stood up, glancing over his shoulder as though he half expected and feared to see someone coming up behind him. He said crisply, "Keep an eye turned toward the *ethereal,* girl, and get off on your own as soon as you can! *He* will know his stroke missed, and he'll strike again as soon as he may."

"*He,* as in the witch-king? *He,* as in Tai-Enchar, who

destroyed the High Kingdom and then died himself, two hundred years and more ago, when the sea came in and drowned Moran Diorr? That's who you mean?" Meridy wouldn't have believed any of this if it hadn't been for the strange double-shadowed witch who'd tried to bind all the ghosts. As it was . . . she thought she did believe it. Anyway, she couldn't disbelieve the ghost boy.

Everyone stared at her. Jaift said tentatively, "But surely that's impossible."

The boy spared Jaift a glance. "The witch-king has been dead a long time. That's true. But witch as you are—you stepped right out of the world, did you? Changed the color of your eyes in a dream and then brought the dream into the *real*? That's sorcery, girl, and no mere witchcraft. If you're so clever as to manage that, you should surely know that *dead* does not mean *gone*."

"But—" began Jaift, and stopped because the boy was shaking his head, faintly scornful and more than faintly impatient.

"I fear that Tai-Enchar does not quite comprehend that his time has passed." The ghost boy's voice fell into a storyteller's rhythm. "For him, it is still two hundred years ago. For him, Moran Diorr is still falling; the sea is still rushing in. For him, victory still lies near enough to grasp in his hand. He seeks to step out of death into life. He still believes he may seize the High King's crown with one hand and immortality with the other. He may be right."

Meridy was starting to have a cold feeling that she might actually know the ghost boy's name. She started to say so and then stopped, caught by an unexpected shyness.

Before she could speak, the ghost boy warned her, "He

may *particularly* be right if he takes you into his hand, and therefore me, since you're now my primary anchor."

"And whose fault is that?" demanded Meridy.

The ghost boy gave her a scornful look. "You'd not have remained immured in your little village for much longer, girl. Even had the God not dropped my anchor at your very doorstep, our enemy would have found you eventually. For many years he has gathered witches to himself as he might, and made them into his creatures as he could, and likely enough you've the gift of sorcery in you as well. You must not permit yourself to fall into the hands of—"

"I know! You said, and it was *so* helpful—I'm sure I'd never have figured out *the witch-king's servitors* would be dangerous if you hadn't warned me!"

Affronted, the ghost boy raised his chin, but his mouth was crooked too, in plain amusement. "Neither stupid nor unlettered," he conceded. "I do recall it. Very well. Know, then, that the loss of a servitor will give the witch-king pause, but only for a short time, until he may persuade another man to allow him entry to his soul—"

"Wait. They *let* him do it?" whispered Jaift, horrified.

This time the ghost boy's nod was less impatient, as though he thought better of Jaift for her very horror. "Indeed, it cannot be done unless a man agrees to it, and generally only to a witch, and only by a sorcerer who is also a witch. Witchery to take a man's soul, but sorcery to step into his place and look out of his eyes, and pure wickedness even to contemplate any of it. But, you know, there are many ways to cause a man to agree. Or a woman on occasion, of course: compulsion, trickery, lies, threats. . . . The witch may be corrupted or fearful, desperate or merely foolish. It comes to the same thing, in the end: the creation of an emptiness for Tai-Enchar to fill."

"And now he's after me," Meridy said, knowing it was true. "Because of you."

"For my sake, I admit it, but also on your own account. Carad Mereth is seeking even now to frustrate all the witch-king's aims; you should understand that, girl, since of course he made you my anchor not only because you had the capability to hold me but also so that he might himself be freed to go about the God's business elsewhere. But the time for fearful retreat is giving way now to the need for bold action."

"And you, between the two of you, you've pulled me into your battle with Tai-Enchar himself!" Meridy could hardly believe this even now, but the ghost boy was looking impatient again, so she said, with as much sarcasm as she dared, "Oh, well enough, well enough! But now the witch-king won't wait long to strike again. All right, but what should I *do*?"

"Go north, of course! Everything lies north. You may have one day or two, but likely not more than that, so don't dither about, girl." And the ghost boy vanished, *flick,* gone, as though blown out by a sharp breeze.

Shaking her head, Meridy looked at Niniol.

"Arrogant youngster," the guard captain agreed, frowning. "Older than he looks, I'll be bound, and keeping plenty of secrets behind his teeth for all he seems to speak out. This witch-king, you mean *the* witch-king, do you, as wanted to set up witches to rule ordinary folk and himself to rule over all? The one as gave witches a bad name straight through to this moment? That's him, is it? It sounds bad."

Meridy nodded reluctantly, resigned to everyone's hearing all about this. Jaift already knew, after all. She agreed with Niniol about the ghost boy, too. Older than he looked, yes, and she thought she might understand the arrogance as well. She wished she could slip away somewhere quiet to think, but if the witch-king was going to send more outlaws . . . or another servitor . . .

Then Derren Gehliy stepped forward and said with surprising dignity, "I don't think any of us know much about . . . about witch-kings, or any of that, but I know we have more wounded, Meridy, and I know that some of our men will likely die without a witch to heal their wounds."

Meridy stared at him. She looked around, taking in Niniol's frowning concern and Jaift's trusting gaze; Derren's steady resolve and Maraift's somewhat flurried attempts to shelter all her younger children simultaneously. The man who had cut the quarrel out of Jihiy's leg, Inden, was hovering nearby, uncertain and worried. He edged forward a bit at the merchant's request and said apologetically to Meridy, "Ceir's arm is near off at the elbow. He's a young'un, miss, and that's a hard thing for a young man, losing half an arm. . . ."

"Of course I'll help Ceir," Meridy said helplessly, seeing no choice at all, no matter what dire warnings the ghost boy might issue. "Of course I will."

eight

She woke up much later, in stifling darkness pierced through by a dazzling line of light. She had a headache, but it was just a faint pressure at the back of her skull—vague memory suggested it had recently been much worse. Dark and that tight pressure at the back of her skull: those were the first things she was aware of. Only after a timeless uncomfortable interval did she become aware that she was being roughly and continuously jostled. This startled her at last into an attempt to sit up. She lost her balance before she was half up and toppled helplessly forward, grabbing blindly for support.

Jaift caught her. "Easy, Mery! You're all right."

Meridy blinked at her. She could barely make out the other girl, but Jaift's tone was reassuring. She wanted to ask where they were, what had happened, but her mouth was cottony and dry and her tongue didn't seem able to frame intelligible words.

"You're in a wagon," said Jaift patiently. "We're still several days south of Riam, but we thought we'd better go on north as quick as we could, what with, um, everything. Father said it was silly waiting for you to wake up, since we didn't know when that would be. You've slept a long time, almost twenty-six hours. But nothing terrible's happened yet." There was a rustle as Jaift pulled the canvas back to let more light and air into the wagon.

"Twenty . . ." Meridy's voice failed her.

"You were exhausted after healing Ceir. And then there were all the others—both Demarr and Tiranas turned out to be almost as badly hurt as Ceir. . . ."

"I don't think I remember that part," Meridy admitted. Her words sounded thick and strange to her own ears.

"Have some tea." Jaift handed her a flask. "It's cold, but it has a bite."

Meridy sipped the tea obediently. The astringent taste of redneedle and sourgrass cleared her mouth and her mind. She said cautiously but much more easily, "In Cora Tal, witches are supposed to be given over to the prince, aren't they?"

Jaift met her eyes. "Well, yes. But after all, we're from Harann, not Cora Tal, and so are you. Father says he's a merchant, not a White Swan guardsman, and it's not his business to hunt up witches for anybody. All the men swore by the God not to say a word. Niniol was a popular commander, and Ceir's like a younger brother to most of them."

This sounded promising, but Meridy knew she had better get up and get moving. She was sinkingly certain that the wagons could not be moving fast enough to evade any new blow the witch-king—the witch-king! it still seemed impossible—might aim at her. Or at the ghost boy through her; she still was not clear exactly what was going on.

She did have one or two ideas about the ghost boy, though. She began, "Jaift, I think I might know who—"

Bur Jaift, clambering to her feet in the dim heat, was

already going on and didn't hear her. "I was worried it was taking too long for you to wake up, but Mother said you were resting normally and you'd wake up when you were ready. She'll be glad to see you up, I expect." She offered Meridy a hand and helped her climb to her feet, steadying her against the jolting of the wagon.

The woman driving the wagon looked around as the girls pushed the curtain aside and came out. "Ah!" she said. "Good! Want down?" She drew up her team of horses.

"Thanks," said Jaift, and clambered deftly to the ground. She offered a hand to Meridy, who jumped down beside her, then looked around, blinking in the molten light of early afternoon. No wonder it had been hot in the wagon, with all this sun. On top of the next wagon, Niniol sat cross-legged, dust motes limning his hands and face, so Meridy knew she could bring him into the *real* if she tried. He was turning an *ethereal* knife over and over in his hands as he kept an eye out for trouble from every direction. He frowned at Meridy but didn't get up.

"He's been worried," Jaift said, seeing the direction of Meridy's glance. "So have we all. But nothing's happened so far."

Iëhiy bounded up, tail waving wildly, and danced along beside them. Meridy reached out, letting her fingers trail affectionately along his back. Iëhiy barked once, voicelessly, then dashed after the third wagon, leaping up to join Niniol.

"He's rather splendid, isn't he, your dog?" Jaift asked, a touch wistfully.

"He is." Meridy found herself smiling. "I didn't try to bind him on purpose, but I'm glad . . . I'm glad he's with me." She cleared her throat. "I'd better go talk to your father, I suppose. I wonder if he would let me have a horse. . . ."

"You can't go off on your own! Father's been talking about

it with some of the men. Obviously the wagons are too slow, but Ceir would go with you, and I'm sure others, too."

Meridy hadn't thought of this at all, and she blinked, nonplussed. A couple of the men to go with her! What a fine idea, although on the other hand she had no idea where she was going or what she was supposed to do. But she had all too clear an idea what enemy she might find set against her. She found herself seriously annoyed with Carad Mereth, who hadn't warned her about any of this. And she was annoyed with the ghost boy, too, although . . . being annoyed with *him* seemed like temerity. The next time she saw him, she would *make* him tell her his right name so she would *know* who he was instead of guessing and wondering and feeling strange about her suspicions.

Maraift was riding, as always, in the first wagon. Her husband, unusually, sat beside her rather than riding alongside. The cut on his cheek had scabbed over and looked like it was healing well. Jihiy perched between her parents on the driver's seat, chattering away with enthusiasm.

"Oh, look!" she said cheerfully as Meridy and Jaift swung up and found places to sit in front of the canvas that covered the load, "Meridy's all better! Aren't you all better, Meridy?"

"All better," Meridy assured her.

"So's my leg," said Jihiy. "Look!" She pulled up her skirt to show the smooth skin. "All better! See?"

"A very nice leg," Meridy agreed.

"Jihiy, sweet, put your skirt down," Maraift said firmly. "Why don't you go see what Little Derren is up to for me, please, dear."

"All right," said Jihiy agreeably. She jumped down from the wagon and ran off.

"We'll make camp in an hour or so," said Derren Gehliy, his tone a little tentative. "But why don't you let Jaift get you something to eat before we halt? You must be starving."

Meridy realized that she was. "Thank you, excellent sir." Jaift gave her an encouraging smile and climbed into the back of the wagon to rummage through the stores there.

Meridy glanced after Jihiy. "I'm glad Jihiy's well," she said, a little awkwardly, wondering how to open the conversation.

"The young are so resilient," Maraift observed comfortably. "Which is probably good, considering the things the children do get up to. Not that older people can't get up to just as much mischief, to be sure, but then they often do take a bit longer to recover. You're looking much better, too, if you don't mind my saying so, but of course you're still so young yourself. Quite terrifying, what happened."

"Yes, um . . ."

"And I suppose we're expecting more trouble," Derren said, his manner becoming brisk, which by now did not surprise Meridy. "It's clear you mustn't stay with my family— the children, you know—but you certainly can't go off all by yourself, my dear. It's not safe. Obviously. We've decided— Maraift and I and the men—that it would be best if you took a couple of the men and some of the better horses and rode on ahead. With enough money to see to your keep for a bit. Now, I've a notion your best move is likely to seek out the sanctuary in Riam and lay all this out before the priests. It's priests' business, right enough—I think we can agree on that! And then they can take care of this Godless witch who's making trouble. But you'll need an advocate, of course, my dear, because what with one thing and another you might be in an uncomfortable bind yourself. So first you must visit the office of my own advocate, or at least, not my personal advocate, of course, but the Riam partner, and we'll arrange to have you declared a guest of my family, which ought to clear up any little problems you might otherwise encounter."

Meridy stared at him. He meant, obviously, to protect her from the rule that witches had to present themselves to the prince in Cora Diorr. "But—" she said. "I mean, thank you, excellent sir, thank you very much, but aren't advocates expensive?" She had the coins she'd taken from the brigands, but she was sure that wasn't enough. "I couldn't—"

"My dear!" Maraift said warmly. "You healed Jihiy, not to mention any number of the men, and from what Jaift tells us, you saved poor Niniol from being enslaved by that awful witch. The least we can do is arrange for an advocate, which won't be so terribly expensive, I'm sure. And a decent inn, of course, and letters of introduction where they're likely to do the most good—Derren already wrote them; Tiranas has them. You'll quite like Tiranas, I'm sure. You healed a dreadful gash across his face, you know. He insists he be permitted to escort you to Riam."

"Oh," Meridy managed, overcome by this organized flood of plans and assurances, almost as much as by the unexpected kindness of the Gehliy family and their whole company.

"You may ride on ahead in the morning," Derren told her. "I'd rather you'd woken earlier, but there, we have outriders keeping an eye out in all directions, and everything's fine and peaceful. We'll post a proper guard tonight, you may be sure!"

Meridy had no doubt of that. She looked around at the quiet hills through which they were traveling. The sinking sun spun heavy gold across the woods and gilded the dust stirred up by the wagon wheels and the horses' hooves. The air lay hot and quiet across the caravan. High overhead, a hawk turned in slow circles. It was hard to believe the ancient malice of witch-kings or sorcerers could still cause trouble in the world in the face of all this measureless peace.

Jaift had made her way back to the front of the wagon, carrying a packet of dried fish and a larger packet of dried apples, plus one of the hard rounds of travel bread. "The fish would be better cooked into a chowder, with cream and dill," she told Meridy a touch apologetically. "But this will do, I suppose. Come on, Mery, it's crowded up here." Tucking the food into the pockets of her traveling skirt, Jaift jumped from the wagon and held up her hands to help Meridy get down.

Meridy was glad of Jaift's steadying hands. She hadn't realized quite how hungry she was until just this moment, and now she felt shaky and insecure. Although maybe that was nervousness from talking to Jaift's parents. Yet she felt so much better, now that she'd been handed a reasonable plan and knew she would have help. She gave Derren and Maraift Gehliy each an awkward nod, hoping she looked grateful and not too stupid. Derren nodded back, smiling, and Maraift said comfortably, "Have a nice snack, dear, and we'll try a chowder when we get to Riam, if the milk comes with decent cream on top. You can't ever tell. I remember when— But never mind, go on, go on, I know you're starving."

Jaift pressed the packet of fish into Meridy's hands. "I left the flask of tea in the other wagon, but the wagon will come up in a minute and we can get up or just collect the tea and walk alongside, whatever you like."

Meridy opened the packet, not really listening. She wasn't sure what chowder was, other than it must contain fish and cream, but she was more than willing to try the fish plain. She wasn't sure she'd ever had dried fish before in her life, and she certainly hadn't ever had a chance to get tired of it, as she gathered people must in Tamar. It smelled interesting—strong but not bad, like smoke and salt and what she imagined must be the sea. It tasted interesting, too. Like fish, but not like ordinary fish. Stronger, and just . . . different. She ate another piece, trying to decide if she liked it. She'd never heard of anyone smoking the trout they caught from the streams near Tikiy. If you smoked trout, would it taste like this?

Iëhiy trotted up, his head cocked meaningfully to one side, his eyes on the packet, and Jaift laughed out loud. "He's so big, but sometimes he acts like just like a puppy, doesn't he?" She gave Meridy a shy look. "I've never been able to talk to anybody about . . . you know. Except my uncle sometimes. I mean, about seeing . . . you know."

Meridy met the other girl's gaze. She did know. She felt she might understand Jaift after all, at least a little bit, even though they were so different. "I could talk to my mother. But then she took the White Road. After that, there was no one. Except ghosts, and that's not the same."

"Were there a lot of ghosts in Tikiy? The priests in Tamar always send the quick dead on their way if anger or regret or love makes them linger. I mean, they do it in case a witch might bind a ghost, which I suppose is only good sense, but I've hardly ever even met a ghost. I didn't know animals could stay quick at all. You call him Iëhiy? Is that Viënè?"

Meridy gestured assent. "It means things that are lifted by fire to the God. Sparks, or smoke, or souls. Dogs belong to the God, you know, and they love life, so I think they come and go as they like. Iëhiy . . ." But Meridy had no idea how to explain about the ghost boy or how the wolfhound was really his. About how she'd only met either of them a week ago. Or about Carad Mereth, who said he wasn't a sorcerer but surely must be.

It all seemed too complicated. She asked instead, "Didn't you say your uncle turned your eyes blue? How? Is it something anybody could do? Wait, are your *uncle's* eyes blue?"

Jaift shook her head. "I don't know how he did it, but he doesn't mind having black eyes, he says. He says people don't mind a witch if he's also a priest, and anyway, I think maybe it has to be done when you're a baby, before your nameday, or people would notice, don't you think?"

Meridy agreed, to be polite, but she thought that, really, if you walked out of your village and never went back, who would ever know what color your eyes had been when you'd been younger? She wished Jaift's uncle were handy. Maybe if she stayed with the Gehliy family until they went back to Tamar, she could meet him and find out how he'd done it.

If Jaift's parents didn't mind her staying with them that long. Maybe she could make herself useful. Somehow.

She ate another piece of fish and started to say something to Jaift, something about eyes or uncles or usefulness. But Iëhiy suddenly turned his elegant head toward the rocky hillsides falling away from the road, toward the west and the setting sun. His ears pricked alertly, then flattened as he showed his teeth in a silent, uneasy snarl. Both Meridy and Jaift stared at him, and Meridy realized, despite the sudden sharp dread that ran through her, how different and strange and pleasant it was to have another girl see the same things she saw herself.

Then the ghost boy flickered into view. He stepped forward, scanning the hills alertly, and laid his insubstantial hand on the hound's neck. Iëhiy, tail waving in welcome, turned his head and licked the boy's hand. Jaift stared at the newcomer, fascinated, but Meridy felt a sense of tightening dread.

The boy told her, breathless and severe, "You are yet in this company? Fool girl! Did I not say Tai-Enchar would find you? Another of his servitors is all but upon you, and you stroll the road at the pace of the stolid cart horses!"

Meridy looked around quickly, but she saw nothing out of the ordinary, not yet. She snapped, furious, "And what should I—we—do about it? Is it brigands again, or just the servitor alone this time? Can't you explain right out like a normal person, in time to actually *help*? What *are* these servitors? Is your enemy really Tai-Enchar himself? What's actually going on, and who's Carad Mereth, and why did he involve *me*? None of this makes *sense*!"

"*Our* enemy is indeed Tai-Enchar, the treacherous witch-king himself, and none other." The ghost boy flicked a mistrustful glance around the surrounding hills and empty road as though half expecting Tai-Enchar to step directly out of some old story and strike him down—or bind him, as Tai-Enchar was said to have bound many, many ghosts, for he had been the greatest of witches and a sorcerer besides.

But nothing happened. The dusty road stretched out before and behind them, and the nearest wagon creaked past. The muffled thud of the horses' hooves and the creak of the wagon wheels only accented the quiet peace of the afternoon. Iëhiy's head was still cocked and alert, but the hound looked to Meridy as though he were trying to pin down a threat he wasn't quite sure was truly out there.

After a moment, the boy said curtly, "Walk a little aside, then; let us three have some space around us. There is nothing else to do now save step a little apart and wait." He led Meridy and Jaift at an angle away from the wagons, but just before Meridy exclaimed with impatience he went on abruptly. "Would you know of Tai-Enchar, of his servitors and his servants and his allies? Listen, then. Men served him in my father's day, shortsighted and prideful, and such men serve him still, some aware of what they do and more in ignorance. You wish to know what is afoot today? Then listen: Diöllonuor, prince of Cora Tal, served the enemy no less than any and more deliberately than some, for power is difficult for any prince to let lie, and the witch-king deploys many subtle designs to trap the ambitious."

"Prince Diöllonuor is dead, though," Jaift objected. "I'm sure we heard he died—wasn't he killed by a fall from a horse or something?"

The ghost boy jerked his head impatiently. "Dead, yes, and gone to the God. In the end he would not bend his head to Tai-Enchar, yet he had compromised far enough to make himself vulnerable. He would not forbear to speak with the witch-king, and thus he opened the way for the woman who now stands in the place of his wife."

Meridy shook her head, trying to get this all straight. It sounded terribly confusing to her.

Jaift at least knew the names of all these people, because she asked, startled, "His wife? You mean Prince Diöllonuor's wife, Princess Tiamanaith?"

"So she was," agreed the ghost boy. "Tiamanaith was a fool. A fine daughter she had borne already, an heir for the throne, yet she would have a son as well, a living son, though her body was no longer fit for bearing. When her babe began to quiet in her womb, she bargained with powers she did not understand—with a long-dead sorceress, Aseraiëth, who had been and still was Tai-Enchar's ally. Tiamanaith did not think to ask why her babe, hers in particular, might draw such powers to bargain, or what price would be demanded in return for his life."

"She *was* a fool, then!" Jaift, exclaimed.

Meridy had to agree. She could hardly believe any woman would be so stupid. *Everyone* knew better than to bargain with the long dead. Surely Princess Tiamanaith's own mother must have told her those cradle stories, the ones every child heard. Even her cousins raised by *Aunt Tarana* would have known better—even they knew those stories.

The ghost boy answered Jaift impatiently. "As I say, yes. Heartsick for her unborn son, and so a fool. She promised Aseraiëth what the sorceress asked, yet for a price surely more dear than Tiamanaith would willingly have paid: a living daughter in exchange for a living son. Thus I surmise," the ghost boy added. "But I am near certain something much of that kind must have passed between them."

"Yes, but surely not?" Jaift hesitated, plainly trying to wrap her mind around this. "A living daughter? She was willing to give up her own daughter to this dead sorceress?"

"I do surmise she did not understand what bargain she had made," the boy told her, almost gently. "But then Prince Diöllonuor died, and his daughter, Diöllin, died also, and this I much doubt was anyone's intention—her death confounded us all, I believe, not merely Aseraiëth."

"Wait," said Meridy. "Diöllin? But I met a ghost named that!"

The ghost boy gave her an impatient nod: *Of course you did.* "When she might have lost herself, I guided her to you. She will lead you to her brother. It is Prince Herren who now stands at the cusp of every ambition." He went on with fierce urgency: "You've interfered in no small way with Tai-Enchar's intentions, but you must do so again, for above all you must find and protect the young prince. But first you must protect yourself! You killed Tai-Enchar's servitor last time; this time, I warn you, his witch-servant won't be so easily defeated. You have dawdled here in the sun like a spring lamb waiting for the blooding knife! It is too late now to evade the servitor's sight, so you must be ready to take another path out of his reach."

"Well, but—" Meridy began.

Lifting a hand, the boy went on forcefully, "The witch-king may come himself, in the body of his servitor. You daren't face him directly; this is not the moment or the place, nor have all the pieces yet fallen upon the board as they must. You're helpless if you stay in the *real*. Step sideways when you see your moment, but you daren't linger in the realms of dream, or you'll find no way out save the witch-king's path or the God's Road, and the first would be dire and the second taken far too soon and for too little gain. Hold hard to the *real* world, do you hear? Don't approach the tower, and *don't follow the White Road*."

"Who *are* you?" demanded Jaift. "You're not like any of the lingering dead I ever met or heard of, not like any ghost my uncle ever described. Meridy, who *is* this?"

The ghost boy said impatiently, ignoring Jaift, "Your road lies north, girl, but take your witch-bred friend with you, blue eyes or no. Take her with you all the way. If it goes ill, you may yet have need of her."

Iëhiy growled, the fur along his back rising, individual hairs sparkling in the sunlight. It was a voiceless growl, rumbling below the level of hearing, but a sense of threat rose up to choke Meridy. The boy's hard, too-adult gaze flicked to the dog, and he said sharply to Meridy, "He is all but here! I can't protect you! *I* least of all! Remember, step sideways as you see the chance, but don't linger in the realms of dream, and hold with all your strength to the *real* world!" Then a soundless concussion seemed to shake the world, and the boy jerked around, eyes narrowing, and was gone, as suddenly as a blown-out candle flame.

nine

Meridy took a step back, though no threat was yet perceptible. Iëhiy began to bark: deep and aggressive.

In front of the wolfhound, not nearly far enough away, the
light folded back. The drying grasses and rocky earth there
turned all to powder, and a curving swath of air and soil and
rocks and all blew away on a dry wind that hissed with emptiness and smelled of hot metal and of dust.

A man stepped through the folded light and rippling
air. This was a bigger man than the other servitor, and much
older, his face deeply lined and his hair quite white, including
his eyebrows, which were thick and striking over his black,
black eyes. But he stood very straight and held his head with
the arrogance of a man who knows he is the superior of everyone he sees.

Except for his hair and his eyes and his attitude, the old
man looked like anyone. Or anyone of pure northern blood.
He looked perfectly ordinary. But he cast two shadows, one
normal and one that trailed at an odd angle, wavering like
heat haze in the summer. It was as though the man walked
under the ordinary sun and at the same time some other sun
from some realm of dreams.

Then he looked straight across the road and met Meridy's eyes, and she saw that he was not ordinary at all. Whatever looked at her out of his eyes, it was *terrible.* Meridy thought maybe she was actually dreaming, maybe she'd never woken from the deep sleep after healing the wounded men. Maybe she'd never healed anyone; maybe everything since she'd left Tikiy was a dream. She felt exactly like she was in a dream: like she was frozen in place, unable to even back away. She wanted to be asleep and dreaming, because this was too awful and she wanted to wake up.

But she knew she *was* awake. *She* wasn't the one who was dreaming. The man had stepped out of the *ethereal* into the *real,* and now he was *right here.* Behind her, Jaift made a little sound, not a scream, but a kind of shrill gasp, yet Meridy still could not move.

Then Jaift stepped in front of Meridy, her chin up in determination, and Meridy suddenly found she could move after all, for sheer shame at Jaift's courage and her own cowardice. Stooping, she gathered a handful of dust, though she could hardly see how she could face a terrible man like this with nothing but dust—

Niniol threw himself right through the nearest wagon and ran toward them, an *ethereal* sword naked in his hand.

The double-shadowed man swept up an empty hand, and Niniol cried out and stumbled abruptly to one knee, wavering around the edges as though the sunlight might burn him away like mist. Meridy took a step toward him, trying to gather him up as he frayed away into memory. She flung her handful of dust over Niniol, and caught him and pulled him into the *real.* Gaining solidity, Niniol began to push himself back to his feet, but he also snapped over his shoulder, grimly, "Fool girls, run!"

Ignoring Niniol, the man met Meridy's eyes once more, and his were black, black, black, and she knew that if he touched her, she would die, or do something worse than die.

But then Iëhiy hurled himself forward with a snarl and the man turned, lifting a warding arm. In that moment, Jaift seized Meridy's hand and dragged her, not away, but forward, dodging right around the black-eyed man. Meridy understood almost at once, and ran with Jaift toward the patch of folded light. Past that gap in the *real* lay no ordinary rolling hills: Meridy could see now, as through a pane of rippled glass, a wide desolate plain, with one stark white tower spearing up out of the plain, far in the distance. *Don't approach the tower,* the ghost boy had warned. She had absolutely no desire to approach that tower, but there wasn't any other way to get clear, not out here surrounded by nothing but hills and empty country, blameless men who would try to protect her, Derren Gehliy and friendly, voluble Maraift and all the children.

Step sideways, the ghost boy had commanded. And something like *You daren't linger in the* ethereal. *Hold hard to the* real *world.* Meridy hoped she understood what he'd meant—she'd *better* understand, or both Jaift and she herself might be lost in that realm beyond the *real* world. The idea was terrifying.

Then somewhere one of the little girls screamed, and Maraift called out incoherently. Meridy didn't understand her, but Jaift threw a look that way and dragged Meridy along with her, straight out of the *real* world, straight into the *ethereal* realms. Meridy bent at the last second to snatch up another handful of dust, though dust seemed a poor weapon to meet whatever might wait beyond the *real.* Light folded around them and folded back . . .

. . . and all around them, dust-dry air hissed through dead grasses. The very light in this place was different: chill and bleak, not with winter, but with emptiness. There was no road, no caravan of wagons, no guardsmen, no children. Meridy and Jaift had run together into an empty realm—empty and silent and dead except for that single bone-white tower.

Meridy pulled Jaift to a stop, gasping with terror of that tower—she wouldn't have gone another step closer to it for anything, yet they couldn't stand still, because surely the double-shadowed man would come after them again. She pulled Jaift a dozen quick steps away from the tower, but the empty plain swung dizzyingly around them and the tower rose up in the distance, still before them, now a tiny bit closer.

Of course it was closer. Meridy understood suddenly. That tower was the only thing truly present in this realm. She saw this *ethereal* country now as a wide and trackless wasteland on which wandered neither wild cattle nor tame, in whose skies flew neither bird nor dragonfly; so empty that nothing at all existed here save the towering presence of the witch-king himself. The wind sighed through the emptiness. The breeze smelled of heated iron, of blowing dust, of crumbling years and grim silence. And no matter what direction they tried to go, the witch-king's tower would lie before them.

Then Iëhiy leaped out of nowhere and ran past the girls, and somehow the dog was running *away* from the tower, not toward it. Meridy followed him, another dozen steps and a dozen more after that, pulling Jaift along with her, and she flung her handful of dust out into the dead, empty air. With it, she seemed to throw more than dust; she threw light and air, and this light was the familiar comforting sunlight of a *real* summer, nothing like the bleak, lonely light of this terrible realm. And they ran through the dust and light and out of the dead land . . .

. . . and stumbled to a halt on the shore of a glimmering

river of moonlight. Light splashed and tumbled like water, bright currents glimmered out in the fast-running depths— but it wasn't a river, it was a road, a road of light that flowed like water. The full moon poured down light, and the light flowed like water, and though it was absolutely silent, somehow there was a sound underneath and behind and beyond the light, as though somewhere far away a great bell had been lifted and struck.

Jaift took a step toward the road, but Meridy held her back and looked around for another way to go, another patch of folded light, of wavering air, a place where the light was the ordinary light of an ordinary summer day. But she could see only moonlight and the White Road.

Iëhiy barked, not that deep warning bark this time, but peremptorily: *Let's go!* His ears were up now, and his tail jaunty. He trotted firmly away. Meridy ran after him, pulling Jaift along with her, and then staggered sideways as the whole angle of the world seemed to change around them, and she fell to her knees in the perfectly ordinary dust of a perfectly ordinary road, Jaift stumbling to a halt beside her, still gripping her hand. For a long moment, both of them stared around, panting and shaking.

This was the *real* world again at last, by the grace of the God. There was no sign of the double-shadowed man, which was even better. Here there was no ghost boy, no white tower in a desolate land, no shimmering road of moonlight that ran like water. But there was no sign of the Gehliy caravan either, or of anything familiar.

Instead, before them, not too far away, rose the bulk of city walls, and above the walls the tops of heavy-looking squared-off buildings with sloped roofs, and before and beyond the walls a distant clamor of life and movement. Mountains stood against the sky to the left, not the jagged peaks of the Southern Wall but rough, low mountains, heavily forested. To the right, where the land was gentler, fields of grain stretched out, tall and green in the warm breeze. The road dust was silky under Meridy's hands. She nervously gathered a handful, but there seemed nothing to do with it here. Iëhiy had vanished again. Niniol . . . Niniol was nowhere in sight. She was his anchor, and since she'd left him, he would be lost . . . but she had to hope he might somehow find her.

There seemed no immediate peril anymore. Meridy could see wagons behind them, approaching, but a good way off, and men riding horses out from the city, but they were hardly closer. She let Jaift help her to her feet and said in a hesitant tone that hardly sounded like her own voice, "Where do you think we are?"

"Oh," said Jaift, a little blankly. She was ash pale, her blue eyes wide and stunned, but then she blinked and swallowed and said, "That's Riam. That's Riam up ahead there. We've come three days' travel in thirty steps. How did we—how did you—was that the *White Road*?"

"We didn't follow it," Meridy said.

"I know! Obviously! But it was the White Road! Where was that other place? Who was the man with the—with the double shadow? He wasn't *actually* Tai-Enchar himself, do you think? Or was he? Tai-Enchar was of Southern blood, isn't that right? That man wasn't, obviously, but could the witch-king truly put himself into someone else's body? Even if he's been dead for two hundred years?"

All good questions. Meridy shook her head, let her handful of dust sift away between her fingers, and looked around.

Ordinary mountains and green fields and a road that rolled out in an easy hour's walk to the city of Riam, and nowhere anything uncanny or *ethereal.*

"I'll tell you," she said. "I'll tell you everything I know, but I don't know much. Let's walk on, all right? And let me think a little, because I'm not sure . . . I'm not sure about anything."

Jaift gave her a close look. "You think about the spooky man with the eyes and the shadow, then, and I'll think about Riam, because we have to be practical, don't we, even if there are ghosts and sorcerers everywhere."

Meridy nodded. She was intensely glad that the other girl was with her, because there was Riam and *she* certainly had no idea where to go or how to handle herself in a city. The two of them alone in a big city . . . She shivered. She would rather think about ghosts and sorcerers.

But she did wish Iëhiy would come back. And she was worried about Niniol. But there was nothing she could do about either of them now.

Riam, Gate to the Deep South, was overwhelming. Meridy had known everybody in the Tikiy-up-the-Mountain by name. True, Tikiy-by-the-Water had been bigger than the living village, but not nearly this big. And ghosts didn't *crowd* so.

The people of Riam dressed in bright colors; they shouted and laughed and screamed conversations over the racket. The streets teemed with petty vendors crying apples, pickles, roasted nuts, or hot sausages at the tops of their lungs; and with women carrying baskets and jugs, some escorted by servants in livery who carried bundles for them. Children dashed past in groups of three or four; Meridy watched a pack of ragged children younger than she race by and clamber up the side of a narrow building, pouring over the edge and away over the rooftops just as a pair of guardsmen rounded the corner after them. The men shouted curses after the last of the children and stalked back the way they'd come. Meridy wondered what the children had done, and whether they were all orphans.

Carriages rattled by, and mounted parties of wellborn young ladies and lords clattered through the streets, some with men-at-arms to clear their paths. Officers of the watch stood alertly on street corners, each with the bronze dragon of Riam on a badge at his shoulder. Jaift and Meridy passed a carpentry yard where men worked at building furniture and a potter's workshop where women shaped jugs and bowls out of damp clay.

The noise was disorienting, even a little frightening, though it didn't seem to upset Jaift. The smells were worse than the noise: horse droppings, at least animal and familiar, but also other things more noisome. And hot cooking oil, and unfamiliar spices, and occasional pockets of sweet, heavy air from incense burners, and most of all thousands of overheated people.

"Down this way, I think," Jaift called, tugging Meridy out of the eddying crowd toward a quieter street. On Jaift's confident advice, they were looking for a bank. This, apparently, was a place where the people would give you money. This certainly sounded like a good thing, because they'd run away from Jaift's family's caravan with nothing but the packet of dried fish, the clothing they were wearing, and the handful of coins Meridy had taken from the brigands. Meridy didn't quite understand how a girl in a plain traveling skirt was supposed to persuade the people at the bank to give her money, but Jaift seemed confident, and the relative calm of this wider street was welcome.

In this part of the city, though the streets were still busy, most of the carriages were smaller and fancier, and the road was wide enough for horse-drawn vehicles to keep to the left, so that people could walk safely on the right. Here, the crowded shops and work yards gave way to larger, more graceful buildings painted eggshell blue or soft green, madder pink or rich buttercup yellow. The colors glowed in the afternoon sun. Shops displayed bright bolts of silk or crystal goblets that were, no doubt, ruinously expensive. Strings of prayer bells swayed from the eaves of most of the shops, chiming gently. The sigil of the God was not only carved above most of the doors but often inlaid with silver or mother-of-pearl. Everything looked far fancier and more elaborate than anything Meridy had ever imagined.

Jaift led Meridy around another corner. Here the street was wider still, the rough cobbles smoothed out to tightly fitted paving stones. Broad ditches and drains appeared on either side of the road, and flowering trees leaned over the walls that separated one graceful building from another.

"Ah!" Jaift said, nodding toward one particularly large building, its walls painted ivory and dove gray, strings of porcelain bells hanging from the carved portico.

"That's a bank?" It looked, Meridy thought, like a particularly intimidating lord's house. It was set off from all the other buildings by gardens of raked gravel and flowering trees. There were iron grills over the windows, but the bars were shaped into flowers and birds. Private guardsmen, each armed with a crossbow and a short sword, stood at the top of the short stairway that led to the wide double doors, now standing open. The guardsmen were watching the street—one of them was looking directly at the two girls. Meridy stared back uneasily.

A woman trailed by two servants came out through the doors, gathered up her elaborate skirts—honey gold and very full—descended the stairs, and was handed up into a waiting carriage by one of her servants. The woman, though clearly carrying more than a dash of Southern blood, looked rich and disdainful; Meridy wouldn't have dared say a word to her. She could imagine a bank giving money to a lady like that but looked askance at Jaift in her plain, dusty traveling skirt. She couldn't help sounding doubtful as she asked, "They'll really give you money?"

"See the owl over the door?" The bird was carved in full relief, its feathers etched with gold. Jaift said confidently, "This is a branch of Tair's, which is my family's bank in Tamar. Don't worry, Mery! It doesn't matter whether you drive up in a carriage inlaid with gold. What matters is if you know the right codes."

"And . . . you know these codes?"

"Of course! Accounts are women's business. My mother gave me the family codes when I took over the candle-wax and honey accounts when I was fourteen. Those are small accounts, good for a girl just learning, but I know the codes for the drawing account, too. Come on!" And she strode toward the door as though she had no doubt in the world about being welcome.

Perhaps because of that confidence, the guardsmen at the door barely looked at the girls—though Meridy drew a thoughtful glance, maybe for her black eyes or maybe for her travel-worn shabbiness. But Jaift knew exactly how to talk to the people at the bank of Riam, and she rapidly disappeared through an interior door with a cool-mannered young man. Meridy perched on a fancy chair in a corner and waited uncomfortably, watching ladies in lace and satin come and go.

In a surprisingly short time, Jaift returned with six gold coins and a larger handful of silver. She gave Meridy three gold coins and half of the silver, which Meridy tucked away carefully before they left the bank. Jaift touched her elbow, guiding her down the street, not the way they'd come but the other way, alongside the narrow garden of gravel and flowers. "Now, you know, of course, that twenty-one copper pence make one silver," she told Meridy. "And ten silver make one thin gold, and eighteen thin gold make one heavyweight gold, except in Tian Sur, where they clip the thin gold so it takes twenty. But prices are different in big cities than in little towns, so you might not be used to gold."

Meridy had never seen a gold coin in her life. "The ones you gave me must be thin?"

"Oh, yes, heavyweight gold is almost always carried as bank drafts and notes of credit, because it *is* heavy, and anyway no one would want to risk having it stolen. Besides, no one is likely to calculate sums in heavyweight unless they're buying, you know, an estate or something. Smaller coins are a lot more practical. Now, in Riam, I'd think that one thin gold would probably buy, oh, say, a decent horse. One silver coin ought to buy a meal and lodging at a town inn, or two nights at a public house on the road; one copper penny should be enough for a loaf of bread stuffed with cheese and sausage; one halfpenny a plain loaf."

Meridy nodded and didn't mention that in Tikiy a copper halfpenny would purchase one's whole supper plus a loaf to take home from Mistress Lireft, a widow who cooked meals for those without the time or inclination to cook for themselves.

Jaift also hired one of the bank's messengers to take a sealed letter to her father at the Derem house. "Because they'll be coming along in a few days, and they'll be so worried," she said. She didn't say, *Unless that double-shadowed man dragged them all into the dead realm and they're all lost there . . .*

Meridy didn't suggest anything like that, either. Hopefully Jaift hadn't thought of the possibility. She only asked, "But you're *sure* don't want to go to the Derem house to meet them?" Though if Jaift did want to go to the Derem family for shelter, Meridy wasn't at all sure *she* would be welcome there as well. Why would those people welcome her? *She* wasn't part of the Gehliy family or promised to a Derem son, and besides that she had black eyes. Not to mention having servitors of the witch-king pursuing her.

"I've never met them, you know," Jaift said, and paused. Then she said in a lower voice, "It's true I was looking forward to meeting Timias Derem. From what my father said, I think I would have liked him. But what we need now is a place to think. Somewhere quiet and private and safe. Because your . . . friend . . . said something about everyone in your company being in peril. Isn't that what he said? So I don't think we dare get near my family. And if you're marked out, am I, now, too? And did your friend *really* mean Tai-Enchar himself is after you? Because that seems . . ."

It did seem impossible. Meridy had been thinking about that. She shook her head, not in denial but in bafflement. "I know! At least this time the ghost boy explained a little, only I didn't understand anything. And every time he appears, something terrible happens." She wondered for the first time whether bandits—or worse, some terrifying black-eyed man out of some dreadful realm of dreams—might have terrorized Tikiy after she'd left, and for the first time she almost wanted to go back just so she could see whether everyone was safe.

It was a stupid idea, of course. She didn't even care if Aunt Tarana or her cousins were all right, or whether they'd all been . . . She couldn't quite make herself complete that thought, so maybe she did care, a little, after all. She bit her lip and said in a lower voice, "I don't know."

"Right—we both need time to catch our breath, after everything!" Jaift nodded firmly. "So I asked at the bank, and there's a decent inn up this way. I thought we could have something to eat and a bath and then think what to do."

Meridy had to admit that sounded like an excellent idea.

ten

The inn was a nice one, nice enough that even with gold and silver weighing down the interior pockets of her skirt, Meridy wouldn't have dared suggest staying there. The smooth plaster walls were painted carmine and ivory, the steep-pitched roof was pine shingle, and the numerous windows were protected by wooden shutters carved into a lacework of leaves and flowers. The courtyard in the front, like the area around the bank, was all raked gravel and flowers; and, as at the bank, there were private guards at the door.

"That's how you know it's safe," Jaift explained with easy confidence. "It's a bit pricier than I'd have liked, but mother wouldn't begrudge it—safe lodging is important! There's a couturier's across the street; I asked particularly. We won't want to wait for tailoring, but they'll have prepared garments that can be altered."

A couturier turned out to be like a dressmaker, such as Meridy had heard they had in Sann and other towns, only even fancier and more expensive.

In Tikiy, two different families made their living carding wool, making and dyeing thread, and weaving cloth; they'd also make up simple garments for anyone who didn't have time or good enough eyes for needlework. Meridy had known, or she'd thought she'd known, how much fancier clothing was in towns. But she hadn't really understood just how much fine cloth and clothing could cost until Jaift dragged her into the couturier's and made her try on a beautiful new dress that hadn't been worn by anyone else before, ever.

Jaift had asked to see only clothing suitable for travel, but even so the dress was the nicest Meridy had ever worn. It was all the colors of autumn, creamy yellow and rust and toast brown, colors that looked good with the brown skin and nearly black hair of a girl with a lot of Southern blood behind her. There was a little embroidery on the bodice and a simple skirt, not too full.

"Easy to put on and take off, with a skirt meant for riding if the excellent miss should wish, though of course a conveyance may be less dusty," murmured the woman assisting them. She hadn't flickered an eyelash at Meridy's obviously common background or even more obvious Southern coloring.

Meridy took an experimental step, watching in the mirror as the weighted hem swirled heavily about her ankles.

"Very nice," pronounced the woman, and then bowed her apology as another customer summoned her. She slipped away, promising she would soon return.

The autumnal dress was irresistible, though Meridy couldn't help but lean toward Jaift and protest quietly, "I'm sure it costs far too much. How can I let you spend all that money on me? My own things aren't new, but they'd do—"

Jaift took her hands, cutting her off. "Mery," she said patiently, "your old dress *wouldn't* do; people don't trust a woman who looks poor, and it's worse if you've got dark eyes. A dress is a small thing. You're my friend. You saved the twins, or at least you made it possible for Niniol to save them; and you healed Jihiy and the guards; and if you have ghosts bringing you warnings of dire danger and horrible sorcerers trying to kill you, at least you'll be able to face them all knowing you're decently dressed!"

Meridy blinked hard. "I've never——" she began, and stopped, because it was too embarrassing to say *I've never had a friend before.* She said instead, "But I'm the one who drew you into the . . . the dire danger from horrible sorcerers! I don't know—I think maybe you *should* go find the Derem family's town house and get away from me."

"Mery, I will die of curiosity if I never find out about the ghost boy and Tai-Enchar——"

The woman came back with a dress of blue and brown and turquoise for Jaift, murmuring that it ought to be nearly the correct length and that it would take but a moment to let out the hem a trifle, and so it was impossible to talk about ghosts or long-dead witch-kings or sorcerers with dead black eyes and two shadows; impossible, too, for Meridy to urge Jaift to leave her. Meridy was selfishly glad of that and let the subject die. She let Jaift pay for the autumn-colored dress, and also for a tray of pastries and fruit to while away the time it would take for the other dress to be altered. All this seemed terribly self-indulgent, but Meridy was utterly unable to resist.

The suite at the inn was small and pretty, its walls painted pale gold and coppery red. The bed was bigger than the one Meridy had shared with two cousins in her aunt's house, and the mattress softer, too. A wide doorway led to a second room that seemed intended to serve as a sewing room or sitting room, and a private bath let off one side, with brass plumbing and—luxury indeed—hot running water. The window in the sitting room even had a tiny balcony overlooking an interior courtyard of raked gravel and flowers, roses and mallows and pinks, all blooming in neatly kept beds.

"It's all so . . . nice," Meridy said hesitantly, looking around. "Is your house in Tamar this nice?"

Jaift smiled. "It's really not. My family does well enough, but there are so many of us, things do get . . . cluttered. And smudged." She perched on the window seat, the setting sun giving her honey-colored hair a gold nimbus and washing the color out of her blue eyes. The waxing moon was already visible in the sky, high up above the city.

Jaift looked at Meridy expectantly. "Here we are! Safe, or safe enough, or at least as safe as we're likely to be. So tell me all about your ghosts, and that horrible empty wasteland, and the white tower. Tell me everything."

Meridy sat down opposite Jaift, tucking her feet under the chair and running her fingers over the old-gold velvet of the cushion. She glanced out the window toward the moon. The sun was lower now, the horizon carmine and orange, the moon bright against a paler flaxen sky, the first stars glimmering faintly in the lavender blue above the sunset colors. Meridy said, "I think I might know who he is—the ghost boy." Then she hesitated.

Jaift straightened her back attentively, folding her hands in her lap. "Well? Yes?"

Meridy bit her lip. Then she said obliquely, "It seems impossible. Only who else would Tai-Enchar, the witch-king himself, hunt all across the world after death? And the boy is the right age, and dressed like a young lord, did you notice? And Iëhiy is his dog, really, not mine, and there's breeding in that hound—you just have to look at him. They even call dogs like that king's hounds, you know, in stories." All this seemed so impossible and yet, when she laid it out like this, obvious. Almost inevitable.

"Yes," Jaift said, not quite patiently. "Who *is* the boy, then?"

"I think," said Meridy, and paused again. Then she said out in a rush, "I think he's Inmanuàr." But Jaift only looked at her blankly, so Meridy went on, trying not to sound impatient, "Inmanuàr—the High King's son. High King Miranuanol. You must know the story! About the Southerners, and how High King Miranuanol gathered all his sorcerers together and did the great working to cast the Southerners back and raise up the Wall. But at the very height of the High King's great sorcery, he was betrayed—"

"By Tai-Enchar, yes, but I never really paid attention to all that ancient history."

Meridy waved a hand. "He was Enchaän, called Tai-Enchar, a petty king who ruled a little kingdom in the south of the High Kingdom. He had a good deal of Southern blood himself, as you might expect since he was both a witch and a sorcerer, and some tales say he'd bargained with the Southerners on that account. Most of the tales agree that his ambition was to raise up a new kind of kingdom, where witches ruled over lesser men and where he himself ruled over all. That's how the stories put it, that he wanted to *rule over all.* So Tai-Enchar struck down the High King in the midst of that great sorcery. But the High King couldn't protect both himself and his working at the same time, so he raised up the Southern Wall and fell—and when he died, all the violence of that freed sorcery poured down on his heir, Inmanuàr Incuonarr, who was too young and couldn't contain it, so he died, too, before he could ever be High King in his turn. And that's who Inmanuàr is."

"That's so sad!" Jaift protested. "It's a terrible story."

"Yes, and you must know this part, that under that storm of sorcery, all the land, for a hundred miles and more around, sank down and the waters rushed in to cover Moran Diorr, and everyone drowned. They say you can still hear the drowned bells ringing far below the waves, on moonlit nights. . . ."

"I *have* heard that one." Jaift rubbed her hands over her arms as though she were suddenly cold, and Meridy surprised herself by shivering as well. Both girls fell silent for a moment, half listening for the muffled ringing of thousands of bells.

Meridy had told the whole story before she remembered how her cousins had loathed her knowing stories and said she was putting on airs. *A village girl trying to make believe she's highborn, like making a bell out of straw and expecting it to ring,* her cousins had said, scornful, and thrown handfuls of straw at her. *Your voice isn't so sweet that anyone wants to hear it.*

"I think the twins like that kind of story more than I ever did. I always just did figuring and accounts and things," Jaift said at last, a little apologetically. "The High King and the Wall and everything, that was all so . . . so long ago. Can ghosts truly linger so long?"

"You must have seen how old the ghost boy is. It's like he's more dense or heavy or something than most other ghosts, but less *real*." Meridy waved a hand, giving up on expressing the idea, but Jaift nodded in understanding and agreement. It was so strange, taking to someone who *understood* about things like that. Even if Jaift didn't know anything about history.

Meridy went on, "So I think our ghost boy *is* Inmanuàr. Because if Tai-Enchar's pursuing him, there has to be a reason, and I think being the High King's heir is reason enough. The witch-king could bind ghosts—"

"But you said Tai-Enchar drowned too?"

"Well, yes, that's the way the tale ends. But he was a sorcerer as well as a witch, and powerful, so who knows? Maybe he stepped out of the *real* before the sea came in and saved himself. They say sorcerers can do that—step out of the *real* themselves, and not just bring the *ethereal* here the way witches do." It occurred to her that she and Jaift had actually done exactly what sorcerers were said to do, fleeing the witch-king's servitor out of the *real* into the terrible empty land. But then she shook her head, realizing that wasn't the same. It was the servitor who had opened the way between the *real* and the realm of dreams; she and Jaift had simply stepped through a door that already stood wide open.

She leaned forward to explain the important part. "And, listen, if Tai-Enchar *didn't* die with the rest, then who *knows* what he might want with the ghost of the High King's heir? I wonder if he could still be all caught up in that long-ago battle. Although"—and Meridy leaned back again, considering, then said more slowly—"none of this explains Carad Mereth."

Jaift lifted her eyebrows, an invitation for Meridy to go on.

"Inmanuàr's anchor. Or *an* anchor. I would have said he wasn't a witch, but then, your eyes are blue, so I don't know." Meridy sat up straight. "Jaift, *could* you show me how to turn my eyes blue, do you think?"

"I really don't know how. Truly. My uncle—"

All this time the sun had been sinking, the sky darkening, the moon brightening, and now out of moonlight and shadows stepped a ghost, indistinct at first, which made Meridy jump to her feet with a cry half of relief and half of alarm, thinking it must be Niniol and he had found her, or else it must be the ghost boy bringing disaster at his heel.

But it was neither Niniol nor Inmanuàr Incuonarr. It was Diöllin.

"Diöllin!" Meridy said in astonishment. "*Princess* Diöllin? You *are* the princess, aren't you? Are you lost *again*? Don't you know if you get lost, you'll start to fade and maybe never find the White Road? You can't depend on anybody helping you find me every time, you know! Why don't you stay with your brother, Prince Herren? He's your first and best anchor, isn't he?"

The ghost gave Meridy an affronted look. "Of course I know that!" she said. Her voice was the murmur of a ghost, but she spoke with a clear, brittle arrogance that all by itself confirmed her identity. "I'm not going to get lost, not this time. I know my name and my way, but they've got him! My brother! Of course he's my anchor, but our enemies have him now. It's pure wickedness, that's what it is! He calls to me, but I can't help him, I can't *get* to him. But I found you. You—you're *heavy*. The moonlight runs around you like water around a stone. So I found you—"

Jaift had backed away, alarmed. Now she came forward with a curious step. "Who?" she asked. "Who has your brother? Not—not your mother?"

"Her!" Diöllin said with furious scorn. "She's not my mother, not anymore! That sorceress took her—she wanted *me,* but then I died, so she took *her* instead, and it serves her right! But then she gave *Herren* to Tai-Enchar! You have to help him!"

She sounded really determined about this last, which made Meridy almost like her despite her peremptory tone.

Then the princess looked Meridy up and down and added more doubtfully, "You *will* help us, won't you? I mean, you're of Southern blood just like *him*—anybody could see that."

Meridy changed her mind about liking her.

But Diöllin went on, quick and imperious, "Well, if you

weren't, you wouldn't be so heavy and strong in the *ethereal*, I suppose, and besides"—her voice strengthened, as much as a ghost's voice could—"besides, I *know* you're not his servant. You showed me my way when I was almost lost; you helped me hear Herren's voice. That *was* you, wasn't it? You must help us again now, when it matters most. You must!"

Meridy scowled at the princess. But Diöllin's plea was clearly sincere, despite her arrogant manner. "If the witch-king's your enemy and he has your brother, what can I do to help?" Meridy asked. Another thought struck her, and she added more hopefully, "What does he want with your brother, anyway? Do you know?" The ghost boy had explained so little, but surely Diöllin must know everything about what had happened. . . .

The princess cried impatiently, "How should I know? What do I understand of sorcery? I only know he took him! I thought Roann—Roann Mahonis, my father's seneschal—I thought he would be able to help me, but I can't find him either—he's not where he should be, and he's not a strong enough anchor for me to find him. And if I go to my brother, the witch-king will bind *me*." There was more outrage than fear on that last. But then Diöllin wrapped her arms around herself, shuddering, and added in a small, tight voice, "Then he'll use me against Herren, somehow, and against our people. I can't let him do that. You have to help me. You must anchor me yourself before *he* can do it. You have to anchor me and save Herren!" Diöllin held out her hands in a gesture not only of entreaty but also of command. "He is *your* enemy, too," she warned Meridy. "If you're my anchor, you can use me. That would be better for us both. I'll help you as much as I can, but you have to be the one to bind me!"

Meridy looked helplessly at Jaift, who stared back, eyes wide.

Diöllin took an urgent step forward. "You have to bind me! *Bind me!*"

Meridy definitely didn't want to set herself up as Tai-Enchar's enemy, and yet she thought it was probably too late to avoid that. Besides, what else could she do? She could hardly let some horrible witch-king bind a ghost who was right here pleading with her—and kidnapping Diöllin's little brother, that was *terrible.* It would be awful for any little boy, but whatever Tai-Enchar intended to do with the new young prince, surely it would be worse.

"Please!" said Diöllin. "You have to anchor me!"

At least Meridy knew how binding was *supposed* to be done, in stories. She stepped forward and held out her hands, letting the ghost lay her insubstantial hands against hers, palm to palm. "Diöllin," Meridy said to her, exactly as witches did in the old tales. "Diöllin. Diöllin! By your name I call you and by your name I anchor you and by your name I bind you to the world."

She didn't feel anything happen, but Diöllin must have, for she cried, "Yes! Thank you, thank you! May the God defend you! Take care. Take care for yourself and take care of my brother. He's north, north of this place. I'll find him—I'll show you—"

And she was gone, flicking out like a candle, or like moonlight when a cloud comes across the moon.

Meridy stared at the empty place where the ghost had stood. Then she looked cautiously at Jaift, who stared back at her, eyes wide and shocked. Probably Meridy looked just as shocked herself. She had no idea what to say.

"Do you realize who that *was?*" Jaift asked, sounding stunned. "You're anchoring *Princess Diöllin?*"

Meridy scrubbed her hands across her face. She wanted to

laugh. Or maybe scream. In the end, she only said, "I think that sorceress, Aseraiëth—I think if she'd gotten Diöllin the way she wanted, she'd have had her hands full. I hope *I* can hold her. It would be bad to lose her after all this." She just hoped that Iëhiy and Niniol would be able to find her as easily as Diöllin seemed to be.

Jaift wasn't listening. She shook her head in dismay. "But how in the world are we supposed to save Prince Herren from the witch-king?"

"*We* aren't! You are going to wait here for your family, and I'll go—" Meridy looked around vaguely. "North, I suppose," she finished, rather weakly, because she honestly had no idea where she might be going, and wouldn't until Carad Mereth or Inmanuàr or someone turned up to explain what was going on and what she should do about it.

In the meantime she could head for Cora Diorr, maybe, and see if she could find Diöllin's brother. Cora Diorr! The City of Spires, the city that rested in the bowl of the sky. Ambica had told her the tale of how the mountains around Cora Diorr had been raised up by magic by the first prince of Cora Tal, who wanted to make sure his city was the greatest after Moran Diorr drowned and the High Kingdom broke into pieces. Meridy wanted very much see the City of Towers, although . . . she wasn't certain she wanted to see the famous city by herself.

But Jaift was eying her dubiously. "Oh, is that what you suppose? Well, it's easier to see a question from all sides in daylight, my father says, and my mother says arguing at bedtime brings bad dreams. Are we going to have any *more*, um, visitations, do you think?"

Meridy opened her mouth, shut it again, and shook her head helplessly.

"Right. Well, let's assume not. This day's been long enough, and tomorrow, who knows? I guess you can blow out the lamps now. But you can tell me some poetry, because otherwise neither of us is going to get any sleep at all! Something peaceful. Soothing." Jaift decisively closed the balcony window and beckoned Meridy to come into the other room.

Meridy hesitated. Sleep seemed impossible, but . . . she *was* very tired. She blew out the sitting-room lamp and followed Jaift, sure she wouldn't even be able to close her eyes for fear of dreams and ghosts.

Old poetry. Peaceful poetry. Soothing. Meridy knew a long epic about a woman who fell in love with the sea and built a boat of white wood with blue sails and swore never again to set foot on land. It was sad, but it was a peaceful kind of sadness. Maybe she could tell that one to Jaift, in a minute, as soon as she remembered exactly how it started.

She dreamed about a dusky-skinned Southern girl who fell in love with the sea, only the girl was not living, she was a ghost. Then the sea became a wide white river. The ghost stood in the center of the river, cool moonlight pouring over her like water and splashing into the river. The river flowed away from her left hand to her right, so smoothly its motion was indistinguishable from stillness. It had neither beginning nor end, and nothing broke its flow—no matter what she did, the girl couldn't check the river's course by so much as an inch or an instant. Meridy knew that, and somehow the knowledge was soothing.

eleven

Meridy woke with the familiar sensation of a half-remembered dream pressing at the back of her mind, but she was instantly distracted because Iëhiy was standing with his front feet on the bed, staring at her intently. As soon as she opened her eyes, he yawned eagerly and licked her face. Meridy fended him off, but she was so relieved to see him that she couldn't mind his enthusiasm. "Where have you *been?*" she whispered to him. "I was *worried*!"

"Not half so worried as I," Niniol told her, and Meridy sat up, even more relieved to find the guard captain leaning in the doorway, his translucent shoulder blending into the painted wood, his mouth crooked in a wry expression that was not quite a smile. He lifted a hand in a salute-like gesture. "The dog seemed to know where to find you. Thankfully. I'd have had no idea. I do beg your pardon for the intrusion"—a flick of his hand took in the bedchamber—"but I fear I couldn't rest without being certain you were here, and safe. Both of you."

His glance went to Jaift, a curled blanket-covered shape on the other side of the bed, not yet waking despite the voices. Or, really, Meridy's voice; Niniol's voiceless murmur wouldn't have woken anyone.

He said, "When the two of you ran out of the world, it was . . . upsetting."

Meridy was sure it had been. "Jaift sent a letter to the Derem household. It's too bad it'll take days for her family to get here. But I'm so glad to see you, and I know Jaift will be relieved, too. Everyone—the caravan . . ." She hesitated, afraid to ask.

"That cursed sorcerer wasn't interested in anyone but you," Niniol assured her. "Ah, I'll tell you in a moment, shall I?" As Jaift stirred, he straightened and stepped back into the other room to give the girls their privacy.

Meridy poked Jaift, tossed back the blankets, beckoned to Iëhiy, and headed for the bath as the other girl sat up, yawning and looking around in blurry puzzlement. "Where—? Oh. Was someone here a minute ago? Oh, Iëhiy!" She patted the wolfhound carefully, shaping her hand around his half-present head and neck. She wasn't as practiced at this as Meridy, but the dog licked her face anyway.

The growing humidity of the morning made Meridy's hair unmanageable, though after she dressed, she spent some time trying to twist it up into a knot.

"Let me braid it," Jaift said, and did so with quick authority. Then she produced a fine copper chain from somewhere, twisted it around the braid, and put Meridy's hair up in a neat coil, which was not something Meridy could have managed for herself. "Copper is definitely your metal," Jaift told her. "That's handy, since it's mine, too. I have—had—some copper earrings that would look good on you. I still have them, I suppose, somewhere." She put her own hair up with expert speed, studying the effect in the mirror. She added, "I wonder if the couturier has any earrings? Or ribbons? Well, it'll do, I suppose."

"You're always beautiful," Meridy said, a little enviously.

It wasn't exactly beauty, but she didn't know how else to describe a girl like Jaift, so much more assured than a village girl. Maybe that was why princesses were always described as beautiful in stories: because they grew up with that kind of confidence.

Jaift smiled at her in the mirror. "So are you," she said cheerfully, without regard for Meridy's obvious Southern blood.

Meridy didn't believe her, but . . . if confidence could make Jaift beautiful, maybe Meridy could at least pretend. Her new dress was very pretty. And her hair was up properly, for once. Straightening her back, she lifted her head.

"That's the way!" approved Jaift. "Are you ready? Niniol said everyone was fine, right? But I want to hear all about it for myself! And I'm starving. I'll get someone to send up a tray, and we can hear about everything and decide what to do."

Meridy only nodded, though she was privately resolved that whatever she had to do about Diöllin and Herren and the witch-king and Inmanuàr and everything, Jaift wouldn't be involved.

Niniol now occupied one of the chairs in the sitting room, his back decently turned to the bedchamber, the sunrise turning his colorless form to light. His legs were stretched out comfortably and he was idly flipping a dagger over and over. But when the girls came in, he straightened and put the dagger away, getting to his feet and turning to offer another of his wry salutes. Despite the morning light, the weapon became far less distinct as soon as he stopped paying attention to it, though it didn't quite dissolve back into memory.

"Jaift—" Niniol began, cut that off, and said more formally, "Excellent miss—"

"Jaift," the girl said firmly. "It seems silly the other way, now. Meridy tells me you said everyone is all right? Please assure me nothing happened to my family! Or anyone else," she added conscientiously.

The guard captain gave her a nod. "They are well; they were all well when I left them. The sorcerer or witch, whatever he was, he hadn't any interest in the caravan once you and Meridy were away. He left us all and went after the two of you, but the hound was through the gap and away before him, and I hoped he'd be some use to you—more use than I managed. Me, I guess I was already fading by then." He added to Meridy, "I can't see the world too clearly anyway, and the longer you were gone, the worse it got. It was like being lost in the thickest fog you've ever seen, till the hound came back and found me."

Meridy patted Iëhiy, who was leaning against her knee, his eyes half shut, looking sleepy and contented. "He's a knowing one, isn't he? I'm sorry, Niniol. I didn't mean to bind you, but since I did, it was terrible to abandon you. I'd let you go now and show you the White Road, but I don't know how to do that either." All the ghosts she'd ever really known had been old dead, but surrounded by and held to the *real* by memories of their familiar lives. She could just imagine what it must have been like for Niniol, cut off from every anchor, aware that he was fading and would be lost to both the world and the God.

"Ah, well." Niniol lifted a shoulder in a sardonic shrug. "The dog found me, eh? I think I . . . that is, I don't much mind your binding me. If you're going to be attacked at odd moments, best you have a decent sword by you. Though you might consider making enemies of ordinary brigands and leaving the sorcerers be."

Meridy was relieved and surprised by his stoic acceptance of . . . everything. But then, thinking about it, maybe she understood. Niniol had been working for the Gehliy family for a long time; he obviously cared about them. Of course Niniol would set himself to protect Jaift until she could get back to the safety of her family. That made sense, after all. She didn't question it but said instead, "You called the man a sorcerer. By his eyes, I think he must have also been a witch. Did he try to bind you?"

Niniol shrugged, cordially enough. "I wouldn't know a sorcerer from a milkmaid. But it's not a milkmaid who can open a way out of dreams and make the very air crumble away to a memory of dust, is it? He might have tried to bind me, but he was away too quick to make a real effort at it, I think. Witch or sorcerer, if you've got him as an enemy, you surely need a sword at your back."

Meridy couldn't disagree. She said to Jaift, "You see how dangerous—"

"Breakfast," Jaift said authoritatively. "And then *we* will find the public conveyances and see about getting a ride north. Don't *argue*, Mery! As if I'd let you go alone! *Or* risk leading this sorcerer or servitor or whatever he may be right back to my family, and don't tell me that's impossible! Besides, do you think I'd let you go off with that snippy princess and try to rescue the young prince by yourself? Although," she added, "I suppose I'll have to write another letter to my parents, though what I'll put in it I really don't know."

Meridy looked at Niniol, but he only raised an eyebrow at her, as much as to say, *Princesses as well as sorcerers, is it?* So she had to suppose that since he was bound to her, he would just as soon Jaift stay close to her, so he could protect them both.

And she had to admit, she would be lost without Jaift.

And Inmanuàr . . . if it *was* Inmanuàr . . . had said she should take Jaift with her. So in the end, she only drew a breath, let it out, and said, "All right, if you're sure. Um . . . what *is* a public conveyance, anyway?"

The conveyances proved to be big, heavy carriages with benches that could seat more than a dozen passengers. Jaift, of course, knew all about them, and precisely whom to ask to find out where the yard was and how often conveyances left for Cora Talen, which was almost due north of Riam and so ought to suit Diöllin, no matter whether they eventually headed for Surem or Cora Diorr or wherever. Each conveyance was drawn by a team of four heavy horses. They were slow, Jaift explained, but faster than a merchant's caravan and definitely faster than walking—and safe from brigands, because the driver and many of the passengers were always armed with crossbows and because the Riamne Highway was heavily patrolled.

"The lords of Cora Talen and Riam send guardsmen to patrol," Jaift said. "The lord of Riam is supposed to patrol the Tamared Road all the way to the Yellow River, but he's lazy about it, my father says; that's why there are so many more brigands along that road. Though it's also true, brigands along the Yellow River Road can fall back and hide in the mountains, but it's hard for brigands to stay out of the way of decent men in farm country like this."

Meridy was glad to hear it. She felt she had had more than a sufficiency of brigands in the past week. She only wished she thought the lords' men also patrolled the roads against sorcerers.

. . .

But they saw neither sorcerers nor brigands on the Riamne Highway. It was busy and cluttered, that wide highway; one could hardly go any distance without passing a train of slow wagons or a private carriage with outriders or another heavy conveyance like their own.

They didn't see Diöllin at any time during the six-day journey from Riam to Cora Talen. But though the princess did not appear, Meridy had a faint, continual sense that if she turned her head suddenly, she might glimpse her out of the corner of her eye. She was surprised the princess didn't hover by her side during all the six days of the journey, urging haste, but then Diöllin had wanted Meridy to anchor her specifically so she would be safe to go to her brother, so no doubt she was hovering near him instead. No doubt the young prince needed his sister.

They didn't see Inmanuàr either. If the ghost boy *was* Inmanuàr—Meridy had to remind herself that they still couldn't be absolutely certain of it. On the one hand, Meridy wished the ghost boy would come, now that she knew what questions she wanted to ask him. On the other hand, if he was likely to draw Tai-Enchar's attention to them, then she wanted nothing more than for him to stay far, far away.

Niniol had been with them all the time, though, and Iëhiy. Niniol was watchful, obviously conscious of his responsibility as their sole guard, aware that he could not defend them against any *real* threat unless Meridy helped him do it, and that anything of the kind would completely betray her as a witch. She was more aware of the suspicious distance other travelers kept from her than she had ever been in her life, especially when she so clearly got more room in the conveyance than anyone else, or when people sharing a table at each public house shifted away from her when they stopped for meals or for the night. Jaift pretended not to notice, and no one could be wary of Jaift, who was effortlessly friendly with everyone. Again and again, Meridy was forced to realize how much she depended on Jaift to break through the reserve everyone felt toward a black-eyed girl. She tried one night to turn her eyes blue, but whatever the trick was, she didn't discover it.

Iëhiy did not seem to worry about anything. The wolf-hound ranged to one side and another during their days on the road, not troubled by either the sun or the rain, for it began to rain as they approached Cora Talen, a heavy gray drizzle that did not seem likely to stop any time soon. But the rain fell right through Iëhiy, except for the occasional drop that splashed off his back or head and made him shake vigorously as though he'd had a dunking.

There were thousands upon thousands of people in the town of Cora Talen. Nearly all of them were alive, and the clamor was frightening. Six days on the road, and Meridy had nearly forgotten what actual cities were like. She was sure Cora Talen was even bigger and busier than Riam.

They descended from the conveyance onto a busy street filled with carriages and horses and people afoot. It was still raining. Meridy and Jaift ducked their heads and tried to keep out of the mud, but both girls also turned one way and another, trying to look at everything at once, because Cora Talen wasn't much like Riam at all. Meridy had thought that one city must be much like another, but where the people of Riam had built heavy, square buildings with steep shingled roofs and plaster walls, and painted all their homes in bright colors, the people of Cora Talen built narrow and tall, with umber-colored brick and slate.

Not far away, a rider sent his horse lunging through a hole in the crowd, forcing a harassed-looking girl carrying a bellowing toddler to jump aside. Blind to ghosts, the girl scurried right through Niniol without blinking. Niniol gave Meridy a long-suffering look.

"You shouldn't complain," Meridy told him, lowering her voice from habit, although there was far too much bustle for anyone to notice her speaking to the empty air. "At least the rain does the same thing."

Even so, the moisture in the air seemed somehow to glisten in a peculiar way where it touched Niniol and Iëhiy, creating, to the perceptive eye, a faintly visible image where they stood. It was hard to believe that no one in this crowd could see them. At least, Meridy firmly hoped that no one but she and Jaift could see them.

"An inn," Jaift said firmly, taking her arm. "A cozy inn, with decent food, and girls to do laundry, and shops nearby. We can find out what time tomorrow a conveyance leaves for Cora Diorr and buy cushions for those awful benches."

They all looked around the street. There were three public houses in sight, but Niniol said authoritatively, "Not those! Travelers who don't know better stay at the first place they see. The decent inns will be a street or two farther on." He cast an experienced eye one way, then another, and said briskly, "This way, I think," and strode away.

Meridy and Jaift shrugged at each other and followed Niniol, Meridy taking Jaift's hand because she was nervous about managing to follow anyone in the busy streets.

"There's so much," she said apologetically when Jaift tugged her out of the way of two men on horseback and then caught her elbow so she didn't step into the gutter. "I thought after Riam I would be used to it."

"We weren't in Riam long enough to get used to anything." Jaift stepped adroitly to the side to let a handful of children run past and looked around, her eyes bright. "Oh, you can see, they must have the open market over there. There are the awnings rolled up out of the way. I wonder when the next market will be."

"Probably it will still be raining," Meridy muttered. "And anyway, we don't have *time* for a market day."

Jaift didn't seem to notice her irritable tone. "I know, the rain is awful, but I would have liked to look just a little. Preferably on a day with sunlight and less mud, I grant you. I *do* want to get out of this rain!"

"You may both cease fussing," Niniol said over his shoulder. "We're there."

"Where?" asked Meridy.

"Here." Niniol put out one insubstantial hand to guide Meridy around a corner and into an unexpected pocket of quiet. "This one looks good. See the sign? It wouldn't be embossed like that except the inn is prosperous and secure."

The sign showed a half-moon over a white poppy, and indeed, both moon and flower were embossed with silver. "Can we afford to stay here?" Meridy asked, trying to remember Jaift's explanation about the different coins.

"Certainly for one night," Jaift declared, and strolled toward the inn's main door.

Heat blasted from the inn's common room as Jaift shoved the door wide and ushered Meridy in. Meridy felt as though all eyes ought to be drawn to them as they dripped their way into the inn, but in fact none of the patrons seemed much interested. No one leaped to his feet exclaiming, "Witches! Quick dead! Send for the priests!" After a moment, she began to relax.

They claimed seats at the unoccupied end of a long table. Iëhiy crawled under the table and lay down with an inaudible sigh, although, being a ghost dog, he couldn't actually be weary. Niniol leaned against the wall behind Jaift. Smoke from the fires of the inn gave him a peculiarly solid appearance, as the rain had not, and at the same time made him seem less part of the *real* than ever. By this time, Niniol had been dead long enough not to fall through the wall. But he watched wistfully as a serving girl brought bowls of thick soup and a platter of bread and cheese. Meridy glanced around warily, but no one in the common room seemed to have any idea Niniol was among them.

"I can tip some into the *ethereal* for you," Meridy murmured once the girl had gone.

"Could you?" said Jaift. "Isn't that more sorcery than witchery, pushing things from the *real* into the *ethereal* instead of the other way around?"

"I don't know," Meridy said, surprised. Thinking about it, it did seem Jaift was right. Witches brought the *ethereal* into the *real*. Sorcerers stepped from the *real* into the *ethereal*. She knew that. It really was confusing, since she'd been feeding Iëhiy tidbits all along. "Maybe such little things don't count—a spoonful of supper for Iëhiy or Niniol—"

"Too risky to fool with right now, either way," Niniol warned her. "Let's not draw attention. There are far too many eyes here." He tilted his head gently to the side.

Meridy followed the gesture and found herself looking into the face of a man several tables away. The man looked away unhurriedly, but not before Meridy caught the gleam of a priest's medal at his throat. Her heart jumped. She couldn't tell for sure whether the priest's eyes were black, but she knew they were dark.

Leaning forward, she whispered, "What are we doing at this public table at all, then?"

"Because I didn't see him at first. He has dark eyes," Niniol added. "But perhaps not black. If he's got the eyes to see, it's too late to stay out of his sight; and if not, it'd look more suspicious to leave now than it does to stay put and have supper. Just you have a bite and then go upstairs."

"He's all right," Jaift murmured. "If he thinks you've bound Niniol against his will, he can ask and Niniol will explain and it'll be fine."

This was altogether too optimistic, by Meridy's estimation. She gave the priest a suspicious look, but he, applying himself to his food with excellent appetite, showed no interest in any of them. Even so, she was glad to finish the last slice of bread and retreat from the common room.

The private suite was small and sparingly furnished, but pretty and comfortable. There was a narrow sitting room that boasted a couch and two tables, each holding an oil lamp already lit against the gloomy evening. The bedchamber offered a bed big enough for three girls and generous for two. Meridy found, when she touched the thin mattress, that it was stuffed with straw. But the mattress had a linen casing to stop the straw from pricking, the blankets were abundant and clean, and there was no sign of bugs. A large wooden basin took up at least a third of the floor space left by the bed.

The servant who had showed them to the rooms told Jaift, "Hot bath comes with the room; bathe before you touch the bed and the room's two pence cheaper. That's true for every night you spend here, miss. Soap comes with the bath, no extra charge. Laundry is four pence extra, but it's a good deal, though it's me as says it: your things will be dry by morning or you get a penny back. No cooking in the rooms, no loud noise after dark, and though you'll naturally want to bar the door, you've no need to worry about thieves. This house is respectable."

Meridy revised her estimate of the servant's rank upward. Maybe she was a member of the owner's family? She certainly sounded decisive.

Jaift said gravely, "We are reassured."

The servant smiled, as everyone always smiled at Jaift. As she left, she added over her shoulder, "Hot water'll be up shortly."

Hot water was a luxury beyond price, Meridy thought a short while later. She and Jaift had each volunteered to bathe second, but though Meridy had succeeded in making Jaift go first, the water was still warm. The soap was even better, grainy and coarse as it was, and privacy was best of all; Jaift had gone out into the suite's tiny parlor to investigate the plum tarts the servant had brought. The inn's laundry provided towels, not only clean but warm from resting near a fire. The faint scent of wood smoke clung to Meridy's towel. She decided she liked that, too. She hadn't noticed how tired she had become of the indifferent grime of the public houses.

Meridy smiled at the ghost dog as Iëhiy rose gracefully to his hind legs and placed his forefeet on the edge of the bath to peer interestedly at the bowl of soap; if he'd still been alive, he would surely have tipped the bath right over, and her with it. She flicked drops of water at his nose, smiling again as he snapped at them.

Then there was a knock on the door.

twelve

Muttering under her breath, Meridy reached for a towel. But then she paused. It must be Jaift wanting something—to explain the schedule for tomorrow, maybe—but if it was Jaift, why didn't the other girl simply come in?

While she hesitated, Iëhiy shouldered between her and the door, head down, an inaudible growl trembling in his chest.

Clutching the towel around herself, Meridy stepped out of the bath, backed up, and found herself at the window. She fumbled with the shutters. Warm air, moisture laden, rolled in as she flung back the shutters and looked out into the deserted courtyard. The wet cobbles gleamed in the lantern light from the inn. The drop was only one story. But she thought of Jaift—what was happening to her friend? She hesitated, torn.

Niniol threw himself through the closed door—or was thrown, judging by the helplessly off-balance way he was trying to catch at the walls. He fell heavily, halfway through the floor before he managed to stop himself. Meridy could see no opponent, no enemy, but she knew who, or what, this must be from the frightening urgency with which Niniol scrambled to his feet. His long *ethereal* sword glowed like blown glass in his hand as he made it upright. There wasn't nearly enough steam left from the bath for Meridy to pull him into the *real*—

Iëhiy vanished through the closed door with a great snarl of rage. Niniol cried, "Get out!" to her over his shoulder, and strode grimly after the dog.

The door shook in its frame from the force of a soundless blow. A cry of pain, equally without sound, reached Meridy. She could not tell whether it came from Niniol or Iëhiy, or from someone else entirely. Spurred into action by pure fear, Meridy wriggled backward through the window, clung to the sill for an instant, and dropped into the courtyard. The cobbles were wet and slippery under her bare feet, and she realized she was out in the weather with nothing but an extremely inadequate towel. There was no time to worry about it. Clutching the towel to herself, she ducked across the courtyard toward the deep shadows by the stables.

Niniol hurtled through the wall of the inn behind her and hit the cobbles, far too hard. No ghost should be so affected by stones in the *real* world, but he moved only dazedly to get to his feet. Changing direction, Meridy fell to her knees at his side.

"Niniol—"

"Get up," he said faintly. "Get up and run."

"To where? Give me your sword, Niniol—"

He had not had it when he fell, but his reach after its familiar hilt brought the *ethereal* weapon glittering to his hand and he pushed it toward her. Meridy looked at it slantwise, looked at the way the rain fell through it and past it and caught gleaming on its faint outline, and pulled it gently into the *real*. It felt like ice and nothing in her hands as she closed her fingers around its hilt, but she *could* lift it; it didn't melt away into the air.

Meridy turned back to face the inn in time to see a black-eyed sorcerer-witch come silently through the door into the yard—not either of the servitors she had seen before. This was a younger man, handsome except for the stillness of his face and his empty black eyes. He wore quality clothing, like a lord, and his skin was fine and pale like that of a lord, too, but his hands were translucent, as though he existed partly in the *ethereal*. The breeze that ruffled his light summer cloak smelled not of rain, but of dust and loneliness.

Through the door, Meridy had a glimpse of firelit normalcy: travelers and inn staff going about their ordinary lives, oblivious to the drama being enacted so little distance away. The contrast with the rain-misted peril of the courtyard made the threat seem so unreal, Meridy had to glance down at Niniol again to prove to herself the events of the past moments had actually occurred. The ghost was trying with fading strength to get to his feet. It was clear he would not succeed. Meridy looked up again.

During that brief glance away, the servitor had come much closer—covering more ground than ought to have been possible, and more quietly. His eyes were not black *all* the time, she saw; sometimes they were no color at all, like the eyes of a ghost. Somehow that was worse than the solidity of the other servitors. But half in the realms of dream or not, she was sure she could hear the soft scrape of his boot soles on the cobbles, and where the light of the inn's lamps fell across him, he cast a shadow like a living man. But just like the others, he cast another shadow as well. The other was an uneasy thing, too big and diffuse and not dark enough, owing nothing to the lamps.

Meridy held Niniol's sword in front of her body, awkwardly. It was not heavy—it barely existed—but she feared to close her hands too hard around the hilt, lest it fall out of the *real*. The towel slipped, and she pulled it back together impatiently. It was ridiculous to die wrapped in nothing but a *towel*.

Expecting no answer, she cried aloud, "Inmanuàr! Carad Mereth! Help me! Help us!"

The man laughed and told her, "The boy's powerless, and the poet is too fond of his own voice to hear yours now, girl." He moved forward.

Meridy braced herself, knowing perfectly well it would do no good.

Niniol made it to his knees and tried to get up, but the man merely looked at him and he fell back, gasping in what seemed like pain.

Since the shadowed man seemed distracted, Meridy stepped forward and swung the *ethereal* sword at him, but he turned smoothly and caught it in his hand. It was like striking iron. Meridy gasped with the shock, and with a ringing chime, the sword shattered as though it were truly fashioned of glass, and the shards of it dissolved into air and light.

Meridy fell back, shaking a hand gone numb. The man laughed and reached for her, but casually, so she managed to duck away. But in the effort she slipped on the cobbles and sprawled clumsily on the ground; she froze there, in the certainty that she could never make it back onto her feet before he seized her.

Then Carad Mereth came gravely and easily through the door of the inn, with Iëhiy pacing, barely visible, at his side, a dog of smoke and mist, and the moon rode free from behind the clouds and shone through the rain. Somehow it was a full moon again, though it had passed full and begun waning during the journey from Riam to Cora Talen. The moonlight shone now more coldly than torchlight, but neither did it falter when it fell across the shadowed man; he cast no shadow from its light.

Carad Mereth walked forward, murmuring, and as he came closer, Meridy could make out his words. His voice was soft and rich as velvet. "'What shall I say, what words will ever come, when all my words are done, when words have gone astray? What shall I give, what can my need sustain, when nothing else remains, when nothing else shall live? What light is there, what light shines through these years, when, darkened by my fears, there's no light anywhere?'"

"Poet," said the shadowed man, "wouldst thou challenge me?" His voice had become strange: it sounded somehow darker and deeper than before. It fell oddly on the ear, grating and somehow discordant, as though it weren't a proper voice at all but something that tried to imitate a true human voice. There was a dark power in it, but a wariness, too, as though the man took Carad Mereth far more seriously than he took Meridy, which seemed reasonable enough. She backed away to Niniol's side, watching in hope and terror to see what would happen.

Carad Mereth laughed. At the sound of his laughter, the rain stopped and the clouds parted. "Look!" he said, raising one hand. "The moon is high. You have missed your chance. Go back! You must wait for the dark or the day."

The man tilted his head back and stared into the sky, and, like a blown-out lantern, the moonlight failed. But Carad Mereth held out his hand and the moon was in it, actually cupped in his palm, round and fat and full. Moonlight shone all around him, silvery on the cobbles, which were no longer ordinary cobbles but made of glass or crystal or ice, something that burned coldly underfoot.

Except then the shadowed man reached out with his own hand, and his hand's shadow rose up, both shadows, dark fingers weaving together and closing around the little moon. Far above, clouds raced across the sky. He said, "I am here with my servant. But thy master hath abandoned thee, poet. *Thou art alone.*"

"Unlikely," Carad Mereth said, but his voice was strangely muffled, as though Meridy heard it from a great distance. He looked at Meridy and said, his voice still distant but his tone lightly mocking, "Not for you this hither shore of dreams." She stared at him, and he told her, still in that light, mocking tone, "Fly, little bird, for the near shore and the world of men!"

They had stepped out of the mortal world, Meridy realized at last; at some moment lost in fear and confusion, she had stepped out of the *real* and into the *ethereal* realms that lay beyond. She looked around, searching for the courtyard of the ordinary inn, the ordinary lanterns with their warm yellow light shining by the door and in the windows, the fragrance of the evening loaves and heavy scent of the rain-wet cobbles. . . .

"She's not for you," Carad Mereth said to the shadowed witch. "She's in the hand of the God. You should know better. Yes, even you."

The man said coldly, "All her kind belong to me. Thou art presumptuous. For a man out of his place, thou hast become too bold. There will be a price exacted for thine impudence, poet."

"Perhaps," Carad Mereth answered softly. "But this is neither your time nor your place. Be certain that if you raise your hand against me now, you will pay a price as well. Are you willing to bear that?" Above them, the moon slid from behind clouds or shadows, and Carad Mereth held out his hands, moonlight pooling in his palms.

But the man did not back away. He stepped forward, saying, "All places and times have become mine now."

Once again the moonlight went out. This time the darkness that closed in seemed absolute.

Carad Mereth made a low sound chillingly like dismay, or fear. Meridy, blind in the dark, heard him, and her whole body clenched up in terror. She tried to run forward, to find the sorcerer, but Niniol caught her and wouldn't let her go. He gripped her hand so hard it hurt and closed his other hand on her wrist, and Meridy couldn't break away from him.

And then Iëhiy came out of the dark, and following the hound, the light came back as well: not moonlight but plain lantern light shining across the wet cobbles, and Niniol's grip, suddenly insubstantial, had no power to constrain her. But it was too late. Carad Mereth was gone. So was the shadowed sorcerer. The courtyard of the inn was empty, except for the rain, still falling gently. Ordinary sounds came out into the courtyard, the talk of men and the stamp of a horse in the stable. She was alone with Niniol and Iëhiy, and no sign of anything uncanny anywhere.

"You stopped me!" she said to Niniol. "He took him!"

Then Iëhiy insinuated his head under her hand, and Meridy turned her face away from Niniol and petted the wolfhound hard, blinking fiercely.

"I'm sorry," Niniol said, not arguing.

Meridy shook her head, not looking at him. She admitted much more shakily, "I couldn't have helped him. You were right to stop me from trying." Realizing suddenly that she still wore nothing more adequate than a towel, she straightened, clutching it. She wanted to ask Niniol about Jaift, but she was afraid that if she opened her mouth, she might burst into tears or start screaming. "I—" she managed. "Jaift?"

"*She's* too sensible to pitch into a battle between ghosts and sorcerers." Niniol gave Meridy a look that was hard to read, but not unsympathetic. "Next time, you might follow her example. For now . . . *are* they gone? Gone altogether out of this world? Can you tell?"

"I think so. I'm not sure. I think so. I don't—I don't think Carad Mereth was lying about the other one also—also paying a price." Meridy meant to speak firmly, but all this came out barely above a whisper. She was trembling, she discovered, and couldn't stop.

Niniol shook his head. But he only said kindly, "Let's get you back inside where it's warm and dry, and have some tea, and decide what to do next."

The tea was hot and sweet, and it came with honey cakes, brown bread, and salted butter. Meridy, dressed once more and prepared to pretend the towel had never been a problem, sat on the bed with her legs tucked up, wrapped her hands around the mug, and breathed the warm steam gratefully. Jaift sat in a chair beside the bed. Whatever she had seen or experienced during the recent alarm, she now looked somehow perfectly comfortable and unshaken. Meridy wished she knew how the other girl did it.

Niniol sat on the floor and leaned against the wall near Meridy, gripping a mug Meridy had tipped into the *ethereal.* Iëhiy rested his great head on the mattress next to Meridy's thigh, accepting bits of cake from her hand with featherlike delicacy. Meridy tried to pay attention to what she did as she passed the fragments of cake from the *real* into the *ethereal,* but it seemed like just a normal thing to her, and not very important anyway considering everything else that was happening all around them.

Jaift buttered a slice of bread and frowned at Meridy. "I want to know more about this blue-eyed sorcerer, Carad Mereth. You've said he's Inmanuàr's real anchor, assuming the ghost boy is Inmanuàr, but who *is* he and what does he want?"

"What I want to know," Niniol said, firmly practical, "is how our enemy found us here. Inmanuàr, or whoever he may be, hasn't come for a visit, so I don't see how he'd have drawn the shadowed sorcerer here to us. Nor Princess Diöllin, either. This other one, the poet, who knows what he might have done, or why? But he came after our enemy, not before him."

Meridy shook her head because she didn't know and couldn't guess. "Carad Mereth . . . he *is* a sorcerer, I'm almost sure. Or maybe a priest. Or I think maybe both. He *is* Tai-Enchar's enemy. That, I'm sure of."

"So that makes him our friend, I suppose," Jaift said doubtfully.

Niniol snorted. "The enemy of our enemy may be pleased to have found a tool apt for his battle. His, mark you, and a fight that should be none of ours, save by his doing, making you that boy's anchor, Mery, and likely sending the princess your way as well, or why else would you be at the center of all this, eh?"

This was all true and reasonable, but Meridy didn't think it was quite right, either. Diöllin hadn't said anything about Carad Mereth. But besides that . . . She said, "Except if Carad Mereth's enemy is Tai-Enchar, then the fight belongs to everyone. Doesn't it? Because the witch-king is everyone's enemy."

"Huh," muttered Niniol, not sounding convinced. "Sounds to me like this Carad Mereth went out of his way to make him *your* enemy in particular."

Jaift took a bite of bread and chewed thoughtfully. Finally she said, "Yet it seems to me we can be sure this Carad Mereth is the God's servant, whether he's a priest or not. There's all this with the moon, you say, so that right there tells us something, doesn't it, because after all the moon belongs to the God. Whatever else, we can be sure Carad Mereth truly is Tai-Enchar's enemy. If that's so, then his fight belongs to everyone, just as Mery says. It might have been nothing but ill chance that brought us here to find the shadowed sorcerer waiting for us, but ill chance can make a way for good, my uncle says. So maybe we're supposed to be here."

"We can hope so," Meridy agreed, relieved at this support.

Before she could say anything else, Diöllin flicked into existence and cried, "He's here!"

Meridy jumped to her feet, horrified. "Already? Again?"

"Not the witch-king!" cried Diöllin. "He was, or his servitor was, but the servitor's gone now, so I came, I came, but at first I couldn't find you, you'd faded into dreams and I couldn't find you! But here you are at last!" Putting her hands on her hips, she stared accusingly at Meridy. "He's here! Herren, my brother! You've found him, so why are you *sitting* here drinking *tea?*"

"Wait, your *brother* is somewhere here?" Meridy asked, bewildered. "In this inn?" Despite herself, she looked around as though the young prince might prove to be tucked away in some corner.

Niniol took the one step necessary, closed his hands on Diöllin's royal shoulders, and shook her firmly. "*Collect* yourself and report *properly,*" he ordered her, exactly as though she were a new young guardsman under his command.

The princess gasped, straightened, jerked herself free, and declared, affronted but also far more coherent, "Herren is here, yes, right here! I couldn't get to him because of Tai-Enchar's servitor, but then you made the servitor go away. So then I could go to Herren, and I did. But he's still with *them,* and you're not even trying to get him free!" She gave Meridy an even more offended look.

Meridy said, starting to understand, "Well, that's why the sorcerer was here, maybe; not because he'd found us, but because he'd brought Herren from Cora Diorr. And we're in exactly the right place after all." She would have to think about that later, if she got a moment. It might be reassuring to think they'd been in the God's hand all along—or terrifying. Or both. But for now she only went on, "So we're here, and Herren's here, and now Carad Mereth has taken the witch-king's servitor away into dreams with him. Or even if it was the other way around and the servitor took Carad Mereth away, they're still both gone, aren't they? That *is* a stroke of luck!"

"If you call it luck," muttered Niniol.

"The God's hand can tip the dice," Jaift pointed out. "That's what my uncle says. But we daren't stumble around looking blindly here and there; what if they take the poor little prince away somewhere before we find him? If we miss him here, we'll likely have to chase after them, and surely that's no good. Much better to find him tonight and . . . get him away from his captors, I suppose. Hmm." She subsided, tapping the arm of her chair in thought or frustration or indecision, plainly not so confident as she saw where her argument was leading.

"They're probably just ordinary men, though," Meridy pointed out. "I mean, that's why Diöllin could come, because the servitor isn't here anymore. Isn't that right? I think finding Herren right now might be the most important thing we can do."

Niniol didn't disagree, though he was still frowning. "But what if there's a sorcerer or a witch with them, still? The boy's captors may be ordinary men, but it's never wise to assume your enemy is as weak or ill prepared as you'd like him to be."

This was sensible. Meridy nodded.

"I'll find out," Diöllin declared, fiercely. "I *will* find out." She took a step toward a blank wall and vanished.

"*Foolish* girl," snapped Niniol, moving as though to follow her and then halting, wary and annoyed. "And if Tai-Enchar's got another witch here in this house, she's put herself right in his hands!"

"Then I suppose we'll find that out, too," said Meridy.

Iëhiy swung around, ears pinned back, facing the far wall. Meridy stiffened, and Jaift jumped to her feet and took a step back. Niniol stepped forward, his imaginary sword gleaming in his hand as though it had never been broken.

Diöllin ran back into the room through the wall, moonlight flaring around her, as though someone had suddenly lit a candle with a cool silvery flame. She had her hands up defensively and she was gasping, quick desperate breaths as though she were still alive. She said urgently, "He's right here! *Right* here! But there's no witch or sorcerer—I don't think there is!" She pointed at the wall through which she'd come. "He's right here! Help him! Help him!"

thirteen

No one argued, or even hesitated. Niniol was the first out into the hallway, even though he'd been farthest from the door, but Meridy and Jaift were hardly slower. Everything seemed calm in the inn's corridor; the lanterns hanging along the walls glowed with their soft light, and from the common room downstairs came the murmur of voices. But to their left, a short distance down the hallway, Diöllin stood, lantern light shining through and around her, limning her face and her hands. She was pointing at the nearest door, her colorless eyes wide and terrified.

How to get that door open was a question. Just knocking was a stupid idea. Meridy knew it. No doubt all of them knew it. Knocking on that door when they had no idea what was on the other side except surely enemies and hopefully the young prince and probably some imminent disaster was *stupid*. She should have come up with a better idea, even an actual plan. Or Niniol should—he was an adult, after all—or Jaift, who was so practical and sensible.

But Diöllin was so frantic that Meridy couldn't think of anything else to do. The ghosts could go right through the door—Iëhiy already had, with an voiceless snarl—but without her to make them *real,* a ghost couldn't do anything useful on the other side. If Niniol had been a living man, maybe he could have forced the door, but neither Meridy nor Jaift had a chance at anything like that.

So Meridy knocked, loudly and confidently. They'd *have* to answer the door, wouldn't they? Because they wouldn't know—

The door swung open, and a man was there, big and unfriendly.

There was light in the room, not much, a single lamp hanging from a chain that cast confusing shadows in all directions. Meridy grabbed a lantern from its niche high on the corridor wall and threw it past the man into the room. Flaming oil spattered everywhere as the lamp broke, and men jumped and cursed. Something caught, cloth of some kind from the smell of the smoke that suddenly billowed. In a minute, the smoke would make it hard to see, but for now Meridy could use it and she did use it, dragging Niniol and Iëhiy into the *real.* The curses of the other men took on a different, angrier tone. Meridy ran forward, Jaift behind her holding another lamp, ready to throw it, though it seemed she might not have to; already something was thoroughly on fire, burning viciously. All around her, men seemed to be tangled in a bewildering violent struggle, and everyone was shouting or cursing or screaming.

Diöllin was whispering to her insistently. Meridy could hardly make her out in the madly shadowed confusion, but she pulled Jaift along the edge of the room. A man reeled back against the wall right in front of them, a knife gripped in his hand, and she ducked and pressed back, but the man pushed himself up and hurled himself into the struggle again without seeming to notice the girls at all. Diöllin whispered, "Hurry, hurry!" and Meridy tried.

Then Jaift cried out and dashed forward, first throwing her lantern and then hurling herself bodily against a half-seen man, and Meridy finally caught sight of Prince Herren.

The young prince was pressed against the wall, tucked on the floor in a corner of the room, bound hand and foot. He'd been struggling to get clear of the fight, but the struggle had trapped him in a corner. Now he was unable to get up, unable to flee or try to fight. He was gagged, too—Meridy could see the strip of cloth across his face.

Jaift was struggling with the man she'd attacked. She might be taller and stronger than most girls, but she was certainly no match for a grown man; when he hit her, she went sprawling. Niniol was here; Iëhiy was *somewhere*—Meridy could hear his terrifying snarls—but she'd lost track of them both.

Then Diöllin was there, hovering by her brother. Meridy could only half see her, there was all the smoke—she pulled Diöllin into the *real,* and the princess flung her arms around the man struggling with Jaift, dragging him back and down. The man shouted in surprise, and Jaift grabbed a chair someone had knocked over, whirled around, and smashed the chair over his head. The man grunted and sagged. The young prince squirmed out of the corner and rolled under a narrow bed that had been shoved against the wall below the window. It was a tight space, but he was not very big and managed to wriggle out of sight.

Then Niniol strode past Meridy, his face grim. He didn't even look at her, but he didn't have to: Diöllin let go of the man, scrambling out of Niniol's way, and Niniol ran the man through without compunction.

Suddenly it was much quieter.

Meridy turned, almost afraid of what she might see, but from overwhelming noise and confusion, the room had become . . . not peaceful. But, yes, much quieter.

Flames flickered here and there, but all the fires seemed to be small ones. One man lay at Niniol's feet and a second over by the doorway. Another man had been flung to one side, against a wall in a horrifying pool of blood; his throat seemed to have been torn out, which was awful. Meridy could see the feet of a fourth man through the open door that led to another bedchamber, but that man was plainly dead too. She was glad she couldn't see him better. She wondered who had killed him—it must have been Iëhiy, who was standing alertly against the wall near that doorway. There was no blood on him, but he'd faded mostly out of the *real* again, so there wouldn't be.

Though people *were* out in the corridor—Meridy could hear them—she thought they sounded angry and scared; not enemies, then, but people alarmed by the sudden sharp battle. It was probably the innkeeper and his staff, and they were going to be very, very upset. She couldn't blame them, she *didn't* blame them, but she had no idea how to deal with them, either.

"I'll take care of that," Jaift said, her tone shockingly normal amid the carnage. She ran her hands over her hair, took a breath, and strode toward the door, pausing only to stamp out a flicker of flame trying to climb up a table leg.

It occurred to Meridy that Jaift might have been *killed*—*she* might have been killed herself. She could hardly believe that they'd come through without a scratch, and suddenly she understood, truly *understood,* why witches might bind the souls of the dead, and what kind of power it might give them.

"Mery!" Niniol said, peremptory, and Meridy, recalled to the moment, turned quickly.

While she'd been distracted, Herren had wiggled back out from under the bed. Diöllin hovered over him, murmuring, her hands moving as she tried to touch her little brother's shoulder, his face; tried to untie the cords that bound his hands and feet. She couldn't, of course, not without help from Meridy. Maybe Herren could feel a featherlight brush of her hand, no more than that. But he could obviously hear his sister. He looked like he wanted to throw his arms around Diöllin and cry. Meridy wouldn't have blamed him a bit; she felt close to tears herself, and she was much older and not tied up. The young prince didn't seem to have been hurt, though. Not really *hurt*. His face was either smudged with dirt or bruised, and she could see from where she knelt the red marks on his wrists where the cords had rubbed, but she didn't see anything worse. She went quickly to help the young prince get free of his bonds.

Niniol swung around, grimly ready, as a man shoved the door wide and came in, with Jaift and two other men crowding behind them. But there was obviously no need to fear these newcomers. They were, Meridy gathered, members of the family that owned the inn, but though they were exclaiming to one another in horror at the dead men and worse horror at the remaining fires still burning here and there, they seemed to be perfectly in sympathy with Jaift and with young Herren, who was white, thin, bruised, and silent. Meridy had known he was Diöllin's *younger* brother, but once he was freed from his bonds and on his feet, the boy looked even smaller than she'd expected—no more than ten, maybe, if that.

"In our inn!" the tallest of the men said in outraged tones, pointing an accusing finger at Herren—but after the first instant Meridy saw that he meant Herren was *evidence* rather than *at fault*. The man was big as well as tall, rather stout, his coloring suggesting a touch of Southern blood. His round face was set in what seemed unaccustomed lines of dismay. "Kidnapping, extortion, arson, who knows what, right here in Cora Talen! In *our* inn! Why, we might as well be in the lawless hills as in a respectable town! What *is* the world coming to?"

One of the other men moved hastily to fetch a pitcher of water and douse the remaining flames, while Jaift went to fuss over Herren and murmur in his ear, "You're our cousin." Then, more loudly, she went on, "Everything's fine now! Moraf and Tomas here have sent for the town guard. I expect they'll hang these thugs from the town gates as a warning to any others who might think to bring their lawlessness into Cora Talen."

"That's exactly what the guard'll do, and good riddance!" agreed one of the other men, who was thinner and shorter and gloomier and must, Meridy gathered, be Tomas. "What do we pay taxes for, eh, with goings-on like this?" He sounded glumly satisfied, as though he'd been complaining about *goings-on* for years and was now pleased to be able to point to something even worse than he'd ever complained of. Kicking the nearest body, he added pessimistically, "None of 'em alive, I guess. Too bad, but it can't be helped, I suppose, and the guard can hang their filthy bodies at least. Here, boy, you all right?"

"You can see he's been treated badly," declared Moraf, patting Herren clumsily on the shoulder.

The young prince flinched slightly, though Meridy didn't think the man noticed. He looked shaken and pale and stiff and exactly like a little highborn boy who had been kidnapped by brigands and held for ransom. But he inclined his head to Moraf and said collectedly enough, "Thank you, sir, and my father will also be grateful for your kindness as well, I know."

Diöllin was making fierce gestures toward the door, but Meridy hardly needed the princess to point out that they needed to leave right away. She stared at Jaift, hoping the other girl had some notion of how to get out of this inn so they wouldn't wind up dealing with the town guardsmen and ten thousand curious onlookers, and possibly another terrifying double-shadowed sorcerer. Surely the witch-king must soon discover that something had happened here to balk him, and then he'd send another of his servants. . . .

"Well said, lad!" declared the first man, patting Herren's shoulder again. "You're a brave one, aren't you? Poor lad, but you're safe now."

"Yes, and I'm most grateful my cousins found me," Herren said steadily. "They've been very brave, especially when they got ahead of their proper guardsmen and had to act on their own." Turning to Jaift, he added, his voice quivering just a bit, "But I want to go home, now, cousin, please."

"Of course, cousin!" Jaift declared without hesitation, taking his hand. She said warmly to the men, "We'll be sure to speak well of you and your inn, where the God moved us to find our poor cousin and save his life."

"Ah, the God's hand *is* in this and no mistake," declared Moraf, with a sidelong glance at Meridy. "Yes, yes, no doubt of that, one could hardly miss it! Eyes as can look sideways will spot what other eyes overlook, as they say, and a good thing for your little cousin, eh?" But he also added, "Just let's wait for the guard and take care of all this proper, right?"

"We can't wait!" Diollin objected.

"Tell them to send the captain to your father's house,"

Niniol whispered to Jaift. "Let them know he's a lord—tell them Lord Saranuol. They'll believe that—he's got a house in every city in Cora Tal and a family that goes off in all directions; no one will be able to say you aren't his daughter."

"Oh, yes, that will do," Diollin agreed, relieved.

"You must certainly send their captain to my father's house," Jaift said smoothly. "Lord Saranuol. We'll take my poor young cousin there and send immediately to his family. I think we'd better go on now, though. I'm sure my cousin must greatly desire to be away from all this." She glanced around meaningfully at the carnage. "We're so grateful for your help and understanding, and do please let me pay for the damages to your suite." She didn't pause but took Herren's hand and headed straight for the door as though it didn't occur to her that anybody might get in their way. Meridy trailed after Jaift, admiring her technique.

"We couldn't permit anyone else to bear the expense!" declared Moraf, but he seemed enormously pleased, and no wonder, considering the charnel atmosphere in the room.

He and Jaift argued politely, while Meridy hastily gathered up their few belongings, about who should pay to clean up the mess. They were still arguing, no less politely, when Moraf led them past the curious faces at all the doors. Jaift refused to relent until they reached the inn's front door, when Moraf finally let himself be persuaded to accept a single thin gold coin.

"I'm sure the guard'll trust you'll send a deposition, excellent lady, but you'll never find a conveyance at this time of night!" Moraf protested one last time, following them out to the street. Lamps glowed on either side of the inn's door, casting their warm light over the courtyard, but there was not yet any trace of dawn in the east. Beyond the illumination of the lamps, the whole city seemed dark and still. The silence made Meridy shiver. Herren was shivering too, even though the night was warm. She didn't blame him a bit.

"Oh, we'll hire a private carriage," Jaift assured Moraf with blithe confidence, and led Meridy and Herren through the inn's courtyard and into the shadowed streets.

Once they'd gotten a little distance away, Herren tugged at Jaift's hand, pulling her to a stop. "We can't hire a carriage," he said, surprisingly decisive for such a little boy. "People would talk. *He* would find out." The boy didn't shout; he showed no sign of childish temper, but he spoke with a kind of flat exhaustion that was worse than anger.

"Hush! I know," Jaift murmured, and led them aside, a bit farther down the street and then into the mouth of an alley, out of the way of casual passersby or, more importantly, of the guardsmen who must any moment arrive at the inn. It was even darker here, though Meridy was standing close enough to the prince to be aware that he was still trembling, with fine little shudders that racked his whole body.

But he said, collectedly enough, "Tai-Enchar isn't afraid of guardsmen or priests or—or anyone. He'll kill anyone who tries to protect me and bind their ghosts—he *will*," he insisted, though no one had disputed this. "He can do that— bind unwilling ghosts, so fast they can't get away. Or the souls of living men. I've seen—I've seen him do it."

"I have, too," put in Diöllin, as though her brother needed support.

Meridy didn't doubt either of them. Besides, she could tell that in another minute, the young prince would finally

lose all his hard-held control and burst into tears. She knew
he would feel humiliated after he'd worked so hard to keep
his poise, so she said as briskly and coolly as she could, "Well,
we'll keep you safe, but even if you have some perfectly splendid ideas about what we should do next, this is not the time
to hear them. Let's *go somewhere else* first and *then* plan what to
do next. Where do you suppose this alley goes?"

"Oh," said Jaift, as though surprised Meridy hadn't realized. "This alley has to lead to Cora Talen's market. You remember we saw the awnings earlier, and how else would the
inn staff get to and from the market? If the market is like the
one at home, it'll open at dawn, but a lot of people will be setting up already. It's a good idea to go there. We can get rolls
or something and figure out what to do next."

"We can get horses," Herren said, still with that startling
decisiveness. "We need to go to Surem."

There was a pause.

"Surem?" Meridy asked at last.

"Well, sort of. Moran Diorr, really. *He* was taking me
there," the prince said, his voice tense and young in the dark.
"That's a place of power for him, but—"

"Then we should go anywhere else!" said Meridy, thoroughly exasperated.

"Listen!" the young prince said. "It's not *only* a place of
Tai-Enchar's power, it's a place of power for Inmanuàr as well."

"Oh!" Meridy supposed she should be getting used to
being startled, yet she couldn't help but ask, "*You* know about
Inmanuàr?"

"Of course! Listen! If I go to Surem under the witch-king's
power, it'll be terrible, but if I meet Inmanuàr there, then it's
different! *He* will know what to do."

"But why—" Jaift began, and at the same moment Meridy said, "Carad Mereth said—" and Niniol said sharply, "You may be—"

All their voices tangled up, and then Herren said, "Enough!"

He sounded young. But somehow he did not sound childish. His tone made this an order. It was not much like the tone an ordinary little boy would take in an argument.

There was a pause. Then Niniol asked, his tone dry, "How old *are* you, Your Highness?"

"Nine," answered the prince. "Almost."

Diöllin put in, exasperated and affectionate: "Our father hates—hated—to have anybody dispute his decisions. Herren is a lot like him. Everyone says."

"Yes, I'm sure that works out well for them, especially when they're making a mistake," Niniol retorted.

Meridy admired Niniol's confidence, if he was willing to argue with a prince, however young. But she was also becoming more and more uneasy with the way they were all standing here in an unfamiliar alley, in an unfamiliar town, in the dark, arguing. Anybody might come this way—the inn's servants, anybody. She said, "I wish we dared call Inmanuàr here and *ask* him, but of course we can't, and he probably wouldn't explain anyway. I don't think it's likely we'll be finding our way to Moran Diorr unless we all learn to breathe like little fishes, but Surem, then. That's fine. I don't have a better idea, anyway. And we can figure things out on the way, I guess. I suppose the first step is probably finding this market."

"Someone there will certainly be selling horses," Diöllin agreed. "We can buy as many as we need, and supplies and everything, and be on the road in just—"

Jaift interrupted the princess. "Oh, we don't want to buy

horses! That would take a lot of money, and worse, people would notice us on the road if we rode out like so many scions of princely houses, especially dressed like this! We'd need new clothing and servants and guardsmen and *everything,* so that won't work at all. You know what we should do? Farmers will be coming to the market with"—Meridy felt rather than saw Jaift wave an impatient hand—"cabbages or turnips or whatever. Some of them will stay in town all day, but plenty of them will go home as soon as they've sold their goods, so we can quite easily get a ride with someone going north. Then no one will look twice at us."

"You want us to ride in a farmer's wagon?" said Diöllin, without a lot of expression in her voice. "You want *my brother* to pretend to be a farmer's brat?"

Meridy, tired and scared, snapped, "There's nothing wrong with asking a farmer for seats in his wagon! People do it all the time!"

The first gray light of dawn was beginning to filter into the alley, so she could see Diöllin lift her chin in arrogant disdain. "Yes, other farmers!" she retorted.

"Meridy is right," Niniol said firmly. "She's right and you know it, Your Highness, or you ought to. If anyone's seeking His little Highness, then looking like farmer's children is perfect. Breeding doesn't make a man stupid—nor a princess, I should hope—so have some sense!"

Diöllin sniffed soundlessly, but she didn't answer, either. Meridy had some hope Niniol had settled the matter, until Herren said stubbornly, "I don't care how it looks, but wagons are slow. We could *walk* to Surem faster than a farmer's wagon will get us there. We daren't be slow. Inmanuàr—"

But before the young prince could finish whatever he had been about to say, Iëhiy suddenly lunged forward, barking furiously. Meridy had half a second to grab Herren's hand, and Jaift's, and start to step back, and then the dark alleyway folded around them and the princess-regent herself rode out of a sudden cold wash of *ethereal* light.

Though she had never seen Princess Tiamanaith before, never even seen an image of her, Meridy knew at once that this must be the princess-regent. She *looked* like a princess, with long strands of white pearls looped through her black hair and more pearls, tiny black ones, swinging from her ears and from the bridle of her horse. It wasn't an ordinary horse, either: Meridy would have known the princess just from that. She rode a fire horse, a black mare, the slit-pupiled eyes blazing with fury and bloodlust. The mare fought the rein, wanting to slash at them with ivory tusks as long as a girl's thumb, wanting to rear and lash out with clawed forefeet, and Meridy jumped aside with a small, embarrassing scream.

But the princess-regent jerked the fire horse's head up with a hard rein, calling out in a high, clear voice, "My son! Here you are at last!"

Meridy couldn't tell whether Princess Tiamanaith even saw the rest of them; certainly she didn't seem to. But she reined the fire horse around and reached down to her son. She was smiling, though there was something strange about her smile, about the tilt of her mouth and the look in her ice-blue eyes. As far as Meridy could see, there was no relief in her; neither joy nor fear, but only a cold and glittering triumph.

Meridy had lost her hold on his hand, but far from running to meet his mother, Herren ducked back and away. Jaift grabbed for him, and she was too late as well. Iëhiy snapped at the fire horse, and Niniol strode forward with his sword blazing in his hand, but Meridy had neither smoke nor dust nor strong light with which she might pull them into the *real,* and there was nothing they could do. The fire horse leaped forward, and the princess-regent reached down and seized her son and dragged him up and across the front of her saddle. At once the fire horse sank down on her haunches, whirled around, and lunged back into the scintillating light through which the princess-regent had made her path into the *real* world, and—

—the light failed, and Meridy jumped after it, but it was too late to bring it back even if she'd been sure how to do it. Iëhiy raced into the dark and vanished, a sharp flicker of light and memory, there and gone, and Meridy and Jaift, and Diöl-lin and even Niniol, were all left standing like fools in the alley, with empty hands and stunned expressions and nothing at all saved out of the violent night. Prince Herren was gone.

fourteen

"*That* was Princess Tiamanaith?" Jaift sounded stunned.

"I guess we know now what kind of bargain she made with Aseraiëth." Meridy tried to keep her voice from shaking, not very successfully. "Inmanuàr said you have to agree to let a sorcerer do that to you. But she did agree. And look what happened to her. What she's become."

"She was desperate," Jaift whispered. "I know she was desperate. But she can't have understood what bargain she was making. She can't have. Did you see her *face*?" Her voice rose in horror and outrage. "That was her *son*!"

Meridy rubbed her own face, trying not to cry with fury and fear and grief for both Princess Tiamanaith and her son. "Not *hers*. Not anymore."

Diöllin had flown to defend her brother, but ineffectually, as they'd all been ineffectual. Her insubstantial hands fluttered as though she tried to reach after the vanished light, after her brother. Now, turning to Jaift, she whispered in the thin voice of the quick dead, "Our mother killed our father. I saw. I couldn't believe . . . but she did it. And now she has Herren. . . . the witch-king stole him, but now she's stolen him back, and I don't know what she means to do with him.

And I don't know what to *do*. I don't know what to do anymore."

"Just how did your father die?" Meridy demanded. "How did *you* die?"

"People *said* it was a riding accident," Jaift said in a low, sickened tone.

Diöllin tossed her head, recovering a trace of her customary attitude. It was mostly a pose, Meridy saw, at least right now. But her tone was haughty as she said, "A riding accident that killed two people? It was that fire horse, that same one, my father thought he could tame her, men of royal blood are supposed to be able to tame them, maybe he could have, my father could ride anything and horses always loved him, but the girth was cut half through, I saw it go, and then—" She stopped. Then she went on, "So then I ran into the corral. I was so stupid, but I thought maybe . . . maybe I could save him. But it was too late. I thought I could climb the fence before . . . but I wasn't fast enough." She shuddered helplessly.

This gave Meridy far too complete and horrible a picture of exactly how the so-called riding accident must have happened. She said, "The fire horse killed your father, and then you, and it was your mother who cut the girth in the first place?"

"She did. I know she did. I saw my mother's face when he fell. She *expected* it to happen. I could tell." Diöllin pressed her hands to her face. She would have been weeping, if ghosts could weep. But when she lowered her hands and glared defiantly at Meridy, her translucent face was unmarked by tears.

"And now she's riding the *same* fire horse herself?" Jaift plainly found this detail unbelievable. "How can she? Don't people think that's, well, creepy and awful?"

Diöllin shook her head. "Everyone understands that part,

even if it is creepy and awful. She wanted to make sure she was made regent. You know people say only royalty can tame fire horses. She was never—she was never a princess by birth, you know. She wanted to show everyone she was royal."

Niniol said quietly, "With her husband and her daughter gone to the God and her son merely a child, Princess Tiamanaith would rule for a long time, I suppose. Or the sorceress, in her place."

"Sorceress?" cried Diöllin. "What sorceress do you mean?"

"An ally of the witch-king's, who took your mother's place, we think." Meridy explained as briefly and simply as she knew how. "But listen, allies or not, the sorceress can't have wanted Tai-Enchar to take the young prince, or why snatch him up the minute we got him away from the witch-king's servants?"

"But if that's not really my mother, that's even *worse*! We have to save him!" declared Diöllin.

"What, you mean we have to save him *again*?" said Niniol, the dryness of his tone not altogether without justice, Meridy had to admit.

But Jaift said firmly, "Of course we have to save him. Poor little boy! Did you see that woman's *face*? She was *scary*. We can't simply abandon poor Herren to her!"

"Iëhiy went with him," Meridy offered. "I think."

"Well, that's something, but even if it weren't for the young prince, we can't let that woman be regent, either. It's not right! We have to *tell* someone what Princess Tiamanaith did, and who that is in her place!" Jaift sounded fiercely determined about this.

"Oh?" said Niniol, crossing his arms over his chest and tilting his head. "Who, exactly, and why would they believe us?" But then he added thoughtfully, "Though that's a reason to find the young prince again, I suppose. Whether we're to thwart the witch-king or unseat the princess-regent or both, it's His little Highness as will have to do it, young as he is."

"Yes!" cried Diöllin. "The *first* thing is to make sure Herren's safe!"

"You're right," Meridy said, relieved to find they could agree after all on what they had to do. She had no idea how they could do any of that, but agreeing on a direction was almost like figuring out the first step of an actual plan.

But Niniol was going on, "Still, I don't see your friend Carad Mereth anywhere, do you, Mery? He challenged Tai-Enchar's servitor—and where did that get him? And now we've got to worry about the princess-regent of Cora Tal? You know what we ought to do: we ought to find the nearest priests' sanctuary and turn all this over to the priests. They're far better suited to deal with this than we are."

"Oh, *can* we?" Jaift said wistfully.

Meridy took a breath, let it out, and said, "I don't think we can, you know."

"Oh, but—"

"No. I mean, I'm the one who's bound Diöllin, and she's the one who can find Herren—can't you, Diöllin?"

The ghost murmured assent. "I always know where he is. He's east of us now, a long way away—oh, she took him home, of course, to Cora Diorr. And the priests wouldn't believe us anyway," she added earnestly. "Who would believe that *Tai-Enchar* is still alive? Or quick, even if he's not alive. Who would believe that a sorceress has taken my mother's place?"

"Well, you are the princess," observed Niniol. "It's not like you're just anybody with a wild story. Although . . ." He paused. "Umm."

"Yes," agreed Meridy. "It's not very believable, is it? And

the quick dead don't always clearly remember their own deaths. Princess Diöllin could be confused. Blaming her mother, well, she's distraught. Prince Diöllonuor's death *could* have been an accident, you know. A broken girth—those things happen, and when you're trying to ride a fire horse, well, there you go. And Carad Mereth didn't seek help from the priests, either. Or if he did, he didn't mention it to me. I expect it was because he knew they'd argue with him or one another and nobody would do anything until it was too late."

"Who'd want to believe *any* of this?" asked Niniol, his tone resigned. "*I* wouldn't, sure enough. So, then, say Her Highness may be able to find Herren, what are we supposed to do once we find him?"

Meridy had no idea, but she declared, "We'll figure that out when we get there."

"I have friends," Diöllin put in earnestly. "My father's seneschal, Lord Roann, he'll help us, I know he will!"

"If he was your father's seneschal, he owes the princess-regent service now," Niniol pointed out.

"No, Lord Roann will help us. He'll know something's happened to my mother, I know he will! I trust him!"

Niniol shrugged. "Well, maybe. But you know, the histories are filled with stories about the trusted servants and close friends and reliable allies of royalty. Exciting, dramatic stories."

"Do you think *I* cannot distinguish a flatterer's tongue and heart from those of a true friend?"

Niniol didn't seem convinced. "It'd be a brighter world if we could all do so, Your Highness. And yet—"

Meridy said hastily, "Let's not start arguing again! One thing we know for sure is that we're not safe *here*. We need to do *something* and go *somewhere,* and does anybody have a better idea than getting seats in a farmer's wagon and heading east toward Cora Diorr?"

Not even Diöllin argued this time. By this time it was light enough to make out her expression, so Meridy could see she looked profoundly skeptical. But the princess said with an exasperated little shrug, "All right. All right! A farmer's wagon will do for now, I suppose, and since it'll take forever to get to Cora Diorr in a *wagon,* we can figure out the rest of it on the way. But don't say anything to *me* if you don't like sleeping in barns and washing at a pump!"

Meridy let her breath out in relief that they could start moving at last. "A barn is good enough, as long as no one looks for us in barns."

"I'd like to find a pump right now," added Jaift, also sounding relieved. "Or even a fountain. We need to make sure we look respectable if we're going to chat with strangers!"

Meridy gratefully let the older girl take over, thinking instead about Cora Diorr—the prince's city, the City of Spires. She knew that Cora Diorr lay in the midst of a plain, but that the city itself was surrounded by a ring of mountains. And she knew that Herren's father had been collecting witches in Cora Diorr for years and years, so in that one city, a girl with black eyes might not stand out at all.

Diöllin was right about a farmer's barn not being as comfortable as a room in a decent inn. But on the other hand, Meridy thought this particular barn was actually fairly nice. There might not be beds, but the barn smelled of clean hay.

And it was a lot more pleasant than her aunt's crowded cottage in Tikiy, where she'd had to sleep in a bed with cousins who hated her. The hands at this farm slept in the stable, not the hay barn, so she and Jaift—and Niniol and Diöllin—

could talk without fear of being overheard. That was important. They had so much to talk about.

And the farmer's wife let them take bowls of stew and thick slabs of bread out to the barn, where she and Jaift had heaved bales of hay and straw around to make a fair approximation of a table and benches; and with blankets to throw over the loose straw later, it would actually be quite comfortable, in Meridy's opinion. Which didn't stop Diöllin from turning her nose up at the arrangement, but honestly, it was perfectly pleasant. The stew was good, too, filled with chunks of mutton and turnips.

Meridy missed Iëhiy begging for tidbits, but at least she was beginning to trust that the dog went where he wished and would always be able to find his way back to her. She hoped she was right about him going with poor Herren. She broke a slice of bread in half, dipped a piece in her stew, and ate it. Then she said, "I have a new game we can all play. It's called Let's Figure Out What's Going On."

"What, just like that?" Jaift said doubtfully. "We still don't really know much. . . ."

Niniol raised his hand in disagreement. He was leaning against the wall near the door of the hay barn, quite automatically keeping an eye out for trouble. The farm seemed perfectly peaceful, but Jaift had already commented matter-of-factly that they should shove bales of hay against the door at night, which was something Meridy wouldn't have thought of.

"We know a good deal, I think," Niniol murmured now, his voiceless utterance decisive for all it could not precisely be heard. "We know plenty to go on with. We know Tai-Enchar is trying to achieve something and needs His little Highness for it; and we know Inmanuàr is trying to stop him and also needs the young prince for that purpose. And we know the princess-regent made a bad bargain with a sorceress. Your Highness, no one noticed the change?"

"It happened this spring," the princess answered immediately. She was perched on another hay bale. She had been looking faintly resentful at the lack of velvet cushions and servants, though since she was quick instead of living, she could hardly complain about the prickle of the straw. But now she seemed to forget her disdain of hay barns and farmers, the expression on her translucent face becoming troubled. "But no, no one realized, not even my father. Not even me, then. I mean . . . for years, my mother had been . . . unpredictable. She would be cheerful one day and then the next . . ."

"Morose?" suggested Jaift, with ready sympathy.

"Cruel," Diöllin said, quietly, looking away. Then she took a deep breath and faced them again. "I know that sounds terrible. But she would fall into these moods. It's not so bad, really. Or it wasn't. You'd leave her alone and the mood would pass off. Except this spring, it came on her worse than usual, and then it didn't lift. I thought . . ."

"Yes?" Meridy prodded her, impatient.

"Well, she's not young anymore. Not truly *young*. But she's not old, either. I thought maybe she was pregnant. Because that's when her moods started. When she was carrying Herren. She wanted a son so much, and prayed so hard, and the pregnancy was so difficult. . . . But after Herren was born, it was like she was herself again. So this spring, I thought she might simply be pregnant again. But if she was, she must have lost the babe early, because nothing ever showed. And this time the mood didn't pass off." She looked at Meridy, trying for haughty, but behind the hauteur, Meridy could see how wretched she truly was. "A sorceress, you said? My mother made a . . . a bargain? Who is—was—this Aseraiëth?"

"A servant or ally of the witch-king's. And I suppose she must have," Meridy said. Saying so was surprisingly difficult in the face of Diöllin's distress. "I'm sure she didn't mean to," she added lamely.

"But why would the . . . mood . . . come and go for so long?" Jaift wondered. "Instead, I mean . . . of the princess just changing and staying changed?"

Meridy had to shake her head. "Maybe that was the bargain—that Aseraiëth herself could come and go?" she guessed. Or part of the bargain, because they already knew another part had involved giving up her own daughter to the sorceress. Maybe Princess Tiamanaith hadn't realized that, though. Maybe she'd thought Aseraiëth only demanded that she share her own body. That wasn't as bad as giving up her daughter on purpose. Meridy imagined the sorceress stepping into and out of Tiamanaith as though into and out of a living mask. For years. Of Tiamanaith sometimes being herself and sometimes being pushed aside to make room for Aseraiëth.

Had she even known what was happening? Maybe to her, she just seemed to look aside for a moment and then back, to find time had stuttered and her children were treating her differently, warily. That would be . . . horrible enough, surely, even in the times when she was herself. "I'm sure she must have realized long ago she'd made a terrible bargain," Meridy said out loud.

"My mother made a bargain," Diöllin said slowly. She rubbed her forehead as though that might help her grasp this horrifying idea. "My mother made a bargain with a long-dead sorceress, an ally of the witch-king. Nine years ago. To save my brother. And the sorceress did save Herren. But now this Aseraiëth has . . . possessed my mother. Is that what you're saying?"

Jaift said gently, "It seems she did. It seems very likely that when your mother was carrying Herren, when she prayed for a living son, someone answered her prayer. But it wasn't the God."

Diöllin was shaking her head, but not in denial. She said weakly, "She wouldn't have, it's impossible, she couldn't have done . . . anything like that." But it was clear she knew her mother *had* done something very much like that.

"She was desperate," Jaift said, even more gently. "Imagine how she must have felt as the baby she carried gradually stilled. You must have known women to whom such terrible things happened. My aunt miscarried four babies; she's never had one live. A mother can be truly desperate." She added to Meridy, "But I wouldn't have thought it was possible to bargain with a sorceress to bring a living child to term, not once it stilled in the womb. I mean, sorcery can be powerful, I guess, but only the God can actually bring the quick dead back to true life!"

"Well, none of us know what Tai-Enchar might be able to do," Meridy pointed out. He had been truly a king of witches and sorcerers, and no one knew what he might have done had he lived. Or what he might be able to do even now that he was dead. Meridy didn't have to say so. It was obvious, though if Tai-Enchar could reach between the realms of the living and the dead . . . it was an appalling idea.

Though what had happened to Princess Tiamanaith was almost as bad. Praying to deliver a living child, and having a wicked sorceress answer your prayer . . . ugh. Pieces slotted together in Meridy's mind like lines from half-remembered poetry. She said, "I expect Tai-Enchar wanted to do to Inmanuàr what Aseraiëth has done to Princess Tiamanaith. Except I doubt he wants to *share.* He needs a living boy, not a ghost. And he hasn't ever been able to restore Inmanuàr to life, not in all this time. Carad Mereth stopped him, I bet. Then here was Princess Tiamanaith carrying a son of the High King's line, willing to make any bargain if she could only have him live. So if the witch-king couldn't have the High King's heir, he would make another heir, a little boy he could take into his own realm so he could do anything he wanted with him." She could imagine it, after all. It was horrible, but she could imagine it.

Jaift looked ill. Then she lifted her chin and said firmly, "We can't let him take Herren, that's all. And, listen, even if Princess Tiamanaith made a bargain with the sorceress, I'm sure she regrets it and is sorry. But Aseraiëth can't simply be Tai-Enchar's ally now, either. Because she snatched Herren from Tai-Enchar's servants the minute his attention was drawn away. If she already gave everything for her son and now the witch-king wants Herren . . . I think they must be enemies now, not allies."

This made sense. Meridy started to nod, but Niniol leaned forward, tapped one insubstantial hand firmly on the table they'd made of hay bales, and warned them all, "Never depend on your opponent to do anything you wish."

Meridy blushed, because she could see how they had started to do just that. She *so* much wanted Jaift to be right.

"But still, they *might* be enemies now," protested Jaift. Jumping to her feet, she started to pace. "Or even if they're not, as long as they want different things, they could be *set against each other.* If we get Herren away from Tiamanaith, *both* Aseraiëth and Tai-Enchar will want him back—we know that much, don't we? Maybe we can set it up so they're both distracted long enough for us to—" She had sounded confident, but now she broke off, turning to face the rest of them, looking suddenly uncertain.

"What?" demanded Meridy. "Don't stop there!"

Jaift opened her hands. "I was only thinking . . . if Tai-Enchar was distracted, if he thought we were going to give Herren back to his mother instead of him, if he was focused on that, then maybe someone might find a way to slip past his attention and into his realm and find this Carad Mereth of yours and free him, and then *he* can . . . do something, I hope, or at least explain things to the rest of us. I mean, if Diöllin can find Herren, surely Inmanuàr can find Carad Mereth. You can summon Inmanuàr, since you're his anchor, even if you're not his first or strongest anchor. Can't you?"

For a long moment, Meridy just stared at her friend.

Jaift said apologetically, "I know, it would probably be too dangerous—" and at the same time Diöllin exclaimed, "No one is going to use *my brother* as *bait*!"

"No," Meridy said to them both. "No, hush, Diöllin, of course no one's going to risk Herren! But going on without any kind of a plan is dangerous, too. Isn't it better to have some idea in mind than nothing at all? All we have is guesses, but I bet Carad Mereth knows about everything, if only we could find him." She hesitated and then added, "Besides that, in Cora Talen, when the witch-king's servitor had me, Carad Mereth rescued me. If I'd been quicker, if I'd gotten away, he wouldn't have had to. If Tai-Enchar has him now, it's my fault." She looked at Jaift. "Your plan needs to be built up a little, but it's a good plan."

Jaift gave her a small nod, looking faintly surprised.

"It's mad!" Diöllin protested.

"It's a *plan,* and we didn't have one before," Meridy insisted. "Listen, Diöllin, the first thing is still to find Herren and get him away and safe—that hasn't changed. I'm sure we won't need to stake him out as bait, though, so don't fuss! We just— Look, both Tai-Enchar and your mother have to *think* we're about to let the other one have him. Then they ought to focus on that, even if your brother's hidden somewhere safe." She hesitated. "Honestly, it's probably not safe for anybody *except* Herren," she added at last. "Because we'll tuck him away somewhere, but if I'm the one who's going to try to slip by Tai-Enchar and find Carad Mereth, *someone* will have to keep the witch-king's attention fixed elsewhere."

Looking from one of them to the next, she found that Jaift was nodding, and Diöllin was shaking her head, but not actually arguing. Niniol was gazing at Meridy with a small, intense frown. But it wasn't disapproval or condescension or anything like that. It was something else. *Oh.* Oh, it was *respect.* Blushing, Meridy looked away.

"Well," Niniol murmured, his tone impressively dry. "It is indeed a mad idea, so it's got that going for it: no one would ever expect it. Most travelers use games to pass the time, but I'm sure this notion of yours will give us *all* something to think about till we reach Cora Diorr."

Meridy was sure it would.

fifteen

Cora Diorr was very different from Cora Talen, different again from Riam, and despite its ring of surrounding mountains, nothing at all like Tikiy.

Tikiy, tucked into the foothills of the Southern Wall, was always overwhelmed by the mountains rearing up to the sky. Generally the people of Tikiy set their doors facing to the north so that they would not have the Wall's immensity before their eyes the moment they stepped from their cottages. Aunt Tarana had scarcely even *looked* south, and she wasn't the only one in Tikiy who kept her attention turned resolutely away from the Wall.

In Tikiy, in the depths of the winter, the moon rose and set behind the Wall, so it was never visible even on fine, crystalline nights filled with stars. For that reason, it was said to be unlucky to die in winter, for how could a ghost find the way to the White Road of the Moon when the moon never rose? So people hung extra strands of prayer bells from the eaves of their cottages. They set flat white stones into the earth before their front steps to invite the God into their homes, and they lit white candles beside the sickbed whenever anyone grew ill. As far as Meridy had ever been able to tell, some of the dead went straight to the God while others lingered, and she had never noticed that bells or stones or candles or the season made the least difference. But those were the customs in the shadow of the Wall.

The country around Riam had been different. There, ordinary mountains lay to the west—nothing like the Wall, but low, rolling hills, heavily forested because the ground there was too rocky to bother farming. Jaift said that her father said that except for lumber and coal and furs and the occasional fire horse foal captured by a daring trapper, everything of interest came and went from Riam to the east and the north.

Then, as they'd seen as they traveled north from Riam, the northbound traveler left the mountains behind and all the country flattened and opened up until the sky stretched out forever above endless farmlands. Meridy had been wide-eyed to see the vast rolling pastures around Cora Talen, and Jaift had been fascinated at the size of the early melons in the fields and the heavy crops of apples in the orchards they passed.

Cora Diorr was not like anything Meridy had yet seen.

Mountains surrounded Cora Diorr, all the way around, a single ring of mountains in a nearly perfect circle. They were not tall, but they seemed to rise up high enough in the midst of all that flat country. People said Prince Tirnamuon, the first prince of Cora Tal after the shattering of the Kingdom, had raised up those encircling mountains with the remnants of the magic that had been used to create the Southern Wall. Now that she saw Cora Diorr for herself, Meridy believed it.

Cora Diorr, the prince's city, seemed huge to her. Maybe that was because from above, where the road ran across the saddle between two of the encircling mountains, the travelers could see the entire city spread out before them. But she thought the city also seemed so vast and intimidating because it was so . . . *Grand* was the only word that seemed to fit.

From the first moment it had been laid out, Cora Diorr had plainly been intended to reflect Prince Tirnamuon's ambition. Far from growing up and out in haphazard fashion, the city had been laid out in a series of concentric circles, each circle pierced by long, straight streets paved with white stone. From above, it was obvious that none of the straight avenues wandered into blind alleys or curved around obstacles; they ran through Cora Diorr like the spokes of a wagon wheel.

Meridy had never imagined such a city. She knew that the prince's city was sometimes called the City of Spires and sometimes the City of Circles, but she had not come close to picturing what the city might actually look like.

Cora Diorr truly was a city of spires. That was Meridy's first impression, though actually there weren't so many—fifteen tall, slender towers, that was her first count. Then, as the road turned and descended and the view shifted, she saw some had at first been hidden behind others; there were actually nineteen.

The towers stood in the center of the city, lancing upward from amid the low sprawl of lesser buildings. Each tower was shining white, but with a cinnabar-red roof rising to a sharp point. The towers seemed too narrow for their height, but there they stood, shining white and red in the sunlight. Meridy couldn't decide if she loved them or hated them, but they were unquestionably stunning.

The tallest spire stood in the center of the city. It was surrounded first by a ring of seven towers and then by another ring of eleven, with all the towers in each ring linked one to the next by the graceful arches of porticos and bridges. Beneath the towers stretched out gardens filled with flowering trees and fountains. A narrow white wall gracefully looped around all the towers of the outer circle, setting the spires apart from the city proper. Each of the straight white streets ran from the edge of the city to the wall, ending at a gate. Just to set the spires off a bit more, the rest of the city had been built of gray or yellowish stone. The other streets, the ordinary ones, seemed to be paved with plain gray cobbles, and the houses and shops roofed with gray slate or maroon tile. Only the circular avenues and the arrow-straight streets that ran through them were paved with white stone; only the towers were white and red.

"Our prince's palace," said the carter in whose wagon they were all riding. "Nothing in Cora Talen to match it, is there? Nor in Riam, I'll be bound." He sounded smugly pleased about this, as though he'd personally designed the city and set all nineteen of those towers in place with his own hands. He clucked to his mules, drawing the animals to a slower pace as the road crested the highest point to let his passengers look their fill before they took the long downhill slope to the city.

The carter was a decent man overall, though Meridy could have done without his opinion, expressed often and forcefully during the five days they'd been traveling with him, that Cora Diorr was the finest city in all the principalities—the handsomest and cleanest, the most elegantly designed and most secure, the wealthiest and most prosperous, the most broad-minded and tolerant, and just generally a favorite of the God in every possible way. It did get tiresome, although Diöllin preened a bit.

On the other hand, seen from above like this, with its wide white avenues and its white towers gleaming, everything the carter said suddenly seemed as though it might be true.

The carter had only recently carried a load of fancy glass

to Cora Talen and sent it on its way to Surem, picking up bales of fine wool in place of the glass, and now he was heading back to Cora Diorr.

They'd been glad to meet him, because by then they'd traveled a day's slow journey from Cora Talen and needed another ride from the farm where they'd spent their first night on the road. Plus, the carter's mules were young and strode out with a will, so his lightly loaded wagon was quite a bit faster than a farmer's wagon. Besides, the carter was a friendly, vain, self-satisfied man who didn't blink at Meridy's black eyes, or look about uneasily as though he might see ghosts nearby, or trace the God's sign over his heart when he thought she wasn't looking, in case she should plan the theft of the soul from his living body. He was, if anything, proud of Cora Diorr's reputation for witches.

"Witches aplenty in Cora Diorr!" he'd told them cheerfully when they'd approached him about riding in his wagon to the capital. "The witches in Cora Diorr live under the law. Nobody's going to be stealing anybody's soul in our city, see, and it's helpful, you know, being able to get the haunts out of a place after a tragedy, or send some poor grieving soul to the God."

They had all looked at one another. Suddenly it seemed obvious where Tai-Enchar had gotten witches to make into his double-shadowed servants. Meridy could see it all: the law that for years, maybe, had brought witches to Cora Diorr and kept them there, vulnerable to the witch-king, ready for his use. And then the princess-regent—the sorceress Aseraiëth—had murdered Prince Diöllonuor to get him out of the way, so she could seize power in Cora Tal and help Tai-Enchar with . . . whatever he meant to do next. It was ugly, but she thought it had probably happened just like that.

"Well, but how about the priests?" Jaift had asked, sounding a little doubtful. "I mean, I know the priests can't *always* clear a haunting, but—"

"But the witches of Cora Diorr can!" The carter had sounded even more smug when he explained that. "They manage what the priests can't, see, so His Highness that was, he sent most of the priests out of Cora Diorr, to tend to the towns and villages as don't have our law and can't have witches about."

Jaift had drawn a breath to say something, probably something tart about thinking witches, no matter what law might rule them, could take over the priests' role. But then she'd closed her mouth again without arguing. After all, they needed a ride—and there was nothing they could do about any of it now, anyway.

"That's why you're on your way to the capital, eh, girl?" the carter had added to Meridy. "You've heard how the princess-regent's called up all witches out of the whole principality, have you? Of course you have! Well, have no fear, you're right to go to the princess-regent. She'll welcome you and teach you the law and you'll love our beautiful city. And your friend is going with you, is she, to see the sights? Wonderful! Always better to have friends about you, and everybody ought to see Cora Diorr once in their lives! I've a light load and room to spare. A silver coin each, you say? Good, that's ample, especially for a pretty pair of girls like you!"

So the journey to Cora Diorr had been pleasanter than it might have been, and at last they came over the saddle between the mountains. The carter—whose name was Jans, it turned out—checked his team of mules and gave his passengers their first real look at the concentric circles and white spires of Cora Diorr.

"How about that, eh?" Jans said in a genial tone. "Cora Diorr's the only city in the world with towers like that. You've heard it called the City of Spires, eh? Well, there you go! Built 'em by sorcery, the prince did, so they say. Prince Tirnamuon, that was, of course." He saw Meridy's nod and went on with enthusiasm, "You've heard the tale, eh? Yes; Prince Tirnamuon built those towers, and laid out the streets, and made a law that everything else in Cora Diorr must be made of local stone quarried right out of these mountains. Nor can anyone raise up other towers—nothing over ten times the height of a man. Though I don't know as he had to set that into law; these days there's not so much sorcery floating around loose as to spend it building towers!" Jans chuckled and nodded and waved the driver's whip vaguely over the backs of the mules, which flicked their ears and started forward again.

The road ran down from the saddle between the mountains to the gates of Cora Diorr in a series of long, lazy curves, so the distance took longer to cover than seemed reasonable. But the road here was good. The slope was gentle and all downhill, so everyone could ride if they wanted. Meridy perched on a bale of wool yarn beside Jaift, and they both watched the city grow gradually larger and more distinct. Meridy found her attention caught as well, as they drew closer to the city, by another group of travelers on the road before them.

They had seen other wagons now and then as they came closer to the prince's city; in fact, there had hardly been an hour when they hadn't seen other travelers of one sort or another. Just on this last day, besides the wagons of tradesmen and farmers, they had seen two companies of guardsmen and, three times, small high-wheeled carriages drawn by high-stepping horses and escorted by outriders carrying banners depicting birds or fish or crescent moons. Meridy didn't know any of those signs, but she could see why brigandage was of little concern on the Coramne Road if there was always so much traffic and so many guardsmen.

But they were coming up on a group now that wasn't like any of those. These people were gathered off to the side of the road doing . . . something. Something that involved a lot of jumping around and shouting. Meridy started to stand up, to try to see better, but the mules, suspicious of all that commotion, pinned their ears back and started to balk and sidle sideways, and the wagon was suddenly nothing like steady enough to risk standing up. Jans, his hands full of reins, cursed the mules good-naturedly but didn't use the whip.

"What *is* it?" Jaift asked, craning her neck. "Can you tell?"

Meridy tried again to get to her feet, steadying herself with a hand on her friend's shoulder. "Not quite . . ."

Diöllin murmured in Meridy's ear, "That's Lord Taimonuol—but I can't imagine what he's up to."

"You know him?" Meridy asked, and then guiltily remembered the carter couldn't see Diöllin and pretended that she'd been talking to Jaift, though of course there was no reason in the world Jaift would recognize anyone. But the carter, busy with the mules, didn't seem to have noticed her slip.

Diöllin was laughing, a little scornful but amused, too. "Everyone knows Lord Taimonuol, trust me on this! That's his banner, but even without that, I'd recognize his horse— that white one. And his hair, that bright gold, look there. Wait till you see him properly; he's worth a look, believe me! I can't see what he's up to, but it'll be something flashy and dramatic, and all the men in Cora Diorr will wish they'd done it and all the women will fall in love with him. That's what he's like."

"That must be some lord or other—you can see his banner, but I can't make out what's happening at *all*," Jaift said, though she was too prudent to attempt to actually get to her feet.

But Niniol, standing in the road with the sunlight streaming through him, his hands on his hips and a disgusted expression on his face, said, "Ah, those fools! They've got a fire horse. Or they *did* have a fire horse. It's gotten loose; that's the trouble."

"A fire horse!" exclaimed Meridy and Jaift and Diöllin all together.

"Ah, no, a fire horse, is it?" said the carter, interested despite the trouble he was having with the mules. "Takes a fool or a king to ride one, as they say."

"But," said Jaift, "after what happened with Prince Diöllonuor?"

"You might think so!" cried Jans. "But I guess the princess-regent is still offering the bounty, or at least them as caught this one must be hoping she is."

"I know why she wants this one," whispered Diöllin. "She wants it for Herren, I know she does! He can ride anything—he's like our father that way; she won't have to *coax* him to try it, but God's grace! My brother's only eight!"

"Every year or two some fool tries to bring one in for the prince's bounty, and like as not gets his guts ripped out for his trouble," Jans continued chattily, not hearing the princess. "Not but that them there haven't got this one farther along toward Cora Diorr than most, I'll give 'em that."

Niniol gave a disgusted little nod. "Men will be fools. But

if the princess-regent lets one of the creatures kill her son, she won't be regent long, I imagine."

Diöllin shook her head. "She won't let that happen. She'll have a plan."

Meridy couldn't resist getting to her feet, craning to see, and never mind the mules' continued restiveness. "Can't we go closer?"

"This's more than close enough, my girl!" the carter put in hastily. "*Far away* is the best place for those monsters, believe me!"

"I'm sure Jans is right," Jaift put in, sounding worried. "What if it breaks away entirely? Poor thing, I hope it does," she added, not very consistently.

"Now, now, you shouldn't wish it turned loose on the countryside!" Jans exclaimed. "I'll tell you what, we'll just turn around, take the wagon back a little ways, get clear of all that nonsense, and let them up there sort it out. . . ."

Meridy jumped down out of the wagon. She'd seen illuminated manuscripts with pictures, but that wasn't the same as a living fire horse. And she'd been too terrified to see anything properly when the princess-regent had ridden the other one out of light and air to snatch her son from Cora Talen.

Jaift, too, climbed down from the wagon at last, half reluctant and half curious. "Really, Mery, I don't think this is safe. . . ."

"'*Nàmàru kiën y daha manet siän*,'" Meridy murmured. *Blood-red shadows falling from the sunset . . .* How did the rest of it go? Something about *Blood-red shadows falling to rend the earth.* That was how a famous poet had described his first sight of fire horses, a wild herd pouring down the slopes of the mountains. She remembered those lines, but somehow she had lived her whole life in the shadow of the Wall and never yet actually gotten a good look at one of the famous creatures. Now she felt how unfair that was. "There's no need to be frightened, with all those men, don't you think?"

"I suppose you're right," Jaift said, though she didn't look happy about it.

Jans was brave enough to try to come after them, but his mules were having none of it. "My mules have more sense than the pair of you girls!" he shouted. "Listen, those fools don't have it under control or they wouldn't be jumping around like that! There was one not long ago, last year maybe, I heard it killed five men and near a sixth before archers put it down—"

Meridy stopped listening. Niniol was speaking to her, too, but his voiceless murmur washed over her. She couldn't see Diöllin, though she supposed the princess must be around somewhere and hoped she was not too worried about this delay. But surely an hour here or there couldn't matter set against a journey of days, anyway.

sixteen

Fire horses were usually blood bay, though a few were black from nose tip to tail tip. Any ordinary cart horse might be bay or black, but no one would ever mistake a fire horse for a normal horse, not for a second, not even if they were exactly the same color.

An ordinary horse might have a flying mane and tail and thick feathering on its fetlocks; an ordinary horse, if it was a fancy riding animal, might have an elegant head and small ears and an arched neck and move like it was dancing. But fire horses had eyes like a cat, slit-pupiled and yellow. They had clawed feet instead of hooves, short tusks set in the upper jaw and longer tusks in the lower, and a killing instinct that made wolves look like sheepdogs. You could train a horse to the saddle, or to pull a cart or plow a field, but no one could train a fire horse to do anything—except the Southerners, of course, who had brought the fire horses to the Kingdom in the first place. And those of royal blood, if one could believe the stories.

Jaift caught Meridy's hand and pulled her to a stop. "Isn't this close enough?"

Meridy shook her head. "It won't be *too* dangerous to go just a little closer. . . ."

But then Niniol snapped, so forcefully she couldn't ignore him, "May the God forgive the stupidity of children! Stop right here!" He had his sword in his hand, naked blade glittering like ice in the sun to Meridy's eyes, and strode forward, back stiff with annoyance, to put himself between the girls and the commotion.

Meridy felt her face heat and was glad Niniol had his back to them, because she could imagine his expression. She was embarrassed, but she still wanted to *see.* She stood on her toes, peering ahead.

The fire horse was contained, barely, by a circle of men, a circle that bowed outward when the animal charged and bent forward again when it gave back. The men had long spears—that was how they were keeping the fire horse in the circle. Other men had heavy, powerful crossbows, but they weren't shooting, not yet.

The fire horse had been chained, Meridy saw, but now the broken length of chain dangled from its neck, whipping around dangerously when it whirled and lunged in a different direction. It had been hobbled, too, but the hobbles had only been ordinary leather and it had broken them—or probably bitten them through. Its powerful jaws certainly looked up to the job. The beast had savage tusks longer than a man's hand, jutting upward like those of a boar. Now Meridy remembered the princess-regent's fire horse had had tusks like that, too, but this one's tusks were much heavier and longer. They were grotesque yet somehow didn't ruin the elegance of its head. When it reared and screamed, the sound resonated with fury, not fear or pain.

This one was blood bay; a brighter red than any horse, only a little darker than the fresh blood running down from the narrow wounds scored across its chest and heavy neck—it must be a stallion, with a neck like that; yes, that would explain the vicious tusks, too.

The stallion's mane flew as he reared and screamed and slashed with his tusks, trying to catch and break the spears. His claws flashed ivory amid the black feathering of his feet. He was terrifying and magnificent, and now that she saw him, she understood why kings and princes would pay a bounty for the chance to try to tame one of these monstrous creatures. But she couldn't imagine little Herren trying to ride this terrible beast. The idea would surely terrify a child. It would certainly terrify *her*.

"My lord!" shouted one of the men. "We'll never get a chain on it again! You must give the order to shoot!" This wasn't one of the ones with a spear but a man standing back a little way, near Meridy and her friends, in fact. He stood like someone important: with his hands on his hips and a thunderous expression on his face.

The man to whom he spoke was younger and a lot more elegant and quite astoundingly handsome. Meridy understood immediately exactly what Diöllin had meant by declaring, *Everyone knows Lord Taimonuol, trust me on this!* She could imagine that every girl in all Cora Diorr would recognize this man. He had the most beautiful golden hair and fine hands, and even now he wore a fancy sapphire-blue shirt with black and violet ribbons lacing up the sleeves. His eyes were blue, too, almost as dark and pure a blue as his shirt. She exchanged a look with Jaift, who raised her eyebrows and mouthed, discreetly under her breath, *Worth a look!*

Meridy would have laughed, except she was sorry for the

fire horse stallion and afraid for the men trying to keep him under control. She could see the older man was right: no one was ever going to be able to get another chain on the stallion. She wasn't even exactly sorry that recapturing the beast seemed impossible; chains and captivity seemed a miserable fate for him.

But the golden lord did not seem quite ready to admit defeat. "Let's not be hasty, Connar," he said to the older man. "We can run him back and forth, wear him down, let thirst work on him. He'll not keep this show up long." *He* didn't shout but spoke in a cold, level voice that somehow carried better than a shout.

Niniol snorted, plainly skeptical of this assertion.

Diöllin agreed scornfully. "Just like Taimonuol. He's always been too arrogant to see plain sense."

"My lord—" the other man, Connar, began, but he got no further because at that moment the fire horse reared, whirled, lunged—then twisted unexpectedly to the side and snapped twice, first catching and shattering a man's spear, then closing his terrible jaws on the man's side, just above his hip. The stallion jerked the screaming man off his feet, flung him aside, and attacked the man's neighbors while they struggled to close their ranks. Suddenly there was a tangle of screaming fire horse and shouting men, everything far too fast and violent and confused for Meridy to follow—she backed away, only realizing she was clinging to Jaift when she stumbled and the other girl put an arm around her to steady her.

Then the fire horse broke free of the ring of men and raced away, clawed feet digging into the earth, hurtling toward the city, head high and mane flying.

The lord cursed, low and bitterly.

"Shoot it down!" ordered Connar. "Shoot!"

The lord shook his head in disgust and gestured assent to the crossbowmen. Quarrels flicked out from the heavy crossbows. Two men missed, but four quarrels struck the fire horse in the back and haunches and side, and he screamed—still a sound of fury rather than fear—as his rear legs collapsed under him.

"Oh!" whispered Jaift, turning her face away.

The fire horse flung his head up, raked the earth once more with his terrible claws, and died as another half dozen quarrels followed the first. But almost at once, his ghost pitched himself violently up and leaped into furious flight toward the mountains surrounding the city. Meridy felt better, seeing this evidence that the beast might have died but that death was not the end.

The fire horse's ghost didn't take the Moon's Road out of the *real,* however. His path curved in a long arc away and around, and Meridy didn't see the pearly white of the Moon's Road open up before him. She was surprised, but the fire horse must have been too angry and distraught to go to the God's hand right away. Until she lost sight of the translucent ghost against the sky and the mountains, he fled faster and more lightly than any living animal, seeming hardly to touch the earth at all.

"May the God have pity on the poor beast, and take it gently!" Jaift murmured, her gaze also following that flight. Meridy nodded in agreement, though he didn't look much inclined to go gently even to the God.

Beside her, Diöllin said caustically, "Well, that was certainly worthwhile. I trust you enjoyed your little expedition. Nothing like *keeping a low profile* and *slipping quietly into Cora Diorr.*"

Meridy tightened her lips against the urge to reply, since

now a handful of the men were turning to regard her and Jaift. Not the lord—he was striding away toward the dead fire horse, everything about him eloquent of disgust and anger even from the back. But the older man, Connar, did not seem best pleased to see spectators in among his people. He swept one summing look across the two girls and frowned at them.

Meridy straightened her back and met Connar's hard gaze.

Before she could speak, Jaift cleared her throat. "What a terrible disappointment," she declared with ready sympathy. "And after getting it nearly all the way! What a magnificent beast it was!"

Connar shifted his frown to Jaift. "A fool's errand from start to finish," he said flatly. "The other one did enough harm, didn't it, and now, *now* nothing will do but to bring in another." Losing his temper, the man began speaking more loudly and more quickly. "And for what? More than like to kill His little Highness, the God forfend! But try to persuade Her Highness of that! No, she must have a fire horse and she must see her son on its back, and never mind no one's challenging his right to the throne, never mind how many men are savaged in the doing! She's got half the privy council paying Southern hunters to leave off trapping useful fur in order to capture one of these monsters, and now my lord's lost his senses and joined in—" He bit that off, breathing hard, apparently realizing that he was ranting about his lord's affairs to perfect strangers.

"Terrible," said Jaift, shaking her head.

"Terrible enough! Just as well it's dead; no one would have tamed that one. Well, it's done and the show's over." He eyed Meridy. "On your way to the city to present yourself to the princess-regent, are you? Yes, well, better she collect any black-eyed girls those Southerners left behind them than fire horses! You'd best get on your way, you and your—sister, is it?" But Meridy didn't look anything like Jaift, so he added, "Or your friend, as may be."

Meridy bobbed her head in agreement. "Yes, excellent sir, thank you."

"Don't thank me, girl, and don't be behindhand to attend on Her Highness. If you mean to dwell in Cora Diorr, get a proper badge so folk know you've been counted and added to the rolls." But after this curt instruction, Connar turned back to his own affairs and seemed to forget about Meridy and Jaift completely.

Meridy was relieved by his lack of interest. She said to Jaift in a low voice as they turned away to rejoin the carter, "I never thought people would be *less* interested in a girl with black eyes! But obviously a witch must be on her way to Cora Diorr in answer to the prince's law. Everyone knows that!"

Jaift frowned at her. "I guess you need a badge to blend in, though."

"A Black Swan," Diöllin said in her bodiless voice. "The White Swan for guardsmen and the Black Swan for witches. I thought you knew."

"How could we, if you didn't say?" Meridy demanded, exasperated.

Jaift said peaceably, "It doesn't matter. If anyone asks, we'll tell them you're on your way to present yourself to Her Highness and haven't a badge yet. Who would know otherwise?"

Meridy shrugged.

"And we'll find a place to stay out on the edge of the city," added Jaift, "and then keep close while we decide what to do, and how to find poor little Herren. Diöllin will know where *that woman* has him, I suppose. Or how to find out." She hadn't called the princess-regent by name or proper title since finding out how horribly she'd betrayed her own children. She said now, "Diöllin, I wonder—" But Jans had brought his wagon forward, his mules not objecting now that the excitement was over. So Jaift raised her voice and said instead, artlessly, "It was a blood bay stallion, but they had to shoot it. What a shame, everything going wrong after they'd got it so far!"

"Everything going wrong! I should say so, if the monster got away from them this close to the city!" exclaimed Jans. "Just as well, though! I can hardly see as Princess Tiamanaith would want her little son anywhere near the creature, after what happened last time! But royalty are always a bit touched, you know, so you never know, do you?"

Diöllin set her hands on her hips. "A bit touched. Really?"

Meridy said hastily, "Yes, it was a terrible accident."

Rolling her eyes, Diöllin turned her back on them both.

"Indeed, terrible! After that, you'd think Princess Tiamanaith, princess-regent now, of course, would have had the beast killed. But she didn't, you know. She rides it herself now, so they say, though I haven't seen it with my own eyes. But I heard she had poor Seneschal Roann arrested after the accident and appointed a man of her own to his place—"

Diöllin whirled back toward him. "Roann Mahonis! Arrested?"

Of course Jans didn't hear her. He went on matter-of-factly, "And I must say, though I don't know anything to the new man's discredit, everyone knows Lord Roann was always a good, careful seneschal to the prince, and it seems awfully high-handed to me—"

"High-handed!" cried Diöllin. "It's a sin against the God!"

"—to put in a new seneschal when nothing that happened was Lord Roann's fault, by anything I know. If anyone should have known the girth was worn, it's the stable master, that's plain enough. Princess Tiamanaith had him arrested, too, and maybe she wasn't wrong there. Me, though, I doubt it was any man's fault. No one's ever said fire horses are easily mastered! No, Prince Diöllonuor knew his risks, I grant him that. But Princess Tiamanaith had to blame someone, I suppose, and Lord Roann ought to have known better than to call down the God's curse on her, especially as he's a priest—"

"He did *not*!" cried the princess. "As if he *would*!"

"—and that's why the princess-regent had him taken up by the palace guard," concluded Jans, with some enthusiasm at the dramatic tale. "A bit harsh, one might say, but it must have been a terrible blow, losing her daughter as well as her lord. I'd have thought, myself, the princess-regent would've had enough of the monstrous beasts! But she's an ambitious one by all accounts—"

"Oh! This is impossible!" Diöllin stood, fists clenched, with the sunlight streaming through her, a girl of air and ice, but passionate and furious as though she were made of fire. All at once Meridy realized she and Jaift had been turning back and forth between the ghost and the carter in fascination. She quickly nudged Jaift, who jerked in surprise, then realized what Meridy meant and fixed her gaze firmly on the carter.

The man only went on, unstoppably oblivious, "Anyway, it's true the little prince would be guaranteed his father's place if he could show himself astride a fire horse, ride it through the city, maybe do an entire progress through Cora Tal, show everyone whose blood he carries. You can imagine! Otherwise who knows, a child like that, a long regency with a woman on Cora Tal's throne, any mischance might—"

"No!" cried Diöllin. "I won't let it happen!"

And at the same moment, speaking over the ghost, Jaift said fiercely, "Don't speak of such things!"

The carter snapped his mouth shut, looking astonished. "Well, now," he said. "Well, now. I didn't mean anything by it, I'm sure. I'm sure I wish the little prince the God's good fortune!"

Meridy said quickly, "It's a fascinating and terrible story, and I guess we can be relieved this other fire horse had to be put down. What a tragedy for us all, and for Her Highness Princess Tiamanaith! But, um, as we're coming up on Cora Diorr, perhaps you can recommend a place near the edge of the city for us to clean up before I present myself."

As a means of turning the topic, this seemed terribly clumsy, but Jans did, of course, know of an inn near the edge of the city, and a chatty discourse on the superior quality of the inns and public houses of Cora Diorr was a small price to pay for a ride to the nearest. It was no trouble, he assured them, just a bit out of his way, well worth a few moments of his time so the girls wouldn't have to walk an extra mile. Though he declared he also knew a much better inn a few streets farther in. "Not grand, mind, but plainspoken girls like you aren't looking for grand, I shouldn't think. The Rose and Lark is clean, and the food's good. That one off there"— and he gestured in casual disdain toward the sign with its two stars and two moons and two leaping fish—"well, it'll *do,* I suppose, but it can't compare. Anybody in the city would tell you the same."

Jaift said diplomatically, "I'm sure you're right, and we do thank you for your guidance and advice, but after all, we won't stay there long. I see there's a bathhouse, and that's all that matters. A bath and a change, you know, and then we'll make our way to the palace. . . ." She glanced significantly at Meridy.

"Of course, of course," agreed the carter. "Very wise of you both; it's best to start as you mean to go on, and nothing makes an introduction go off better than a few ribbons and a bit of lace, as they say. So, then, look there, that's the way to Fifth—the straight streets are numbered, you know, starting from the direction of sunrise at midsummer round about that way, so it's easy enough to keep track of where you are. Clever, isn't it? Now, ask for the seneschal, the new one is Kais Norren, did I tell you? Well, mind you keep a courteous tongue with him—he's already famous for his short patience with country folk—"

"Wonderful," Meridy muttered, and then remembered that of course they wouldn't be seeking out the new seneschal at all, so his temper didn't matter.

"You'll get on very well with all them up there," promised Jans. "We're friendly folk in Cora Diorr, even the witches. You'll see." And he clucked to his mules, which strode out with a will, knowing their stable was nearby.

Meridy, at least, felt both deeply relieved and oddly bereft to lose sight of the carter and his wagon. She looked around—at the public house and the street and the city beyond. The street here seemed crowded, but not like Riam. Here, even right on the outskirts of Cora Diorr, with the circle of mountains rising up seemingly directly behind them, when they faced into the city, there were already a lot of buildings close together.

Everything was built of that grayish and yellowish stone;

there was almost no wood, and little plaster to soften the stone. Slate roofs, not cedar shingles; here and there maroon tiles not only on the rooftops but set into the gray walls. The city of Cora Diorr had been laid out within the encircling mountains and so of course it had been built of the same stone. It wasn't *unattractive,* she thought, but . . . she couldn't imagine feeling comfortable here. This city seemed cold and hard, and if you turned your back on it and looked outward, the horizon was too close and too steep. She thought if she lived here, she would start to feel confined and then trapped. She wondered if Prince Diöllonuor had ever let his witches leave, if they didn't like Cora Diorr. Maybe not. Everyone knew the prince had wanted his witches to stay under his eye. Even she knew that.

Good thing she wasn't planning to actually meet the princess-regent. No. All they had to do was find Herren. Well, find Herren and then . . . after that the plan seemed a little indistinct. But once they had Herren with them and safe, surely they could sort out exactly what to do next. Herren had sounded like he had an idea, just before the princess-regent snatched him away. . . .

"Maybe you'd like it if you grew up here," Niniol muttered beside her, squinting first at the mountains rising up at their backs and then at the city rising up before them. "Maybe it'd make you feel safe instead of . . . closed in."

He sounded exactly like she felt: stifled and a bit dismayed. Meridy found herself somehow relieved to have her own feelings echoed so clearly, but Jaift, looking around eagerly, said, "What do you mean? It's so interesting. I'd like to find one of the white streets—numbered from the sunrise, Jans said. Isn't that so interesting and organized? But numbers aren't very pretty, so that's a shame. They ought to have named them after . . . I don't know. Clouds or white flowers or something. I want to see the palace better. It must be beautiful, don't you think?"

"But we shouldn't actually go there . . . ," Meridy said doubtfully.

"Oh, no, I don't think that would be wise! Not without thinking things through."

"Thinking things through," Diöllin repeated, her tone sardonic.

Jaift tilted her head, her eyes narrowing. Meridy said quickly, before they could argue, "So what should we do first?"

"We must find out what's happened to Herren!" snapped Diöllin. "And Roann Mahonis! I still can't believe she had him *arrested*!"

Niniol said firmly, "*First* we need to get out of public view; that would be *my* suggestion."

"We'll take a room," said practical Jaift, with a cool look for Diöllin and a smile for Niniol. She went on briskly, "We need to get out of the street, especially Mery and, um . . ." She meant Diöllin, who might be spotted by any of the city's witches, but was too sensible to say the princess's name out loud now that they were in the city. "Then we must find out where there's a branch of my family's bank."

"Your mother won't have changed the numbers on the accounts?" said Niniol. "If they'd hired couriers, they could have already changed the numbers in all the important towns in Cora Tal and Harann both. . . ."

"No, no, of course not! My family wouldn't have done that!" Jaift sounded shocked. "Cut me off? Hardly! But . . ." Her tone became more thoughtful. "Asked for a message to be sent if I make a withdrawal . . . they might have done that. Hmm."

"Does it matter?" asked Meridy. "I mean, we have enough, don't we?"

"Well, yes." But Jaift didn't sound happy. "I should have drawn out more to start, but then you have to worry about pickpockets and things. . . . You don't want too much in your pouch, Mother always says. . . ." She was starting to sound uncertain.

"As long as we have enough for now," Meridy said quickly. "What should we do, then?"

"Well . . ." Jaift rubbed her lips, considering. "I suppose once we know more clearly where Herren is, it might be useful to know what rumors are running through the city about the princess-regent. The servants who work for Cora Diorr's noble families will know who's trustworthy, I expect, and who's still loyal to the old seneschal. Servants always do know things, Mother says. Anyway, we can find out, and then we can decide what to do and where to take Herren once we get him back. But first we should make sure we have a place to stay." She looked without enthusiasm at the public house with its two stars and two leaping fish.

Very practical, all of that, Meridy agreed. She wished she had some general idea what it *was* they actually needed to do—what they could do, what they *ought* to do.

She wished Carad Mereth would come back. She hoped that, despite all their fears, he was actually all right. She wished she could believe that he had bested Tai-Enchar's servitor and hadn't fallen into the witch-king's power himself.

More, even, than that, she wished Iëhiy would come back. She longed to be certain the wolfhound was all right. Well, of course Iëhiy wasn't alive anyway, but that wouldn't protect him from Tai-Enchar. She wished she knew *everyone* was all right, no matter how mysterious and annoying they might be.

But she and Jaift only had each other, and the hope that the God favored them. That would have to be enough.

The others were all heading toward the public house now. Before she followed them, Meridy turned once more to look back. A haze seemed to fill the warm air between the city and the encircling mountains, as though a transparent curtain had been drawn closing them all away from the open road. Closing them all into Cora Diorr.

Somewhere far away, between the city and the mountains, she almost thought she glimpsed the ghost of the fire horse, rearing against the sky with sunlight streaming through his transparent mane and limning the lines of his elegant head and long neck. He raked his claws against the sky, in defiance of men or perhaps death or the God, and flung himself forward.

Then the sun went behind a wisp of cloud and the sunlight dimmed, and she was no longer certain whether she'd seen anything after all or only imagined it.

"Mery! Are you coming?" called Jaift, half turning, and Meridy spared a second for one more searching look across the cluttered roads to the empty land beyond, turned her back to the fire horse—free now, unlike the rest of them, of life and the living—and went to follow her friend.

seventeen

Meridy wiggled her way around a corner tight enough that she had to let out her breath and twist through sideways. It wasn't as though she were big. Secret passages sized for children! It was ridiculous.

Though that wasn't quite fair. Most of the time the passage was wide enough; it was only some of these corners. It must be trickier than she'd imagined to fit secret passages into walls. Not that she'd ever actually thought about it one way or another, the cottages in Tikiy not being well suited to such creative architecture.

The important point was that the passages were here below the palace and that Diöllin knew about them.

That first night they'd spent in Cora Diorr, Diöllin had made her way carefully all around the palace in the dead of night, when ghosts were hardest to see even for witches, and when she'd come back, she'd said she was certain her brother was beneath the palace, in the upper dungeons. "Where else could he be?" she had asked rhetorically. "He's definitely within the outer palace walls and way down low beneath the earth, and there isn't any place down there except the dungeons."

"Your mother put her little son in the . . . dungeons." Jaift spoke, not exactly as though she didn't believe Diöllin, but as though she didn't *really* believe it. Not even after all they knew and had guessed about the princess-regent.

Meridy agreed with Jaift. It *was* terrible. How must he feel, snatched away from the witch-king's terrifying servitor by his mother only to have her lock him up in a *dungeon*? Or at least, to be treated so by the sorceress who wore his mother's form. Meridy didn't want to imagine Aseraiëth pithing poor Tiamanaith like a reed and filling her up again with her own soul. But it was impossible to put the image out of her mind.

"The upper dungeons, at least, aren't so horrible," Diöllin had said, but tentatively, more as though she were trying to reassure herself than convince anyone else. At least, Meridy was fairly certain no one had been convinced.

But then Diöllin had told them about the secret way in and out of the upper dungeons, and promised them no one knew about that passage except herself. "My father showed me," she had explained, drawing a confusing sketch of lines and angles with the tip of one finger on the coverlet of the bed in the room Meridy was sharing with Jaift. The image lingered, shimmering faintly with *ethereal* light, after she drew it. "He said his mother showed him, and her father showed her. From ruling prince or princess to firstborn heir. Only we knew. No one else."

Meridy had hesitated, but Niniol had asked bluntly for them all, "You're *certain* your mother never knew, are you?"

That was an ugly question, and it had produced an ugly pause. "We shall have to hope not," Diöllin said at last.

Niniol had shaken his head in disgust. "Fools depend on *hope*. What if His little Highness isn't in the upper dungeons after all? Have you a secret way into the lower dungeons as well? Or, say you know exactly where he is, have you a way to slip past the guardsmen? Surely there are guardsmen. If I had that duty, I'd be ashamed to let children come and go under my watch, far less prisoners. Or, say you manage to get the boy out; then what? Her Highness found him easily enough once the witch-king lost him; what's to stop her from doing it again?"

Diöllin had not been able to answer him. None of them had been able to answer him. It had all been very uncomfortable.

But then Jaift had lifted a tentative hand. "All that is true, everything Niniol says. But there's no point in trying to think of everything at once when we don't know anything, is there? The only way to find out just where Herren is or whether you can slip past the guards and reach him is to try. Then at least we'll know that much."

There had been a little pause. Then Meridy had said, "If Diöllin finds the right cell, I think she could help me open the door. And for after—Diöllin, don't you know people who would've been terribly offended by Lord Roann's arrest? They might help Herren against the princess-regent, isn't that so?"

"Yes," Diöllin had agreed eagerly. "Lord Perann—Roann's brother. He would certainly help us!"

So after that even Niniol had agreed grudgingly that, as plans went, it was terrible, yet maybe not so terrible as doing nothing. "But it's lucky I'm here to go with you," he'd told Meridy and Diöllin. "You'll both swear to listen to me and *take advice* and never mind one of you is a witch and the other royal. Hear me?"

Diöllin had been offended, but Meridy had agreed fervently, and made Diöllin promise, too, though the princess had been a bit stiff about it.

"This way down into the dungeons worries me most,

whatever Prince Diöllonuor told Princess Diöllin," muttered Niniol. "Just the ruler to his heir, that's all well and good, but no one can truly be certain of secrets. It's always wisest to assume your enemy knows more than you would wish."

But they had to do *something*. So now Meridy found herself sneaking through hidden passages right inside the smooth white walls of the palace and wiggling her way around obnoxiously tight corners.

Coming to the end of the current passageway, she slipped back the spy panel for a quick look at the outer hall. She had to stand on her toes to peek out. Made for thin, *tall* people, this passageway. If she'd known, she might have brought something to stand on.

But she was definitely glad she'd had a chance to look. Because there was, most annoyingly, a kitchen boy or some such on the landing, kissing a girl who was probably a young maid. Cursing inwardly, Meridy wondered whether it would be a greater risk to delay, hoping the two of them would go away on their own, or to try to frighten them off with some well-selected ghostly noises.

A door slamming on the landing above fortunately decided the matter for her; the pair ducked giggling down the stairs and vanished. Whoever had come onto the stairs above went up. Meridy listened long enough to be sure of this, then slipped the catch on the hidden door and stepped out into the stairway. She ran down the stairs to the third landing from the bottom—four nerve-racking flights. Fortunately Diöllin seemed to be right about these stairs being little trafficked, which had no doubt been the appeal to the maid and the kitchen boy. Meridy met no one and made it to the third landing without incident, with Diöllin whirling around her and pointing imperiously at the steps to show her where the hidden panel was.

"I *know*, all right?" Meridy whispered. "Just keep a lookout for anybody, will you? *That* would be useful." She didn't know how useful Diöllin would be as a guard, in fact; what did a princess know about such tasks? But Niniol, steady as always, was right beside her. Him Meridy trusted.

The hidden panel was actually built into the steps themselves. She had to get the first riser up from the landing out of the way before she could lift the step, which was a good deal more difficult than Diöllin had implied. It was set in so solidly that at first Meridy thought the princess had counted stairs or landings wrong and the stone was truly immobile; but Diöllin insisted, and at last the stone moved a fraction, so Meridy knew it was the right one after all. She ought to have brought something to pry with, but no. And had anybody suggested it? Again, no. She pried harder, her stomach knotting up at the idea of having to admit defeat and sneak back out of the palace without anything to show for the whole effort. She'd been tense since they'd all decided on this ridiculous plan, but she'd *said* she would do it and now if she couldn't—well, she was sure Jaift would sympathize, but Meridy didn't even want to imagine what Diöllin would say.

Jaift had come to the palace along with Meridy and the ghosts, because Diöllin said Lord Perann had an apartment in the outer ring of spires and that was where Jaift was most likely to find him. They'd separated at the outer ring, Jaift to find Lord Perann and Meridy going on toward the central spire of the main palace. But Meridy had been glad to have Jaift's company on their way through the city anyway. Cora Diorr had been confusing, crowded even as dusk crept through the narrow streets and laid shadows across the streets. There were lanterns along the alleys and in windows and below the eaves along with the prayer bells, and as far as Meridy could tell, the people of Cora Diorr simply never went to bed at all.

She didn't like the crowded streets; or the tall, narrow buildings that seemed to lean over them; or the frowning, unfriendly glances both she and Jaift drew. Somehow the City of Spires felt . . . not just closed in. It felt lonely. As though despite the noise and hurry and crowding and dirt, everyone in this city was essentially alone.

No doubt Meridy felt that way because she and Jaift were strangers to Cora Diorr. But besides that, Meridy had the sense that they were being followed. Niniol said not, and so she knew she must simply be feeling nervous and jumpy in this strange city.

But at least, unpleasant as she found the city, Meridy had to admit that a pair of girls did seem able to make their way through the city at dusk, and then along the white street right up to the palace, all without drawing attention.

The white spires had looked tall and delicate from a distance, but from beneath they looked much taller and considerably more massive. Perhaps especially by night, the palace didn't look like something that had been built by ordinary men. Meridy thought the towers must really have been raised up by sorcery—she had suspected the carter might be making up that tale just because it sounded impressive, but it just did not seem like any normal effort of men could build anything so smooth and graceful and perfect.

Diöllin showed them one of the servants' entrances to the lower levels of the palace, and from there she'd directed Meridy to the deep cellars and the entrance to the secret passages. "There were already caverns here," the princess explained.

"Filled with water, some of them, but that was all to the good: like a wonderful deep cistern for the whole city. But Prince Tirnamuon used the caverns in his building, and of course that's where he got all this white stone. My father said—" But she had fallen silent then, and she wordlessly showed them where to go.

So Meridy had thought, her stomach clenching, *Well, that's the easy part right there.* Because no matter how nervous she'd been to that point, once they were in, everything got more frightening. Meridy had to sneak into the dungeons and find Herren and get him away, while poor Jaift had to go all by herself to find Lord Perann Mahonis. Diöllin had sworn that Lord Perann would never believe that his brother had betrayed Prince Diöllonuor; not possibly. She was certain he would help them. Meridy wasn't so sure. Jaift was good with people and good at managing things; she insisted she would be fine. But if she couldn't persuade Lord Perann . . . well, the plan got more nebulous after that.

It really was a stupid plan. Niniol was right about that. But none of them thought they dared wait and wait and wait until they got every single bell lined up to ring at exactly the same instant.

At least Meridy had Diöllin to show her where to go and how to get in and out of her ancestor's secret passages. And more comforting still, she had Niniol at her back. Though neither Diöllin nor Niniol could actually *open* a stuck panel or pry a stone out of the way, either.

In the end, Meridy broke a fingernail getting the stone out of the riser. It hurt, but she couldn't complain because Diöllin might have understood, but she didn't want to look like a baby in front of Niniol.

So then Meridy had to lie on her belly on the landing

and wiggle through feetfirst. It was a tight fit, and not much good for her clothing, either, but at least she'd put her village homespun back on, as closer to what one of the palace servants might wear. Anyway, awkward as it was, this particular passage, according to Diöllin, led in a straight fall directly to the upper dungeons, with stones set out of the wall to form a kind of ladder. There were no more than four inches of grip for each stone, and those few inches gritty with accumulated dust and sometimes fouled as well with other substances that did not bear imagining. Even worse, the webs of spiders crossed and recrossed the narrow shaft, clinging to and winding about anything that touched them.

The climb was awful. A fall would be a serious matter; so far as she could see, there would be no chance to catch yourself before you hit the foot of the shaft nearly eighty feet below. Meridy went straight down without a pause, drawing a quick breath of relief when she at last reached the bottom safely. There was just room to stand and stretch her arms out, but she knew one of the walls was false and led into one of the cells. Besides her *ethereal* light, there was a little *real* light here, too. It fed in from chinks between the stones of the false wall. The air, circulating gently from those cracks, smelled of rats and damp and growing fungus.

"Ugh!" she whispered, though even that small sound echoed and reechoed alarmingly, little breathy *uh uh uh* sounds, and she froze, listening in case anybody might have noticed. But she heard nothing.

She couldn't see through the chinks very well, but enough to be fairly certain the cell was indeed empty. It looked about four or five strides across, not really square but oddly shaped. Two of the walls looked like they might even have been part of the original cavern, the stone folded and rippled; a third was made of the same kind of stone, but carved into ordinary blocks and mortared together. The bars that formed the fourth wall were close set in a grid, the spaces almost too small even to put a hand through. It all looked thoroughly secure and escape-proof, if you didn't know about the hidden way out.

She had asked Diöllin why in the world the princes of Cora Tal might have built secret ways into and out of their own dungeons.

Diöllin had shrugged. "You never know what might come up, I guess. Prince Tiranann once imprisoned his own daughter in this very cell, when she tried to run off with a common lover—didn't you ever hear that story? But he also must have told her about the way out, because she escaped and rescued her lover and they ran off together to live in Tian Diorr, in the far north of Tian Sur, as far from Cora Diorr as they could get. Herren and I still have distant cousins in Tian Diorr, though officially our two families aren't supposed to know about each other."

And now here Meridy was, studying the very same cell. She ran her hands over the false wall, looking for the catch that was supposed to be . . . yes, here. She began to press down on the catch, hoping that it wouldn't make any noise or, if it did, that no one would be near enough to hear the sound. But Niniol stopped her, holding up an imperative hand and stepping through the wall. Meridy let her breath out, feeling stupid. Of course she should have thought of that.

She waited for Niniol to come back, mentally running through the endless list of disasters that could occur. One of the guards might turn out to be a witch, since there were so many in Cora Diorr, and he'd see Niniol and give the alarm. Or despite what Diöllin thought, Herren might not be in this part of the dungeons at all; he might have been imprisoned lower down, in the lower dungeons, utterly out of reach. Or a special guard might have been mounted outside his cell. Or the guards might patrol frequently, so it would be impossible to get past them without being caught. Or another prisoner might wake up and raise a shout, out of either surprise or despair that he wasn't the object of the rescue. Or, most unbearable of all, Princess Tiamanaith or even the witch-king might already have done something dreadful to Herren and they might just *be too late*—

"Stop that," Diöllin said, her attenuated voice in Meridy's ear.

Meridy twitched guiltily. "What?"

"You're thinking terrible thoughts," the princess whispered. "I can tell."

Meridy gave her a look. "I have a right! Look what you got me into! That awful climb, all those spiders and that horrible slimy fungus or whatever—"

"Oh, please! You're a village child; you can't tell me you worry about a little dirt!"

Perhaps fortunately, Niniol came back as suddenly as he'd gone, interrupting Meridy before she could answer this as it deserved. He tilted his head ironically, but all he said was, "There's a guard station at the far end of the corridor, and three men on guard there even at this hour. Sound will carry down here, so try to be quiet!"

Meridy nodded understanding and pressed gently on the catch. Then harder. Then harder still and never mind if it made a noise; it was stiff with grime and disuse. The grinding snap when it gave was gritty, muffled, and louder than she would have liked. She eased the panel out of the way a little at a time and hoped the noise she made sounded ordinary to the guards. Niniol, glowering in annoyance, stepped through the wall and out into the corridor, then put his hand back through the grate at the front of the cell and beckoned, so she knew the corridor must still be clear. Intensely grateful for his presence, she edged out of the shaft into the main part of the cell. It was not quite dark; light from lamps in the corridor caught on the iron and brass of the bars and was reflected from the stone where moisture had seeped through the floor or slicked the walls.

"There's a key hidden in the shaft," the princess whispered. "A key in the shaft and another key hidden behind a stone out in the corridor, so someone can get either in or out of this cell." She pointed, lamplight barely showing the lift of her arm.

Reaching back into the shaft, Meridy felt across the wall at the edge of the open panel and almost at once located the little packet of waxed canvas and leather that held the key. She unwrapped the key as slowly and carefully as she could, the canvas crinkling alarmingly. Then she crossed the cell to the door. Niniol was still waiting, tense but patient, so she knew no guard had come closer yet. She couldn't resist laying her cheek flat against the bars and looking for herself. But Niniol was right, of course; no one was in sight. She could hear masculine voices, but only faintly.

"They'll patrol now and then," Niniol murmured. "Or I would. Let's be quick."

Meridy nodded. She found the jar of oil—Jaift's idea, of course—and reached awkwardly between the bars to oil the hinges. The oil spilled a little, but she didn't care as long as the odor wasn't too noticeable.

She unlocked the cell door and pushed it gently open—wincing at the quiet *scriiik* it made, but in fact the noise wasn't bad; she was very grateful to Jaift for thinking of the oil. She took a moment to hide the key back in its place. Then, stepping out into the corridor, she closed the door again behind her. Niniol put out a hand to stop her closing it quite all the way. "Shutting it will make more noise. Leave it a little ajar."

Meridy nodded again. That seemed best anyway, in case a rapid exit should be required. Then she stepped cautiously into the corridor.

Nothing happened. No one jumped out at her, as she'd half expected. She could still hear the guards' voices, an indistinct, lazy mutter. There was no sign at all anyone had heard her. Her heart, which had been racing, slowed to something nearer nervousness than terror.

"This," Diöllin murmured voicelessly in Meridy's ear, "is almost too easy."

"Hush! You'll bring down bad luck on us," Meridy whispered back, only half joking. "Listen! No one's coming, are they?"

"No," said Niniol, his head tilted, listening too. "Not yet. Careless bastards. Be quick, now. The last thing we need is to fall afoul of a Godforsaken routine inspection. If I were their officer, I'd require one at some random time each night."

Meridy agreed but turned in a half circle, uncertain. It was all very well to determine that they had to find Herren and then climb down here to do it, but now it seemed rather another thing to walk openly up and down before all the cells *looking* for him. The guards couldn't be so very unalert as to fail to notice someone doing that, and anyway, what about other prisoners? If any of them called out, that would probably draw the guards' attention too.

Meridy looked at Diöllin, who flickered away without

hesitation, down the corridor away from the guard station. Twice the ghost princess paused, clearly uncertain, but then she went on. The corridor angled around as it got farther from the guard station; not a normal angle, but a gentle curve followed by an abrupt jog to the left; it was obvious this whole level of the dungeon had once been part of the caverns. It was much darker down that way, with fewer lanterns and some of those not lit. Diöllin vanished from sight entirely among the dim shadows. Meridy hoped the princess would find her brother in one of the cells that lay around that curve, that Diöllin hadn't been completely wrong about where he'd been put. They all just had to trust that Diöllin always could find her little brother.

She was shivering. Well, it was cold. There was nothing to be afraid of. There were only three guards, after all, and Niniol was right here. Though she didn't quite know how she might draw him into the *real* with neither smoke nor dust nor strong light to work with. She realized now that she should have brought a handful of dust with her. Though without better light, dust might not help much. How stupid not to think of that earlier.

Then Diöllin came back and waved, and Meridy let her breath out and tiptoed in that direction.

"They've got him in the *farthest cell*!" Diöllin whispered indignantly when Meridy reached her. "And you know who's imprisoned with him? *Roann Mahonis!* In the farthest cell of the lot! It's outrageous!"

Meridy stared at her, wanting, suddenly and astonishingly, to laugh. The princess had explained that the cells nearest the guardroom were the least damp and best furnished, and got the first and best food and the first and cleanest water, and were therefore by far the most desirable, on the limited scale of comfort that the upper dungeons offered. The seneschal, and even more the young prince, surely ought to have been given one of the better cells, but anybody could see that would have made breaking out much more difficult, that the fact the two were imprisoned together was a huge, unlooked-for stroke of good fortune. Meridy had never hoped for so much luck. Diöllin, too, must realize how amazingly lucky they'd been. She'd just forgotten for a moment.

"That sounds extremely convenient to me!" Meridy whispered. "I suppose your mother thought she'd guard them both at once, since they're both important, but to me it sounds like the hand of the God has stretched out over us. This way we've a chance of getting them both out right now! Listen, we *can* trust the seneschal, can't we? You're *sure?*"

"Roann Mahonis? Of *course* we can!" Diöllin declared indignantly. "No one more!"

"Oh! You're in *love* with him!" Meridy realized she should have guessed long before. "Why didn't you say so in the first place?"

"I am *not*," protested Diöllin, drawing herself up. "I am not in love with *anybody*. Anyway, it's impossible; he might be a seneschal, but he's only a petty lord—my father would never permit . . . Anyway, I'm *right*. We can trust him. Lord Roann is the most faithful, the cleverest—"

Niniol made a curt gesture, cutting her off. "Your Highness, we don't care! With luck it'll make the man more trustworthy rather than less. Now hush, both of you! The God grant I never again have to slip by a guard post with a couple of prattling children, living or quick!"

Diöllin, with a resentful sniff, fell silent. Blushing, Meridy waved for her to lead the way, but Niniol brushed past the princess, disappearing into the darkness around the angled corridor. Meridy gave Diöllin her best stern look, one she had copied from Aunt Tarana, and followed.

There weren't many cells in this direction, which was surely a good thing—the fewer restless or wakeful prisoners they passed, the better. Meridy couldn't stop herself from peering into each cell as she passed it, with a horrible, irresistible curiosity. No one seemed awake, but some of the cells held shapeless heaps of rags, which must really be prisoners tucked down on their thin pallets. It was awful. These dungeons were dark, and cold, and frightening, and Meridy didn't want to leave *anybody* here, even though she knew that was foolish.

But it was still awful.

Between the poor lighting and the barely suppressed terror, she was afraid she would never have found Prince Herren by herself. Meridy passed two cells and then another and another, at odd intervals, plainly set into natural alcoves rather than carved out according to any deliberate plan. As she passed the next-to-last cell, she became aware of a low scratching sound emanating from the final one in the row. It was a peculiarly stealthy sound, which was not quite the same as merely not being loud. She glanced at Diöllin, who shrugged as though to say, *Well, yes, but what did you expect?* The princess said, her inaudible voice sounding a little defensive, "I did tell you. Roann is clever."

Sneaking forward the last little distance, Meridy saw that this sound was in fact being produced by the seneschal, who, so far from being resigned to his imprisonment, was engaged in the unpromising task of defeating the lock of his cell. For this purpose, he was using a piece of straw and a bent length of wire, and it was the pressure of the wire against the iron of the lock that she had heard. Herren, tucked against the wall on a pallet, was visible only as a lump beneath several blankets. A brazier stood at the foot of the pallet, coals glowing dully, so evidently the princess-regent had not wholly disregarded the surviving heir's well-being.

Niniol strode ahead and stood outside the cell, his hands on his hips, watching the seneschal's efforts with a somewhat nonplussed expression. Now he turned his head and gave Meridy a sardonic look. "He does seem resourceful, I'll grant," he observed.

Meridy nodded. She wasn't sure she thought fiddling around with that wire was exactly useful, but at least it showed a lot of determination.

Meridy had been sufficiently silent on her approach that Lord Roann had not become aware of her, and priest or not, he obviously wasn't a witch because he hadn't heard the ghosts. Thus, he was still working on the lock even when she was only a few feet away. The lock was, of course, on the outside of the cell door, with the key meant to be inserted from the front, and this made it difficult to achieve any sort of access to the keyhole from within the cell. Lord Roann's hands and arms were therefore pressed rather awkwardly against the bars, his fingers twisted to what must have been the point of pain in order to use straw and wire against the lock.

As Meridy watched, he dropped the wire. It fell on the floor outside the cell door. Judging by the strict patience with which the seneschal knelt on the floor and began to try to fish it back within reach with a length of straw, it was not the first time that this particular accident had occurred.

Unable to resist the temptation, Meridy whispered, "Let me get that for you," and picked up the wire.

eighteen

Lord Roann, with a stifled exclamation, first recoiled in shock and then stood up, peering through the dim light as well as he could. Of course he had no idea who Meridy was. He plainly couldn't see Diöllin, who had slipped through the bars to hover protectively over her brother. The princess tried to touch Herren's shoulder and stroke his hair, but of course she couldn't. Giving up, she came back and tried to lay her hand on the seneschal's arm, but she couldn't do that either. From the way she turned to glare at Meridy, she was obviously frustrated. "You didn't have to scare him!" she said.

The seneschal jerked and turned, searching for Diöllin. His lips shaped her name—Meridy couldn't have mistaken it. He had plainly not only heard her voice but recognized it, soundless though it had been. His eyes were dark, but despite the poor light, Meridy was certain they weren't black. She raised her eyebrows at the princess. "Just how many anchors do you *have*?"

The seneschal gave Meridy a swift, gauging look and said to Diöllin, in a low, tense voice, "Ah, Liny! You've found a true anchor, then, a witch who can keep you safe in the world. You trust her?"

"She's braver than you'd think, and her manners are decent, for a village girl."

"Oh, thank you so much," Meridy said drily, though actually from Diöllin that seemed a near paean.

Diöllin ignored her, laying her imperceptible hand on the seneschal's arm, looking into his face. "Roann, I'm so sorry. I would have told them it wasn't your fault, only I couldn't, and they wouldn't have listened anyway." Then she gave Meridy a haughty look. "If he can serve as an anchor, that's all to the good! He's not heavy enough in the *ethereal* to keep me safe from Tai-Enchar, but he's heavy enough to keep me from getting lost, at least unless I get too far away from him. You have to agree, it's much safer for me to be anchored by a *dozen* different people than to allow myself to be lost. Anyway, I'm not—Roann isn't—and besides, it hardly matters *now*."

Meridy had to agree that a dozen anchors couldn't be too many for a ghost who'd caught Tai-Enchar's eye. Stepping closer to the door of the cell, she informed Lord Roann, "Diöllin and I came here to rescue you. Well, Herren, but here you are, too—isn't that lucky?"

Lord Roann took a breath to collect himself. "I admit, I'd welcome a more practical option than picking the lock with that bit of wire. But, listen . . ." His eyes searched her face, assessing.

Meridy felt the strength of his gaze and knew he saw more than she liked. Certainly he must see the Southern blood, obviously running far stronger in her than in the folk of these northern cities. And even in this dim light he could hardly miss her black eyes.

But he said only, "You're a witch, of course, and you've bound Diöllin. How could you dare? And how could you dare bring her *here*?" His voice, neutral on the first few words, sounded increasingly outraged. He went on fiercely, "Don't you realize how dangerous this is for her?"

"*I* brought *her*," Diöllin corrected him. "I asked her to bind me, so don't fuss! I need you, Roann—I mean, we all need you, of course! It's true! Don't *argue*." She said to Meridy, casting her eyes upward, "He always *argues*. But he's not such a fool as to argue about something stupid *now*."

Lord Roann opened his mouth but closed it again without speaking. He took a deep breath instead, probably, Meridy guessed, counting to ten. Or a hundred.

He was not as tall a man as Meridy had expected, and not as handsome. Once she'd realized that Princess Diöllin was in love with him, she had instantly imagined a man more like the unbelievably handsome Lord Taimonuol. But Roann Mahonis was only middling tall and middling good-looking. His hair, cropped sensibly short, was brown and wavy, not golden and smooth; and his face was round rather than aristocratically chiseled; and his hands, where they gripped the bars, were broad and strong, like the hands of a farmer or craftsman. And he was old; over thirty, Meridy thought.

But his gaze was intent, alert, intelligent. She could see how a girl might be impressed by the strength of it.

Leaning forward, he murmured, "Who *are* you? A witch, obviously, but not one of Tiamanaith's. If you've protected Liny—Her Highness—then I'm grateful. But it *is* dangerous for her here. Don't you know there's always at least one witch among the guardsmen? If one of them, an experienced adult, contested you for Diöllin, do you think you could hold her and keep her safe?"

Meridy glared at Diöllin. "Why, no, I don't think Diöllin mentioned about the witches."

"You have to get her away again immediately! Look, let

me wake His Highness—he's a little thing, he may be able to fit between the bars, there's a gap against the far side where the wall's uneven. You can take him and get out—"

"Not without you!" declared Diöllin.

The seneschal flinched and turned back, saying in a low, intense voice, "I'm not—it isn't—what matters is that you get His Highness clear away."

"Yes, and then what? I need *you,* Roann! I don't trust Lord Taimonuol! And Perann's all very well, but he can't get the court behind him the way you can. *You're* the one we need." She added plaintively, "Oh, it's been so awful, Roann! My mother—"

"I know," the seneschal said to her gently. "I know."

Niniol rolled his eyes. "Ah, young love. Perhaps we might open this door sometime soon?"

But Diöllin was already going on and of course Lord Roann hadn't heard Niniol at all. "Roann, what *happened*?" the princess asked. "How could it have happened?" Her voice was low and pained.

Lord Roann's hands moved restlessly across the bars, as if he sought some obscure comfort from the cold metal. But he only shook his head. "The beast seemed under control to me. I'd have suggested a stallion, myself. Fire horse stallions are straightforward, mostly; if they hate you, they show it. A mare can seem easy until she suddenly bites your throat out. Your father did seem to have gentled her. I suggested another month or so to be sure, but you remember how your mother said a showy gesture at the harvest conclave would let your father take precedence over the other princes—"

Diöllin clutched her hands together, shivering with distress. "She did? I didn't know that *she* suggested that."

"That's right. There was that trouble with Larian of Moran

Tal putting on airs at the spring conclave, you remember. If your father had a fire horse under bridle, well, so much for Larian. I thought your father could perfectly well wait for spring, but he wanted to show his beast off this fall. Even so"—and though he did not raise his voice, he leaned forward and spoke with intensity—"Prince Diöllonuor was not careless, and *I* certainly did not slice the girth half through. Nor did the stable master. I think now—" He cut that off, looking at Diöllin.

"You think it was my mother," whispered the princess. "I think so too. Except it wasn't her at all. Not by then. It was a sorceress, a long-dead sorceress. *She* took her."

Lord Roann bowed his head, but to Meridy's astonishment he did not seem surprised. "I'm sorry, Liny. Your mother was never . . . We didn't get on. As you know. But this spring, she seemed . . . though I couldn't see how any witch or sorceress could dare do what it seemed might have been done. I spoke to your father, but he wouldn't hear me."

"You guessed? You didn't tell me."

"Ah, Liny, I wasn't certain; how could I be? Then, that day, the girth broke on the beast's first good plunge, which it shouldn't have. I saw her face when it happened, and I knew. But then you—" He stopped, rubbing a hand hard across his mouth.

"I don't remember," Diöllin said, shuddering. "I don't remember that part."

"I wish I could forget."

"I think we can all imagine," Niniol said, almost gently, though he also added, "But we should save all the tales for later, surely. Tell them to stop all this babble and let's get moving, eh?"

Meridy nodded emphatically. "You're right. Oh, hush,

Diöllin; you know Niniol's right." She could see the shadows of bruises on the seneschal's face, though, and asked worriedly, "But can you walk, Lord Roann? Can you, um, climb?"

"What? You're hurt? They *beat* you?" said Diöllin furiously. "How *dare* they?"

Lord Roann smiled. "I must admit, I have been a little obstreperous. I didn't realize I might have to walk, or climb." He reached out a little, then drew back, as though remembering that he couldn't touch Diöllin's hand. He settled for giving Meridy a short nod instead. "I promise you, I would be delighted to walk, run, climb, or *crawl* out of this place—but if it's going to take more than a moment, then it's too dangerous. What's important now is protecting Herren. Listen to me: you can leave me here—that's all right. Diöllin will know whom you should talk to, whom you can trust. It's His Highness who needs to be taken out of here—"

"Is he all right?" asked Meridy. "Shouldn't he have woken by now?"

Lord Roann glanced over his shoulder toward the young prince, frowning. "They've been giving him a drug. Sweetleaf, I'm nearly certain. Her Highness commanded it, fearing, I think, that he'd begin issuing commands of his own and manage to get someone to listen. . . ."

Meridy frowned, guessing that the actual purpose of the drug, which encouraged deep and dreamless sleep, was to keep a boy like Herren away from the eye and the attention of Tai-Enchar, whose realm lay almost entirely in dreams and memory.

Turning, Lord Roann went swiftly across the cell and knelt beside Herren's pallet. Diöllin fluttered anxiously around him as he gathered the boy up and came back to the front of the cell, where he scowled intently at Meridy. "If you *can* open the door . . . ," he murmured.

"Yes—yes, of course we can open it." The princess flitted toward Meridy but whirled back again as her brother, rousing at last, began to try, vague and wavering as he clearly was, to stand on his own.

Lord Roann laid a finger across Herren's lips, supporting the boy as he struggled to get his balance. Herren didn't fight him; he didn't make a sound. It was terrible that so young a boy should have learned such caution even when he was drugged and half conscious, but he slung an arm over Lord Roann's shoulders and blinked silently around to see what was happening.

"Hush!" Roann murmured. "Sit here—or stand if you like, but softly. Can you do that?"

Herren rubbed his face hard, trying to wake up. Meridy thought again how old he seemed for an almost-nine-year-old—how steady and quiet, though his face was white with nerves and he was surely sick with the drug. She thought his hands were trembling, but she could hardly blame him for that. Hers were too, a little.

"Here, Your Highness," Lord Roann whispered. "That gap by the wall—"

Herren laid a hand on his arm, and the seneschal stopped, looking down at him. "I need you," the prince told him in a low voice, firm for all he could hardly stay on his feet. "Liny, are you—you're here, aren't you? Can you open the door?" He looked at Meridy. "Do you—do you have a key?"

"A *real* key, no," said Meridy. "But . . ." She looked past him, at Diöllin. "Another option, maybe. If you're ready?"

The princess nodded and came quickly back to Meridy's side of the bars.

"Oil the hinges," Niniol reminded them.

Meridy pretended she hadn't forgotten. "Of course." She got out the jar of oil and handed it through the bars to Lord Roann, who was taller. The seneschal took it without further argument and stretched up to oil the hinges of the cell door. Meridy left him to it, laying her left hand on the lock and holding out her right hand to Diöllin.

Diöllin wasn't able to touch the lock on her own, far less shift the tumblers. But she took Meridy's hand, then frowned at the lock as though it had suddenly come into focus for her. Then Meridy had to wait for a truly agonizing period as Diöllin did . . . whatever the quick dead did, to make an *ethereal* object. In this case it was harder, because Diöllin wasn't trying to make something she knew well, or even something she had glimpsed once. She was trying to use the lock itself to make its own *ethereal* key.

Meridy knew she and Diöllin should be able to do this. Ghosts could make *ethereal* objects, the lock itself would shape its own key, it should work. It *should*.

And at least she knew what Diöllin was trying to do. Lord Roann finished with the hinges, tucked the little jar away in a pocket, and then simply had to wait with tense patience for something useful to happen. He put an arm around the young prince's shoulders—Herren was practically swaying. The boy leaned against him, not exactly trustingly, but as though he couldn't stand up entirely on his own and was marginally willing to let the seneschal support him. Meridy suspected Lord Roann's air of edgy quiet was better than she could have managed, if she'd been the one waiting for someone else to open her cell door with magic and sheer force of will.

The wait seemed interminable. The only sounds were a slow trickle of water from somewhere not too far away, and a sudden, disturbing low moaning from some unfortunate prisoner a little way back along the row of cells. Meridy shifted her weight carefully from one foot to the other, trying not to fidget. No doubt this experience was character building—

Dim light from a spell glow slid along something that did not exist. There was nothing there. There was. Meridy squinted, trying to decide whether she was seeing more than merely her own hope. On the other side of the bars, Lord Roann drew in his breath, and Herren straightened shakily, gripping the seneschal's arm. A key, long and pale, limned with light, shaped itself out of the air and rested on nothing, glimmering.

"Try it," Diöllin whispered, her voice in Meridy's ear seeming even more muted than usual.

Meridy reached out with her free hand and touched the key.

For an instant it was hard and cold against her fingers. Then she closed her hand about it, and it puffed into nothing as instantly and completely as though it had never been there at all. Meridy only barely stopped herself from groaning aloud in disappointment. Herren turned his face aside, and Lord Roann gripped his shoulder encouragingly. Meridy looked helplessly at Diöllin.

"Wait," murmured the princess. "Just wait a moment. It's my fault, I let you touch it too soon—it wasn't ready, but I can do it, I know I can. Let me try again."

Another wait, not so long this time. Another key, drawn out of air and imagination to tempt the hand and mock the attempted touch. Gone like the first, a breath of cold solidity lost to the first brush of a living hand.

"It's not going to *work*," Meridy whispered.

"You're both trying too hard, likely," Niniol said impatiently. "Take it slow, touch it gently."

"I can't touch it lightly enough—it isn't going to *work*."

"It will!" Diöllin whispered. "Roann will make it work!"

Meridy, startled, saw for the first time that the seneschal was no longer standing on the other side of the bars. He had turned slightly away and retreated a few steps for what privacy the cell could afford him, leaving Herren, who had crouched down and was leaning against the bars but had made no protest.

The seneschal was kneeling silently, facing one of the cell's stone walls, head bowed. He wore no priest's medal—the warden must have taken it—but even if she hadn't known he was a priest, Meridy could hardly have missed it now. His hands were cupped at his throat where the medal should have been. His neck and shoulders were tight with tension, as though he were attempting some arduous physical task. His voice, in low entreaty, was a thread of sound against the buried silence of the dungeon. Meridy couldn't clearly make out his words, but she could tell he was calling on the God. He was calling the attention of the God, in the name of justice and truth, to the lie the princess-regent had told, the lie that wore Tiamanaith as its face.

"We'll try it once more," Diöllin whispered. "The God's hand will be above us." She sounded quite certain about it.

Meridy wished she were that sure, but maybe . . . maybe it would work now. "Do you think it's safe for you, though?" she asked Diöllin.

Diöllin laughed, a half-audible sound with real amusement in it. "Mery!" she said, though she had not usually called Meridy by that little-name. "I don't know! But Roann is right: what else can we do?"

"Trust the God," Niniol said quietly, but Diöllin was already working on making a third key, which began taking tenuous shape almost at once. The key solidified as Meridy watched, pale and gleaming as if it held an immanent light of its own within its slender form.

Lord Roann had fallen silent. He was perfectly still, as though prepared to stay exactly as he was for hours, or for days. It was not exactly a stillness of waiting; there was nothing in it of either patience or impatience. In some indefinable way Meridy thought it seemed to go beyond any such familiar concepts, to touch a form of stillness greater than mortal men should know. She wanted to say something, anything, just to break the silence. This was surely not the time. She bit her lip and didn't make a sound.

It took a conscious effort to conquer that quiet sufficiently to reach out yet a third time for the key, where it glittered among the shadows of the dungeon hall. As it had been before, it was cold and hard to the touch: but this time there was something more than that first solidity. A tight stinging raced up Meridy's arm and made the back of her neck prickle, as though her hair were trying stand on end; a cold that chilled her hand to the bone as though the key were made of some more unearthly substance than any ice. It burned like the winter made into fire and given form. Meridy came appallingly close to dropping the key in shock; and whether she could have retrieved it or whether it would have fallen instead back into the *ethereal* realm from which it had been created, she had no idea.

Then she closed her fingers about the slender bar of it,

steadied the lock with her other hand, and shoved the key home. It turned with a gritty scraping sound, but once it turned, the lock sprang open as though eager to yield to an irresistible force. Meridy gasped once, in pain and relief, and let go of the key: despite the pain of it, it took a conscious effort to force her hand to open, as though some part of her craved that coldly burning touch. The key, released, fell from the lock and struck the floor. It rang once against the stones, shredded into light and air and silence, and was gone.

nineteen

Meridy simply could not believe she had dropped the key. What a *stupid* thing to do. That golden tone must have been audible all through the dungeons, maybe all through the city. It had sounded exactly like a prayer bell—worse, it had sounded exactly like a prayer bell that the very hand of the God had lifted and struck. The tone, absolutely pure, lingered on the ear even after it had faded into silence, as though the silence were somehow part of the sound. It was the sort of ringing chime that seemed as though it must have been heard everywhere in the entire *world*. Meridy clenched her burned fingers in her other hand, fiercely blinked back tears as the sharp pain faded, and stared at Niniol.

Niniol drew his sword, a whisper of *ethereal* sound, and took a few steps back along the corridor. He stood now, alert and poised at the point where the corridor turned. He didn't say, *Hurry.* He didn't need to.

But there was actually no sign, yet, that the prison guards had heard the sound, though it had rung out so clear and sharp and perfect to Meridy. She stood still, listening, trying to breathe quietly. There were no alarmed shouts, no sound of rushing boots, nothing.

Within the cell, Lord Roann got awkwardly to his feet, as though needing to remember and carry out each necessary movement separately. Diöllin hovered by him, trying to help him, though her hands only passed through him. Herren, though stumbling himself, was more use, half supporting the seneschal and half forcing Lord Roann to focus and support himself. Meridy swung the door of the cell open—it made a scraping sound, but nothing too loud. By then, Lord Roann, with Herren's help, had made it to his feet.

"Are you all right?" she asked, very low, offering the seneschal her shoulder to lean on.

Dismissive of pride, he let her take his weight. "I will be. Is anybody coming? They must have heard that. . . ."

"The guards don't seem to have," Meridy said doubtfully. "Maybe it wasn't a *real* sound."

Herren was trembling with cold or fear or the drug. "If it wasn't *real,* my mother will have heard it. Tai-Enchar probably heard it, wherever he is."

"I would say there's no chance they didn't both get an earful," Niniol agreed, his tone grim. He still had his sword naked in his hand, but he had to know as well as Meridy that it would do no good against their true enemies.

Lord Roann said, "Please tell me you have a plan for the next part of our daring escape."

"Yes," Meridy agreed fervently. "I hope so! Hurry. Try to be quiet." She helped the seneschal back down the corridor toward Tiranann's special cell with its hidden way out. She hoped Lord Roann would be able to manage the climb—he was putting a lot of his weight on her, almost too much, and she staggered, trying to be quiet.

No guards intercepted them, so Meridy was more and more certain that the ringing tone hadn't been a *real* sound.

She half expected, as they came around the curve of the wall, to find a guard standing outside Tiranann's cell, but no one was there. She opened the disguised panel and waved Lord Roann and Herren into the hidden chamber at the base of the long shaft that led up and out of the dungeons. Then she hurried back to close and relock the door.

"Rub out the marks in the dirt," Niniol ordered shortly. "Hurry. There *is* a guard coming, now. I'm not sure those fools know even yet that anything's wrong—I think it's a routine change of shift. It's likely dawn, or nearly."

Meridy scooted out of the cell into the bottom of the hidden shaft with deep relief, pushing the panel closed behind her and summoning a wisp of *ethereal* light to let everyone see better. Then she leaned against the panel for a moment to catch her breath. She almost felt safe.

"I had no idea," Lord Roann murmured, glancing around at the constriction of the shaft.

"*I* didn't know," Herren said tensely.

"I should have told you," Diöllin said to her brother, penitent. "But Father said only his heir was supposed to know. But I *would* have told you, only how could I know she would imprison you down here? Or Roann, either? And then it was too late."

"We're not out yet!" Meridy reminded them. "And, I'm sorry, but the only way out is straight up, about eighty feet."

"I can do it," Herren said at once, with the confidence of youth or possibly desperation.

Lord Roann drew in a slow breath and released it. "I can make it."

"There's no good place to rest along the way," Meridy warned them both. "I mean, if you fall—" She broke off, because it wouldn't help to say, *If you fall, there's nothing to catch you.* She said instead, "There's no landing at the top. I'll have to go first to get the panel open. Then Herren, then you, all right?"

"I understand," the seneschal agreed. And if he understood that if the young prince fell, he would have to try to catch him and break his fall, well, that was exactly what Meridy meant.

"I won't fall," Herren put in, also understanding this. "I won't."

Meridy studied the boy worriedly. He looked white and exhausted. So did Roann. There was a tremor in the seneschal's hands, and a muscle under one eye showed a distressing tendency to twitch. He didn't look like a man who should be climbing an ordinary flight of stairs, much less an eighty-foot shaft with poor handholds and no way off save at the top.

Lord Roann must have seen her worry, but he only leaned his head back against the wall and whispered, "I'm fine. Go on." And Herren seconded this: "Yes, go. Go!"

Meridy knew neither of them was anything like fine, but she saw no other choice. "Follow me as close as you can." Turning to the rough stones of the shaft, she began the climb.

It wasn't exactly difficult, but it seemed to take a great deal longer than coming down, far longer than could possibly be safe. She found herself trying to count the falling of grains of sand in her head: time passing far too quickly. She wanted to climb fast, but she made herself stay one step above Herren, hoping that if he started to lose his grip there might be time to try, somehow, to steady him before he fell. Diöllin hovered behind her brother and the seneschal, murmuring encouragement, and though she had no way to truly help either of them, they both continued to move upward steadily, with only a little hesitation now and then to find a new grip where the stones were especially rough.

They came at last to the top of the shaft. Meridy pressed one hand against the far wall and bent down to touch Herren's hand. It took a long moment for the boy to stop trying to climb, to understand that he must be still and wait for the panel to be opened. Niniol, fortunately, was able to make sure that the stair landing was clear without the need to wait, listening, for some interminable interval.

Meridy slipped the catch and pushed on the panel. It didn't yield, and for one horrible moment she thought the panel was irretrievably stuck. She forced herself not to claw at it frantically but to try again from the beginning. It lifted out at the third attempt, and she scrambled through with a convulsive urgency. She doubled around at once and reached back through the narrow opening to help Herren out—his small size was a big help, but then Lord Roann nearly got stuck. The man's shoulders were a good deal wider than Meridy's. He'd never have made it if Meridy and Herren hadn't been there to pull him through. Worse, after the seneschal was out, he lay on the landing with the boneless sprawl of the truly exhausted. His face was white, his fingernails torn where he had gripped the stones during the climb. The pale spell light of the stairway revealed every bruise and cut with unforgiving accuracy.

"Roann!" Diöllin cried, frantic with dismay.

Niniol nudged Meridy and she realized how stupid she was being. She wanted sand or dust, mist or smoke, or at least strong sunlight, but there was a lamp on a hook not too far away. She hastily opened the glass and fed the little flame with bits of cloth hastily torn from Lord Roann's shirt. It didn't make enough smoke, not nearly as much as she would have liked, but it was something. She cupped her hand over the lamp and blew the drifting smoke toward Niniol.

Niniol shivered as he shifted momentarily into the *real*. Then he reached out, gripped Lord Roann's arm and belt, and heaved him up, coming smoothly to his feet and settling the other man over his shoulder, undignified but secure.

Roann stirred, murmuring an incoherent protest, making a fumbling effort to get away from Niniol and get back to his own feet.

"Roann!" whispered Diöllin. "Stop *arguing*. Be still!"

He did stop, too, which Meridy hadn't expected.

"We've got to be quick," Niniol said, his voice almost clear for once because he was that close to the *real*. He strode down the stairs.

Meridy caught Herren's hand and ran after Niniol, frantically feeding the lamp flame with bits of cloth and hoping they didn't encounter anyone coming up the other way. It was three flights to the bottom of the stairs, with doors on each landing.

Niniol, colorless and glimmering with *ethereal* light, carried Roann Mahonis, looking, as in a child's story, like a ghost under the command of an evil witch stealing away a soul in the night—rather too much like that, in fact. Meridy was constantly terrified that someone would cheerfully open one of those doors, step into the stairway, and see them. She was sure she looked just like the mad witch in the story— wild-eyed terror probably looked exactly like madness. She clutched the railing and glanced over her shoulder, trying to decide if she really heard hurrying footsteps behind them or whether that was only her nerves populating the upper levels of the stairway with pursuers.

"Someone's behind us!" Herren said, tense, his hand cold in hers, and Meridy nodded. She only hoped Jaift had gotten the seneschal's brother to help; she prayed they were in place—this stair was near the servants' kitchens; Diöllin had insisted they'd be able to get out that way, through the door by which butchers and cheesemongers brought in their wares. But what if something had gone wrong; what if Jaift wasn't there?

There was nothing to be done except go on. And then Meridy had to duck forward fast and haul Niniol farther into the *real* as he started to slip away into the *ethereal,* and she still had nothing to work with except wisps of black smoke and terror and prayers. Niniol gave her an exasperated glance and started taking the stairs two at a time.

Diöllin flicked back around the last turn of the stairway and beckoned to them. "Here!" she whispered. "Hurry!"

Meridy sent one last wordless prayer to the God, hurried with Herren down the last flight of stairs, stepped around the corner, and found Niniol just easing Lord Roann down, with Jaift and a man she didn't know, surely Lord Perann, taking his weight between them. She darted forward to help, gratefully allowing Niniol to fade into the *ethereal.*

Herren tugged at Meridy's sleeve. "We can't stop! We can't stop here, not for a second! She *knows.* She's *coming.*"

"Oh, no!" said Jaift, jerking her head up.

"Oh, yes!" Meridy gave the other man an assessing look. He looked strong, at least. "Quick—if we can't get him up, we'll have to carry him!"

Jaift patted the seneschal's face, trying to rouse him out of the vague stupor that had claimed him. "Who *is* this? He looks terrible, poor man."

"You didn't *know?*" exclaimed Lord Perann, with a grim

glance that weighed both Jaift and Meridy and found them thoroughly suspicious. "No, of course you didn't, or you'd have used his name to buy my help—and fair weight to the coin at that. Listen to me, Roann, you get yourself up on your feet *right now* or I will *tell Mother you got me in trouble with the princess-regent,* do you hear me? And if I wind up beside you in that cursed dungeon, I will *blame you.*"

Meridy bit her lip, trying not to laugh. Brothers, indeed. And better, Roann was now making an earnest effort to get to his feet. Jaift backed up toward the door behind them, reaching for the latch, but it opened just as she reached it.

For an instant Meridy thought her heart might truly have stopped beating. She'd always thought that was merely an expression, but it actually felt exactly like that. But the two girls who stepped through the door were servants carrying trays cluttered with tea things, not the princess-regent or horrible black-eyed servants of the witch-king, and the door they'd come through opened, after all, just to the servants' kitchen and hope of safety.

They all stared at each other in mutual astonishment and alarm. Meridy knew her eyes were wide and frightened—and black—and she couldn't imagine what her group looked like to those girls: Lord Perann supporting most of his brother's weight; Jaift hovering anxiously; and worst of all, Herren, his young face surely all too recognizable.

And the sound of someone coming down the stairs toward them was now unmistakable. Several people, in fact, their boots clattering, sounding to Meridy's frightened ear a good deal more like guardsmen than servants.

"Excuse us, please," Jaift said composedly, stepping past the two girls and holding the door open for Perann, who huffed in wordless acknowledgment, heaved Lord Roann around, and got his brother aimed, both of them staggering, for the kitchens. Meridy, pretending as hard as she could that everything was perfectly ordinary and unremarkable, hurried after them, still holding Herren's hand.

Then a shout made her glance over her shoulder, and she saw half a dozen men round the corner of the next landing up.

"Here, you!" the one in the lead called out, and Meridy took a step backward, but before she could turn and run, the stairway and half the landing crumbled slowly away to sand and dust. The men fell away into sudden yawning emptiness. They didn't even have time to look surprised. A wind came up, redolent of hot stone and blowing dust, here in this inner stairway where no passing breeze could possibly find its way. And, strolling confidently from the midst of the empty plain that yawned wide, where only moments ago the perfectly ordinary stairway had led up and away, came Princess Tiamanaith.

The princess-regent looked *exactly* like a sorceress. Meridy couldn't see how anyone could miss what she had become. She wore mourning white, a simple, sweeping dress that fell in gorgeous panels to her feet, and over that a long vest of black, its pectoral embroidered with shimmering black thread. Her black hair was looped up with strings of white pearls; her skin was aristocratically pale; strands of tiny black pearls swung from her ears.

Meridy, unable to move in that first moment of astonishment, met the princess-regent's gray eyes and realized at once that that had been a mistake, because she could not look away.

The woman smiled, and then Diöllin whirled in front of Meridy, crying out with the thin, breathless voice of a ghost. Tiamanaith's smile faded, but the thoughtful look she bent on Diöllin was not the look of a mother for her daughter. There was a terrible covetousness to it, an angry, balked possessiveness. She started to speak, but Meridy didn't stay to hear her. She whipped around and fled, pulling her ghosts along with her through the sheer force of her will. One of the servant girls squeaked and dropped her tray. The other, admirably sensible, hurled hers away, grabbed her friend's hand, and pulled her out of the way.

Meridy ran into the kitchens after Jaift and the others, but she felt now almost like she had fallen into a dream, the kind of dream where you run and run but you can hardly move, and all the time something terrible is coming up behind you. Worse, she really *couldn't* get away: in the kitchens everyone was piled up against the door, Jaift standing off a cook twice her size and three times her age while Lord Perann supported his brother and Herren struggled to unbar the door and the rest of the kitchen staff looked on in amazement.

Obviously the bar was stuck or jammed or held somehow. Herren couldn't get the door open. They couldn't get out. There was no way out. Meridy skidded to a halt and turned, helplessly, to face Princess Tiamanaith as the princess-regent stepped with measured grace into the kitchens and gazed across the long room, first at Diöllin, then straight at Meridy, and finally at her son.

Herren, brave though he was, made a thin sound of terror and cowered like a beaten dog.

"He is *mine*!" declared Tiamanaith. "Mine! My son!" But she said *my son* not with love but in a tone that made it clear she claimed possession. She looked beautiful and passionate and just as human and mortal as anyone, but there was nothing human or mortal in her eyes. "Mine!" she repeated. "I carried him in this body and marked him with my sign at his birth, and I will have my price for him!"

"You were his *mother*!" cried Diöllin. "What bargain did you *make* that you would use him like this?"

To Meridy's surprise, Tiamanaith actually answered Diöllin. "She would have lost him," she said coldly. "She *had* lost him, and she had not the arts to reclaim him. Was it not kind of me to offer my aid in her trouble? Was it not generous of me to *share* her life for nine years? For nearly nine years the boy lived and was healthy, and nearly all the time he lived under the affectionate gaze of his mother. The bargain did not require I wait so long."

"She didn't know what she did!" Diöllin retorted. "I know she didn't! She meant to give you her own life, not Herren's! You cheated her!"

Tiamanaith laughed scornfully. "It's not my fault she didn't understand her own bargain. She was a careless woman—careless and vain, but she was the one who accepted the aid of sorcery in her trouble. Stupid woman, you know it's true. Be quiet!"

Meridy realized, with an unpleasant chill, that when she said *Be quiet,* the sorceress, Aseraiëth, was actually speaking to Tiamanaith. The princess-regent was still *in* that body, along with the sorceress.

She couldn't stand it. So she took one long step, grabbed Herren by the wrist, and dragged him and her ghosts the *other* way, the way the princess-regent had opened up, into dust and emptiness. Into dreams and memory.

It wasn't *her* dream, of course. Or her memory. She recognized the white spire in the empty plain, now, and couldn't believe she hadn't recognized it at once as a dream of Cora

Diorr; but this was a Cora Diorr in which all the city—all the *world*—had turned to dust except for that one perfect spire. All else was gone, or had never been. The dust hissed across the wasteland with a sound like loneliness.

In this place, terrible as it was, the quick dead took on color and seeming solidity; Niniol, intimidatingly stolid and grim, had again taken on the semblance of life. Diöllin put her arms around her brother, holding him tight. Her hair, smooth and lustrous, fell in a rich brown cascade down her back, and the golden chain that bound it glittered. Her eyes, narrowed with determination, were the eyes of a living person. Meridy had forgotten their odd color, green bronze like moss on forest loam.

Meridy stared around, searching for anything except dust and desolation, but could see nothing here that could help them against the princess-regent, and still no way out.

"She'll follow!" Herren said tensely. "And this is *his* place, this is Tai-Enchar's own realm. It's the worst place we could have come—"

"I know! Be quiet!" Meridy tried to think. At least Jaift wasn't here; she was glad of that; surely Jaift must be much safer now: the princess-regent would come after Meridy and Herren, and Lord Roann and his brother would protect Jaift. But now she and Herren were trapped here where every place was the same place, and it was all the dream of the witch-king.

"Carad Mereth!" she shouted, and then, "Iëhiy?" But neither sorcerer nor wolfhound came. It was on the tip of her tongue to call Inmanuàr, but some half-recognized terror stopped her; this might be a bad place for her and Herren, but she felt sure it would be much worse for Inmanuàr.

Meridy had brought herself here, brought Herren and

Diöllin and Niniol here, but there was *still* no way out, and Herren was right, this was the worst place she could have brought them—she could almost *feel* Tai-Enchar's attention closing around them, as though the witch-king were an approaching storm—something bitter and terrible that would break across them and turn them all to dust—

Behind her, a step that wasn't a step, and a breath that wasn't a breath, and she whirled, *knowing* it was the witch-king, he was *here* and it was *too late*—

But it was Iëhiy, looking almost like a living hound, brindled and powerful; and with him, beautiful and terrible, a fire horse.

twenty

After that first shocked instant, Meridy recognized the beast. Of course she did. This was the blood bay stallion she had seen killed on the road outside Cora Diorr.

Like the other ghosts, he seemed almost alive here in this *ethereal* realm, shockingly vivid against the empty plain and the colorless sky, red bay half a shade darker than blood, black mane flying as he tossed his head and half reared in threat and warning. But though he seemed poised to attack or flee, he did neither. His yellow cat's eyes were fixed on Meridy, his ears pinned back, his teeth bared—his tusks gleamed like ivory in the dead air. But he didn't snap at her, or tear at her with his clawed forefeet. He did snort at Iëhiy, but the hound only tilted his ears back in a friendly way.

No one else was so sanguine about the fire horse's sudden presence. Diöllin had shoved her brother behind her own body, and Niniol had caught Meridy's shoulder to pull her back, too, but Meridy refused to move. She stared at the stallion. She could tell, now, that she was his anchor. She could *feel* it. She *knew* she was his anchor. She must have drawn him after her without even knowing it, just as she had drawn her other ghosts—no wonder, no *wonder* she had felt in Cora

Diorr that there was someone following them, following *her*. She had been right all the time. It had been this terrible, wonderful, brutal, brilliant, monstrous creature. And Iëhiy, with a dog's sure wisdom, had led him right to her.

And as the empty air opened wide and something—or someone—terrible began to coalesce, Meridy shook herself free of Niniol's half-tangible grip, caught Herren's hand, stepped forward, and flung herself onto the back of the fire horse, dragging the young prince up in front of her.

It didn't matter that she could never have leaped up like that onto the back of an ordinary horse, or that she didn't have the strength to lift a boy of almost nine, or that the living fire horse would never willingly have let either of them touch him. This was a place of dreams, and she *did* leap to the stallion's back and pull Herren up with her; and the fire horse *did* let her do it.

The stallion wanted to run. Meridy wanted that too. He wanted to run forever and never stop, so he leaped forward, and in that first great flying breathless moment, Meridy shouted to Iëhiy, and the dog was there, in front of them, racing across the dead realm. And before the dog, the light twisted open between dreams and the living world, and Meridy shouted again, and in one great bound the stallion carried them though the roiling confusion of light and out of the *ethereal* into the *real*.

She nearly fell. In that first instant, she nearly fell right *through* the fire horse, because in the *real* world the ghost did not have weight or heft or solidity. He was already racing the wind, and if she had fallen, she would have smashed into the ground with terrible force, dragged Herren down with her, and probably killed them both. But the dawn light was streaming through a silvery morning mist, and in one terrified gasp Meridy limned the fire horse with mist and jerked him into the *real*. She might have fallen even then because she wasn't a very good rider and she'd never been on a galloping horse, far less *bareback* on a galloping fire horse. But there Herren saved her, saved them both, because his balance never faltered. Meridy wrapped one arm around his waist and clenched her other hand in the stallion's thick mane—it was like gripping a handful of cloud—and somehow stayed on.

She made no effort at all to guide the stallion, or even see where he was going. She didn't care, as long as it was *away*. But she realized eventually that Herren was somehow guiding the fire horse. It was as though the boy merely *looked* the way he wanted the stallion to run, and the fire horse turned that way. She had no idea how Herren did it, but the fire horse bolted around one white spire and another and then hurled himself for a gate. Thankfully the gate was standing open for a dawn delivery of, she couldn't guess, fresh-baked bread or produce for the kitchens or who knew what. There were wagons in the way. The fire horse did not hesitate but only gathered himself and leaped for a gap between a wagon and the gatepost. The gap would never have been big enough for the living beast. But the ordinary horses harnessed to the wagon shied violently and the wagon tilted to the side, and then the gap was after all wide enough, barely. The white street unrolled before them, straight and level, and the fire horse pinned his ears flat, put his head down, and charged along it with furious disregard for anyone who might get in his way.

Meridy, terrified, saw men and ladies, carriages and ordinary horses, scramble this way and that, and she couldn't help but wonder what all those people saw: two children clinging to what seemed a half-solid burst of red-tinged fog with blazing yellow eyes and clashing tusks?

Behind them, they must have left an uproar, but Meridy could hear only the wind rushing past. All her thoughts jolted and scattered with the speed of the fire horse—she was almost not afraid of falling now, she was almost getting used to shaping the fire horse continually out of the mist and the rushing wind. It almost felt as though she truly was riding the wind, as though there was no *way* to fall, not now. Ridiculous as it was, she almost felt *safe*.

She couldn't tell whether Tiamanaith was coming after them, but she didn't know how the sorceress even *could,* now. How horrible for poor Herren, his mother lost to the terrible sorceress; he must be so frightened, he was just a *baby,* but he felt so steady in front of her. She couldn't see her other ghosts, not even Iëhiy anymore, but she knew she still held them; she could feel the binding between them and knew they weren't lost, they were here, with her.

The fire horse had cleared the edges of Cora Diorr with blazing inexhaustible speed, far ahead of any possible pursuit. He was racing south, his muscles bunching and stretching beneath her; but for all his seeming solidity, she knew they were riding a ghost as insubstantial as smoke, and what she would do when the morning mist burned off, Meridy did not know. She could not imagine holding the fire horse this far within the *real* with nothing but sunlight and a handful of *ethereal* dust.

But, though nothing like tame, he might have realized that somehow carrying Meridy with him meant he was free to run for the mountains. He wasn't fighting her binding, at least; or at least he wasn't fighting her as long as she wanted him to do what he wanted to do anyway, which was run. He wasn't afraid of her, or she thought not. A fire horse didn't have any reason to fear a mere girl, even if she was clinging to his back; a fire horse didn't have reason to fear anything less fierce than a dragon or a griffin. Or maybe he didn't fight her because Herren was royal and thus, as all the stories claimed, naturally able to tame and ride a fire horse.

Meridy, lifting her gaze, looked west, toward the road and the gap in the encircling mountains. She shouted in Herren's ear, "West! We have to go west before we can go north!"

The young prince jerked his head in a tense nod, and the fire horse's path curved, racing for the gap.

Of course, even a fire horse stallion couldn't carry Meridy and Herren all the way to Surem in one mad gallop, no matter how fast.

Meridy couldn't hold the ghost far enough into the *real* for so long without a break, for one thing; and then two children riding a fire horse ghost at blazing speed down the Coramne Road . . . Well, it would not be precisely discreet to leave a trail of astonished rumor behind them.

On the other hand, the journey to Surem did promise to be much quicker than any other journey Meridy had ever taken in her life. The fire horse was so much faster than a public conveyance or carter's wagon that it was like comparing mutton with turnips, as the saying went.

Speed was important. She could imagine how many White Swan guardsmen might be on the road behind them. What she could not guess was whether Princess Tiamanaith—the sorceress Aseraiëth—would be after them herself or, if she was, whether she would ride through the *real* world like an ordinary person, or straight through dreams.

Nor could she guess what Tai-Enchar might be doing. Meridy detested the sorceress for Herren's sake, but she was fairly sure the witch-king intended worse for the young prince than even Aseraiëth. And she still did not know what Carad Mereth or Inmanuàr or anyone could actually *do,* at Moran Diorr or anywhere else, or whether it might still be possible to let Herren draw their enemies' attention so she might free Carad Mereth. If she could indeed find him, in Tai-Enchar's terrible lonely realm; and after her recent visit to that place, she couldn't see how to even begin. For all she knew, Carad Mereth had already been crushed and turned into dust and was now blowing on the wind of the witch-king's dreams.

Shuddering, she tried not to think of it. She wished Jaift were with her. Jaift would say something practical and reassuring, and no doubt Diöllin would be sarcastically disdainful, but then Niniol would say something sardonic to Diöllin and they could all argue about their plans, which would make those plans seem so much more normal and . . . and achievable, somehow.

Iëhiy no longer ran with the fire horse. Meridy was beginning to trust that the dog would always be exactly where he was most needed, and she hoped that he'd gone back to help Jaift somehow. Meridy hoped he had. She wished she knew for sure that Jaift had gotten clear of that disastrous conclusion of their escape. And Lord Roann, too, and the seneschal's brother—she couldn't remember his name and didn't care.

The mist lingered long into the morning. That helped a great deal, for it gave Meridy the means to keep the fire horse ghost continually within the *real.* The mist also concealed them from sight and muted the footfalls of the fire horse, though those were already muffled compared to a living animal's, as though he moved half through the *real* world and half through dreams.

The fire horse never tried to throw them off, or reach around with slashing tusks to savage them. Meridy didn't understand that, but she was afraid to question it too closely, in case the stallion changed his mind.

For a long time, neither she nor Herren spoke. Meridy didn't wonder at the young prince's silence; certainly he'd had no shortage of horrible things to deal with. For her part, she was concentrating both on keeping the fire horse as far as possible in the *real* and on staying mounted. The stallion's ghost might not be trying to pitch them off, but every muscle she owned ached from their wild flight, and she was now finding it difficult and uncomfortable to ride bareback, especially without stirrups. It didn't help that Herren seemed perfectly at ease on the fire horse's back.

Though she couldn't see more than a few feet ahead or to either side, Meridy thought they had for some time been moving uphill at an increasingly steep grade. She hoped this was true, since it would mean they had already reached the slopes of the mountains that encircled Cora Diorr. That seemed unbelievably fast, but then the fire horse had been racing the wind from the instant she'd leaped to his back and pulled Herren up after her. She hoped that she was right and that they were even now heading up toward the gap where the road ran between the mountains. She felt that they would be safe once they had crossed the saddle between the mountains and come out on the other side.

She had no reason to think they'd ever be safe again, actually. The sorceress hardly seemed likely to just shrug and let them go. Though as they went on and on, she started to believe that maybe Aseraiëth wasn't likely to catch up with them right this minute.

At last, worries crowding her mind, she asked tentatively, "Herren, I mean Your Highness, do you think, um, the sorceress might be able to find you?"

The stallion's small ears swiveled and tilted at the sound of her voice, but he didn't miss a step. Maybe he thought he could whip around anytime he liked and tear them to pieces. Probably he could, if he tried it and Meridy didn't push him away from the *real* fast enough. She tried to be ready for that, just in case.

Herren didn't turn his head. Nor did he answer, for so long that Meridy had about decided he wasn't going to. But at last he said in a thin, exhausted voice, "Maybe. I don't know."

"Wonderful," muttered Meridy.

Then the boy volunteered, "She knew where I was. Before. She didn't have to *find* me. It's only, she couldn't take me until . . . until the servitor went away. So then the witch-king didn't have eyes or hands right there anymore, so my— So she could come get me."

Meridy thought about this. She hardly wanted to ask about anything that had happened to Herren; it was all so horrible. She didn't want to frighten him by asking more about the terrifying sorceress who had taken his mother's place, or the witch-king who must be even worse. But she needed to know some things. She really did, or how could either of them figure out what to do next? Besides, she was almost sure that Herren knew more about what was going on than she did.

She asked tentatively, "So is the sorceress Aseraiëth, is she an enemy of the witch-king now? Is she working for one thing when he wants another?"

Herren still didn't turn to look at her. "She isn't one of Tai-Enchar's servitors. That's not what she is. She's her own person. I think . . ."

Meridy waited.

The prince was silent for a moment. Then he added, "The witch-king wants . . . he wants to pour himself into me, like the sorceress did to my mother. Except he doesn't mean to share. Just take my life for his. Then he'll be a prince, descended of the High Kings, and he'll still be a sorcerer. And alive. And he'll make himself High King and rule forever, I guess. Until the *real* world becomes a mirror of the dream he's made in the *ethereal* realms."

Herren was gazing straight ahead over the fire horse's translucent head. But he was shivering, and Meridy suspected it wasn't from the damp chill in the air. His voice held a kind of exhausted flatness that was disturbing in a child his age. She had worried in case she should frighten the young prince, but she was fairly sure she couldn't have come up with anything half as frightening as this if she'd thought it out with both hands for half a year. "Are you *sure* you're only eight?"

The boy huffed a tired laugh. "Almost nine."

"Of course." It was all so terrible, she honestly didn't want to hear anything else, but she would be ashamed to be less brave than a little boy who wasn't even quite nine. She said, "That's what he meant to do to Inmanuàr, I suppose. Although maybe not, since Inmanuàr might be the High King's heir, but after all, he's long dead."

Herren turned his head at last to look over his shoulder at Meridy with an actual glimmer of curiosity. "You know Inmanuàr too?"

Meridy was too surprised by this response to answer. Herren went on quickly, "Then you know the witch-king *did* want to do the same to Inmanuàr, but first he'd have to embody him, and he couldn't, he never could, because Carad Mereth kept stopping him."

"I see. . . ."

"Of course." Herren sounded surprised that she could question this. "Carad Mereth anchored Inmanuàr to life so he couldn't take the White Road, and then he anchored Inmanuàr to me when I was born, because—" But he broke off there, not like he didn't know where that sentence had been going, but like he'd changed his mind about telling her. He definitely sounded much older than eight. Or almost nine. He sounded, in fact, just like the kind of little boy who might have been serving as an anchor for a really old ghost all his life. He said, "Inmanuàr's wanted to take the White Road for a long time. But he can't because that would let Tai-Enchar win. He needs to stop Tai-Enchar first. Except it's been so long, and Tai-Enchar's been gaining power, not wearing away. But Inmanuàr has a plan—or Carad Mereth has a plan, or they both do."

Carad Mereth, whoever he really was, must have anchored the High King's heir right at the moment of his death. And held him ever since. And he had the nerve to claim he wasn't a sorcerer. She wondered what his name had been, way back then, at the breaking of one age and the beginning of the next.

But she only asked, "And your . . . mother?"

The young prince flinched slightly, facing front again so that he wouldn't have to look at Meridy. "*She* wants . . . I think she wants to use me to bargain with the witch-king. But I don't know what she wants to bargain *for*, now. She wanted Tai-Enchar to help her do the same as him, but with Liny. Diöllin. Take her body so she could be alive and have the bloodline of the High Kings and sorcery, too."

"She *told* you that?" How utterly appalling.

"No. Sort of. I . . . I figured it out. But Liny died, so now I don't know what that sorceress wants."

Meridy tried to think about that, about what a long-dead sorceress might want, how she might make use of a ghost like Diöllin. It was hard to think, though. Herren tried so hard to be grown-up and fearless and calm, and he *was,* but he was also a little boy and it was all so horrible.

The fire horse came over the crest of the mountain road and started the descent. Meridy wondered if the stallion had realized yet that he would never tire, and wondered if he thought it was worth becoming quick. Probably not. But he sure liked to run. He was stretching out again, faster and faster. Meridy clung to Herren and resisted the urge to suggest that he try to persuade the fire horse to slow down. It wouldn't really help—nothing would help but actually getting *off,* and she knew they *had* to keep moving.

"Don't hold on so tight," muttered Herren, taking Meridy by surprise, so for a second she just blinked at him. But he repeated, "You don't have to hold on so tight. Relax. Like you're sitting in a rocking chair. He's all right."

Meridy tried to do as the prince suggested. She wasn't sure she succeeded.

"How long do you think you can keep him in the world?"

"I don't know. Until the mist lifts, I suppose—or until I fall off or, I don't know, something else happens. I have to . . . It's not . . . I've never tried to keep a ghost so far into the *real* for so long before."

It was both easier and more difficult than Meridy would

have expected: easier because it didn't require constant close attention, harder because she had to struggle against letting her attention drift completely.

She said, "He won't get tired. But he might get bored, I guess. Or angry." She wondered again how fast she could push him away from the *real* if he turned on them.

But Herren shook his head and patted the fire horse on the neck. "He won't. He knows he can't leave you. You're his anchor."

"He can't *understand* that, though."

"He does. He's not like a normal horse. An ordinary horse is afraid of everything. *He's* not afraid of *anything*." The boy sounded envious. "He's not afraid of you at all—of us. He doesn't mind carrying us as long as he can run. and go where he wants. He probably wouldn't like it if you tried to get away from him."

How could the young prince possibly know all that? But on the other hand, Prince Herren had obviously grown up around horses. Maybe he'd always thought of riding a fire horse. . . . Well, he was a prince; of course he'd thought of riding one. She had already realized that the stallion had no reason to be afraid of them. And maybe . . . maybe he *was* smart enough to know about anchors, and to know that they weren't the ones who'd trapped him and dragged him out of the southern mountains and then shot him and killed him. She had no idea how smart fire horses were, not really. Maybe Herren was right after all.

But Meridy doubted she was ever going to sound that calm about the idea of riding a fire horse, even one that was smart and not scared of her and quick rather than living.

On the *other* hand . . . maybe Herren was just so exhausted, or so stunned by everything that had happened to him, that he simply couldn't manage to be afraid even of things that would terrify any normal person. On reflection, that seemed entirely likely.

Meridy said prudently, "No matter how far and fast he can run, *I* can't ride straight through to Surem from here without rest. And I don't think you can, either."

"I can't sleep," Herren said, still without turning. "Because if I fall into dreams, Tai-Enchar will find me. I can't let him. I have to get to Surem. To Moran Bay. But not . . . I can't let *him* take me there. I have to find Inmanuàr. In the place of his power, he says. That's Moran Diorr, I guess, but it's under the bay, so I don't know."

Meridy felt like everything had been moving too fast and now she was trying to catch up. She felt stupid. Maybe the fire horse was smarter than *she* was. He was surely less frightened. How stupid to be envious of the beast for that.

She said, "We'll find you some sweetleaf. It's common enough. Any farmer would have some, I'm sure. We'll stop somewhere after the fog burns off—I mean, we'll have to stop then anyway. I'm not sure I can keep the fire horse far enough in the *real* without it." She hoped dust and sunlight would be enough to manage it. She was sore, but not eager to slow to a walking pace. Nor to walk all the way from wherever they were to Surem. That was a long way. She didn't know how far. But farther than Cora Talen, she knew that.

Herren said abruptly, "The stallion's name is Gonnuol."

Meridy stared at the back of the young prince's head, wishing she could see his expression. "Oh, it is?"

"He's a king of his own kind. Gonnuol is a good name for him." Herren's voice was growing thin again, but he sounded like he meant it.

"Well, I'm not arguing." Meridy supposed she could call

the stallion Gonnuol if Herren wanted. High King Gonnuol had ruled long ago, before the Great War and the raising of the Southern Wall and the drowning of Moran Diorr. She remembered that. If the stories were true, the original Gonnuol had been a violent, dangerous man; an effective leader when it came to keeping the peace in the early, more volatile Kingdom, but a hard man. Maybe it was a good name for a fire horse stallion after all.

"The mist is lifting."

Meridy, startled, looked around. Herren was right. The fog was burning off at last. When she glanced over her shoulder, she could see where the sun was: a diffuse brightness lit the fog behind them, not enough yet to cast shadows forward, but warm on her back. "Can you make, uh, Gonnuol slow down?"

"I don't know. Sit back. More than that. Put your weight right back. Sit down harder."

Herren demonstrated what he mean, leaning back against Meridy so that she had no choice but to do the same. She didn't see what good that would do, but to her surprise the fire horse—Gonnuol—did slow his pace. Unfortunately, the slower gait was a lot rougher than his faster paces. Meridy jolted, slipped, clutched at Herren, jolted again, and lost her hold on the fire horse, who became suddenly as tenuous as the thinning mist.

She hit the road hard, Herren on top of her, and the stallion disappeared into the brightening morning.

twenty-one

The young prince got up again, slowly. Meridy didn't, not at once. She lay on her back on the road, blinking at the lilac-and-pearl sky and trying to decide if all her bones were still where they ought to be. At least the surface of the road was smooth and not too hard. Hard enough, though.

Herren brushed himself off and fussily straightened his sleeves. He didn't say anything, which was nice of him. Maybe he was just too tired. Maybe he was afraid that if he said anything, he would start yelling. Or crying. She could understand that, too. Meridy painfully pushed herself to sitting and looked around.

She couldn't tell how far they'd come. Except the land here was extremely flat. When she turned to look, the haze was still too strong to see the mountains behind them. She could tell there were fields or pastures on either side of the road. . . . There were spotted goats in the nearest pasture, and a big white dog, who was at the moment watching Meridy and Herren suspiciously, and no wonder. On the other side of the road there was nothing but a field of some crop or other, turnips maybe. A vague shape, hardly visible through the remaining haze, might be a farmhouse. Or a barn, considering the goats.

What she could definitely see, indistinct in the haze, were other people on the road. There was a large group some distance away, along the road toward Cora Talen, with wagons and, from the blocky shapes of their beasts, probably oxen. Farther away in the other direction was a smaller group that Meridy was almost sure consisted of mounted men. Not farmers, then, or carters, or, probably, anyone else she or Herren would want to meet.

Now that they'd stopped, Niniol glimmered into shape, colorless and not quite visible. He stood with his arms crossed, regarding Meridy where she sat in the dust and then measuring the half-visible shapes of the approaching men with a cynical eye. "You'd better get up if you don't want to meet those men," he told Meridy, not very sympathetically. "His young Highness is correct. We're safe to presume his enemies will not cease their pursuit of him. We must take effective action to prevent word of him from traveling this road."

Meridy smiled at him, despite weariness and lingering fear and new bruises. Trust Niniol to move right on to practical concerns.

"Herren!" said Diöllin, flickering into view like a pale candle-flame. She rushed to her brother, murmuring. He couldn't see her, of course, but he shrugged away from her voice, from her presence, his mouth tightening. He didn't want sympathy, Meridy could see. Maybe because he was so tired and too much kindness might make him cry. She could understand that, and she looked away to give the young prince a chance to compose himself, if necessary.

Near at hand, outlined in haze and light, stood the nearly

transparent form of the fire horse. He had circled and come back and now tossed his head uneasily, staring at them, his ears pinned back. He tossed his head again, raking the damp surface of the road with one clawed foot, leaving every now and then a long set of parallel slashes in its packed earth. Jerking his head up, he snapped his fanged jaws, tusks clashing in soundless threat. He looked . . . he looked impatient and annoyed, Meridy decided. Like he'd never heard of anything so stupid as girls who fell off his back and lay in the dirt at his feet.

She definitely felt stupid enough. And Niniol was right, of course. She got to her feet, a bit at a time, missing Jaift, who would have hovered and asked if she was all right and probably told a deprecating story about falling off a pony when she was little.

But it was Diöllin who came to her, leaving her brother to recover himself. She stood with her transparent hands on her hips and glared at Meridy. "Of course," she said. "Of *course* once a fire horse became quick, naturally you'd bind him. How else? But how could you let my brother near a monster like the one that killed our father? What if it had torn him to pieces because you held it in the *real*?"

Herren jerked his head up. "I'm not a baby, Liny!" For once he sounded his age. "What else were we supposed to do? Walk? Hide in a corner of that horrible empty dream realm until *she* caught up with us, or the witch-king did?"

"Well, but, Hery—"

"The boy's right, but Diöllin's right, too. The beast hardly seems safe to have so near." Niniol, plainly exasperated, was measuring the beast with a professional eye.

"He's fine," Meridy assured them, hoping she was right. "He's just a little upset."

"You can't blame him," Herren protested. "It's not his fault!"

Meridy started to say that she knew that, she didn't blame the fire horse at all, but the prince stepped forward, ghost blind as he was, holding out his hands and murmuring. Not in a soothing tone so much as a sympathetic one: *I know, it was terrible, you started to fade, didn't you, it's so unfair, I'd be furious too.*

And, even though Herren still couldn't see him and wasn't looking in quite the right direction, Gonnuol calmed. The stallion still had his ears pinned back, but he snaked his long, elegant neck forward, not to bite, but to nose at Herren. He couldn't touch him, not quite, not really, which they all knew, so Diöllin only hissed under her breath rather than panicking.

Meridy, too, trusted the lack of congruence between the quick and the living far more than she trusted the stallion's temper. But the fire horse still didn't try to savage the boy, and now his ears were tipped forward in a more friendly manner. "That's better," she told Herren. "That's a lot better. Maybe it's true what they say about needing royal blood to ride a fire horse! But we daren't linger. The fire horse is all right, but we need to get off the road."

"His name is Gonnuol," Herren insisted.

"Of course his name is Gonnuol," Diöllin said resignedly, but after another suspicious glare at the fire horse, she smiled at her brother. "Of course you tamed him. I'm not surprised at all, actually. Although——" She turned to Meridy. "You must be *careful* if you bring the beast back into the *real*! But you did get Herren away, after all. So . . ." She took a breath as though it actually hurt her but managed almost graciously, "So, thank you." Then she moved again to her brother's side and held her hands out as though to lay them on his shoulders, though she couldn't actually touch him. "I wish you could see me," she murmured to her brother.

"At least he can hear you. Besides, if he were a witch, he might be even more vulnerable," Meridy pointed out, and then hesitated because it was hard to see how Herren's position could be worse whether he was a witch or not.

"Not being a witch doesn't help much!" Herren said, echoing her thought. "*I* wish I could see Gonnuol. The rest of you can see him. It's not *fair.*" He turned to Meridy. "Can't you can make him *real* again?"

"If I do, anybody could see him," Meridy pointed out. "And those men are getting close enough to notice a horse appearing out of nothing." At the moment obviously no one could see the fire horse but herself and the ghosts, or else those goats in the pasture would be upset, and that dog a lot more suspicious.

But it was the men who worried her. She looked at Niniol, who shrugged and murmured, "*Off* the road. Let's go."

Meridy sighed. This was obvious, but in all this flat country, it wasn't obvious how to get out of sight. Jaift would have thought of something clever. She'd probably have hurried to catch up with the wagons, gained the sympathy of the ox drovers with three words, and by the time the riders caught up, she'd be walking along with half a dozen other girls, looking like she'd known them for years, and Herren tucked out of sight among the radishes and cabbages.

Meridy herself seemed entirely out of clever ideas. Maybe she had to be desperate to think of something clever. Maybe she never did think of clever things, only desperate ones. She rubbed the dirt off her hands onto her skirt. She must look like a particularly unkempt farmer's daughter. She studied Herren. His clothing had plainly been better, once. But he certainly didn't look much like a prince. She said finally, "Those goats. I bet we could look like goatherds."

"That'd do," agreed Niniol. "Let's be brisk about it." He took a step toward the pasture fence, giving an impatient little jerk of his head.

Not hearing the ghost, Herren looked at Meridy sidelong. "I don't know what goatherds look like."

"Just like us," Meridy assured him, with another glance down at her disreputable skirt. "From a distance, anyway. We need to find switches. And to get rid of the dog."

At this, the young prince brightened. It made him seem, for the first time, almost like a normal little boy. "Gonnuol could drive him off! And then we could take the goats back to the barn and see if the farmer has sweetleaf. And then we—you—could make Gonnuol *real* again and we could ride to Surem." His mouth tightened at the thought of that long journey, the little-boy eagerness already fading. He was definitely fighting exhaustion, Meridy thought, and probably the lingering effects of terror. She sure was.

But she only said, trying to sound cheerful, "Surem, then. But first, goatherds!" She turned to the fire horse. He immediately arched his muscular neck and half reared, raking his claws through the dirt when he came back down.

"Gonnuol seems impatient," Meridy told Herren. "I think he'd be glad to drive off any number of dogs. I just hope he doesn't send the goats into a mad panic. . . ." That might be tricky to arrange. She stared toward the pasture. Off to the side of the road, the fire horse tossed his head and snorted, mincing away sideways, looking for that one moment so much like an ordinary horse that despite everything, she wanted to laugh at him.

Herren fell into step beside her as she started toward the pasture.

"Gonnuol likes you a lot better than he likes me, even if you can't see him," Meridy told him. "He really is wonderful . . . as long as he keeps deciding to do what we want him to do."

"He knows you're his anchor," Herren told her again. He sounded confident about it. "I just wish I could *see* him," he repeated, sounding for once almost like the child he was.

The fire horse made a series of stiff-legged bucking hops, each one a little closer than the last, and snapped at Meridy, his ivory tusks clashing with a jagged, dangerous sound that she could almost hear. No matter how beautiful he was, those tusks looked at least as dangerous as the killing weapons of a wild boar. Meridy tried not to recoil visibly. She added, "As long as you're right about him not trying to kill us."

"I'm right," the young prince promised. "He won't. You'll see."

Herren *was* right about the stallion, fortunately. Though it proved difficult to get Gonnuol to chase off the dog without terrifying every goat for a mile around. Iëhiy might have done it, surely, but the wolfhound was still missing—having gone back to guard Jaift and make sure she was all right, Meridy hoped. Or perhaps to Inmanuàr, wherever he was. Or even to Carad Mereth—maybe the dog would find him, rescue him from any strange terrible prison in which the witch-king might have imprisoned him so she wouldn't have to try herself. . . . She had no idea what Iëhiy might do, but by now she trusted the hound to be where he ought to be. She wished she were as confident that she and Herren were where *they* ought to be. But heading toward Surem, surely that was right. If it was wrong, Inmanuàr or someone was going to have to appear long enough to *say* so.

But at least Gonnuol turned out to be quite good at terrifying goats, which was fine, for when frightened, the goats quite sensibly fled straight for their barn. It was easy enough to follow them. By the time the riders, whoever they might be, passed by, Meridy and Herren must have been far enough from the road and looked enough like farmer's children that they didn't draw attention.

The actual farmer, a big darkish man obviously carrying more than a trace of Southern blood, and with three equally big sons even darker than he, was puzzled at what could have so frightened his animals. But he was willing to let Meridy and Herren have a little sweetleaf despite that mystery, when Meridy explained her little half-brother had bad dreams.

"Goats ain't so flighty as sheep, usually," the farmer rumbled. "But I guess sometimes they get ideas in their heads." And when Meridy asked, he kindly traded Herren's fine but much-abused shirt for a decent undyed homespun garment that had belonged to his youngest daughter, a girl a year older than Herren and close to the same size. "Nice work in't," he told Meridy, admiring the embroidery on Herren's shirt. "M'wife'll find good use for the cloth, you can be sure."

He was too kind to ask any questions about where Herren might have come by such a fine shirt or what the boy had been up to, to wear it so hard. Instead, he gave Meridy and Herren each a meat pie left from the day before and pointed out a farmer's track—a rutted path that wound between fields.

"That 'un runs mostly north," he told them. "Our tracks, they goes back and forth a bit, but keep'n eye on the sun and mind you mostly go north and you'll come out some're on the Border Road by an' by. No one cares if somebody takes our private tracks, so long as they ain't thieves or ruffians, but mind, those folk up there in Moran Tal, they ain't so easy as us with someone as is carrying more'n a drop of Southern blood, witches or no, even for a girl your age as is looking after her brother just as she ought. But a nice-mannered little thing like you as bespeaks a man all polite, you ought to get along all right."

He brushed off Meridy's promise they were neither thieves nor ruffians.

"Anyone'd see you ain't," he said gruffly. "Mind you ask polite when you come to a house and don't just up and head for the well or a seat in the shade. And you'll likely get on best if you stay out of pastures; there're those as have bulls in 'em. But you'll find we're friendly folk out here, mostly." And with a short nod he turned his back and strode away to see to his goats.

"Who did he think we are?" Herren asked, once they had left the farmer's house and followed the rough track around the pasture. "He can't have guessed anything like the truth?"

Meridy had no idea, but Niniol said briskly from beside her, "You with your eyes, Mery, he probably thinks you're running away from a master who'd got ideas about what use to make of a witch. As for His little Highness, I imagine he's got a notion the master also had ideas about extra duties for good-looking boys."

"Oh," said Meridy, and then, "Oh!" as she understood what he meant.

"He thought *what*?" Diöllin pivoted, drawing herself up

in outrage to glare after the farmer. "How *dare* he think such a thing!"

Niniol said sardonically, "Better you commend the man for generosity to runaways, Your Highness. There's those as would hold 'em and wait to see if someone came looking— especially with the boy's shirt being so fine. You're lucky that one had more than a touch of Southern heritage himself, and likely his wife more than a touch, or he might not have been so generous to a girl like Meridy, with or without His Highness playing her half brother."

Diöllin sputtered wordlessly, still glaring.

"What?" Herren asked. "Liny? What did he think?"

"Never you mind," Meridy told him firmly, feeling her face heat.

Diöllin was still stiff with offense, but Niniol was hard to argue with, and anyway the princess was distracted by the fire horse, who danced around them, tossing his head and snorting and every now and then snapping his jaws so his tusks clashed alarmingly.

"I guess Gonnuol wants to run," Meridy said, glad to change the subject. "You'd think he'd at least *think* he was tired. Listen, Herren, can you make Gonnuol understand that if he wants to run, he has to let me pull him into the *real*"—she only hoped she could—"and get up on his back again? And wait, *are* we going to Surem? If you're sure that was where the witch-king was taking you, maybe we should go somewhere else after all."

But Herren was shaking his head. "We have to go to Surem. I mean, Inmanuàr said Moran Diorr, but I suppose we have to go to Surem first, and then we can think about how to—how to reach Moran Diorr. I never knew how to do that, but, Meridy, you can take us into dreams. . . ."

"Wait," said Diöllin. "*Who* said you have to go to Moran Diorr? Herren, did you say *Inmanuàr* wants you to go to Moran Diorr? You don't mean *Inmanuàr Incuonarr?*"

Though he couldn't see his sister, Herren looked away from her voice.

Meridy hesitated. She asked Diöllin almost reluctantly, "Didn't you know that Inmanuàr's been talking to your brother for years? That long before Carad Mereth made me an anchor for Inmanuàr, he made Herren an anchor for him?"

"What?" Diöllin plainly hadn't known anything of the sort and, from her disbelieving stare at Meridy, wasn't at all sure she believed it now. Her gaze went from Meridy to her brother, snagged on Herren's white-faced stoicism, and jerked hastily back to Meridy. "*Why?*" Then she visibly gathered her wits and went on quickly, "You must have misunderstood. He couldn't have done anything of the kind, or Tai-Enchar would have been drawn after Herren long ago!"

"Well, I kind of think Inmanuàr didn't have to worry about that," Meridy said. She couldn't think of any way to be gentle about this. She said baldly, "From what happened to your mother, and from what Herren tells me, and from one or two things Inmanuàr's said, I'm almost sure the witch-king has actually always had his hand over Herren. Since before he was born."

"Wait, no!" cried Diöllin.

"Listen," Herren said. "She's right, Liny. Just listen." He didn't speak loudly, but the tired resignation in his voice, so wrong for a child his age, struck his sister to silence.

Meridy said, "I think Tai-Enchar has always been ready to reach out and take Herren when the time was right, but I also think Carad Mereth and Inmanuàr had their own plan about how to—how to use Herren against him. Then the witch-king had to move before he wanted to, because you weren't supposed to die yet. Just your father. I think when the fire horse killed you, too, things went wrong between Tai-Enchar and your mother—I mean, the sorceress who's taken your mother's place. Aseraiëth. But I think . . . I think things went wrong for Carad Mereth and Inmanuàr, too, and *everyone* had to move suddenly even though they weren't ready." She looked at Herren, who gave a noncommittal shrug.

"No, but, Herren—" Diöllin began, stopping as Niniol laid a hand on her shoulder, which to Meridy's surprise the princess did not seem to resent. Instead she gave Niniol a look almost of entreaty. "*You* don't think it could be true?"

"It could be," Niniol said quietly. "Who can tell? Does it make any practical difference at this moment? It's clear Surem is a place of power in all this, and I think we must go there."

"Moran Diorr," Herren said. "Moran Diorr's the place of power."

Diöllin shook her head, not exactly disagreeing, but hating everything about the whole situation, Meridy could tell.

The princess said, "I don't . . . Look, keeping my brother *away* from Tai-Enchar, *that* would protect him—"

"He can find me," Herren said thinly. "He can find me in my dreams."

Diöllin stared, struck wordless.

"Ah, well. Of course he can." Niniol rubbed his forehead with the tips of his fingers.

Meridy said apologetically, knowing how much Diöllin would hate this, "That's why I asked that farmer for sweetleaf. I know it's not really good to take every day, but it keeps him from dreaming."

Diöllin said, "Herren . . ." Then she stopped.

"I wanted to tell you, Liny. But it's always been that way, and there wasn't anything you could do."

"There still isn't, apparently," the princess said wearily. She went to her brother and tried to lay her hands on his shoulders, murmuring in his ear so that he would know she was right there with him. Herren sighed and closed his eyes, obviously wanting to lean against his sister, except he couldn't.

Meridy looked away, sorry for them both and more than a little afraid that it was only going to get worse. She said, "We'll go to Surem, then, and think about how to get to Moran Diorr, and if we can find a way into dreams, then maybe we can still follow Jaift's plan. . . ." She wished again she knew for certain that Jaift was safe but tried not to let herself think about it. She made herself finish firmly. "Jaift's plan to free Carad Mereth. Then he can oppose Tai-Enchar, as I guess he has been doing for hundreds of years, and maybe then—"

"Then I'll tell him he has to use someone else for his plans and leave my brother alone!" Diöllin declared fiercely.

Meridy wished she thought that was possible. "I was going to say, maybe we can help Carad Mereth defeat the witch-king once and for all, and then we'll all be safe." She tried to sound like she believed this, but she couldn't help glancing quickly at little Herren.

"Yes," Herren said firmly, but without meeting her eyes. "Then we'll all be safe."

twenty-two

The farmer's track led to another, and that one to another, and if the trampled pathways weren't so smooth or straight as a highway, they were at least far less trafficked. And if an occasional farmer caught sight of Meridy and Herren riding by on the semivisible ghost of a horse, at least Gonnuol was so inexhaustibly fast that the glimpse was probably too brief for anyone to realize what exactly had passed by.

The journey from Cora Diorr to Surem, the capital of Moran Tal, which sprawled along the shore of Moran Bay, ought to have taken weeks by wagon. Or if they'd been riding a normal horse, at least seven or eight days. But they crossed the border into Moran Tal two days after leaving Cora Diorr, and then two days after that, late in the afternoon, struck the Suremne Highway half a day's ride from Surem.

"Three hundred miles in four days!" Meridy said, marveling at such speed. It was almost beyond belief. Though her backside and thighs believed it. She wished very much that Gonnuol had been wearing a saddle when he'd been killed, and she'd have felt more comfortable with a bridle, too, although the fire horse had proved willing to accommodate them once Meridy had demonstrated that she would let him fade back into the *ethereal* if he turned too far away from the route she needed him to take. She knew now that Herren had been right: Gonnuol understood that she was his anchor and that if he wanted to run faster than a person's walking pace, he needed to carry her. If all fire horses were as smart as Gonnuol, no wonder they were so dangerous to hunt and difficult to capture.

But no matter how much he understood, Gonnuol was definitely unhappy about approaching Surem.

They'd had to let him fade into the *ethereal* at last, here where the countryside was heavily settled and travelers ever more frequent. Once they dismounted and started walking, the fire horse circled around Meridy and Herren, dancing uneasily sideways and then lunging forward in a rush, snapping his jaws to make his tusks clash together threateningly. Meridy didn't blame him one bit, even if his violent displeasure was nerve-racking. The idea of walking among all these people frightened her, too, though she tried not to show it. Anyone might be a witch, or a sorcerer, or one of Tai-Enchar's servitors, or something even more dire. Even though they shouldn't need to go right into the city, the thought of so many strangers was hard to face. And what if a priest or a witch or someone saw the fire horse? Word would spread so fast, and anybody who was searching for them would know exactly where to look. . . .

"Even if a witch does glimpse Gonnuol, they'll probably think he's just an ordinary horse," Herren pointed out. "He's not likely to get near enough for any stranger to get a close look at him, even if they've got the eyes to see."

By this time, Meridy wasn't even surprised Herren had guessed what she was thinking; he was amazingly perceptive.

She supposed it was because he was a prince and had grown up knowing that people didn't always say what they meant.

"Gonnuol is trailing us, anyway, not sticking out of your pocket," the boy added. "I'm sure he'll stay as far from strangers as he can."

This turned out to be true, and as their actual goal was Moran Bay, not Surem, they had no need to venture into the city itself. Of course, they had to skirt the entire city to reach the bay, which seemed unnecessarily tedious. Though a fairly decent road of pounded earth encircled the city, it was amazing how easy it was to get used to riding instead of walking.

Also, the road was busy; there was no avoiding that. There were a few fancy narrow-wheeled carriages with high-stepping horses, but there were a lot more dogcarts competing for space with wagons pulled by mules. All this traffic competed with boys leading small herds of goats and girls carrying hens tucked under their arms or baskets of fruit, with men striding out on errands and women strolling more sedately, their skirts turned up against the dust. These were a mostly people of fair coloring, which made Meridy feel terribly conspicuous. Now and then someone, attention caught by her dusky skin and hair, gave her a close look, frowning, but most of the people were too busy about their own affairs to bother noticing a witch-girl.

To the left, the unwalled city of Surem rose up: neither the yellow-gray stone and white towers of Cora Diorr, nor the umber brick of Cora Talen, nor the bright blues and pinks and greens of Riam, but a distinctive style unlike any of those. Here the plaster of the homes and shops was whitewashed, or else painted eggshell-cream or a pale gold like well-beaten egg. The fancy exposed timbers that edged and crossed the plaster were painted dark brown, the color of the best garden loam, or else a russet like oak leaves in the fall. The roofs were dark shingle, mostly a brown tinted with gold, and the strings of prayer bells hanging from the eaves were enameled in warm tones of cream and copper and gold. Even the cobbles were of a tawny brown. It was all very handsome.

Meridy wondered what the wealthier parts of Surem might be like, and wished Jaift were with her, and that the two of them had nothing to do but explore the city. She wished even more that she had some way to know, really *know*, that her friend was safe in Cora Diorr. Surely Lord Roann and his brother would have been able to protect Jaift. . . . She didn't want to think about that too closely, and there was nothing to do about it anyway, and plenty to keep track of here on the outskirts of Surem.

To the right, outside the city proper, cottages and stalls and markets spilled into the farmlands. The cottages were thatched, mostly. If they had window coverings at all, these were of oiled paper rather than glass, and the cottages probably also had floors of beaten earth covered with rushes rather than properly laid wooden boards. But their plaster was neatly painted and mostly in good repair, and many of them looked larger and more comfortable than the general run of the cottages in Tikiy. Beyond the cottages and market stalls, interlaced with the sprawl of humbler buildings, lay the pastures and fields, most of them bordered by tight-planted thorn briar and locust trees and overlooked by low, sprawling farmhouses. No doubt narrow farmers' tracks wove through those fields, though it was hard to see how even such narrow paths could find their way through the forbidding fencerows. Besides, in this close-planted country, it would surely prove impossible to remain unobserved even if it was possible to keep to those tracks—and they would have to go far out of their way to avoid Surem's outskirts, anyway.

Herren, brighter and more cheerful than Meridy had yet seen him, stared around at everything and everyone. He said suddenly, "We could buy a chicken. You could carry it and then no one would look at you twice. I ought to have a goat on a string, like that boy over there."

"A goat!" Diöllin said, her shock obvious even given her faint thread of a voice.

"Well, not an ugly one like that. One of those pretty ones with the floppy ears." Herren looked hopefully at Meridy. "Could we buy a goat? We could give it away again later, to a boy who doesn't have one of his own. It's only right for a prince to give largess to his people."

"We're in Moran Tal," Diöllin pointed out. "These aren't even our people."

"Well, but I'm sure a boy from Moran Tal would still like a goat, if he doesn't have one," Herren argued.

Meridy surprised herself by laughing. She supposed they did have enough money to buy a goat, and almost wanted to see if one of the goat boys would sell an animal just to please Herren. "I expect we wouldn't find a boy when we needed one, and then Gonnuol would probably turn up and terrify the poor goat straight out of the *real* and onto the White Road." But she added, giving the young prince a penny, "Why don't you buy a couple of pies from that stall over there, though?"

She strolled on slowly, keeping an eye on Herren though Niniol, watchful as always, shadowed the young prince.

Then she stumbled in shock as, between one step and the next, she found first Iëhiy and then Inmanuàr himself close beside her.

Iëhiy dashed to Meridy and hurled himself against her

with enthusiasm, ears tipped back, panting happily. If he'd been a living dog, he would surely have knocked her over, but since he had no weight or heft, she stroked his jaw and pulled his ear and patted his neck. But though she told Iëhiy how glad she was to see him, and it was true, she wasn't nearly so happy to see Inmanuàr.

The High King's son looked exactly as always: at once young and old, assured and guarded, impatient and enduring. Sunlight slid along his cheek as though not entirely certain he was there, folding around echoes of the bright violet and sapphire colors his clothing had once possessed. He tilted his head as Meridy thumped Iëhiy's sides and told him what a good dog he was. Though Inmanuàr looked grave enough, there was a hint of humor to his mouth.

Straightening, Meridy demanded, "What are you doing here? And what—or who—is coming after you this time? Tai-Enchar or Princess Tiamanaith?"

"This time I am not leading our enemies to you," Inmanuàr said, and added, "Unfortunately."

Meridy glared at him. "You mean they already know where we are! Tai-Enchar or the princess-regent, or both?"

Inmanuàr was smiling at her. "You are quick. Both, for the princess-regent—or rather, the sorceress Aseraiëth— marks the footsteps of her son, and Tai-Enchar marks the path she draws for him. You have been swifter than she expected, and so for a time she lost Herren, but now she has him again in her eye."

"So if she's on her way, and Tai-Enchar behind her—" Meridy looked around quickly, not only to be sure Herren was all right but also as though she might suddenly see a hiding place, or a bulwark against sorcerous attack.

Inmanuàr lifted a hand. "No; we have a little time.

Enough, we may hope. Aseraiëth's goals are not quite aligned with Tai-Enchar's; each delays the other and so they have not come quite so far upon their way as might be. This works to our gain, because for you there is a swifter road than this to the shores of Mora Bay. 'Ere dawn or dusk, ere breaking or binding, swift upon the noiseless road the traveler proceeds!'"

"'Guided by dream before and reverie trailing behind,'" Meridy said, completing the line. Then she blinked and added, "That poem is a *tragedy*!"

"My good dog will guide you," the ghost prince promised her gravely, and turned to Herren as the boy came up to them, Niniol half a step behind and Diöllin as much to the fore. Diöllin was glaring at Inmanuàr, furious, but if the older ghost noticed, he seemed not to care. Well, he was the High King's son; Meridy could see that the anger of a mere ordinary princess might not move him.

Herren knew Inmanuàr was there, Meridy could tell; or he guessed it. Perhaps he had heard his voice. The boy had brought one of the little pies, wrapped in a mulberry leaf, for Meridy, but he had clearly forgotten he held it. Red mulberry juice dripped into the dust. He said in his thin, tightly controlled voice, so wrong for a boy his age, "She's found me."

Stepping forward, Inmanuàr set his hands on the young prince's shoulders. Herren flinched as though he felt an echo of that touch, but he didn't step back.

Lowering his voice, Inmanuàr said to him, "The sorceress will not have you; she will not bargain with Tai-Enchar over your body. It will not happen. Meridy will keep you safe and bring you to Moran Diorr. Once you are come there, above all, you must come to *me*. To me, and no one else. Do you understand?"

"Wait—" said Meridy, suspecting *she* understood what

Inmanuàr intended to do once he brought Herren to Moran Diorr, and beginning to be appalled.

"What do you mean!" cried Diöllin. "He's not— What do you mean to do?"

But Herren only gave a stiff, tight little nod, and said, "Yes. I will."

"Good," Inmanuàr said quietly, for this moment ignoring the rest of them. "You'll do, when it comes to the moment. You will have to. As will I." Then he turned back to Meridy and added, "As will we all."

Meridy, who had been set to argue, found no way to argue with this.

"So, my friend," Inmanuàr said to her, now more gently. "You mustn't dally on this road—but you know that. I think Tai-Enchar will come before the sorceress. It's true my presence always draws him, and since Aseraiëth had already led him most of the way to this place, he will soon find me, and step through dreams to come to this place. You must be prepared to step away." He held out a hand to Iëhiy, who came and leaned against his side. Inmanuàr looked gravely at Meridy. "Follow my good dog," he said to her. "The God's hand lies over him. He will never guide you wrong."

Then Inmanuàr turned to hold out his hand in the same way to the fire horse stallion, who paced forward as tamely as a dog and shoved his muzzle into the boy's palm. "You, none of us expected," Inmanuàr said to the beast. "Your speed and ferocity might be enough, at the end, if only we can come to the end together."

"The end, is it?" said Meridy. "And you have it all planned, do you?"

"And plans go wrong, you will say, and I can't disagree. Whatever moment you see in which you might oppose Tai-

Enchar, I hope you will seize it, for all our sakes. But not here, and not yet. This is not that moment. The memory of Moran Diorr holds all our hope and all our fear. Do you understand?"

But before Meridy could say no and demand better answers, Inmanuàr stepped back, and back again, and flicked out, gone.

Meridy swung around, trying to see in every direction at once, certain that in another heartbeat, the witch-king would come. She had to find that other road that Inmanuàr had commanded her to take. Or Iëhiy had to show it to her, but she had to be ready to see which way the dog went, ready to follow him—ready to help Herren follow him, even though he didn't have the eyes of a witch. She seized the young prince's hand, casting the mulberry pastry into the dust.

Diöllin said imperatively, "Mery, we have to—" But before she could finish her sentence, the dusty sunlight folded back around them and the summer air dimmed. The fire horse gave a series of aggressive little half lunges, snorting, and Iëhiy, every translucent hair along his spine standing on end, snarled. Niniol stepped in front of them all, his sword glimmering like ice in his translucent hand.

Stooping, Meridy snatched up a handful of dust and said to Iëhiy, "Go! Show us the road!"

The hound snarled again, ignoring her. And then Jaift stepped out of the fold in the light.

It was Jaift. But her eyes were black, and her mien, contemplative and brooding, was nothing like her ordinary cheerful generosity. Meridy couldn't tell at all what the person behind those black eyes was thinking. She shaped Jaift's name without sound. She'd left her friend behind, she'd seen no choice and she'd been so sure that all their enemies would follow *her*—she'd hoped so hard that Jaift, whom everyone liked and who could talk anyone into anything, would be safe. And now she saw that Tai-Enchar had swept poor Jaift up and taken her for his own. This was not Jaift at all. This was a servitor. It was the witch-king himself.

It was unbearable.

Meridy started forward, though she had no idea what she intended to do; though she knew there was actually nothing she *could* do. She was aware of Niniol shouting at her, trying to grip her shoulders and stop her, and she knew he was right, but she strode right through him anyway, and Jaift, black-eyed Jaift, looked her in the face and smiled a faint, chilling smile.

"Get out of her!" Meridy cried. "Let her *go!*"

But the witch-king only smiled, and lifted Jaift's hand toward Meridy, and took a step in her direction.

Iëhiy, with a sound somewhere between a snarl and a whine, whirled and fled, and the fire horse raked his claws across the dusty earth, snapped at the air, sank down on his haunches, and sprang away, following the hound.

"Meridy!" shouted Diöllin, breathless and intense with horror. "Stop! *Herren needs you!*"

Though she was sick with horror, Meridy knew the princess was right. She backed away from Jaift, from the horrible thing Tai-Enchar had made of Jaift, and seized Herren's hand hard in hers, and fled after the fire horse.

She abandoned Jaift to their enemy. It was the worst thing she had ever done, but she did it, fleeing into the *ethereal*, following Iëhiy, who always knew where he was and where he should go.

From somewhere, seeming very far away, came the hound's ringing bay answering her call, and around them, the light tilted. Meridy thought the air opened up and slammed down again in a thunderclap of silence greater than sound, and she was suddenly somewhere . . . else.

She stood in a sleeting torrent of light. Light tangled in her hair, light trailed from her hands and filled her eyes. She found a cold like deep winter striking into her lungs, and that seemed wrong; wasn't it summer? Yet snow crunched underfoot and naked black trees surrounded her, and the light was all wrong, and the air was . . . not right, either, somehow.

She swayed, swept by a wave of vertigo. But before she could lose her balance completely, strong hands closed on her shoulders.

It was Niniol. In this place, he looked like a living man: big and gruff and solid, with grizzled hair and, across his jaw, the thin scar pale on weathered skin only a couple shades lighter than hers. When he tilted his head and lifted a wry eyebrow at her, he looked exactly like himself.

Meridy tried to catch her breath. She managed to say after a moment, in a voice that almost sounded like her own, "Well, so we ran into dreams, but not Tai-Enchar's realm, thank the God!" She glanced around at the leafless winter wood. The full moon rode high above the black trees; its silvery light poured down around them. Iëhiy was nowhere to be seen, and she felt bereft.

"Oh, it's a realm of dreams, all right," Niniol agreed. His tone was grim, even resigned, but he did not seem to think they faced any immediate threat. He tilted his head back, lifting his face to the pale moonlight. "A soldier recognizes this place. We've come to the God's very doorstep. Should we venture farther, we'd take the White Road in truth."

Meridy nodded, feeling that he was right. "If this is the God's doorstep, we daren't stay long, or we'll become echoes of ourselves and then we'll never be able to go back, only on. But where's Iëhiy? And the others?" How had she lost the prince? Hadn't she had hold of him? She was terrified for the boy, but Niniol only nodded past her. Turning, she found the frozen wood stretching back and back and back, endlessly. But coming toward them, Herren and Diöllin, hand in hand. The princess looked just as she had in life, except perhaps angrier and more determined.

"You saw that!" she said to Meridy, as soon as they'd come all together. "That was Tai-Enchar! He's taken your friend for a servitor—"

"Obviously!" snapped Meridy, heartsick at the thought of it and furious at Diöllin for putting that truth into words.

Diöllin, like Niniol, seemed as solid as a living person in this place of dreams.

Herren held his sister's hand, but not like a child clinging to an adult. He held her hand as though he were afraid, but not afraid for himself. He held her hand as though he feared if he let go, she might fall away from him and vanish into the endless winter. He said thinly, "If we defeat the witch-king, we might save Jaift. That's all we can do for her now. But first we need to return to the world of men. How are we going to do that?"

Meridy stared at him. Then she let out her breath and shrugged. He was right. Or she hoped he was right. She wished she knew what happened to the witch-king's servitors when he was finished with them—what might happen to them if Tai-Enchar were actually defeated. She could hardly imagine what *defeat* might even mean, in this context. If being dead for two hundred years hadn't been enough to get rid of the witch-king, then she had no idea what would actually do it.

She wished Inmanuàr would come back. But if Inmanuàr returned, no doubt he would draw the witch-king right to them yet again. Probably in Jaift's body. That . . . had surely been one of the worst things Meridy had ever seen in her whole life. And it wasn't over yet, and there was nothing she could do. Except defeat the witch-king. Somehow.

She looked at Prince Herren. The same thing that had happened to Jaift had happened first to Herren's *mother*. She couldn't even imagine. Herren had faced that, faced everything. If he was overwhelmed now, well, she couldn't blame him for a second. Yet the young prince did not seem overwhelmed. When he had asked how they were going to return to the world of men, she knew he wasn't asking because he'd given up. He was asking because he *hadn't*.

If Meridy was certain of anything, it was that she did not have the strength, or the weakness, to meet the little boy's eyes and tell him she didn't know what to do.

She looked around. This silent realm obviously wasn't meant for mortal men or living creatures. No one had to explain to her they couldn't linger here. She knew that. But how could she find the way without Iëhiy?

"You know the road we must take," Niniol said, gravely confident, and Meridy looked at him.

Diöllin started to say something, but Meridy held up her hand for silence and the princess hushed. Then Meridy stood still for a long moment, listening to the soft, endless hiss of the wind blowing through frozen leaves and over drifts of snow. It was a sound born of silence, a sound that stood behind the silence, and the stillness of this place seemed to grow deeper and longer and wider for that tiny whisper. The pale light of the full moon flooded everything without, somehow, revealing anything.

Inmanuàr would have quoted something. Something old, and appropriate. Meridy thought for a moment. Then she said softly, "'The pale moon rose in beauty, shining like death, the road shining before us, a straight road laid for us through the shadows.'" The rolling lines came back to her easily, and she suddenly saw that a road ran through this winter wood. It stretched away, glimmering like crushed pearl in the moonlight.

The moonlight poured down, and the wind stirred the snow and brushed it, stinging, into the air, and the leafless black trees closed around the road as though there were no end to them and never would be. But it was all an echo. It wasn't the God's true Road. Meridy held both her hands toward this dream-echo of a road and said out loud, quoting a line she dimly remembered from one of Ambica's stories, "'The path that can be found is not the true path.'" Then she closed her eyes, took Niniol's hand, and Herren's, glanced at Diöllin to make sure she had her brother's other hand, and walked straight forward, not along the road that ran out before them, but straight across it, toward the opposite side.

When the air softened, losing its stinging chill, she stopped walking and opened her eyes.

twenty-three

They stood, Meridy saw, with only a faint sense of surprise, on the edge of a high cliff. Herren stood on her left, and Niniol, once again insubstantial, on her right. Below them, a glittering expanse of water stretched out in the sunlit afternoon. The shadows of high clouds raced across the bay, seeming to disappear when they met the land. Where the breeze stirred the bay, the rippling wavelets glittered and flashed as though sparking with inward fire. The sound of the waves against the rocky shore below was softly discernible even from this height.

"Moran Bay," Meridy said. "The waters that drowned Moran Diorr when the High King fell."

Herren shook free of her grip and walked forward, to the very edge of the cliff. Diöllin whipped in a tight circle around him, her worry all but palpable, but Herren didn't notice and she sighed sharply and drew back a little. The princess, like Niniol, looked like a ghost again to Meridy's eye: colorless, tenuous, merely a memory of the living girl. The sunlight here, echoing between sky and water, seemed stronger and more brilliant than the sunlight elsewhere. It shone around and through the quick dead.

Iëhiy appeared in the sudden way that the quick dead sometimes did, glanced around with a jaunty air, and came to sit on Niniol's feet. Light glimmered through every translucent hair of his coat and in his colorless eyes, and then tangled in the mane of the fire horse, which followed the hound out of the air. Gonnuol tossed his head suspiciously and trotted away, pacing along the cliff edge, his head snaking out aggressively when he saw Meridy looking at him. He paused to tear with his claws at the tough grasses that clung to the edge of the cliff. Every now and then, a grass blade stirred in answer to his violence.

On a day like this one, Meridy could not believe anyone in the world could not see ghosts.

"Remarkable," Niniol murmured, studying Moran Bay. "How many miles did we step across with that little detour, I wonder?" He added, with an ironic glint in his eye, "Things like this never used to happen to me, you know, until I met you."

"Yes, well, things like this never used to happen to me, either," Meridy answered. "Then I met Carad Mereth. So this is all his fault." She hoped she would have a chance to complain to him about it. Soon, preferably. She thought of him, trapped somewhere in the witch-king's realm, and winced. It had seemed so practical to find a way to rescue him and then let him deal with everything. Now she guessed that even if she'd managed to find him, it wouldn't have solved anything.

Of them all, she was almost sure Herren had the most to fear. But he looked steady enough. He stood at the edge of the cliff, so near the empty air that it made Meridy nervous, but he showed no sign of fear. Looking down at the blue waves, he said in a low voice, "Moran Diorr is down there."

Meridy nodded.

"Then that's where we need to go," the young prince declared.

"I know," Meridy answered.

Diöllin opened her mouth but closed it again without saying anything. Meridy gave the princess a sympathetic look. Diöllin wanted to protect her little brother. Of course she did. It couldn't be any comfort for her to realize, as she must have by now, that she couldn't, and that Herren wouldn't let her protect him anyway.

"How does one reach a city drowned beneath the salt waves hundreds of years ago?" asked Niniol, but his tone was resigned, as though he had no doubt they'd find a way.

"It's said by all the poets," Meridy said, "that if one should descend beneath the bitter waves of Moran Bay, Moran Diorr still rests there. In all its glory it is preserved, for those who look into memory, for it holds still the ghosts of every man and woman and child who was caught within its borders when the sea came in."

"Good, good," said Niniol. "And did any of these poets ever offer advice as to how one might descend to its drowned streets?"

Meridy couldn't help but smile. "Well, no. But I think I know. I think Inmanuàr did tell us how to reach Moran Diorr. The city lingers in drifts of memory, you know. It's like any ghost town, in a way. What we need is an old ghost, one who remembers the city as it was when it lived. One we can follow so deep into memory that for us, the waters of the bay never covered the City of Bells." And she held out her hand, deliberately, to Iëhiy. The wolfhound, ears up and tail waving, got to his feet and came to her. Sunlight streamed through him, brindling his coat in light and shadow. He seemed to have been poured out of glass and air. He was very old. She'd always known that. Next to him, Niniol and Diöllin were practically invisible.

Beckoning to Iëhiy, Meridy stepped to the edge of the cliff, so that she stood between the infinite sky and the bitter water of the bay. Somehow the rushing sound of the waves washing against the rocks far below made the cliff seem even higher. Meridy took care not to go too near the edge—she had never been afraid of heights, but this was something else.

At her side, the wolfhound stood like a statue. He *was* fearless. Even if he'd been living, even if he might have fallen, she thought the dog would have been just that fearless. She had no doubt that the God's hand was over him and had been all his life, for dogs were sacred to the God, who loved courage and faithfulness, and surely no dog anywhere was braver or more faithful than Iëhiy.

She quoted softly, "'Listen! Beyond the sound of the waves, drowned bells are ringing.'"

It seemed to her that the world grew more quiet still, as though the wind itself had hushed to listen. And it seemed to her that behind the silence, she could indeed hear the sound of a thousand ringing bells. Tiny delicate bells of glass and crystal, their voices like chimes, sang above the joyful clear notes of heavy bronze bells; the sweet voices of bells made of mellow gold rang around and above the brighter notes of silver and brass and copper; and below them all tolled the deep voices of great dark iron bells, heavy and powerful as the sea itself.

Beside her, Herren drew in a breath.

Iëhiy bounded joyfully forward, off the cliff and into the air. He did not fall, being a ghost; but neither did he run straight across the empty air. Instead, a bridge made of light and memory and the ringing voices of ten thousand bells spun itself out of the air before the hound. The bridge reached from the rocks at Meridy's feet down in a dizzying sweep to bury itself in the depths of the bay.

Niniol hissed through his teeth and murmured, "The God protect us!" in a tone that made it clear this was a prayer and no mere exclamation.

"It *will* hold our weight," Herren said determinedly, and started forward—brave as Iëhiy—but Diöllin leaped to prevent him.

"Careful!" she cried. "An *ethereal* bridge—I should think it would need more than a ghost's memory to anchor it against the weight of living feet!"

But Meridy shook her head. "Iëhiy is a very old ghost, you know. He was Inmanuàr's dog, and he knows his way home. No, I'm sure any road he travels is a true road, and any bridge the God lays before his feet is a true bridge. It will hold our weight—as long as it needs to. Long enough for us to walk into memory." She didn't let herself say, *I think it will.* She was afraid of finding their enemy behind them, but she was even more afraid the bridge might fade if clouds crossed the face of the sun. She didn't say so. The clouds now were high and wispy, but there were more of them than Meridy liked—if she couldn't have mist or fog or smoke, then bright sunlight was better than shadow. She shook away her fears, though, and said as confidently as she could, "Come on! Follow Iëhiy and never doubt that the bridge will hold—don't doubt it for a second!" Then she ran forward. She didn't let herself hesitate at the edge of the cliff; she didn't reach forward to touch the bridge with a toe. For a bridge like this, she suspected that belief mattered.

Her foot came down on the bridge, and it did hold. Light poured through and around the bridge, and the ghostly ringing of ten thousand bells rose up around her, and she walked forward, not too fast now because if she ran she might become frightened and fear was the cousin of doubt, and she guessed that doubt would melt this bridge as surely as uncertain light.

The bridge held her and did not fail, but it did not feel like any normal bridge. It felt cold underfoot, and both brittle and springy at the same time, and not at all like it was *real.* It would have been too easy to imagine falling through it and down down down, to the rocks where the waves washed at the base of the cliff. So she did not let herself look down, or back. She went forward, following Iëhiy, and simply hoped the others followed her.

Herren caught up to her before she'd gone very far, Diöllin right with him and Niniol a heartbeat after that, and Meridy took the young prince's hand, gave her ghosts a smile, and walked more surely because they were with her. Risking a glance back, she was not quite surprised to see the fire horse trailing after them. Though he put each clawed foot down with delicate care, he, like Iëhiy, seemed unafraid of the dizzying fall below or the wide sky all around them.

Behind the stallion, Meridy saw the bridge unraveling into light and air, so behind him there was no bridge leading back to the edge of the cliff. This did not seem to concern the stallion, however, and after all they could not go back. So she turned her face firmly forward and followed the high, waving tail of the wolfhound, barely visible ahead of her.

Somewhere in that journey across the bridge of moonlight and imagination, they should have found themselves descending beneath the waters of the bay. But the waves seemed to melt away before them, towers rising up instead. The path of the bridge seemed to flatten until it was nearly level, as though they walked on a road of shimmering ice toward a city and not on a bridge that descended into the bay. Meridy never glimpsed water; there was no sign now that the sea had ever rolled in to cover this land. And, although Meridy did not look back again, she suspected that if she had, she would have seen no dark shadows of rocky cliffs behind them, either. They walked now though memory, and here the land had never sunk down and the sea had never come in to cover the towers.

The voices of the bells rang in the air all around them. Meridy walked forward, following Iëhiy. Color and solidity washed across the wolfhound as he trotted before them, not all at once, but little by little, until eventually he looked exactly as he had in life. Beside her, Niniol, too, once more took on the appearance of a living man, so she knew they had stepped fully into the realm of dreams.

Then Iëhiy stopped and turned back to wait for them, his ears pricked forward attentively, and they were standing in the center of a broad avenue, with tall, graceful buildings to either side. The street was paved with fitted white stone, worn smooth by countless feet, that cast back the light not of the afternoon sun they had left behind, but of the full moon.

The towers of Moran Diorr were white as the stones of the street; white with broad veins of pale gold and smoky gray-blue winding through them. Those towers rose astonishingly high in the air, with domes and balconies, doors of carved and polished spicewood and narrow arched windows. The stone of the towers was carved everywhere, with flowers and leaves and interwoven patterns in delicate relief, and the windows glittered with glass in shades of gold and amber and rose, and flowers spilled over the balcony railings. The towers' height gave them a light and airy look for all their size, and Meridy realized the spires of Cora Diorr must have been built as an echo of these towers.

Around and amid the towers, tall houses glowed in the moonlight, all sunset colors: saffron and carmine, warm orange and apricot, and all of them embellished with elaborate swirling plasterwork. Their rooftops were tiled in red and rust and tawny gold, steeply pitched, with long strands of enameled prayer bells swaying from their gracefully overhanging eaves.

Bells were everywhere: not only the strings of prayer bells but bells of brass and copper and bronze, steel and dark iron, some smaller than Meridy's hand and others taller than she was. Wind chimes of steel and brass hung from lampposts; delicate strings of gold and silver bells trailed from the branches of the trees that lined the avenue; bells of clear glass and lapis from the rising dishes of a many-tiered fountain where water splashed. Several of the towering spires were open to the air, and within them hung tremendous bells of bronze or iron. All the city was filled with the sound of bells, though there was no wind Meridy could feel; but even though they stood within the city, the sound somehow seemed to come from very far away, from hundreds of years in the past.

There were no people in the street at all, or in the windows of the buildings. There were no human voices mingled with the voices of the bells. There were not even any visible ghosts, except for those who had come with Meridy.

"My sweet God," Niniol murmured in a hushed voice, speaking for all of them.

"Are we really here?" Diöllin asked. "Is this really Moran Diorr?" Forgetting her customary disdain, she stared around in open amazement.

"This is one layer of memory," Meridy explained, knowing it was true. She looked around at the graceful empty streets and the deserted towers. "See how . . . empty it is here. This is the memory of the city, but we need to go deeper, farther back, into the memory of the people who used to live here before Moran Diorr drowned, to truly see the city as it was."

"We need to find Inmanuàr," Herren said, and though he had been staring around with the same wonder they all felt, he spoke those words with what seemed to Meridy a kind of disturbingly flat resignation.

twenty-four

Herren was right, though. Meridy knew that, too. They did need to find the High King's son. Meridy looked around, searching for inspiration, and found it in the usual place. She said, "Iëhiy!" The hound bounded to her, whining, then trotted away down the wide avenue. Herren started off after the dog without looking back or waiting for anyone else.

Diöllin called after him, "Herren!" but though her brother must have heard her, he did not look back.

"No, listen, your brother is right," Meridy told Diöllin. "He's older than his years—as you'd expect, since he's anchored Inmanuàr all his life." Though come to think of it, that could not be at all reassuring, so then Meridy simply shook her head, touched Diöllin's hand in sympathy, and hurried after Herren, knowing the princess had to follow.

The High King's palace, when they found it, proved to be a many-cornered structure so vast it would probably have taken days to walk around it, with a white spire at each corner and a tiered roof rising to a swooping dome. Meridy knew this must be the palace; if she had spent a year imagining what the High King's palace must look like, she would have imagined a great and beautiful building exactly like this. But its vast gates—brass and black wood—were standing open, and so were the doors beyond the gates. The city seemed even emptier and more deadly quiet here, where no doubt noblemen and lords, merchants and tradesmen, and petitioners of all stations and degrees had once thronged. Meridy glanced around, half seeing the crowd in her mind's eye. But even here the city stood deserted and empty.

It was all rather nerve-racking. Meridy waited for Niniol, who came up beside her and gave her a reassuring nod, though he also cast a worried look toward Herren, who had already reached the palace gates.

"I know—I know," Meridy said. "I'm afraid for him too, but what else can we do?" She pulled Niniol forward.

Herren did not wait for them at the entrance but passed alone through the gates and then through the doors and so into the High King's palace, leaving Meridy and the others to hurry in his wake.

Once inside, she hesitated, but Herren was already heading for a stairway curving up to the right, the steps of white marble threaded with pale gold veins. Meridy followed him, uneasy but committed.

The great stair proved to lead to a long, vaulted hallway with walls of tawny-gold stone and marble pillars and floors of complicated mosaic. A heavy throne of carved dark wood stood at the opposite end of the hall. When they drew closer, Meridy saw that the sigil of the God was inlaid in pearl on the high back of the throne. And then she saw that Inmanuàr sat upon the throne.

Inmanuàr's head was bowed, and Meridy thought for a moment that he might be weeping, but he straightened as they approached and his face was calm. Yet he seemed somehow more deeply grieved than if he had wept. He seemed even less *real* than before, in this great hall, which had been drowned and destroyed two hundred years before, and yet, like the other quick dead in this place, he was more visible here than he ever had been elsewhere. But Meridy would have known he was a ghost even if she had been seeing him for the very first time. He was *too* solid, too present, far too old for the boy he seemed to be, and somehow it showed. He looked, despite his youth, like a king. Meridy looked into his face and hardly knew how to speak to him, or what to say.

Then Iëhiy, unimpressed by kings or princes or the weight of the tragic past, threw himself at Inmanuàr, ears slanted eagerly and tongue lolling, and Inmanuàr braced himself, caught the insubstantial weight of the dog neatly, and ruffled his ears. "Well, dog," he said, with real affection, "and so you have brought them here for me."

Meridy, drawn by an unexpected stab of jealousy, suggested in her most cutting tone, "Perhaps someday you might tell me his true name."

"His name was Tai-Ruòl," said Inmanuàr, looking up again, one hand still resting on the wolfhound's massive shoulders.

The name meant King of Hounds. Meridy had to admit the name suited the wolfhound. She was being stupid. Anybody could see the dog was his, really. And it didn't matter anyway.

But then Inmanuàr straightened. "Iëhiy is a good name for him," he said more gently. "The sparks of the fire that lift to the God . . . a good name. He has guarded you well, my brave dog. But when we finally face Tai-Enchar, he will not be enough."

"We know that!" Herren said in his thin, strained voice. "*I* know that."

Inmanuàr inclined his head to the living boy. "Of course you do, little brother. So here you are. You have been very brave."

"I had no choice!" Herren was pale, his face stiff. He said again, but more quietly, "I never had a choice."

"You have always had a choice. Tai-Enchar never guessed you would come to me. Yet you are braver than he could have imagined, and here you are, in this place where I died." Inmanuàr's young face was sober and cold in the pale light; the expression in his eyes was ancient.

"I know what you plan to do with Herren," Meridy told him. "I figured it out. You need me to do it, don't you? It's why you needed a witch in the first place. But it's not right."

"That's true," Inmanuàr agreed somberly. "It is not right. But every other choice is worse. You know that. That is why the God put you in my path and gave you the way to come here."

Meridy shook her head, but she couldn't refute this. She knew it was true.

"Wait," said Diöllin. "Wait—"

Inmanuàr lifted a hand, stopping her. He said, with a distant, reserved kindness, "You, too, shall have your part to play, I believe." He swept his gaze across them all. Then he set his hands on the arms of the throne and pushed himself to his feet, for all the world as though he were a living boy with weight and heft. He said, "I was my father's heir. When the half-Southern witch, then called Enchaän, turned against my father in the midst of the sorcerous working, my father could not both defend himself and hold the frame of the sorcery. He chose to hold the sorcery and complete the raising of the Southern Wall, and in that he succeeded. But he still held all the remnants of that working in his hands. He meant to ground the sorcery and let go of that power, but he died too soon and so it came to me." His light voice seemed almost to echo in the great hall, although it was no louder. "I could not hold it. It was too strong, and I was too young, and I had no time. All I could do was keep it from going to my father's murderer. And so all that great sorcery shattered in my hands. And the land sank away beneath us, and the sea came in. And we all drowned: my father's people and I, Enchaän and the witches who were his allies and servants, all of us drowned together. The whole city, and all the lands around."

"Carad Mereth was in the South, wasn't he? He came back, but too late," Meridy said softly.

The High King's son focused on her again. "He was called Laìdomìdan then. Yes. He had gone south to raise up the Anchor for the Southern Wall and be certain it held. As you say, he came back, but he found nothing here but the bitter waters of the bay. Moran Diorr was gone. But he knew Enchaän was not entirely gone. So he called me by name and bound me not to go to the God. And so I am here, now. I am still the key to my father's power. While I linger, no one else may seize the rule that should by rights have come to me. Thus, for two hundred years Enchaän has hounded me across the face of the land. But he has never won what he sought."

"Until at last he seduced enough living people to his side in Cora Diorr," said Meridy. "Princess Tiamanaith wasn't the first, was she? The first to make a bargain with Aseraiëth, I suppose. But not the first to support Tai-Enchar. There were others. For years. The witches who went to Cora Diorr . . ."

"Not all of them. Never all of them. But too many. Prince Diöllonuor was warned. He was warned most strictly. But he heeded no warning."

Diöllin said bitterly, "My father believed too much in his

own cleverness and never enough in the cleverness of anyone else. He let Tai-Enchar into Cora Diorr. He let his ally Aseraiëth take my mother. She was that desperate, and my father never even realized what she'd done. But I didn't understand either. Not soon enough. Not until it was too late."

"I knew it wasn't her," Herren said, not looking at any of them. "It used to be. But not since this spring."

Diöllin put an arm around her brother's shoulders. "I should have listened to you." For a moment, Herren stood stiff. Then he leaned against her, and she bowed her head above his.

Inmanuàr said, more gently now, "Tai-Enchar gained influence subtly, and by the time any of us understood, it was already too late. But the God's hand is still lifted over us, and so now we are not without hope."

"But Tai-Enchar can't find you here," Meridy said. "He can't find any of us here." She tried not to let it sound like a question.

Inmanuàr regarded her steadily. "We have stepped into a lingering moment of memory. But we have not stepped altogether outside time, and, you must understand, our enemy also remembers Moran Diorr. He will come here eventually. Thus we dare not delay overlong." And Inmanuàr held out his hand to Herren.

"Wait!" Diöllin snapped. "What are you going to do?" But she knew, Meridy understood, because she added furiously, "It isn't right!"

"There's no better choice," Herren said, sounding tired and bitter and much older than his years. "Not for any of us. If Inmanuàr doesn't do it, you know, Tai-Enchar *will*. And sooner rather than later, probably."

Inmanuàr gave the princess a sardonic look. It was not the

look of a boy, or even of a mortal prince. It was the look of an ancient king. "We all must do what is put before us to do." He turned back to Herren, held out his hand again, and asked steadily, "Shall you do this?"

"I said I would," Herren said. "I will. I know I have to. What I want . . . what I want is for you to save my mother."

"That may not be possible," Inmanuàr warned him. "But I promise you that if she lingers yet, then I shall try."

Herren nodded jerkily. He took the one step necessary, past Diöllin, who hovered desperately but could not stop him, and took the hand of the High King's son. Meridy thought it was the bravest thing she had ever seen.

Inmanuàr gripped the younger boy's hand firmly in his. Then he turned, as inevitably as a falling stone, to Meridy. "Later, you may find something else to do," he told her gravely. "That is in the hand of the God. But we shall hope for that mercy." Pale light struck through Inmanuàr's eyes, which in this place were a cold gray-blue like shadowed water. Lifting his hand, he shaped a heavy fragrant rose out of air and nothing, as a ghost might do, and held it out to Meridy.

It was very like the rose he had given her, on their first meeting in the ghost town of Tikiy. Ordinarily if one touched such an *ethereal* creation, one's living touch would send it dissolving back into the dreams from which it had been formed. But in this place . . . Meridy reached out and lifted the rose delicately from his hand. It was heavy in her hand, and its thorns pricked her fingers exactly like the thorns of a *real* rose. She frowned at Inmanuàr.

"It is not true sleep that the prick of a rose may grant," the High King's son told her, his tone somber. "It is not true life that the fragrance of a rose may recall. Such sorcery belongs to tales and memories and dreams."

"I know," said Meridy. She did. She thought perhaps Ambica had told her that, or her mother. Or maybe she had always known it.

"Of course you do," Inmanuàr said. "Yet I think you will find a use for at least one rose before the end." He looked around at them all. "From this place, there is no retreat. From this lingering moment, we must step into time and face Tai-Enchar in the world of men. If we fail, we will fail entirely and Tai-Enchar will take every realm for his own and make wastelands of them all. If we succeed, who knows what may come of it?"

Niniol hooked his thumbs in his belt and gave an abrupt nod. Diöllin's lips were pressed thin, but at last she, too, nodded. Meridy took a breath and threaded the rose stem into her hair, tucking the heavy flower behind her ear.

She was just in time, for as she did so, the light in the hall folded back and opened up, and it was too late to argue or question or try to think of something better.

The witch-king came in Jaift's body. Meridy had expected that, of course she had, but it was still a shock. It was her friend's face, Jaift's flaxen hair and fair skin and high cheekbones; but those were not her eyes. Or maybe they were, if Jaift's uncle had never fixed the color of her eyes, but their black seemed endlessly deep now, and the disinterested contempt in them was nothing like Jaift. The witch-king in her body looked past Meridy, past them all, seeming aware only of Inmanuàr; and he studied the High King's son not with anything so personal as hatred, but only with a distant, empty satisfaction.

"My little enemy," murmured Tai-Enchar. The witch-king's gaze shifted from Inmanuàr to Herren, and Jaift's mouth curved in an expression that owed nothing to Jaift's generosity and kindness. The witch-king said, "Thou hast brought me a gift, I perceive." His voice, coming from Jaift's lips, thin and cold and terrible, was not the bodiless voice of a ghost. But it was nothing like Jaift's own voice, either. Meridy had heard Jaift when she was uncertain and when she was confident, when she was irritated and when she was angry. But she had never heard her friend sound cruel, and satisfied to be so.

"If you will act, act now!" commanded Inmanuàr.

"I know!" snapped Meridy, furious and terrified, and she lifted Herren's soul directly out of his body, exactly the way everyone always feared a witch might do. She took his soul out of his body and made him into a ghost and bound his ghost to herself, *exactly* the way everyone had always told her witches would do. It wasn't even hard.

Herren's eyes rolled up, and his body collapsed. Diöllin cried out as her brother's ghost wavered into visibility and then, as Meridy called out, "Herren! By your name I bind you to the world!" he gained definition and an appearance of solidity. Meridy dropped the hand of Herren's physical body and backed away, putting her arms around the boy's ghost instead.

"No!" cried Diöllin, hopelessly. "No!"

"It was the only way," Herren told her. "It had to be the High King's living heir, and it had to be someone uncorrupted by Tai-Enchar. I was as close as anyone else living, so it had to be me." In this place he still sounded almost like a living boy, though far more patient than any normal boy his age.

Ignoring both of them, Inmanuàr stooped over the young prince's abandoned body, his face intent.

Tai-Enchar lifted one hand, and dust seemed to rise up and whirl around them. The witch-king was trying to take them all into his own realm, Meridy realized—or else he was trying to make this echo of Moran Diorr into a part of his own realm. In the next instant she feared she would glimpse endless wastelands stretching out around them. But then Inmanuàr said sharply, "He is not for you!" And he vanished.

Then Inmanuàr opened the eyes of Herren's body, and rose to his feet, and held out his borrowed hands. Light, opaque and sharp-edged, struck through the dust and emptiness, and the witch-king's empty realm shattered all around them into shards of light and shadow and re-formed again into the memory of the High King's palace.

In this violent moment, they all fell deeper into memory—Inmanuàr's memory, or perhaps the memory of the city itself. Meridy saw richly clad noblemen and white-robed priests; she saw soldiers in the High King's livery, bearing the badge of the vermillion fire horse, rampant on a sable ground: an emblem that no living man had raised up since the High King's fall. She saw half a dozen men and one woman of obvious part-Southern blood standing close by a wide, low table; and on the table a map drawn in colored sand, greens and browns and the long blue lines of the rivers, and in the south, sand rising up into sharp peaks too high and jagged for any mortal person to pass, whether of pure Kingdom blood or Southerner, whether sorcerer or witch.

And there, close by the map, she also saw a tall man with eyes of an unusual light brown, and golden skin that suggested a dash of Southern blood. His face was thin, with prominent cheekbones and a bold curving nose. He wore a long tawny-colored jacket over dark green trousers, with the sleeves slashed to show a paler green shirt. He was not young, but not nearly as old as Meridy had expected. He was, of course, High King Miranuanol, the last of the High Kings.

He was a memory of an earlier age, and he stood amid memory and dreams and imaginings, and turned his head, and saw them all.

Meridy saw how the High King's gaze caught first on Tai-Enchar in Jaift's body, and narrowed with recognition. Then the High King looked past Tai-Enchar and gazed upon his son—on Herren-Inmanuàr, the ancient ghost of his son overlaid on the body of his distant heir. He recognized him immediately, and without hesitation stretched out his hand toward him, and said in a voice both deep and soundless, "My son, I see this has become the hall of the dead. Take my strength, then, and do as you must to redeem my Kingdom."

"Not even this will avail thee," said Tai-Enchar, his voice cold and empty. "My servitor is stronger than thine, as I am stronger than thou." And Jaift's hands lifted and a wind rose up, hissing with dust and loneliness.

And then all the High King's power, all the gathered magic of the sorcery he and his allies had been working in their own place and time, the memory of all the strength of the sorcery that had long ago shattered, fell again from the High King's hands as though from that long-vanished moment, as though from a tremendous height, and smashed into his son.

It had happened before. In an earlier age, it had crushed Inmanuàr; he had not been able to hold it. This time it was different. This time Inmanuàr expected that wild torrent of magic and power. He had had centuries to prepare, and Carad Mereth for a teacher, and now he stood, embodied within a new living body, in this place of his father's power and his own death. This time he rode the torrent of magic and took it for his own, and all around them he built a clear and solid memory of Moran Diorr as it had been. Inmanuàr raised the city up: white towers and sweeping galleries, graceful avenues and wide gardens, flowers and fountains and deep, still pools, and everywhere the sound of bells. And in this memory, he left no room at all for Tai-Enchar.

Meridy had half expected Inmanuàr to fling Tai-Enchar out of Moran Diorr, but the witch-king was flung out of Jaift's body as well, and she was not quite fast enough to break her friend's fall. And Jaift fell as bonelessly as the dead, with no effort to catch herself. A second after Jaift crumpled, Meridy skidded to her knees beside her on the polished floor, laying her fingertips against Jaift's throat to see if she could find a pulse. She almost thought she felt a flutter, but it was feather-light and fading. She wasn't even surprised, though grief rose up into her throat. She had known the moment Jaift fell that it was already too late.

Inmanuàr did not even glance in their direction. Jaift might have fallen, but Tai-Enchar, though disembodied once more and cast out of this memory of Moran Diorr, was not *gone*. The witch-king had only fled back to the new seat of his power in Cora Diorr, so of course Inmanuàr had no time for anyone now save his enemy. He shouted, with joy as well as rage, and put out his hand, and the fire horse stallion was there, as he had been in life, a glorious blood bay with an elegant head and gleaming tusks, a flying black mane and thick black feathering on his feet that did not quite hide his savage claws.

"Gonnuol!" Inmanuàr hailed him, calling the stallion by the name Herren had given him, in Herren's voice, and the beast, snorting, came to him with small, mincing steps. He snapped at the boy, but not seriously—a warning, maybe, that he was not by any measure tame. But Inmanuàr only laughed. He leaped up onto the fire horse's back, and Gonnuol began to leap forward, but Prince Inmanuàr checked him after all, wheeled him in a tight circle, and brought him back. "Follow your friend!" he commanded Meridy. "Bind her ghost and let her be your guide out of this memory and into another! She has harbored Tai-Enchar, and what she has learned you must use! You must find Carad Mereth and free him—that is your road now, and you must follow it! Tell him we are well begun, but now we are come to the end. It is the ending of the age! Tell him just that!"

"You intended this to happen to her!" Meridy cried. "How *could* you?" She meant to shout, but her voice sounded to her own ears like the barest whisper.

Inmanuàr gave her a tense nod, not of apology but acknowledging that she wasn't wrong to feel so angry and so bereft. "That something of the kind might come to pass, that possibility I foresaw. But we all do as we can and as we must. Take comfort from this certainty: Tai-Enchar erred in letting her go, for now she is out of his power and in the hand of the God, and so she can show you the way even into the witch-king's realm. Don't allow grief to blind you to the gift she has yet to give!"

Meridy stared at him, speechless. Before she could gather her wits, Inmanuàr let the fire horse wheel about once more, and this time he allowed Gonnuol to plunge forward, leaping out of light and into dreams, and suddenly there was a great host that rode behind them. They poured past Meridy out of the air, more and more of them, on and on. The hoofbeats of their horses were the ringing of bells, surely as audible in the *real* world as here in the realms of memory. Some were kings or princes; she saw their crowns, but the signs they bore were mostly unfamiliar. These were the old dead, the long dead, who rode past her now. They had been loosed from the hand of the God to ride out to battle, and they went eagerly, as though flying from a tightly strung bow.

Leaping straight through the wall of the Great Hall, Inmanuàr and the stallion and all that host vanished from Meridy's sight. She knew they wouldn't stop now, not until Inmanuàr had brought Tai-Enchar to bay in Cora Diorr. And then one of them would drive the other out of every realm and leave him with no refuge but the White Road of the Moon. Meridy only wished she knew which of them would win that final battle. She was certain Inmanuàr would win, but what if she was wrong, what then?

She knew she still had to find Carad Mereth. That was *her* task, either way. *The ending of the age.* She felt that it was, one way or the other.

But Jaift was still dying, and there was nothing Meridy could do to save her. Far from *saving* her, she had to *use* her friend's death. That was the worst thing of all.

twenty-five

Niniol, recovering his wits or maybe his nerve long before Meridy could scrape hers together, came and dropped a sympathetic hand on her shoulder. "Well," he said, his voice a little rough. "Well. I thought when they met here in Moran Diorr, that was supposed to end everything. And instead, here we are." He paused and then said, even more softly, "I failed her. I can't imagine what I'll say to her parents. How could I let this happen?"

Meridy looked down at Jaift, lying discarded, her head on Meridy's knee. She felt dull and stupid. She shook her head, but after a moment, she managed to say, "It wasn't your fault. It was my fault. I left her there. I left her in Cora Diorr, even knowing what I knew about the princess-regent, and about Tai-Enchar, and about how he makes the . . . the servitors."

"She's free of him now, at least," Diöllin offered tentatively, approaching side by side with the ghost of her brother.

They might look like living people, but in all this memory of a kingdom, Meridy knew, no one was alive but she. Or in merely another moment, that would be so.

"But she's still dying," Meridy said, dry-eyed and bitter. "Can you save her? Then don't say her death doesn't matter."

Jaift drew one last faltering breath, and died.

Before Meridy, the White Road of the Moon glimmered into view.

Jaift's ghost pulled free of her body and got to her feet. She stood in the middle of the White Road, moonlight shining down from above and billowing up around her feet like water, until she seemed almost to be made of light herself. The moon, full and heavy, stood above, its cool silver radiance pouring down to create and illuminate a long, pale road of light that ran through the darkness.

All this Meridy saw through and around and above the City of Bells, one dream overlaying the other. Finding herself on her feet, she took one step forward and seized Jaift's hand in hers. "Jaift!" she said. "By your name I call you and by your name I anchor you and by your name—by your name—I bind you to the world."

Jaift turned her head to gaze at Meridy, blinking.

"Where is Carad Mereth?" Meridy asked her. It wasn't what she wanted to say, but she didn't *know* what she wanted to say, and so she asked the question Inmanuàr had laid on her. She asked it again, "Where is Carad Mereth, and how can I free him from Tai-Enchar's power?"

Jaift tilted her head, blinked again, and then shivered all over, a swift convulsive shudder so that Niniol put a hand on her arm to steady her. "Jaift!" he said gently. "I'm so sorry."

Jaift frowned at this, seeming at last more like herself. "What do you mean? It wasn't your fault, Niniol!" Then she turned her frown on Meridy. "Or yours. Tai-Enchar did this to me, not either of you." Then she looked around at the splashing light and added uncertainly, "But I need to go. You've bound me, Mery, but I need to go."

Meridy wanted to weep. Even though she knew it was

wrong to hold a ghost who longed to take the God's Road, she wanted to keep Jaift's ghost bound so close and tight that her friend would never take the White Road and never leave her. She knew that would be wrong, but she *needed* Jaift.

She really did; not just for herself, but to help her find Carad Mereth. She whispered a scrap of poetry: " 'Look to the vivid sky, which strikes through the night! The face of the sky is the moon's face.' "

Moonlight rose around them like a tide coming in, washing past their knees. Meridy said again, urgently, "Where is Carad Mereth? We must free him!"

And Jaift said, "Of course we must." She took Meridy's hand and began to walk forward, not following the Road but heading at an angle across or through or somehow past its foaming light.

Meridy followed. But she waved Niniol back when he would have come with them, and she gestured to Herren to hold back Diöllin, because she feared any ghost that was once swept away upon the White Road of the Moon would never return to the realm of men. Jaift she hoped to keep hold of; but she knew she had no chance of holding so many ghosts against the tide of the White Road. "I'll find you!" Meridy called to them over her shoulder. "When I come back into the world, I'll find you, or you'll find me! Take care of them, Niniol!"

"I will," he promised her, his expression grim.

But Meridy, now breasting the current of the White Road with Jaift, hardly heard him. And whether the White Road of the Moon would run both ways in the end Meridy didn't honestly know. Except that Inmanuàr had told her to follow Jaift. So she did that, not quite blindly.

Meridy knew she would never have found the way by

herself—not unless she, too, had died—but now she followed Jaift. And her friend didn't merely follow the White Road but bent their path through numberless realms of dream and memory, and so they walked not only into the moonlight but out of the moonlight. Meridy held tight to her hand and Jaift gripped her back and would not let go, and so when they stepped out of the moonlight again and into the dark, they were still together, hand in hand. Dust blew around them in a wind that whispered of solitude and despair.

They had come into the heart of Tai-Enchar's realm. Dread ran through Meridy. Though she turned and looked again for the White Road, nothing now but darkness and emptiness surrounded them.

Then a voice, light and quick, taut with strain hidden beneath the lightness, spoke suddenly from behind her: " 'What lies in the shadows the full moon casts below? Under the hand of the God, under the bright shadow they lie; from day to night to day again they flow.' "

Meridy caught a breath in relief so intense that it was almost painful. Still gripping Jaift's hand in hers, she turned. Behind her, where a moment before had seemed only darkness, stood Carad Mereth. They had found him after all.

The sorcerer stood surrounded by darkness, but it had not yet mastered him. He made his own light, and it might be pale and flickering, but it was a light in the dark. She could see his golden hair and brilliant cornflower-blue eyes. Yet if the darkness had not overcome him, neither had he defeated it. He had begun to lose himself to the emptiness. His hands were translucent, his form indistinct, shredding softly away at the edges. His eyes were open but blind.

" 'The souls of the dead,' " Meridy said to him, answering the riddle the sorcerer had posed.

Carad Mereth smiled. His blind eyes drifted shut and then slowly opened again, veiled by settling dust. He told her, his voice strained, " 'I dreamed a rushing river flowed. On its swift wave the new dead rode, nor did not pause, nor turn to stay, but straight and fast they flowed away. And whither then? I cannot say.' " As he spoke, dust and ashes fell from his mouth and stained his lips. His words dissolved into silence a heartbeat after he spoke them.

" 'The River that is the Road!' " Meridy answered. "Jaift is our way to the White Road, but how can we free *you* to take it? And how can any of us take that Road back into the world of men rather than to the hand of the God?"

" 'The path that can be found is not the true path,' " Carad Mereth told her, his voice husky, ashes pluming on his breath. " 'The way unbarred is not the true way.' "

Meridy snapped, frustrated and terrified, *"Can't you talk like a normal person?"*

"No," said Carad Mereth, and bowed his golden head. Dust shifted across him, and he became more indistinct still. "Not here. I am thorn-caught in this world of dreams."

*"Thorn-*caught?" Meridy stared at him. When she lifted a hand to her hair, the rose fell into her palm, but it had become brittle. As she touched it, three petals cracked and fell away into gray dust barely touched with the memory of crimson. Meridy cupped the flower carefully, the faint memory of the fragrance of roses rising around her. She held it out to Carad Mereth. She said to Jaift, "Find the Road! Show us the Road!"

The fragrance lifted around them, but Jaift only gazed at her blankly.

Then Carad Mereth murmured, " 'I turned away into the darkness, and the pale moon rose in beauty, shining like death, the road shining before me, a straight road laid for me through the shadows.'"

"Oh. Yes," said Jaift, sounding surprised. She took the rose from Meridy, turning away into the dark as the rest of the petals fell and drifted into dust. But when Jaift took a step, it was out of the darkness and into the moonlight.

Meridy looked up at the full moon where a moment before there had been no moon. She thought she could hear ten thousand bells ringing in a darkness that was suddenly not empty, but a crystalline darkness filled with stars. It seemed to her that the sound of the bells was quite clear, a swelling sound that rang against the very moonlight.

The God's moon stood above the White Road, its light silvery and cool and comfortless, yet infinitely more inviting than Tai-Enchar's emptiness. Meridy gasped in hope and terror, and caught Carad Mereth's hand, and gripped Jaift's hand hard in her other hand. The thorns of the rose stem stabbed into Meridy's thumb as they grasped it together, but she did not loosen her grip, and when Jaift stepped onto the White Road, Meridy threw herself forward into the rushing silver light alongside her friend and dragged Carad Mereth after her.

The White Road of the Moon was not like any ordinary road. Nor like any ordinary river. Its light swept you up and onward and poured through you and around you, and yet you never lost your footing or drowned in the rushing light. Like a river in flood, it carried you where it would.

Yet Meridy had stepped from it once, into Tai-Enchar's dark realm; and now when she could neither think nor see, Carad Mereth gripped her hand and pulled them all together, in some way she did not understand, inexorably, to some other shore. She clenched her fingers hard around his, and held on to Jaift with her other hand, and staggered to a halt.

Gasping for breath, or for something like breath, Meridy tried to understand where they had come. She still stood between Carad Mereth on the one hand and Jaift on the other; each still held one of her hands. Jaift shifted as though she might let the White Road carry her away, but Meridy clung to her and refused to let go.

All three of them stood on a long, shining road of light that stretched out infinitely far, but now that they had stopped, it seemed again more like a road and less like a river. To each side stood a wall of darkness, infinitely deep, but this was not like Tai-Enchar's darkness. Sparks of light floated around them like stars, touching Meridy's hands and face, cold and stinging, like snowflakes, but with a brilliant living cold that was nothing like the cold of any ordinary winter. Jaift was gazing down this road, her expression abstracted and a little sad.

"Oh, well done. Well done," Carad Mereth said to both Meridy and Jaift. He stood taller already; by anything Meridy could see, he had recovered himself entirely. He said to Jaift, more gently, "But you have paid the price for this chance we have won at last from the teeth of disaster."

Jaift blinked and after a moment smiled, so much like herself that Meridy could hardly stand it. She answered, "We all paid the price. You not least."

"Yes, but you know, I am a servant of the God."

Jaift patted his hand. "Aren't we all? I'm free. Tai-Enchar's carelessness and arrogance freed me, for he never dreamed Herren would give up his own life willingly to Inmanuàr and so he never planned for that."

Jaift sounded perfectly certain of this, and Meridy winced, afraid to ask *How much do you remember?* She already knew the answer. But she said, "That's good, of course that's good, but you know, we left Inmanuàr—Herren—Inmanuàr—we left him pursuing Tai-Enchar. But the witch-king will turn at bay in Cora Diorr, and then I don't know what will happen—this is the ending of the age, Inmanuàr said—"

"Indeed, it *is* the ending of the age," Carad Mereth agreed. "Though Tai-Enchar has not yet been cast out from the world of men. He will remain dangerous so long as any part of him lingers in the world. But now, I think, we have at last come to the moment in which it will be possible to defeat him. This is the moment the God has fashioned out of the brief lives and bright courage and tiny, bitter agonies of men." His gaze lingered on Jaift.

Meridy said sharply, furious with grief, "If we've paid the price for it, then why aren't we *finished*?"

"Nearly finished," Carad Mereth told her gently. "Nearly finished, I hope." And, stretching out his hands, the sorcerer recited in his expressive voice, " 'What shall I say, what words will ever come, when all my words are done, when words have gone astray? What shall I give, what can my need sustain, when nothing else remains, when nothing else shall live? What light is there, what light shines through these years, when darkened by my fears, there's no light anywhere?' "

Then he stepped forward into the light and into the hand of the God, drawing Meridy and Jaift after him . . . and out of the light, and into life.

Though they returned to the realm of men, they were no longer in Moran Diorr. Meridy knew it at first because this time they were not greeted by the harmonious ringing of ten thousand bells. But for that first moment, she was blind—all light seemed to have failed and she could see nothing. She heard a low murmur of voices and an indistinct shout, and neither seemed far away, but she couldn't *see*—

Then Niniol gripped her shoulder, the light touch of a ghost—she knew him, steady and reassuring as always, and her vision began to clear. "You're here," she said, turning to him, relieved, and then was relieved again to glimpse the pale shadowy forms of Diöllin and Herren beyond him. And Jaift was still beside her—Meridy still held her hand, though Jaift's hand was tenuous now, and hard to hold.

"*He* brought us," Niniol said grimly, with a nod, meaning Carad Mereth.

The sorcerer glanced at them sidelong, his cornflower-blue eyes as secretive as the eyes of a witch. "A small exercise of sorcery, simple enough, as Meridy is your true and proper anchor. We'll need all our friends before the end, I think." He added to Meridy, "You can always bring your bound ghosts to your side. You'll learn that, eventually."

She supposed she might, if they lived through the next hour. She would hardly be able to help learning such things, if everyone she knew died and became quick and she bound them all. But there was terribly little time for grief, because as her vision recovered, Meridy realized that they had stepped off the White Road into a fabulous and crowded chamber. The room was wide and open, round rather than square. All the walls were smooth and white, oddly slanted inward toward a high, pointed ceiling, pierced by narrow, arched windows. The floor was a beautifully inlaid marquetry of different woods. It took Jaift's voiceless murmur of surprised alarm for Meridy to realize that she might recognize this place, and then she understood, with piercing fear, that this must be one of the tall white spires of Cora Diorr, and that they had stepped straight into the witch-king's stronghold.

Nor was this hall empty. The witch-king himself was not here, not yet, for they had stepped through the realms of dream and shadow and come to this place before him. But Meridy knew he must be coming. Even now, noblemen and a few noblewomen, men of means and soldiers and all kinds of people cluttered the round hall. They comprised nothing like the graceful gathering Meridy might have imagined, though, for the air was filled with a violent sense of fury and fear. Among the ordinary people, appearing untouched by any human emotion, Princess Tiamanaith sat elegantly perched on a heavy chair—probably a throne, Meridy realized. The princess-regent wore a simple white gown, clasped at the waist with a girdle of silver set with tiny black diamonds, and one earring that was a strand of tiny black pearls and another that was a single ruby drop.

Princess Tiamanaith was very beautiful, of course, but although she did not seem old in face or body, her eyes were ancient. Meridy couldn't see how anyone in this place could fail to know what she was, that she was a sorceress and not the proper tenant of that body. Surely any witch should be able to tell, save that all the witches here but Meridy herself were the servants or allies or victims of the witch-king. For there were other witches here: half a dozen black-eyed men and one black-eyed woman, all wearing the Black Swan badge. They terrified her.

The sorceress and her witches terrified everyone, judging by the angry stillness that gripped this hall. Once she looked around more deliberately, Meridy recognized the extremely handsome man, Lord Taimonuol, who had almost succeeded in bringing the fire horse stallion to Cora Diorr—or had succeeded, in fact, in a way. Yes, and there was his man, Connar. And there, among the others, Meridy recognized the seneschal, Lord Roann Mahonis, and beside him his brother, Lord Perann. All these men looked furious and wary, but none of them seemed to have challenged the sorceress or her witches. Plainly none of them dared. She guessed Lord Roann and many of these others had come to this place to challenge the princess-regent, and guessed as well that they had found themselves helpless against Aseraiëth and her witches.

Carad Mereth did not pay attention to anyone but the sorceress. Stepping forward a pace, he said, with an odd kind of constraint in his tone, "Aseraiëth. I thought . . . I thought you might have gone."

The sorceress who was not Tiamanaith inclined her beautiful head. "No. As you see, my old, I am here. No, when Enchaän comes, he shall turn and face your new-made champion. And here in this place he has made for himself, with me beside him, Enchaän will take the heir and the heir's power for his own at last, whether or not Inmanuàr has taken Tiamanaith's brat for his own renewal."

"Inmanuàr has taken nothing that was not freely given."

"Do you think that matters, my old? No, it matters not. Enchaän may not have won all that he wished with this play, but he has not been defeated, and the ruin coming will not be his." Her voice was as beautiful as her face, clear and warm and seductive.

Carad Mereth answered almost gently, "Enchaän has already been ruined. He has done it to himself. Now comes the end of the long game. There are only a few moves left to play out."

The sorceress tilted her head and answered, "You shall find

that the board belongs to Enchaän, and all your hopes shall go down to dust. No, Laìdomìdan, you have badly overplayed your hand." And she laughed, a delicate, scornful laugh.

Beside Meridy, Jaift flinched, and Meridy looked from her friend's ghost to the embodied sorceress and realized that what she heard in Aseraiëth's voice was worse than scorn. That show of derision lay over something else, and she remembered the tales that spoke of the great sorcerer Laìdomìdan and the love that lay between him and the sorceress Aseraiëth, until Tai-Enchar's great betrayal of the High King and the Kingdom sundered them from each other and made them enemies. Meridy stared at Carad Mereth, recognizing in him the sorcerer of legend, and understanding that behind Aseraiëth's disdain lay ruined love. That was worse than if she and Carad Mereth had always been enemies.

"Is Enchaän's victory truly what you desire?" Carad Mereth asked Aseraiëth. *His* voice shook, just perceptibly. "Are you so unwilling even yet to go into the hand of the God?"

"That is not my Road. Not any longer, if it ever was. Ah, Laìdomìdan, my fair. You always have such hope. How can you bear it?"

"I suppose I bear it because living without it would be . . . truly unbearable."

"Do you think so?" asked the sorceress, and laughed. Behind the warmth of that laugh lay a deep shadow of cruelty; and behind the cruelty, a deeper echo of bitterness and despair.

Taking a step forward, Carad Mereth said, quietly and intensely, "You are wrong, and you will lose everything. It needn't be that way. You may still repudiate Enchaän. There will be time. The hand of the God is over me, it is over us all, but I will wait that long."

Aseraiëth lifted her head with a swift, arrogant movement, but when she laughed again, this time she did not trouble to disguise the bitterness. "You are always so kind, Laìdomìdan! You needn't bother. I will not stray from the path I have chosen. It will be interesting to bear witness to this confrontation, I have no doubt. And when it is over, I will rule here beside Enchaän, but you will have gone to your God. Does that not comfort you?"

Carad Mereth drew a breath that sounded pained. Meridy, recoiling from the depth of anger and grief between the two sorcerers, could see that the hand of the God was indeed over him, and over Jaift. A brilliant pressure poured through her friend and infused the very air surrounding Carad Mereth, until it seemed almost easier to cease breathing than to bear it.

Then the light folded open. Meridy had seen this often enough now—she could hardly mistake it. Or maybe she recognized the way Carad Mereth lifted his head, the mocking twist to his mouth meant to hide fear. He was afraid, she knew that—she was afraid, too, not only for herself and for her ghosts, vulnerable to all these witches and to their terrible king, but also for all the ordinary people here in this place.

Aseraiëth took an eager step forward, lifting her hands.

Flinching from the sorceress and the rippling light, Meridy said to Carad Mereth, half a cry of protest, "But what will *happen*?"

"We shall no doubt shortly discover," he said, not quite smoothly. "I suspect there may not be much of Cora Diorr left at the end. That's yours to manage, young Mery, if you find the way to open the White Road for the living as well as the dead. I won't have the attention to spare. Besides, Jaift is *your* friend and will make an effort to listen to you even while she has one foot set on the God's Road."

He smiled at Jaift, who seemed, to Meridy's worried glance, to have *both* her feet on the White Road.

Meridy began, worried, "But—"

"Make no mistake, child: it is indeed the ending of an age."

Meridy had no doubt of this. She was almost certain Moran Diorr had risen from the waters of the bay—the *real* and the *ethereal* had been impossible to sort out, there at the end—but she found she could quite easily believe that the City of Spires might fall. She wanted to say, *But what will you do?*

Then Tai-Enchar stepped out of the air, and he was here, and there was no more time for questions or for fears.

twenty-six

"Enchaän! Welcome," said Aseraiëth, lifting her hands, which were filled now with light.

The witch-king had been disembodied, and so his insubstantial form was hard to see. But it took a moment to realize this because even dead, the witch-king held power that loomed across and through the tower like a black storm. Like Inmanuàr, he seemed both more strongly present in the world than an ordinary ghost and at the same time less *real*. Meridy could hardly bear to look at him. She wanted to back away, but she couldn't move. She tried to hold harder to Jaift's hand, but it was cool and insubstantial in hers, and Meridy found her fingers closing on air.

Then Tai-Enchar passed across the chamber like a wraith and held out his hand to one of the witches, who drew back, but not quickly enough. The witch-king's ghost seized his hand and vanished, and immediately the witch blinked and opened eyes that were blacker and emptier than the eyes of any natural man. His shadow spread out above him and before him, not like an ordinary shadow, Meridy saw, but simultaneously there and not-there, like a ghost. It was Tai-Enchar's soul, too powerful to be entirely contained within his stolen body.

"No," whispered Jaift, taking a small step toward the possessed man. "No."

Meridy gave her an agonized glance, knowing that this was exactly what Tai-Enchar had done to her friend, and that seeing him do it to someone else must be so much worse for Jaift than for the rest of them. She tried again to take her friend's hand, but still Jaift was too insubstantial and she couldn't even manage that.

The possessed witch had been an older man, stocky and strong, with dark hair and a grizzled beard and weathered skin. But the presence that now looked out of his eyes was nothing that belonged to that face or that body. He said to Carad Mereth in a voice like iron, "One is hardly astonished to find thou hast come here to this place before me, poet. But this is a place of mine now, and all your effort will not avail thee. I shall take for my own the champion thou hast made, and thou wilt witness the crumbling of all thy hopes."

"Not my champion, but the God's," Carad Mereth answered evenly. "Or why would you have been forced to flee to this place?"

Before the witch-king could answer, if he intended to, Aseraiëth stepped forward, demanding attention. "Tai-Enchar! I will serve you, lord! Together we can still defeat our enemies. All I ask is that you restore Tiamanaith's daughter to life! Look, there is her soul." She pointed to Diöllin's translucent form with a terrible, covetous ambition. Diöllin glared, but the sorceress ignored her and went on, speaking to the witch-king, "You need only make a body for her—for me! A daughter of the High King's line, bearing the right to his power and his sorcery and his kingdom; am I not due that? Then I will help you defeat Laìdomìdan, for all he fancies himself the servitor of the God. And when Inmanuàr arrives, you, too, will take the body that is rightfully yours!"

"Little though I require thy labor on my behalf," answered the witch-king, "yet thy service over these long years does deserve recompense." And he turned his terrible gaze thoughtfully upon Diöllin.

Meridy ran to Diöllin and grabbed her hand, a hand that returned faint and desperate pressure, not quite tangible, not enough to hold her. So Meridy caught the princess with her will and her heart to hold her, but despite all she could do, they both cried out as the binding between them snapped. Dust whirled and condensed, and almost at once another body lay there, a second Diöllin, more solid and *real* than the ghost Meridy still tried to hold, but empty. It should have been impossible—it was a sorcery beyond anything Meridy had ever imagined—but Tai-Enchar had done it. And so fast. It was wonderful and terrible, this untenanted body that had never lived and was not truly dead; truly a thing of dreams and of nightmares.

"No!" cried Diöllin, soundless and desperate, but Aseraiëth only laughed.

"How dare you?" Jaift whispered. "How dare you?" But no one heard her except Meridy, and there was nothing either of them could do. Diöllin took several small, reluctant steps toward the new-made body. It was plain that the body drew her, plain that the witch-king or the sorceress or the sheer weight of the newly created body could compel the ghost to enter it.

Meridy could not believe how fast everything was unraveling. She looked around desperately, but Inmanuàr still did not come.

"Aseraiëth, listen to me," Carad Mereth said, low and urgent. "You made no bargain with Diöllin! It is not fitting that you should bend your efforts to take her life for yours, nor did Tiamanaith ever have the right to give away any life but her own. You act against the natural order and against the God, in whose hand the dead rest."

The sorceress ignored him. She knelt over Diöllin's new body and impatiently held out one hand toward Diöllin, who helplessly took several more steps toward her; and very quickly, even though both Meridy and Jaift tried to hold her, the ghost of the princess faded as she entered the body Tai-Enchar had prepared for her. The body opened her eyes and sat up, Diöllin once again a living girl—but she flinched away from Tiamanaith, shuddering. "Mother! No!" she cried, and then Herren, hovering translucent and intangible over his sister's new body, said it too, half a sob, in the all-but-noiseless voice of a ghost, "Mother!"

The sorceress opened her mouth to speak, then threw back her head and made an inarticulate choking sound instead. From reaching out toward Diöllin her hand went to her throat, and Meridy, fascinated and horrified, watched vivid expressions of fury and grief and outrage chase across the sorceress's face, and realized that Princess Tiamanaith was fighting to reclaim her own body from the sorceress to whom she'd given it—that she was fighting Aseraiëth in a last desperate effort to protect her daughter. Meridy could *see them both* in that struggle, like seeing both a living person and her ghost at the same time, except that Meridy was really seeing two people struggling for dominion within a single body, both Tiamanaith and Aseraiëth, one overlying the other. It was unspeakably horrible, and worst of all, she could tell that Aseraiëth was going to win. She was almost certain that Tiamanaith was able to resist for this one moment only because the sorceress had been preparing to leap from her body to that of her daughter, and she could see that Tiamanaith's strength was already failing—

"Mother!" said Herren, voiceless and desperate as any ghost, helpless as any ghost to reach out into the solid world and touch his mother. He pulled away from Meridy, flickering toward his mother in the quick not-quite-there movement of a ghost. Meridy reached for the binding between them, to stop him, but she was too late, they were both too late. The sorceress had already laid her hands on Diöllin's shoulders, and the princess stood frozen and helpless.

Meridy couldn't stop Aseraiëth; she'd been too slow. But she did something else. In the moment the sorceress's soul leaped free of Tiamanaith and began to enter Diöllin's body, Meridy laid her will on that soul and lifted it free of *both* bodies. She held Aseraiëth's furious soul, and cried out, "Aseraiëth! By your name I bind you to me and to the world!" And she held and bound and ruled the ghost of the sorceress exactly the way she would have held and bound and ruled any other disembodied ghost.

Aseraiëth and Tiamanaith alike cried out, but the voice of the ghost was a high-pitched furious whisper, while the living woman gave voice to an alto cry of anguish. Tiamanaith, once again alone in her body, crumpled to the floor. Herren, for once as frantic as any little boy, hovered around his mother, patting her arms with his insubstantial hands, desperate to comfort her and be comforted though she could not see him and showed no sign that she could hear him, either.

And Diöllin, no longer under siege from Aseraiëth, ran her hands down her new body and then raised her living hands and stared at them, overcome to the point of speechlessness.

"Well done!" Carad Mereth said to Meridy. "Hold the sorceress fast. But I must warn you, ghost or no, she is still dangerous, and it's unlikely you'll be able to hold her long."

Meridy was sure he was right. She could already feel a strange kind of tension in the binding. Aseraiëth was not only ragingly furious but also doing something to the binding that Meridy didn't even understand. She could hardly spare a second to worry about that, because now the witch-king was studying at her. He had noticed her, maybe for the first time, and she would have given almost anything to be unnoticed again.

As though he'd picked Meridy's greatest fear out of her heart, Tai-Enchar said to her, "As yet thy strength is but little. Yet it shall grow, and thou shalt become a most valuable servitor."

"No!" whispered Jaift.

Meridy wanted to shout defiance, but she couldn't make a sound. She shook her head, denying the possibility, yet she knew if they didn't defeat the witch-king now, today, in this moment that had brought everyone together in this place, he would do it. Tai-Enchar didn't even mean it as a threat. He would make her into one of his servitors just as he had done to Jaift, just as he'd done to that poor man he possessed now, because he thought she would be useful, and because she couldn't stop him, and he would think no more of it than a normal man would think of bridling a horse or chaining a dog. Less.

Dismissing Meridy from his attention, Tai-Enchar said to Carad Mereth, "Though thine allies may purchase for thee one moment and another, it will never be enough for thee. Thou and I are aware that thou hast not the strength."

"Though a cup of water is nothing, no one can hold back the tide when it rises," Carad Mereth answered. "The tide has turned, Enchaän, and even you will not stand against it, no matter how you may plant your feet and rail against the moving sea."

Tai-Enchar laughed and moved forward. All his witch-servants moved with him, to encircle Carad Mereth, who stood quietly, making no obvious move to defend himself. Meridy shrank back, but Diöllin leaped forward, catching one of the servitors by the arm and slapping him across the face with a sound like the crack of a whip. The man shook his head impatiently and hit her, an open-handed blow much more powerful than hers, and Diöllin stumbled back and fell, trying unsuccessfully to catch herself, and hit the floor hard.

Immediately Roann Mahonis, though he was unarmed, stepped up and hit the servitor, not any casual slap but a hard twisting blow aimed up under the ribs, a brawler's move that even in that moment startled Meridy for what it implied about the man's past—suddenly he seemed a great deal more like the kind of man Diöllin might have fallen in love with.

The witch staggered, gasping, and went to one knee, glaring up at Roann. He lifted a hand—he was going to snatch out Lord Roann's living soul. Meridy caught her breath, feeling that she should be able to stop him, but even after all that had happened, she did not know how. And then Aseraiëth made an effort to break free, and Meridy was caught up in a different and even more imperative struggle she didn't know how to answer.

But Lord Roann's brother, Perann, swearing at Roann and the servitor with equal violence, kicked the man in the back from behind, and suddenly it *was* a brawl, ordinary men against the witch-king's servitors, nothing like any high battle in a tale, but ugly and confusing and brutal. The handsome Lord Taimonuol had snatched a slim dagger from some hidden sheath and efficiently stabbed one of the witches, but then he fell himself as his soul was flung violently from his body. Meridy, staggering from Aseraiëth's assault, nevertheless tried to catch Lord Taimonuol's soul and keep him safe from the witches, while his man Connar, plainly too furious to be afraid, bludgeoned the witch with both fists coming down against the back of the witch's neck, and then Meridy lost track of that fight because too much else was happening.

A small knot of stillness had formed around Carad Mereth. He was backing slowly away from Tai-Enchar, one quiet step and then another, as though he moved through an empty room and not a brawl, as though he and the witch-king were the only two men present.

The witch-king moved forward, one slow stride and then another. Niniol tried to strike at him, but there was the high sharp sound of breaking glass, and a swelling chime that snapped suddenly into a dissonance, like a bell had been lifted and struck so hard it had shattered, and his *ethereal* sword shattered and was gone, leaving Niniol weaponless. He leaped back, but Tai-Enchar tilted his head and Niniol staggered to a halt and cried out, a terrible thin sound.

"Niniol!" cried Jaift. She flickered forward, trying to catch Niniol as the witch-king's will forced him to his knees—one ghost trying to support another—and they both flickered and faded before Tai-Enchar's cold assault. There was no blood, for ghosts couldn't bleed, but Niniol was shredding around the edges. He gripped Jaift's arms, shuddering. Meridy cried out, and in that moment Aseraiëth twisted somehow and broke the binding Meridy had laid on her. She shook herself free, hissing with triumph and rage.

Whirling on Meridy, Jaift commanded, "Let me go! This is enough, it's too much! You have to let me go." Her voice, though soundless, was filled with passion. Jaift glared at the witch-king, her expression fierce with revulsion and simmering fury. "He thinks he owns me," she cried. "He thinks he'll possess me—he thinks I'm his to give away! But I was *never* his, and I make my *own* choices. Let me go, and I'll open the White Road wide right here! It *will* run both ways, Mery! I'll open it and you'll hold it open, and let Tai-Enchar face the very God! He won't have everything his own way *then*!"

Meridy knew Jaift *could* open the White Road of the Moon, exactly as she said. She knew she had to let her. But then, whatever else, once Meridy let her friend go, Jaift *would* go. And then she would be gone. And Meridy would never see her again.

If Meridy held her, then Jaift could stay with her forever. She need never be lost entirely from the world of men. Let ancient ghosts and ruthless sorcerers contest as they would, let Inmanuàr and Carad Mereth defeat their enemies without dragging everyone else into their battle. She would get Jaift away somehow—and Niniol, and—

"Mery!" cried Jaift. "Let me *go.* I have to open the way! This is the time, this is the moment, Inmanuàr is coming, can't you feel him coming? He'll be here any second! The White Road *has* to be open when he comes—it has to be open if anyone living is to have a chance to get out of this, get away—"

"I *know,*" Meridy snapped furiously. And as Aseraiëth had unwittingly showed her, she lifted the binding she had laid and let Jaift go.

Jaift gave her a decisive little nod and gripped Niniol's arm briefly in farewell. Then, despite Tai-Enchar's grasping power, which tried to claim and possess her, Jaift turned and stepped forward, and where her foot fell, that *was* the White Road of the Moon. The witch-king did not stop her; maybe he could not stop her. Moonlight fell over Jaift, and the White Road spilled around her, a river and a road that ran from life into death, from the *real* into the God's own realm. Jaift lifted her hands, and they filled with moonlight that ran over and splashed around her feet, and then the river that was the road carried her away and she was gone.

Though she had known that was going to happen, Meridy wanted to cry out her grief and anger. But she had no time for that, not now, because once Jaift had brought the White Road into this place, Meridy found she knew exactly how to open it wide for the living as well as the dead. It was sorcery, but it was something she had learned how to do. It was just like tipping a tidbit from the *real* into the *ethereal* for a dog; it was just like that. Only bigger. Wider. Wide as moonlight. But she could do it, and it would get them all away from this terrible place and save everyone from Tai-Enchar.

Except if she didn't do something to make the White Road lead from this tower back into the *real,* then it would surely carry the rest of them away to the God's realm, living and dead alike, and while they would then be safe from the witch-king, that would also ruin what Jaift had tried to do, waste all her generosity. Meridy couldn't bear that.

Lord Roann, appearing at her side, closed a powerful hand on Meridy's shoulder, giving her a small shake. "It leads to the God's realm, that's where it leads—"

"I know. But it also leads *everywhere*," Meridy insisted. And, kneeling, she set her hand upon the glimmering light of the road and bent it around until it ran straight between Cora Diorr and that low place not so far away, the saddle where the road ran between the mountains.

Then she looked for a way to anchor it, and a way to make it broader—broad enough for everyone in the palace, everyone in the city beyond, broad enough that all the people of Cora Diorr would find it opening up before them, between one step and the next—she didn't know how to anchor it, but she knew she had to find a way, that if she couldn't, she would never forgive herself for wasting the gift Jaift had given her, given them all.

"Oh," said Lord Roann. "Oh, I *see*." And he held out his hands, palm up, in the gesture of supplication, and said in a different, fervent tone, "Look on us with favor, O God! O God, be merciful to your servants!" And pale moonlight poured over and across him, and out of him, too, until it seemed the living must be half blinded by the light.

Roann, and through him the God, was anchoring the White Road. Meridy knew it. She could feel it. She had bent the Road away from the God's realm and made it leap through the mortal world, and the hand of the God reached out to support all her effort.

She had just time to know it, and to cry out in her heart, *Then why did Jaift have to die to open the way? Couldn't the Road have been opened without that cost?* But there was no time for more than that, for at last Inmanuàr came, pursuing Tai-Enchar out of the realms of dream and memory and into the *real*, and there was no more time for rage or grief.

twenty-seven

The fire horse stallion leaped out of shattering light, for all the world as fierce and vital and vivid as a living beast, Herren-Inmanuàr high on his back, leaning forward, small and pale and equally fierce. Light broke before him like a wave and scattered behind him like sparks, and with him like a flood tide came the host of the ancient dead loosed from the hand of the God, and Meridy was both relieved and terrified by what she saw coming down upon the world of mortal men.

"Get out!" she cried to everyone in the tower, everyone living, and Roann Mahonis seconded this, commanding in his deep, authoritative voice, "Run, run, go!" And from somewhere far away, somewhere even Meridy couldn't see him, she heard Iëhiy bark thunderously: *This way! This way!* as clear as could be. She shouted, "Follow him! Follow him! Don't you know dogs belong to the God? The God's hand has opened for us all!"

And at last the White Swan guardsmen and their lords and the servants and all the mortal people in the chamber who had been fighting against Tai-Enchar's witches began to struggle instead toward the glimmering light of the White Road. Meridy waved them all urgently onto the road and opened it all through the palace—it was strange, but the White Road *wanted* to open everywhere at once. It did not have to limit itself to the palace, either: it could perfectly well open before every threshold in Cora Diorr, and at the mouth of every alley; it could roll out before every traveler upon the avenues and streets of the city. Where any of the folk of Cora Diorr walked, their very next step could carry them into moonlight.

"Hurry!" Meridy called out to them all, to everyone in the City of Spires. The moment stretched out and out; the God was allowing the moment to linger, or maybe Meridy's own furious terror only made it seem that way. But she could feel the wave about to break and cried loudly, "Hurry, hurry! It's the ending of the age! Run, if you want to see the next age dawn!" And all through the city, some men listened to her and some fell back; some mothers snatched up their children and ran forward into moonlight and some caught up their babies and ran away; some craftspeople and tradesmen and merchants abandoned their tools and shops and coins and leaped into moonlight and some could not bear the loss and would not. All through Cora Diorr, some folk trusted the God and ran forward and some feared too greatly and fled, lords and common people, guardsmen and servants; and if there was any pattern to who went forward and who refused, Meridy could not distinguish it.

And in the high white chamber where long-dead sorcerers strove against the living and the dead for victory . . . for a long, stretched-timeless moment that might have been measured in seconds or in hours or in days, Meridy could not tell how the battle progressed or even where it was taking place.

She knew that Inmanuàr fought Tai-Enchar, but she could hardly perceive anything of that. It was not a battle of blade against blade, but she did not understand what it *was*. She knew, though, that they battled partly in the *real* world but mostly in the layered realms of the *ethereal;* in memory and in dreams.

Her own perception had become fragmentary and uncertain. Sometimes it seemed to her that she still knelt within a round chamber high up in a white tower; but sometimes she thought that she hovered above Cora Diorr and looked down upon the whole city spread out below her. Or sometimes again it seemed that she knelt in the midst of an infinite empty plain where the wind hissed through the dust with the sound of aching loneliness.

In certain confused moments, she thought moonlight washed around her like water, breaking around her knees and flinging light like spume past her face; sometimes she thought bitter ash and smoke rose up around her, so she choked on it and could hardly catch her breath.

She glimpsed Tai-Enchar's servitors. There seemed a lot of them, now that she could look out over the whole city at once. She thought of all the witches Prince Diöllonuor had brought to Cora Diorr, who let themselves be made into the kind of creatures that caused normal people to fear witches; and for what? To serve Tai-Enchar and bring down all the world under his rule? She was furious with them, and horrified by them. But even through the fury and horror she still also pitied them, because there was so little left in them save their master's will, and after all, the witch-king had taken Jaift for his own as well and she knew her friend had never chosen that. Maybe it had been like that for all of them.

But no matter whether they had surrendered to Tai-Enchar willingly or not, none of Tai-Enchar's witches would take the White Road now, and there was nothing Meridy could do to make them. The God never compelled anyone to take the Road into his realm; there was nothing she could do to make the living risk such a journey. They fought for their master, and if the long dead hadn't poured forth to challenge them and press them back, Meridy doubted Inmanuàr would ever have made it fully into this confusion of *real* and *ethereal* to challenge the witch-king. She glimpsed High King Miranuanol, and she was intensely relieved to glimpse Niniol at his back, but then even with her wildly expanded vision she lost sight of them both.

Even so, however, even with the old dead holding back Tai-Enchar's servitors; even with Gonnuol under Inmanuàr like a living banner . . . even so, Meridy was more and more afraid that the witch-king could not be defeated. Even now, he was being held back only just enough to stop him from crushing them all. She could see plainly the desperation on Herren's living face, the face that Inmanuàr now inhabited. He was too young—the witch-king's ambition had come to fruition too early and too fast, and despite his driving will, the body he had taken was simply too young. She had known that—they had all known that—he didn't have the strength. She looked, desperately, for Carad Mereth.

He met her eyes through all the mad tumult, a long look that somehow contained both terror and hilarity. He gave her a brilliant, vivid smile and held out his hands, palm up, and his hands were filled with light and also with shadow, and he cried out, "Inmanuàr!"

"Yes!" Inmanuàr cried, and in that instant he abandoned Herren's body, which crumpled immediately, falling from Gonnuol's back as a wild storm of uncontrolled sorcery broke across the city. Meridy cried out, and the fire horse screamed in rage, but High King Miranuanol was there, striding out of the tumult to catch Herren and lay him down gently. Then the High King leaped to the fire horse's back in the boy's stead, and the stallion reared and screamed again and lunged away in answer to his will, and Meridy lost sight of them.

She wanted to go to Herren, see if he might somehow have survived Inmanuàr's use of him. His body looked so small and crumpled, abandoned there in the midst of all the turmoil. But she tumbled off her feet the instant she left the White Road, struck by the storm of sorcery that Inmanuàr's sudden capitulation had released. She had not known what that could be like until she was out in it, and then she didn't know how anybody could possibly hold on to balance and sanity in the wild storm. It was as though lightning struck all around her. She was blind with it, blind and deaf and left without any sense of where she was.

Only she *did* know where she was—she knew she was in the round white chamber high in the spire of the palace, and Herren had fallen . . . he could not be far away . . . she remembered the young prince's desperate surrender of his living body to Inmanuàr; she could *not* believe Inmanuàr had abandoned Herren now, either his body or his soul. . . .

"Here," said a crisp voice near at hand, not a *real* voice, she could never have heard any actual sound, not now. But she didn't hear the voices of ghosts with her ears, and she heard that call. So she turned toward it, and only a second later she practically stumbled across Herren's body. She patted the boy's body and face until she found his wrist, and then heaved him up, glad for once he was so small and young. But then she did not know how to find the White Road again, she couldn't see anything, she was lost—

"*Here!*" Inmanuàr said again, not far away, and she stumbled after that inaudible voice and staggered into the silent serenity of the White Road of the Moon just before her strength gave out. She fell to her knees, Herren's body in her arms, and tried to understand what was happening.

Inmanuàr's abandonment of the battle had left Tai-Enchar facing no opponent at all. The witch-king stood within the raging sorcery that filled the world, and for once Meridy could recognize the expression in the witch-king's eyes, on his face. He was baffled, and he was beginning to be afraid. She shot Inmanuàr a glance—he knelt beside her, translucent, one bodiless hand gripping her wrist to keep himself from following the road, his other hand resting on Herren's limp body. Meridy opened her mouth, meaning to demand, *What have you done?*

Before she could speak, Carad Mereth cried, "Aseraiëth! I loved you once. If you ever loved me, if there is anything that remains of the woman you were, now is the only time left!"

But Aseraiëth cried out passionately, "Damn your fool's kindness, and the mercy you offer in your blind arrogance! Do you think I want it, or would take it? If the age must end, then bring it down!" And the sorceress flung out her hands and reached out into the *ethereal,* striving to gather up the loosed sorcery. But it swept away from her, spinning around Tai-Enchar. It was he, Meridy understood, who would impose order and pattern on it, and force all the *real* and *ethereal* realms to bend to his will.

Carad Mereth made no such effort. He did not try to hold or even guide the storm of magic. Instead, he put out both his hands and sent it exploding outward, and Meridy saw power leap through him in a blazing, scouring rush—he burned with his own internal light as the God flung limitless power through him and broke Tai-Enchar's withering pattern.

Carad Mereth cried out, a sharp wordless shout, and deep black cracks rushed across the fine marquetry of the floor and the white plaster of the walls; only these cracks widened rapidly, each becoming an abyss that had no limit to its depth.

Aseraiëth stood, bodiless and yet looking almost like a living woman, in the white chamber, in front of the white throne, until the fine marquetry of the floor shattered under her feet. Then she fell without a sound, and whether she fell beneath the crashing stone or fell upon the White Road and was swept away, Meridy could not tell. All around, the white spire crumbled and came down upon Tai-Enchar. Even then, the witch-king might have held himself together through the destruction, but he had no chance. Because the other spires of the palace shattered, one after another, in a slow cascade of cracking stone and breaking glass. At first Meridy couldn't see whether any of this happened in the *real* or only in some terrible dream, and then she understood that for this moment the *ethereal* and the *real* had spilled into each other and all the layered realms had become one.

The destruction spread out in concentric circles, as the ripples of a thrown stone spread out into a pond; the destruction ran out into the city and the surrounding land. While Meridy knelt safe amid the rushing light of the White Road, clinging to Herren, the earth itself opened up, and at last, all around the city, the encircling mountains that sorcery had once raised up swayed and cracked and came roaring down in one enormous avalanche after another, burying Tai-Enchar within Cora Diorr, the City of Spires, until no sign of sorcerer or city was left there.

And as the broken mountains settled across the bones of the city and whatever might be left of the witch-king's soul, the long dead rode across the wreckage and faded out of the world, passing again out of time and memory, going back into the hand of the God. The last to go was the High King, Miranuanol Incuonarr. He rode Gonnuol through the *ethereal,* across the tumbled stones and the shattered spires, the fire horse treading down the dead and the ghosts of the dead. But High King and fire horse wheeled then to face Meridy. Gonnuol tossed his head and reared, arrogant and fearless as ever, and the High King lifted his hand in grave salute toward Meridy, or maybe toward his son, who still stood beside her in the midst of the pouring light of the White Road, resting a steadying, insubstantial hand on her shoulder. Inmanuàr returned a nod to his father, and after a second, so did Meridy.

Then the realms slid apart from one another, and High King and fire horse were both gone. All around, the tumult began to subside. It was over.

twenty-eight

"A buried city for a grave marker," Meridy observed, gazing down upon the rubble that covered Cora Diorr. "I don't know whether that seems a fitting cenotaph for Tai-Enchar, or whether it seems . . . indecent."

"It seems appalling, to me," Niniol said. He was standing behind her, leaning his hip against a ridge of stone, looking precisely as always: practical, stolid, reassuring, and unimpressed by anything, even broken mountains and buried cities and the defeat of immortal sorcerer-kings.

"The theology addressing this situation seems ambiguous," murmured Roann Mahonis.

His brother, Lord Perann, rolled his eyes.

They were all sitting on the edge of the cliffs where so recently half the mountains had sheared away and toppled down into the valley upon the City of Spires. The whole valley had become a mass of broken stone and torn earth. Eventually, Meridy supposed, seasons would turn and turn again, and all the tormented valley would smooth out into level meadows, and young trees would spring up and grow, and all this devastated land would look . . . ordinary. She could not quite imagine anyone trying to plant orchards or fields over that buried city, though, no matter how many years passed. She thought that even in a hundred years, or a thousand, any fruit grown there would surely taste of bitterness and grief.

Diöllin was sitting beside Lord Roann, leaning against him. She hadn't gone so far, yet, as to rest her head on his shoulder, but his arm was around her waist and she seemed quite comfortable to have it there.

Diöllin, like all of them, looked drawn and weary, but she was alive. She owned her own body again, she and no one else, and it was a living body, as though her soul had never been cast adrift. That was one good thing to come out of these terrible days. Meridy didn't think it was enough, but . . . it was something.

The princess said, "It *is* appalling. That's what makes it a fitting grave marker. What would you use, flowers? Broken stones and broken bones are more fitting."

"Too many broken bones," said Niniol. "Too much death."

"Some did live," Meridy said quietly. "Because of what Jaift did. She was just going to meet that boy and get married, and now . . ."

Niniol shook his head, his expression somber. "Jaift never had a chance. Not once the witch-king took her."

"She did have a chance," Meridy answered. "And she took it. She opened the way." She rubbed a hand across her mouth. After a moment, she went on, "Jaift opened the White Road for me. Without her, I would never have been able to make a way for all those people to get out of Cora Diorr. So many got out."

"So many didn't."

"Without a flood of the dead to carry the witch-king away with them, who knows whether he might still be down there?" said Roann.

Perann added, "It was a high price to pay, but if it was the last of the price, we can be grateful for that."

"Yes. But I'll have to tell her mother," said Meridy. "How will I ever tell her mother?" She bent her head, not weeping because she was too spent and sad for tears.

Niniol laid a half-visible hand on her shoulder. "Her uncle is a priest. He'll understand. Maybe he'll be able to explain it to them."

Meridy shook her head. "Maybe he'll be able to explain it to me. And what about Herren? That's not fair either."

Everyone glanced beyond Meridy, to where Herren's body lay, cool and waxen in the tentative, hazy sunlight. He looked even smaller and younger like this than he had when he'd been alive. Meridy didn't look at him herself. She stared steadfastly down at the buried city because she couldn't bear to look at the body of the young prince. She had carried him out of Cora Diorr, but what did that matter? He was still dead.

The eastern faces of the mountains were now broken cliffs, which made the undamaged road leading away westward and the smooth, sweeping fields all across the western flanks of the hills seem all the more peculiar. Hundreds—thousands—tens of thousands of people, maybe—wandered across those fields or were already making their way west along that road. A few, braver or more reckless, were slowly picking their way down the eastern cliffs to investigate the shattered rubble that covered the remains of Cora Diorr.

Meridy would not have ventured into that valley for anything. If she turned her head and looked sideways into the valley, she was certain the sunlight fell at an odd angle across the buried city. To her, it seemed that the very dust settling slowly through the air sparkled with glittering traces of sorcery.

She was sitting, her legs drawn up, close by the edge of the cliff. Iëhiy lay beside her, panting as though he had actually felt the effort of leading all those people out of Cora Diorr. She was glad that he, at least, had not taken the White Road. Glad that he had found her again. She sat with one hand resting on his insubstantial shoulders.

She had been the last person, the very last, to make it out of the city before the mountains had fallen. She had no idea how many people had been left behind. Hundreds, or thousands, or tens of thousands; she did not know. It looked like so many, cast homeless out onto the lands beyond Cora Diorr's encircling mountains. But Niniol was right: there must have been so many left. They had all had a chance to get out; Meridy had done that much—Jaift's sacrifice had let her do that much. It did not seem like enough.

Lord Roann had made no comment when she'd staggered off the White Road and come back into the *real* in this place, carrying Herren in her arms. But the seneschal's eyes had looked bruised with worry and sorrow. He'd touched her shoulder in wordless sympathy and taken Herren's body himself, to lay out in the shade of the broken stones that now stood along the edge of the new cliffs. Meridy had let him do it. He had been Prince Diöllonuor's seneschal and Diöllin's lover and no doubt loyal to Herren. And besides all that, he was a priest. He had the right.

Besides, Meridy couldn't have borne to do it.

Behind her, another voice whispered Herren's name.

Meridy turned.

Princess-regent Tiamanaith stood there, looking drawn and ill but also determined. Her gaze went from Diöllin to Herren's body, and then she didn't seem able to look away.

Diöllin gazed up at her mother, her expression studiously

blank. Lord Roann got to his feet, straightened his shoulders, and set one hand protectively on Diöllin's shoulder. Niniol crossed his arms, frowning, but even he didn't say a word.

The princess-regent didn't meet anyone's eyes. She only walked past them all and knelt, slowly, as though she were an old woman, beside her dead son.

Meridy shifted back to give her room. She knew that everything that had happened—or at least, a lot that had happened—was Tiamanaith's fault. Yet Meridy couldn't hate her. Tiamanaith simply looked too blankly devastated. It was Diöllin's place to protest, surely, if it was anyone's, and Diöllin did not seem inclined to hurl bitter accusations at her mother. At least not at this moment.

It wasn't fair that Tiamanaith would never have a chance to make peace with her son. Herren was the one who had loved his mother; Meridy was certain of that. Herren had loved her and tried to help her even after what she'd done, even after what she'd let happen, and now he was dead and his mother was alive.

Meridy rubbed Iëhiy's ears and sighed. If they had won, she would have liked to *feel* their victory.

"I tried so hard," Diöllin said quietly, accepting Lord Roann's hand to rise. She moved to stand beside her mother. "We all tried so hard. And it wasn't enough."

"You were with him all the time," Tiamanaith said, her tone only weary. "I betrayed him, I betrayed you both, though I swear I never meant it so. But you were always with him. I'm glad for that, at least."

Meridy looked away, swallowing. Though she had briefly anchored Herren's ghost, she knew that he was now gone far beyond her reach. If only she were a trained sorceress, she might do something useful even so. She might stretch out her hand and wake the boy as though he were merely sleeping. . . . She blinked.

Then she reached up to her hair and let her fingers shape the heavy, nodding form of the rose she found there. When she touched it, the rose fell into her hand, *ethereal,* without weight or heft, but beautiful for all that: a rose out of memory and dreams. Its petals were silken soft against her fingers, and the thorns of its stem pricked her hand.

She held it out, mutely.

"But it's not *real,*" whispered Diöllin. "And it's not . . . it's not true life that the fragrance of a rose may recall. . . ."

"But maybe it's not yet true death that's taken Herren, either," said Meridy. "We don't know. The White Road is everywhere, after all. Maybe . . . maybe it might run both ways for a little while longer, for a little boy who never had a chance to live his own life." She wished she thought it might for Jaift but knew it wasn't possible; Jaift had taken the White Road all the way to the God's realm; nothing else could have let them do what they had done. But maybe . . . for Herren . . .

"Try it!" Diöllin said urgently. "You must at least try!"

Lord Roann said huskily, "It's in the hand of the God."

"And we've all seen that the God can be generous," Perann agreed.

Meridy shook her head, but she laid the rose down on Herren's chest. If there was any fragrance, she couldn't tell. It was too faint, or perhaps too *ethereal,* too much a thing of memory or dreams. But she waited, leaning forward, holding her breath.

"It's not going to work—" moaned Tiamanaith.

"You give up *far* too easily," snapped Diöllin. "You always have! That's the whole trouble!"

Tiamanaith winced and looked down, but though Meridy wanted to agree with Diöllin, she thought Tiamanaith was probably right. She could see not the faintest flicker of an eyelash . . . not the slightest movement of a breath. . . .

Then Herren drew a long, slow breath after all, and put a hand to his chest, his fingers curving around the heavy blossom. The *ethereal* petals shattered and melted at his touch, and his lips moved, and he opened his eyes.

Tiamanaith cried out, but Meridy caught her breath. Herren's eyes were black.

"Well done!" cried a quick, half-mocking voice behind them.

Meridy jerked upright, astonished. "Carad Mereth!"

"Of course!" said the sorcerer, smiling at her. He looked younger now, as though he had been reborn in the cataclysm that had struck Cora Diorr. But his manner had not changed. He said cheerfully, "Carad Mereth, come as always at the very tail of time! Well done, I say, you and all these others, but you particularly, of course, my rose child all thorns! I thought I might have to make another rose for you, but you seem to have made one of your own. Well done, and we shall assuredly make a sorceress of you yet!"

"Inmanuàr made the rose," Meridy said, confused. "But anyway, look! It's not Herren at all! His eyes are *black*! I thought Tai-Enchar was *gone*!"

"Ah! But Tai-Enchar *is* gone, you know. Never fear; the young prince is well enough. Only the White Road carried him nearly to the God's realm. One doesn't return unchanged from such a journey, you know." Carad Mereth held a hand down toward Herren, offering it to the boy, and Herren blinked again, shook his head, and accepted the sorcerer's help.

"And you are mistaken twice," Carad Mereth added to

Meridy absentmindedly. "The rose Inmanuàr gave you was for me, and grateful I was to have it, believe me. But even had you not used up its virtue to wake me from dreams, it would not have done for the young prince. No, you made this one yourself."

Meridy stared at him. It was true. She had used In-manuàr's rose to free Carad Mereth. She *must* have made this one herself, only without quite realizing it.

"And not before time," Inmanuàr agreed, flicking into visibility beside Carad Mereth. Iëhiy leaped up and went to lean against him, and he stroked the dog's head, smiling, the tension running out of him like water. He said to Meridy, "I can't always be making such little trifles for you, you know."

Meridy couldn't help but exclaim, "I thought you were gone!"

"I was delayed merely," Inmanuàr said gravely. "Nor have I yet been freed." He glanced sidelong at Carad Mereth. "Now that all long plans have finally come to fruition, perhaps that may change."

"Yes; that's another reason I thought I'd better seek you out before the day grew much older," Carad Mereth said to Meridy. He smiled at her with a pleased expression, like a particularly self-satisfied cat. "Tai-Enchar is gone at last—gone, or bound beyond any hope of escape, which is satisfactory either way. Cora Diorr has fallen, but Moran Diorr has risen up out of the bitter waters, all its shining walls and graceful towers brilliant in the sun! That, even I did not expect to see, not in this age nor the next. Listen! You may hear the ten thousand bells ringing even from here!"

Meridy opened her mouth to declare that this was nonsense but shut it again without saying a word, because in the moment of stillness that followed this declaration, she almost thought she *could* hear the faint echo of ten thousand bells.

"And now the young prince has also been raised up," Carad Mereth added, smiling at Herren. "And with eyes that see all the layers of the world! As I say, no one comes back from that far shore unchanged, and that's just as well, for any king does best when he can see beyond the mortal realm."

"Any *king*?" Tiamanaith protested. "Is that yours to decide?"

"It's mine, surely," Inmanuàr told her acerbically.

Tiamanaith opened her mouth but closed it again, saying nothing.

Carad Mereth, still smiling, said to Herren, "It *is* just as well, you know. Moran Diorr was never meant to be merely the capital of any minor principality. This new age cries out for a new High King, and here you are! You gave yourself willingly unto death to save your Kingdom and then, by the grace of the God, stepped again from the White Road into the world of men! Very soon all men will know it, for word of Cora Diorr's destruction and Moran Diorr's rise will spread. Who would challenge your right now?"

Herren turned slowly to look down into the ruined valley. Roann offered him a hand, his mother reached out both her hands to him, but he ignored them both and moved another step closer to the edge of the new cliff. Diöllin, ignoring her brother's silence, went to him, but she only stood beside him silently. Herren glanced up at her and drew a slow breath. Turning, he asked, in a voice that was very nearly steady, "Inmanuàr?"

Inmanuàr inclined his head. "You will do well," he said. "I think you may trust my judgment in these matters."

"You should . . . I meant to . . . I didn't . . ."

"I know," Inmanuàr said gently. "But it's not for me. I have been too long dead, and anyway, it would not be right. I thank you for your trust. But I am glad to be able to set back into your hands the gift you gave to me."

"I'm glad to take at least my life, then," Herren said, and smiled at last.

"Good. You *should* be glad of life, for it is a gift of the God. And I think you will do well with your life, and with my city and my Kingdom."

"So!" cried Carad Mereth. "As that's settled! I will ask you, Inmanuàr: will you now go to the God? Or will you linger to look over the shoulder of your heir? He has a generous heart and a brave spirit, but he might not thank you for it."

"I suspect you're right," the ghost boy answered drily. "Ready to go to the God? I've been ready these hundred years past and more. Will you release me?" He ran his hand down Iëhiy's neck and added, "And my good dog?"

Meridy caught her breath.

Carad Mereth held out his hands and did the thing a priest does to release a bound ghost, and Inmanuàr threw back his head and blazed up brilliantly, and went out, like a snuffed candle.

But Iëhiy—Tai-Ruòl—did not. The great wolfhound whined, and paced to Meridy's side, and sat down on her foot. Surprised, she touched his head, delicately, the way one had to touch *ethereal* things, and the hound leaned his head against her thigh and panted happily up at her.

"He's yours, then," Carad Mereth said cheerfully. "Do you know, I thought he might choose to stay with you. He's been quick a long, long time, but often dogs love life too well to understand death."

Meridy looked up at him without speaking and stroked the barely tangible ears of her hound.

"You—" said Herren. "How much of all this was your doing?"

Carad Mereth smiled at the young prince—the young High King—utterly unruffled. "Not as much of it as you might think," he said lightly. "A great deal of it was *your* doing, you know, and most of the rest you owe to one another's efforts. As always, I was in the hand of the God."

"Is there anyone who is not?" Roann asked, his tone wry.

The smile became an outright laugh, full of joy, and Carad Mereth said, "No, indeed. We are all in the hand of the God." He offered Herren, who regarded him warily, a bow that was only a little mocking. "Cora Diorr has fallen, but Moran Diorr has risen again! And here you are, the High King's heir. You will do very well by that bright city, and by all this land. Will you take the throne Inmanuàr grants you? Will you claim your city and your heritage and your title? It is your right, and besides, the dispossessed folk of Cora Diorr will need shelter."

Herren didn't say yes, but he asked, as though he were already thinking of them all as his people, "Is there room for them?"

"And to spare!" But then Carad Mereth added more gently, "Moran Diorr was a great city, you know. There will be room and to spare for all your people in the City of Bells, if you are High King and have authority to offer it to them. Princes will do battle over Moran Diorr, you know, if you do not claim it. They will raise up armies and march to war. But if you claim the City of Bells, it will fall gently into your hand."

The boy nodded, and sighed.

"You *will* do well," said Diöllin, smiling. Now at last she set her hand on her brother's shoulder, dropping a quick kiss on the top of his head.

Herren put his hand over his sister's. He met her eyes, unsmiling but intense, and then said to Roann, "If I will be High King, then Diöllin will be princess of Cora Tal. Until she marries, there will be quarrels among the lords who are most ambitious to rule by her side. If she chose to marry you, I would be glad of it, Lord Roann."

Tiamanaith opened her mouth but then said nothing. Both Diöllin and Roann stared at Herren for a long moment. Then Diöllin laughed and lifted her eyebrows at Roann, and the man bent his head and answered soberly, "My king, I will justify your trust in me."

"Of course you will!" said Diöllin. "That's never been in question!" She sent a cool look at her mother.

Tiamanaith still said nothing. A faint flush had risen into her cheeks. Meridy measured Herren, and Diöllin standing beside him, and Lord Roann, and found herself confident that no one would need to fear Tiamanaith making any unwise bargains in the future, even if somewhere the ghost of another long-dead sorceress might possibly wander the world.

"And you?" Herren said to Carad Mereth. "Where you will go?"

"I?" The sorcerer pretended he was surprised by the question. "I have no place in the Kingdom you will build. I am the Storm Crow, flying always on the breath of disaster. You may be sure, there is always a disaster poised to fall *somewhere*. But not here, not for the coming age, I hope."

Herren paused. Then he came forward to take Carad Mereth's hands and say gravely and formally, like a king, "You have my thanks, then. I think you are due that."

"I think so too," Carad Mereth answered, looking very

pleased with himself. "We shall see. Later years will judge us both." Then, turning to Meridy, he said more soberly, "Well, my rose child? You have become a sorceress; that is not a choice you can unmake. But you have the courage for it, and the determination, and the fortitude to bear the cost. Will you come with me? I will teach you the song of the stars and the language of the earth and the ways that lead from one realm to the next—"

"You think I should want to fly always on the breath of disaster?" Meridy asked him.

Carad Mereth paused. "Well—that is—"

"No, never mind." Meridy found herself smiling, though she could feel that it was a crooked smile, with sorrow behind it, and the acceptance of sorrow. "Yes, of course I'll come with you. I always meant to." Then she looked at Niniol and hesitated.

"Oh, I'll come along," he said mildly. "You're my anchor, after all. I'm not so weary of this world as to be impatient for the God's realm. My wife will be there when I go, however long I linger here. And you'll need a man who can give you practical advice instead of just the song of the stars."

Meridy bowed her head, as grateful for Niniol's stolid assurance as for Iëhiy's good cheer. "Yes," she said in a low voice. "I would be glad of that." Then she looked doubtfully at Herren and Diöllin and the others.

"You'll visit me, of course," Herren told her—nearly an order. The boy added seriously, "Never mind where you might go and what you might learn. You must come visit me in Moran Diorr."

"Visit us," agreed Diöllin, smiling. "I'll establish a new capital in Cora Talen, I suppose. I'll plant a great circle of trees all around the city. Apple trees, maybe. They'd be more welcoming than a ring of mountains, not to mention easier to raise up."

"I shouldn't be at all surprised if you find the trees of your encircling orchards growing taller and more swiftly than ordinary trees, and bearing apples with flesh as white as the light of the moon," Carad Mereth said wryly. "Magic does tend to linger about those who have set foot upon the White Road of the Moon."

Meridy laughed a little because she knew this was true, and because she knew that in a sense they had never stepped off the White Road. She was not exactly happy, not yet. The loss and sorrow and fury of the past days all clung too close to her still for happiness. But she was beginning to feel, cautiously, that happiness was *possible.* "I'll come visit you in Cora Talen and see your orchards," she promised Diöllin. "And you, Herren, I'll see you in Moran Diorr." She looked around at them all: Diöllin and Herren, Lord Roann and his brother, and even Princess Tiamanaith. She said, "Perhaps we can all meet in the City of Bells. In a year, maybe. And it will be *our* city, all of ours, raised out of memory, with all its bells tuned to living joy as well as old sorrow."

"In a year, they will ring to welcome you," Herren agreed, smiling, but serious, too. "In a year, I will set all the bells of Moran Diorr to ringing. Promise me you will come when you hear them."

"Yes, I will," Meridy told him. "One year from today." And she laughed, because she knew it was ridiculous to imagine that even the ten thousand bells of Moran Diorr could be heard not only in the world but all through the realms of dreams and memory. Yet she knew at the same time that it was true.